Nic... ... ...e with strong heroines, heroes who dare challenge them and a ... ... husband, as well as her demon spawn, in Utah. When she's not writing, she's constantly injuring herself running, rock climbing, practicing yoga and snowboarding. She loves hearing from readers through her website, nicholesevern.com, and on Facebook, @nicholesevern

Ever since **Lisa Childs** read her first romance novel (a Mills & Boon story, of course) at age eleven, all she wanted was to be a romance writer. With over seventy novels published with Mills & Boon, Lisa is living her dream. She is an award-winning, bestselling romance author. She loves to hear from readers, who can contact her on Facebook or through her website, lisachilds.com

Discover more at millsandboon.co.uk

DEAD GIVEAWAY

NICHOLE SEVERN

SNOWED IN WITH A COLTON

LISA CHILDS

MILLS & BOON

First Published in Great Britain 2022
by Mills & Boon, an imprint of HarperCollins*Publishers* Ltd
1 London Bridge Street, London, SE1 9GF

www.harpercollins.co.uk

HarperCollins*Publishers*
1st Floor, Watermarque Building,
Ringsend Road, Dublin 4, Ireland

Dead Giveaway © 2022 Natascha Jaffa
Snowed In With a Colton © 2022 Harlequin Books S.A.

Special thanks and acknowledgement are given to Lisa Childs for her contribution to *The Coltons of Colorado* series.

ISBN: 978-0-263-30331-5

0222

MIX
Paper from
responsible sources
FSC™ C007454

This book is produced from independently certified FSC™ paper to ensure responsible forest management.

For more information visit: www.harpercollins.co.uk/green

Printed and Bound in Spain using 100% Renewable electricity at CPI Black Print, Barcelona

DEAD
GIVEAWAY

NICHOLE SEVERN

For Marla for equating my books to
'Hallmark with guns.'

Chapter One

Her keys cut into the palm of her hand.

Genevieve Alexander couldn't move, couldn't think. She hadn't gotten more than two steps into the house before her instincts had warned her to run. The backs of her knees shook as she took in the blood. Shadows distorted the face of the victim, but she didn't need the lights on to identify the woman staring back at her. The killer's MO was already familiar, but crime scene photos were nothing compared to the real thing.

The Contractor.

It was impossible. The killer she'd prosecuted for stringing his victims from their own ceilings like marionettes had been sentenced to life behind bars without parole. This… This was something else. This was her home.

But the holes the medical examiner would find in each joint of the victim's body weren't the worst part. Posed with the help of industrial-strength fishing line and steel eyelet screws, the woman stood there as though she'd simply been waiting for Genevieve to come home from work.

Because she had been. Waiting.

Reality pierced through paralyzing confusion and fear. Unpocketing her phone, she stumbled away from the scene in her once pristine living room. She couldn't contaminate the scene.

She collided with a wall of muscle.

Her scream cut short as a gloved hand clamped over her mouth.

"Hello, Genevieve." The unfamiliar voice grated against every cell in her body as he hauled her back into his chest. "Do you like my gift? I made her for you."

She struggled against the grip around her face and midsection. Head craned back, she couldn't see more than the blood spatter across her ceiling, and panic infused her nervous system. She clutched her phone, stretching her thumb across the screen to dial 9-1-1, but the man at her back was so much stronger, so much bigger. A hit of spiced cologne burned the back of her throat.

He pressed his mouth against her ear. "Drop the phone. I wouldn't want anyone disturbing us until I'm ready."

Genevieve shook her head. No. It was her only lifeline. Her only guarantee she didn't end up like the victim on the other side of the room. Tears burned in her eyes. Pain lightninged through her lower back, and she arched against her attacker. Her protest died in his hand.

"You always try to control the situation on your terms. That's what makes you such a good district attorney, but the only way you're going to get through this tonight is if you do exactly as I say." A prick of pain centered over her throat. A blade? "Understand?"

She tapped her thumb against the screen, unsure if she'd hit the right buttons. She loosened her grip around the device. The hard *thunk* of metal meeting hardwood was as loud as the final nail in her own coffin. Had the call gone through? Her hair tugged at the base of her skull as she tried to lift her head, but he held her secure.

"Good. Now, I'm going to remove my hand from your mouth. If you scream, you die. If you attempt to escape or overpower me, you die," he said. "Any questions?"

Genevieve shook her head. She had to play along, had to do whatever it took to survive. Her exhales warmed the skin around her mouth as he peeled his gloved grip from her face. Closing her eyes, she recalled the layout of the house, where she'd stashed the gun she'd received as an engagement gift all those years ago. Her gaze settled on the brick fireplace a mere three feet from the victim, the one she'd taped her weapon inside. Had he searched the house? Had he already found it? Only one way to find out. "What do you want?"

"To give you one last chance to prove yourself." Her attacker smoothed her hair over her shoulder. Too close. Her gut revolted at his touch, but she'd have to buy her time before making her move. "Ms. Johnson here was nice enough to keep me company while I waited for you to come home. Unfortunately, she couldn't talk much after I drilled the first hole in her knee. I always pegged her for a better conversationalist, but now I know better."

Elisa Johnson? The contours of her assistant's features sharpened against the shadows threatening to consume her, and Genevieve's heart squeezed in her chest. Fire-red hair clung to the curves of an oval face and interrupted the flawless outline of full lips. Pale skin had lightened in the wash of moonlight, but it was her eyes that demanded attention. Impossibly green and empty. Her knees weakened, but the solid mass at her back refused to let her fall. She tried to process his last words, but escape had overridden any sense of logic. "I don't know what you're talking about. What do you mean you're giving me a chance to prove myself? I don't know you."

"But I know you, Genevieve. Did you think the Contractor would be so easy to apprehend? That I'd let some random amateur with a grudge tarnish my name like that?" A growl vibrated through his chest and straight into her. "I've spent a year building my reputation, and one case with all the answers you're looking for comes along, and you just roll over. Is that what it's come to these days? You're supposed to make sense of the evidence. Not make it fit your personal agenda, Counselor."

Thousands of crime scene photos, half a dozen incident reports, countless witness interviews and investigation reports filed through her mind in less time than it took for her to take her next breath. "You're...you're lying. We have the right man. He confessed."

"Everyone wants to be known for something, don't they?" he asked. "Isn't that why you became district attorney? Isn't that why you bury yourself in your work during your sixteen-hour days, why you handle all of your cases personally and try to fill that missing piece you've been living with for so long?"

He'd studied her. Stalked her. Learned about her.

The blade dug into her skin as he maneuvered her back into the living room, but Genevieve wouldn't flinch. Wouldn't cry. She wouldn't give him the satisfaction. Her heels scraped against the hardwood floor. His grip slid to the nape of her neck, forcing her to confront the victim. Genevieve closed her eyes, but there was no erasing the images left behind.

"Look at her, Genevieve." He shook her hard enough to make her back teeth hit together. Leaning in, he leveled his gaze in her peripheral vision, but it was still too dark to make out anything significant. "Elisa Johnson is dead because you disappointed me. Out of everyone who worked that investigation, I expected you to see the lies, but maybe I've given you too much credit. Don't worry. I'm going to give you one more chance to become the opponent I deserve."

Once more chance? Genevieve forced herself to take a deep breath. Her attention cut to the fireplace. Her heart threatened to beat straight out of her chest. She had one shot to make it out of this alive. She wasn't going to fail. "You don't have to do this. You don't have to hurt anyone else."

"Sure, I do. Otherwise, what's the point?" he asked.

Sirens echoed through the large living room, growing closer. Red and blue patrol lights cut through her sheer curtains and sped around the room. Relief and panic combined in a twisted tornado of emotion. She couldn't let him get away. She couldn't let him do this to someone else.

"Seems our time together has come to an end, Genevieve, but I know we'll meet again." The grip at the back of her neck lightened, the pain in her back subsiding. "I promised to give you one more chance, and I'm a man of my word. Show me I didn't make a mistake when I chose you."

Genevieve ignored the bite of pain at her throat as she lunged for the fireplace. The corner of the brick crushed the air from her lungs, but she shot her hand up into the chimney and ripped the gun she'd duct-taped there free. Spinning to confront the killer, she took aim at an empty room. Her breath sawed in and out of her chest. Sweat built in her hairline as shouts penetrated the bubble of fear in her chest. She heard the front door slam against the wall behind it, and in a split second, flashlight beams centered on her. Then the body.

"Drop the weapon! Interlace your hands behind your head!" An officer closed in on her, then slowed. Disbelief hitched his voice an octave higher. "Ms. Alexander, put the gun on the floor, turn around and interlace your hands behind your head. Now."

"He was here." Her fingers shook as the past few minutes replayed in her head. She tried to keep her voice even despite the storm churning inside. He'd said he'd chosen her, that he wanted her to prove herself. What did that mean? What did Elise Johnson have to do with any of it? She released her grip on the weapon, catching the trigger cage around her index finger and slowly placed her gun on the floor. "He was here."

But he'd be long gone by now. Most likely through the trees surrounding the back half of her property, and he'd left Elise behind to remind her of her failure to bring him down. They hadn't been able to connect the Contractor's victims, but he'd chosen her assistant for a reason.

Because of her.

An officer collected her weapon from the floor while another maneuvered behind her. Wrenching her arms at her lower back, he secured both wrists into cuffs. The ratcheting of metal seemed louder in that moment. Two others arced their flashlights over the victim's face, her hands, clothing and legs. They took in the bloody screws installed at each of the body's joints. The drill holes would measure out to be caused by a 5/16 drill bit once the medical examiner had a chance to do the autopsy. Just like the others.

Only that wasn't true. Air caught in her throat. She hadn't seen it before now, she'd been too caught up in the investigation at the time. The last victim, the one they'd connected back to the man they believed to be the Contractor. Corey Singleton. He'd used a 3/8 drill bit.

He hadn't been the Contractor at all.

He'd been the copycat.

"What the hell is that?" one of the uniforms asked.

Her attention slid to the woman at her side, strung up for all to see. The answer to his question settled at the front of her mind. Her voice deadpanned as she realized the outfit she'd carefully chosen this morning before heading into the office had been stained with the victim's blood. She rose to her feet at the officer's cue,

the world clearer than it'd ever been before. Her mouth
dried as she considered the implications of what'd just
happened. "My punishment."

*"ACCORDING TO ALAMOSA POLICE, a suspect in the death of
Elisa Johnson's horrific murder has been arrested and
is in custody for questioning. District Attorney Genevieve Alexander was found at her home, holding a gun
at police as they responded to the 9-1-1 call from Alexander's cell phone. Upon arrival, police discovered
the mutilated body of Johnson and blood matching the
victim's DNA on the DA's clothing."*

Genevieve.

Easton Ford twisted toward the television. He lunged
for the remote, knocking it to the floor in the too-small
cabin, and hit the volume button. The news anchor went
on to warn viewers and small children before plaster-
ing photos from the crime scene across the screen. Hell.
The positioning of the body, the amount of blood left
behind… He'd seen the worst in people stationed overseas—survived the worst—but this was different. This
was sociopathic. B-roll video of Alamosa PD's main
suspect answering questions outside the courthouse
replaced the horrific images of the scene.

A surge of familiarity knotted in his gut. Wavy dark
brown hair, wide almond-shaped eyes and flawless skin
triggered his protective instincts as he watched Genevieve in her element in front of the camera. The deep
red blouse and black skirt clung to her lean frame like
a second skin, but it was the honesty and brightness
in her eyes that compelled him to take a step forward.

The numbers in the corner of the screen dated the video a couple months old, but, even after all this time, she hadn't changed much at all. How long had it been? Fifteen years? More? He'd been a silly kid in love with his high school sweetheart, ready to take on the world for her.

Before the world had taught him happily-ever-afters didn't exist.

Not for him.

Three knocks punctured through the focused haze he had on the TV, and he hit the power button. It'd been months since he'd picked up a weapon, but his instincts automatically had him wanting to reach for the safe under his bed. He was being paranoid. The only people who dared to knock on his door out here in the middle of nowhere were his mother and the pain-in-the-ass police chief of Battle Mountain. His brother.

A growl of irritation built in his chest. As the most recent volunteer reserve officer for Battle Mountain PD, he'd taken the brunt of shifts these past few months since Weston had gone and gotten himself a fiancée, but today was his day off. Easton tossed the remote onto the couch. Three steps. That was all it took to cross his small satellite cabin on his family's property.

Whispering Pines Ranch had become more of a retreat to tourists and strangers than a safe haven recently, but his father's death two months ago had made an increase in reservations necessary to keep the ranch running. His mother was doing the best she could, but his intention to disappear—to detach—from the world and everybody in it was getting harder to accomplish every time some tourist needed directions.

He ripped the door back on its hinges, prepared to reestablish the rules of the ranch.

And froze.

"Hi." One word. That was it. She stood there as though he hadn't seen police escort her from her home in Alamosa in cuffs or the blood staining her clothing on the news mere minutes ago. As though she hadn't left him at the altar on their wedding day. As though she hadn't gutted his heart before an IED had tried to finish the job in Afghanistan. Genevieve Alexander, in the flesh. Her hair whipped into her face as spring struggled to hang on a little bit longer. "I heard you were back in the States."

Easton crossed his arms over his chest and leaned against the door frame. Scanning the property, he pegged what he assumed was her vehicle parked along the dirt driveway. Damn. He hadn't even heard her coming. Too distracted by the news that she'd been found in the middle of one of the most gruesome crime scenes in history. "I heard you were arrested for your assistant's murder."

"That's why I'm here." She swiped her hair away from her face, exposing the delicate pattern of bruises across the front of her throat. "I didn't kill Elisa. I found her dead, strung up like a puppet, when I got home from work. The man who killed her. He was waiting for me in the house."

He pushed off from the door frame, gaze locked on the outline of a thumb print along the side of her neck.

An uncontrollable heat exploded through him as Easton closed the distance between them. He pushed her hair out of the way to get a better look. "Who?"

"I don't know. I was in the middle of calling 9-1-1 when he attacked me. I wasn't sure the call had gone through until the police were breaking down my front door." Genevieve seemed to curl in on herself, deep green eyes distant as she lowered her attention to his boots. "Alamosa PD didn't have any other choice but to take me into custody when they responded to the call. They found me at the scene, covered in the Elisa's blood—"

"With a gun in your hand," he said.

She nodded. "I kept it taped to the inside of my chimney for protection. The work I do and the people I prosecute... I make enemies. I didn't want to be unprepared, but I never expected this. I told the police everything he said to me. They're still trying to corroborate I'd just left the courthouse fifteen minutes prior to the call, but they don't have any evidence to file charges. So I was released a few hours ago."

"And you came here." Genevieve didn't have the inclination or the strength to hang a woman from the ceiling, and the evidence of bruising around the back of her neck said she was telling the truth. Someone had attacked her.

"I didn't know where else to go. I need your help, Easton." She set her chin. "You have every right to hate me after what I did, but whoever killed Elisa Johnson is going to kill again. He's doing this because of me, and you're the only one I can trust to handle yourself while I investigate."

"You want to take on a killer without the support of the police." Battle-ready tension hardened the muscles down his spine. Easton pulled his shoulders back, and suddenly, she seemed so much smaller than a minute ago. "What do you mean he's doing this because of you?"

"That's why he killed Elisa. That's why he was waiting for me in my house." Her voice shook. Unlike anything he'd heard before. "Have you heard of the Contractor?"

His instincts kicked into overdrive, and everything inside of him went cold. Easton stepped back. The victim in Genevieve's home. He'd seen that kind of depravity before. "Serial killer. Strung his victims up from the ceiling using fishing line and steel eyelets. You think he has something to do with this?"

"I think he *is* this." Another tendril of breeze filtered through her hair and released the hint of her perfume as she countered his escape. "The man who killed my assistant isn't the same man I prosecuted for the deaths of those four women. He's…disappointed in me for falling for a copycat, disappointed that I took his reputation from him."

"And you believed him?" he asked.

"I prosecuted Corey Singleton on four counts of first-degree murder. The investigating detectives recovered trace DNA from the last scene that pointed them to Singleton. He had a history of violence, a connection with the last victim and was in possession of the drill bit used to burrow holes into the victim's joints. Forensics matched the blood on the drill to her almost immediately." Color drained from her face. "I had everything I needed to prosecute him for the first three deaths through evidence from that scene alone, but there was something different about the last victim compared to the other three. I didn't make the connection until it was too late."

Pressure built behind his sternum the longer Easton let her work her way back into his life. "What connection?"

"Corey Singleton used a 3/18 drill bit to kill his last victim, but the first three? They were murdered using a 5/16th," she said. "I know it doesn't sound like much, but if the man who killed Elisa was lying, why the change in tools? Serial killers have a compulsion to carry out their kills systematically. There's a ritual behind this, an origin story. Something police were never able to pinpoint with Singleton."

"There are any number of reasons for the change. He could've broken the original drill bit, lost it. Maybe he made the change to do exactly what you're doing right now. Throw doubt on the investigation and his guilt. It's obvious Singleton didn't kill your assistant as he's serving the rest of his life behind bars, but the man waiting for you in your home could easily be the copycat. Why take him at his word?" Awareness charged through his veins as her perfume infiltrated his personal space. What the hell was he doing here? What was it about Genevieve that pulled him in to the point he could momentarily forget what she'd done?

"Because I was there," she said. "I heard the truth in his voice."

"You and I both know that wouldn't hold up in court, Counselor." No. He couldn't put himself through this again. Not after he'd just started to get his balance under the crushing weight of grief. For his father two months ago. For his unit he hadn't been able to save last year. He'd done his part in bringing down a killer determined to rip his family apart. He wouldn't put them through that again. He wouldn't lose anyone else.

Easton forced himself to detach, to take a step back. He set his hand on the doorknob, and that mesmerizing gaze honed on the movement. "You've got an entire police force capable of uncovering the truth and protecting you, Genevieve. I'm not one of them."

He moved to close the door.

She slammed her hand against it. Fire simmered in her gaze, and a responding heat flared under his rib cage. "I read the papers, Easton. I know you had a hand in apprehending that man who killed those three victims here in Battle Mountain, including your father. He targeted your future sister-in-law. Someone you didn't even know." Genevieve let her fingers slip down the weathered wood of the cabin's front door and straightened. "Please. Whoever's doing this… He's not going to stop. He wants to prove he's the real Contractor. He believes I'm a key player in his game, and I'm scared. I can't do this without you."

The old brass doorknob protested under his grip. "Then I suggest you start running."

He closed the door behind him.

Chapter Two

She was on her own.

Genevieve shoved the two-decades-old key into the scratched faceplate and pushed inside. A wall of odor burned down her throat as she closed the door behind her. Battle Mountain, Colorado had once been the state's most industrious mining town. But when the mines went out of business and residents had to leave their birthplace for stable employment and income, the town had taken a major hit. Money had dried up, tourism had yet to recover, and places like Cindy's Motel had started showing their age.

The single-level structure stretched between the dilapidated parking lot and overgrown ring of trees. Light blue paint peeled away from the popcorn ceiling and flaked down into the corners of the room. Worn brown carpet came up at the edges and matted in the center of the room. She tossed her keys on the dresser near the door. The beds had been professionally made up, but there wasn't an inch of her body that wanted any contact with those sheets. Sunlight filtered through the dirty window at the back of the room and from a smaller window in the bathroom on the other side of the dresser.

It wasn't much. It wasn't anything, but the thought of going back to Alamosa, of stepping inside that house, nauseated her iron stomach. The life she'd built since leaving Battle Mountain on her wedding day was over. There was no going back, even if Alamosa PD released the scene. Right now, Cindy's was all she had.

Genevieve unshouldered her bag onto the bed. The white noise of cars traveling down Main reached her ears, but where she'd once found comfort in being surrounded by people she'd known all her life, fear tunneled deeper. Someone had broken into her home three nights ago, had killed her assistant and left her for Genevieve to find. He'd put his hand over her mouth and bruised the back of her neck. Her fingers automatically traced the pucker of scabs along her throat. The blade hadn't gone deep, but it would leave a scar. Something for her to carry the rest of her life.

She closed the blackout curtains over the window, encasing herself in darkness. Too exposed. She fumbled for the lamp on the nightstand between the beds. Light clawed up the walls and across the floor as she sat on the edge of the mattress. Her hair slid in front of her shoulder as she reached for her bag. Tugging the folder of files she'd printed from the backup on her laptop before Alamosa PD had taken it into evidence, she bit back the urge to break. Crime scene photos, investigation reports, witness statements—it was all there.

I promised to give you one more chance, and I'm a

*man of my word. Prove I didn't make a mistake when
I chose you.*

Genevieve shoved the folder back into her bag. Chose her for what? As another victim? If that'd been the case, he would've killed her then. Or maybe he'd run out of time. She tensed against the shiver cascading down her spine and forced herself to her feet. She was a district attorney, damn it. He didn't get to do this to her. He didn't get to haunt her for the rest of her life. She'd prosecuted the worst criminals in the state for more than five years. He should be the one to fear her. A humorless laugh escaped her lips as she confronted the mirror over the dresser. "What are you doing here?"

She'd known Easton wouldn't be happy to see her, but the moment Alamosa PD had finished interrogating her, he'd been the one to cross her mind. Not her staff. Not her friends. Not her parents or brother. Easton. She gripped the edge of the dresser, the ache in her fingers anchoring her to the moment. He'd been exactly as she remembered. Defensive. Evasive. Cautious. All the things that'd made him a survivor of war.

Once upon a time, they'd been dumb and in love. They'd had an entire future in front of them and not a single care in the world. A smile tugged at the corner of her mouth. Only it didn't last long, and it'd all come crashing down around her.

She'd felt the cracks starting between them long before he'd slipped that engagement ring on her finger, but Easton had been her first. Her first love. Her first kiss. Her first everything. She hadn't known anything about the world then or her place in it, not even what she wanted to do with her life. He was handsome, loyal and everything she'd been told she wanted in a husband. He'd loved his family and put everyone else's needs, including hers, before his own as his father had taught him. Then she'd gotten into that beautiful lacy dress the morning of their wedding. She'd always loved beautiful things, had a compulsion to surround herself with beauty as much as possible, but the only thing looking back at her while she stood in front of that mirror had been a stranger. A hollow capsule of flesh and bone she hadn't recognized for years.

So she'd run. She'd left the dress behind, the ring, left Battle Mountain and him. She'd worked two part-time jobs in a town less than three hours away to pay for law school and strived to become her own woman. Not Easton Ford's girlfriend, his fiancée or his wife. She'd heard through the small-town grapevine he'd joined the army two weeks after their wedding day, that he'd served his country all this time until his unit had been ambushed last year. She'd grieved. She'd blamed herself for driving him to escape, and the months had slipped by. Until she'd learned he'd survived.

What was she supposed to do now? The police suspected her of having something to do with Elisa's murder, even though she'd been the one to call the police, and there was no evidence of blood on the tools her father had given her when she'd bought the house. They wouldn't let her near the investigation, and the law prohibited her from prosecuting a case where she was involved. Not only that but the one man she believed she could rely on had closed the door in her face. She was alone.

Genevieve raised her gaze to the mirror. She wasn't a detective. She wasn't an investigator. A single moment of terror had ripped the life she'd built from her hands. She'd relied on her work to get her through the worst lows she'd survived. Now all she had was a case file and memories of that night. It would have to be enough. Because the thought of letting another woman die as Elisa Johnson had…

She slid the folder from her bag a second time and forced herself to open it. Spreading the photos across the bed, she took them all in at once. The similarities in the manner of death, the differences in each victim's appearance, the investigative style of the detectives assigned to each case. She tried to breathe through the sob lodged in her throat as she added her assistant's file to the mass of reports.

The police had already started their investigation. She would finish it.

Fishing the roll of Scotch tape from her bag, she secured the first victim's photo to the right side of the mirror, followed by photos of the scene. Genevieve stepped back. She'd been through these files hundreds of times to prove the evidence implicated Corey Singleton in the four murders. Now she'd prove someone else had killed the first three victims.

Maria Gutierrez. Twenty-eight, single, lived alone with no connections to any of the other victims. Soft black hair framed a heart-shaped face and highlighted the richness of the victim's skin. She'd been beautiful with a wide smile in the photographs her parents had given to police. Genevieve remembered them from Singleton's trial, remembered their tears and heartfelt appreciation for putting the animal who'd killed their daughter behind bars. Only now, she wasn't so sure she had. She couldn't imagine what they—what the other families—were feeling with the possibility she'd been wrong. They'd gotten their closure. But it seemed someone was determined to make them relive that loss all over again. She couldn't think about that. Maria had been the first victim. She'd just graduated with her master's in psychology. She'd been preparing to apply to the FBI as one of their criminal investigators with her eye on joining the Behavioral Analysis Unit.

Genevieve crossed her arms over her chest to control the tremors in her hands. She stepped closer to the dresser, studying every pixel of the crime scene photos as though it were the first time. There had to be something here. Serial killers like the one who'd broken into her home didn't wake up and start killing one morning. Something had set him off. Something had attracted him to Maria Gutierrez and the next three victims. "Why was she so special to you?"

She caught sight of Maria Gutierrez's front door. The LED light on the alarm panel was green. No sign of forced entry. Just as there'd been no sign of a break-in at her own home. Police posited Maria had disarmed the panel to answer the door. From there, the killer had forced his way inside. She pulled the photo free of the vanity mirror. No. That didn't make sense. Maria had been fit, training every day to pass the Bureau's physical exam.

She kept herself in shape because she knew what it would take to become an agent. She would've fought back, but there hadn't been DNA under her fingernails or defensive wounds. "You let him into the house. You knew him."

Why hadn't she seen it before? Why hadn't police?

Genevieve turned back to the investigation file. Detectives would've interviewed the victim's friends, her family, coworkers—everyone in her life—to get a sense of her routine and behavior leading up to her death to narrow down their suspect pool. She shuffled through the case file, speed-reading through handwritten notes and typed reports. Witness statements didn't reveal any unusual activity in the days leading up to Maria Gutierrez's death, but the victim's phone records told a different story.

There.

A call from Maria's cell phone to 9-1-1 two weeks before she'd been discovered strung up by fishing line had been singled out among hundreds of others between the victim and her friends and family. Police had foolishly dismissed it as part of the investigation because of the timeline, but Genevieve's instincts screamed there was a connection. The call hadn't lasted more than thirty seconds, barely enough time to report a crime to the dispatcher, but it was something. She raised her gaze to the smiling photo of the Contractor's first victim taped to the mirror. "What scared you enough to call the police, Maria? What did you see?"

GENEVIEVE WASN'T GOING to run.

She hadn't become district attorney by shying away

from a challenge. Only this challenge was sure to get her killed, and hell, if he wouldn't be the one responsible for it. She might've ripped out his heart the day of their wedding, but his father had taught him better than to turn his back on someone in need.

Damn the old man's sense of honor.

Easton forced one foot in front of the other across the parking lot, the to-go bag in his hand. Word at Greta's on Main, the only diner in town, put Genevieve over at Cindy's Motel down the block. The place wasn't much. Multiple rooms lined up one after the other, and there at the end was the same junker car that'd been parked in his driveway this morning. He'd already run the plates. Question was, had Genevieve stolen the vehicle or borrowed it from the owner legally? He bet the latter, considering she wouldn't have wanted to draw extra attention. No more than being Alamosa PD's main person of interest in a homicide investigation.

He jogged across Main and walked straight up to the door. He raised his fist to knock, but it swung inward before he had the chance. A small gasp reached his ears as Genevieve stumbled back. His awareness honed in on the small differences between the woman he'd watched on TV to the one recoiling in front of him. The lack of makeup, the shadows under her eyes, the slight feralness of her hair. Red ringed her eyes as though she hadn't slept in days. Not to mention the fact that she wore an oversized sweater and jeans instead of one of those power suits she'd taken on as armor over the course of her career. It'd only been three days since the attack, but it was obvious Genevieve Alexander wasn't the same. He offered her the bag. "Figured you probably hadn't eaten. I brought your favorite. Waffles from Greta's. Consider it a peace offering."

"How did you know I was here?" She took the bag and peered inside, careful not to touch him. Her expression contorted into confusion. "And where is my bacon?"

"I think you know the answer to both of those questions." He wiped at his mouth to ensure he hadn't left any bacon crumbs or grease behind.

"You never could help yourself, even after I stabbed your hand with my fork at your family's breakfast one Sunday." The momentary crack in expression revealed the same deadpanned humor he'd come to love about her all those years ago. It electrified his nerves but disappeared before he had a chance to lose himself into her gravitational pull. Genevieve stared down at the white plastic bag. "I know you, Easton. You didn't come all the way down the mountain to bring me waffles, and given what you said to me this morning, I know you haven't suddenly had a change of heart. So what do you want from me?"

The warmth between them vanished as quickly as her smile, and the hollowness he'd carried since discovering her engagement ring in the bride's suite of the church flared. "You were right before. My brother and his fiancée were targeted by a serial offender two months ago, and I was part of the investigation. While I don't have as much experience on the force as the Alamosa PD, I have a key set of skills they don't. Mostly intelligence gathering. So after you left—"

"You mean after you told me to start running and shut the door in my face," she said.

Heat scorched down his spine as defiance claimed her expression. Despite distance and time, some things hadn't changed. But he had. "After your visit this morning, I took a look at Alamosa PD's reports on the Contractor killings in National Criminal Information database and requested the original case files, but they only sent two. Seems the FBI took over after a second victim turned up, and seeing as how you were the prosecuting attorney, I assume you have access to the complete investigation file."

"Right." She stood a bit straighter, her attention drifting somewhere off to her right toward Main Street. "And if I said I have the files? What then? You made it pretty clear you didn't want anything to do with me or this investigation this morning. What changed?"

He set his top teeth over his bottom and tapped them together at the sure horror of Battle Mountain's dentist, Dr. Corsey. Memories of loss, of suffocating, of screams and fire fought to escape the box he'd buried them inside. A low ringing started in his ears, and Easton closed his eyes to get ahead of the flashback. His heart rocketed higher, pounding behind his ears. He just had to ride it out and hope there was a small part left of himself when it ended.

"Easton?" Her voice penetrated through the ringing. Soft skin smoothed over the back of his hand, and in an instant, he was anchored in the moment. "Easton."

The ringing stopped. The panic dissipated, and he opened his eyes. She centered herself in his vision. He studied her hands wrapped around his and pulled back. Damn it. He'd had it under control. He'd managed for months, even after being buried alive in a freezer with his brother the night his father had been killed. But within hours of her coming back to town, his brain felt as though it'd been put in a blender on high power. He forced his breathing to slow, forced himself to stay in the moment.

"Are you okay?" Concern etched deep into her expression.

"I'm... I'm fine." He swiped damp palms down his jeans. Distraction. The case. "If you give me a chance to review the case file, I might be able to pull something on your killer. Something Alamosa PD might've missed."

Hesitation slowed her step back into the motel room, but Genevieve nodded. "Yeah, okay." She left the door open for him, and Easton stepped inside. She motioned to the vanity mirror. "This is everything I was able to download before the captain banned me from investigating the last victim's death and took my laptop as possible evidence. Five total, but the fourth—Kayleigh Winters—I'm positive was killed by Corey Singleton, the man I prosecuted, and not the Contractor."

Crime scene photos and investigation reports had been taped over every reachable inch of the main wall in the room. Five distinct victims complete with hot-pink sticky notes in Genevieve's handwriting, but the fourth—Kayleigh Winters—had been set apart from the others. Hell. She'd gone and made herself her own murder board. Then again, Genevieve always had been creative. "You've been busy."

"Yeah, well, when a serial killer breaks into your home to tell you he's the real killer, you need to see the whole story. Not individual pieces." She set the bag with the to-go container of waffles on the farthest bed from the door. Neither of the beds had been disturbed other than to act as a table for the papers she hadn't gotten around to hanging on the murder wall, but from what he'd been able to get out of Greta at the diner, Genevieve had gotten into town last night. She obviously hadn't slept, or if she had, she'd taken the floor. No evidence of food containers other than the one he'd brought either. The district attorney had trained herself to put on a strong face, but the cracks had already started to show. If she kept this up, she wouldn't last the night.

Easton stepped into the web of photos and sticky notes and reports. Most of Genevieve's work seemed to center around one victim in particular. Phone records indicated the victim had made a call to 9-1-1 two weeks before her death. "What's so special about this call to police?"

"Maria Gutierrez was the first victim killed by the Contractor. This started with her." Genevieve closed the distance between them. "Serial killers rarely kill randomly. At least, the pattern isn't random to them. For the majority of the homicide cases I've prosecuted, the first victim ends up being someone the killer knew. I've gone over all of her friends' and family's statements. No one sticks out yet, but I thought if I figured out what made her so special to him, why he chose her—"

"You could determine a connection to the rest of his victims." It was the smart move and made the most sense. Something had to have triggered the killer. The answer could be in Maria Gutierrez's file.

"Yes." Genevieve folded her arms across her chest. "Maria graduated with a master's in psychology. She was getting ready to apply to the Bureau with hopes of joining one of the BAU teams after doing her time in Criminal Investigation. I'm still in the process of trying to get a hold of the 9-1-1 recording. She might've seen something. Something that scared her enough to call police."

"You think she recognized our killer for what he was." And tried to stop him.

"It's possible. She was training herself to see the signs. I won't know for sure until I can review the recording, but I can't find any other instances in her life where she'd need to call 9-1-1," she said. "No one in her family had been hurt, there were no reports of accidents or break-ins in the area around her home. According to the GPS data from her phone, the call originated from her house, near midnight."

"Thirty seconds. That's not much time to explain you suspect someone in your life is a serial killer." Easton unpocketed his phone and speed-dialed Battle Mountain's police chief. His brother and boss. "I'll see what I can do about the recording. After that, we'll know if your theory is right."

The line rang.

Genevieve set both hands on her hips and stared up at the wall. "Thank you."

Two sharp knocks twisted Easton toward the still open door. A courier stepped into the room carrying a small cardboard box, a familiar insignia on his chest. "Hey, I've got a delivery for Genevieve Alexander."

"I...didn't order anything." Wide eyes met Easton's as the color washed from her face and neck. "No one knows I'm here."

Easton ended the call and reached for the box. "I'll take it."

"Have a nice day." The courier jogged back to his truck.

Turning the package over in his hand, he studied the label. Genevieve's name had been handwritten across the box with the motel's address and room number printed clearly below it in thick black marker. Easton slid his phone back into his pocket and pulled his tactical folding knife from the other. He cut through the tape and pried open the lid as Genevieve took position off to his right.

Packing material exposed the single item at the bottom of the box. Nausea churned in his gut as he set the box on the dresser. "I need to call this in."

Chapter Three

He'd found her.

She wasn't sure how, but there was no denying the box that'd been delivered had been meant for her. Genevieve pressed the crown of her head into the aged brick outside her room. Nothing helped. She could still see the blood, the outline of flesh and cartilage.

Weston Ford, Battle Mountain's police chief, had already swept her motel room and bagged the evidence. The coroner, Dr. Chloe Miles, would be able to tell them how long ago the ear had been cut from its owner once she could do a thorough examination. Maybe even whether or not the victim was male or female, possibly get an ID through DNA.

It didn't make sense. The Contractor had never dismembered victims before. Why would he start now? Why send the mutilated ear to her? Genevieve pressed her fingernails into her palms. It wasn't supposed to be like this. She wasn't supposed to be here.

"Do you have any idea of how he knew you were here?" Easton stepped into her peripheral vision. A day's worth of beard growth shadowed the sharp angles of his jaw. Two distinct lines deepened between his eyebrows as he closed one eye against the afternoon sun to look at her. Penetrating deep blue eyes settled on her, and a slow burn climbed up her spine. He hadn't changed much over the years. He'd always been handsome with a combination of his father's good looks and his mother's eyes, but there was something different about him, something weathered. Tested, to the point she couldn't look away.

"No." She shook her head to break the all too familiar spell he cast onto the people around him, the one that drew her into his eyes and urged her to drown in the depths. "I withdrew cash from an ATM in Alamosa before I got out of town and left my credit cards behind. I paid for the room in cash and purchased a phone that couldn't be linked to me. I even surrendered my laptop to the police so it couldn't connect to any networks without my knowing. He shouldn't have been able to find me."

"And your car?" He pulled a small notebook from his back pocket and scribbled unrecognizable notes into it. The seam of his flannel shirt protested against a breeze funneling down the canyon carved into the San Juan mountains.

"I borrowed it from a family member of another case. I told her I needed it for a few days but didn't say where I was going. She said I could use it as long as I needed." Her voice leveled out of habit, masking the tornado of fear and anger spiraling out of control. "Mine is still parked in my garage."

"Then he followed you." Easton stabbed the pen into

his notebook then pocketed both. "Weston and Chloe are still trying to determine where the box came from and who the ear belongs to. We've got DNA and tissue samples, but Battle Mountain doesn't have a forensics lab. It'll be a few days before Unified Forensics in Denver is able to determine any results. I put a call into the delivery company and got a hold of the driver. The warehouse had already loaded his truck by the time he got to work this morning. The box had all the required labels, but the company told Weston the package doesn't actually exist."

"You're saying the killer could've put it on the truck because it looks like all the others." It made sense, but having the answer didn't settle the agonizing buzz of anxiety under her skin. She bit into her thumbnail, an old habit she hadn't been able to kick. She studied the cars in the parking lot, memorizing every license plate, every scratch and dent and possible location the killer could've hidden. Had he been right outside her door this entire time? "Which makes it impossible to trace. What about the driver? Have you talked to the warehouse employees or pulled the security footage from the warehouse?"

Because there had to be something. A killer didn't just walk into people's lives and right back out without leaving a trace.

"We ran a background check on the driver and corroborated his alibi. He was at home helping his wife and their colicky son when the truck was being loaded. As for the security footage, we're working on it. Unfortunately, Battle Mountain PD is a little short-staffed.

You're looking at one of two officers, and the other one isn't the least bit happy I called," he said. "To be fair, Weston's never happy if he has to leave his cabin these days, but that's not the point. Until we can figure out who the hell is behind this, it's not safe for you here alone."

A humorless laugh escaped up her throat, and she dropped her hand to her side as she faced him. "Where am I supposed to go, Easton? I did everything I was supposed to to make sure no one could track me, but it wasn't enough. It doesn't matter where I go. He's designed some kind of test I don't know the answers to, and he's not going to stop leaving bodies behind."

"Then you're coming back to the ranch with me," he said.

The skin along her scalp constricted. No. She nearly flinched against his suggestion. No. "You can't be serious. A killer has marked me as a potential victim, and you want to bring me home with you. Where your family lives, where innocent civilians will be vacationing. You don't want me on your land, Easton."

"Not permanently, no, but it's the only choice you've got." He stepped into her, every inch the soldier she'd imagined these past few years. Committed. Reliable. Defiant. "We have six satellite cabins. Weston and Chloe are in one, I'm in another. Our last tourist left this morning. Mom is in the main house. You'll have your own space, and there's no chance whoever is doing this will find you there. I might not carry a firearm anymore, but the rest of my family does. We know the land. We know the threat. You'll be safe to investigate this case without the weight of being a psychopath's target under our watch. Isn't that the goal?"

She didn't know what to say to that. The logic of it made sense, but her heart warned her the minute she stepped foot on that ranch, surrounded by his family, unable to escape the pull he had on her—she'd be right back where she started. "Why are you doing this?"

"You're the one who asked for my help this morning, Genevieve," he said. "If it makes it any easier, I could always put you in cuffs. Just got myself a new pair a few weeks ago. Haven't had the chance to test them out." His eyes brightened at his own threat. "Besides, you and I both know Alamosa PD told you not to leave town while they conducted their investigation into your assistant's murder. You might be a district attorney, but that doesn't put you above the law. Having two BMPD officers vouch for your whereabouts if they come calling isn't a bad idea."

Damn his logic. Warmth flared up her neck and into her face. He was right. The police still considered her a person of interest, but she wasn't willing to wait for Elisa Johnson's killer to ambush her a second time. "Fine."

"Good." He headed for the familiar turquoise 1959 Chevy Fleetwood pickup with its bulbous headlights and smooth curves. The paint job was new. At least within the past few years. He'd always had a soft spot for the hunk of junk considering how uncomfortable she remembered the seats were. Calling over his shoulder, he hit her with a half smile that knocked the wind straight out of her. "Grab what you need but be advised. Your little art project probably won't fit in the cabin."

Dr. Chloe Miles, soon to be Ford, stepped from the motel room with the cardboard box in one bag and the ear in another. The coroner's long dark hair had been pulled back, exaggerating her beautiful Latina heritage and deep-set eyes. Pristine slacks and a button-down shirt clung to the doctor's lean frame. "Not a lot of people can find a body part in their mail and hold it together like you have."

"As much as I wish it wasn't true, I've seen my share. I know how these things go." She stretched out her hand. "Genevieve Alexander."

Understanding widened the coroner's eyes for a fraction of a second before Dr. Miles tried to hide her surprise. Too late. The good doctor shook her hand. "I heard about what happened to your assistant in Alamosa. I'm sorry for your loss."

"Thank you." She didn't know what else to say. For as many hours and she and Elisa had spent together going over her court schedule and requesting files to review, Genevieve hadn't known her assistant well. They weren't friends. They barely spoke of anything more than the job, but that small connection had been enough for Elisa to become a target. Genevieve took a single step forward, her voice shakier than she meant. "Dr. Miles, two months ago you were almost killed by a man who buried his victims alive in refrigerators. I've reviewed the police reports. I've read your statement, but what I can't figure out is how you did it."

Apprehension filtered across the coroner's expression, and Chloe hugged the evidence closer to her chest. "How I did what?"

"Survive." She needed to know, needed to see the mind game she'd been recruited to participate in had another outcome other than her death.

Dr. Miles nodded, understanding. "Sometimes I'm not so sure I did. Survive. I still have nightmares. I still wake up feeling as though I'm locked in that container, and I'm running out of air." Police Chief Weston Ford maneuvered around them before heading for Easton on the other side of the parking lot, and the coroner's gaze followed him the entire way. A small tug of the muscles at the corner of her mouth betrayed her inner thoughts, and a ping of envy slithered through Genevieve. "Having Weston there to remind me that the man who hurt us and Easton is behind bars helps, but it doesn't make the nightmares any less real."

Easton?

"What do you do then?" A knot of tension solidified in her gut.

"I force myself to remember. What he looked like, how his voice sounded, the smell of his cologne. I put myself back in that refrigerator, and I make myself face the pain all over again to retrain my body not to react. Sometimes it helps. Sometimes it doesn't. Either way, having someone you can trust to be there with you is key." Dr. Miles's smile slipped away as she raised molten-brown eyes to Genevieve. "The thing about fear, Ms. Alexander, is that you have the power to control it. If you don't, you can guarantee it will control you."

THE TRUCK BOUNCED beneath them as Easton accelerated back toward Whispering Pines. His seat protested with each jerk of the shocks, the passenger side window didn't roll all the way up anymore and there was a smell he hadn't quite been able to locate yet. But damn if Genevieve shoving her hair away from her face from the passenger seat didn't throw him back into the past. When life had been simpler and neither of them had known what was coming. "Weston is interviewing the warehouse workers from the shipping company. He should be able to get access to their security footage, too. If we're lucky, we'll know exactly who put that package on the truck."

"Everything about four of the five murders has been planned down to the last detail. No forensics at the scenes. No witness statements." Genevieve kept her gaze out the passenger side window. "Do you really think he's going to slip this late in the game and risk being caught on camera?"

No. He didn't, but it was a lead they didn't have before.

Main Street shops constructed in various shades of red brick and flowering clusters of previously winter-stripped trees thinned as they left Battle Mountain town limits. Monstrous peaks demanded attention as they headed west, only a few strips of snow still clinging to the mountains.

"Thank you," she said. "For helping me. I'm sure I'm the last person you wanted to show up on your doorstep this morning."

"To be fair, I don't want anyone showing up on my

doorstep." He turned onto an unpaved road a mile or so outside of town and maneuvered through a combination of mountainous ridges and family-owned ranches. Muscle memory kicked into gear as he took in the gut-wrenching openness of Mother Nature stretched out in front of them. He wasn't exactly sure how long it'd been since Genevieve had been out this way, whether or not she'd visited Battle Mountain since running all those years ago. Had it changed? Dense pines climbed higher along the ridge steps of the mountain, and for the first time since she'd showed up this morning, comfort warmed through him. He'd been all over the world as a Green Beret to distract him from what he'd left behind, but when his chips had been cashed in after the ambush that'd killed his unit, there'd only been one place left to go. Home. "Especially tourists."

"Because of what happened a couple months ago?" Her voice softened, and the hollowness behind his rib cage revolted. "The way you reacted before…when your hands were shaking… You said you'd been involved in the investigation, but it was more than that, wasn't it? You were buried, too."

Easton ripped the steering wheel to the right. He slammed on the brakes, throwing them both forward in their seats, as the truck came to a sudden stop. He shoved the pickup into Park. Dust kicked up in front of the hood and blocked out the view of the road. His pulse rocketed into dangerous territory as he prepared for the onslaught of memory and pain. "What the hell are you doing, Genevieve? You show up at my cabin after all these years, and you think because we have a past that gives you the right to pry into my life? You don't know me. You don't know what I've been through or who I've lost. You made it pretty clear you wanted nothing to do with me when you left, so why start now?"

Shocked silence descended between them, and her mouth parted slightly.

Easton struggled to contain the repressed rage he'd carried all these years. He forced himself to take a deep breath, but the pain was always there. Always close to the surface.

"You're right. You don't owe me anything. I'm sorry. I thought…" She shook her head as though the simple action could rewind time, and a wave of shame increased its grip on him. She hugged her overnight bag closer to her. "We don't have to talk about anything other than the case. It won't happen again."

He pried his grip from the steering wheel and let his palms slide to the bottom. The dust cleared, revealing serrated peaks fighting to pierce the bright blue sky. A herd of deer stared back at the truck from their position a few yards away. The soft call of a crystalline river flowed alongside the dirt road before it widened into the impossibly green-blue lake taking over the small valley after this year's snow. So different than the bare, blood-soaked, dust-bowl dunes of Afghanistan. Easton pressed his lower back into the peeling plastic seat. Damn it. He'd nearly managed to move past these spurts of rage and isolation with the help of Weston and his parents, but there was no denying he'd ever had control when it came to Genevieve.

But that had never been her fault.

"It's not because of what happened during that case. The…" He ground his back teeth as another flood of shame rose to suffocate him. "The shaking. Weston and I, we were buried in a freezer barely big enough to contain the two of us, but the flashbacks and the bouts of anger started long before then."

She centered that watery mesmerizing gaze on him, and his heart tapped double time. Hell, his mother and Weston, even his father, had gotten used to seeing him like this, but he'd never intended to expose himself for the bitter bastard he really was. "How long?"

"Since my discharge." Easton compressed the brake to counter the buildup of energy streaking down his legs, and the cabin of his truck suddenly seemed so much…smaller than a minute before. "I was the only one in my unit who made it home after our caravan was hit by an IED during our last mission."

Her mouth parted on a strong exhale as though his words had physically hit her. Sunlight breached through the passenger side window and haloed around her from behind, softening the outline of her face. Genevieve stretched one hand out, sliding long fingers across his thigh, but thought better of touching him and pulled away. Too soon. "I'm sorry. I had no idea."

"Why would you?" His nerve endings protested at the loss of her touch, but it was only his imagination. The connection they'd had didn't exist anymore. She hadn't come to him to make up for the past. She'd showed up on his doorstep to ask for his help with a case. That was it. They weren't friends. They didn't keep in touch. He was the best chance she had of outwitting whoever had killed her assistant. Nothing more. Easton notched the pickup into Drive and pulled back onto the road.

The engine revved higher as he topped the first hill before the landscape dipped and spread out into another valley. He turned the shuddering truck once more up a long dirt drive. Two massive logs supporting the sign over the entrance to the fenced property reading Whispering Pines Ranch stood at attention as they passed underneath. Unsteady ground threatened to slow them down as they drove toward the main cabin ringed by the tree line. The cabin's green roof and trim set the structure apart from the six smaller satellite cabins located less than a few hundred yards in each direction. It wasn't much, but it was home.

Easton maneuvered the truck closer to his cabin and parked in nearly the same spot Genevieve had this morning. It'd only been six hours since he'd laid eyes on her after all these years, but so much had changed. He'd never talked about his time overseas, about the terror he'd witnessed or the side effects of losing his unit, but he'd opened up to her. Why? He reached for her arm as some unknown need drove him to keep her in the truck a little bit longer. "Genevieve."

She turned to face him, her hand settled over the door latch.

Years of imagined conversations, confrontations and accusations vanished the longer he studied her. She'd broken his heart. One day decided she'd had enough of him and this town, everything they'd built together, and disappeared. It hadn't been until he'd recognized her on the news a couple years ago when she'd been prosecuting a big case that he'd even realized where she'd gone. Her sweater gave under a single stroke of his thumb and drew her gaze to his hand. Fire burned up his spine as her pupils dilated, nearly blocking out the ring of color in her irises. Easton cleared his throat, peeling his fingers from around her arm. "I need to make sure it's safe before you go in."

"You think he could've followed us?" Genevieve settled back into her seat.

"No, but the second my mother realizes you're here, she might run you out of town with her rifle. Better to be safe than sorry." He shouldered out of the pickup and slammed the door behind him, cutting off the slight comfort of her warmth and perfume. What the hell had he been thinking bringing her out here? His family was barely recovering from his father's death at the hand of a killer, and he'd immediately thought to bring another to their door. His hand tingled with the memory of how her sweater had felt against his skin, and Easton curled his fingers into a fist as he rounded the hood of the truck. There was something very wrong with him.

The last tourist of the weekend had checked out this morning, but he still felt the need to knock before pushing inside the cabin a few yards from his. As though he expected the killer to answer back. Easton pressed his toes into the wooden door as he turned the knob. The scent of wood smoke and cured meat burned down his throat.

The space didn't allow for more than the single counter space off to his left, a small kitchen table straight ahead with two chairs, a single beaten love seat at the back near the fireplace and a twin-sized bed shoved in the corner, but it'd be enough. Looked as though his mom had already been through to make the bed, empty the trash can and wash the dishes. There wasn't anything else here to distract him from the woman waiting for him outside in the truck.

Nothing but a killer determined to claim her for himself.

Chapter Four

She'd run out of tape.

Despite Easton's warning that her murder board art project wouldn't fit inside the cabin, she'd set out to prove him wrong. And failed. The cabin was everything she remembered and everything she wanted to forget. Cozy, secure, full of memories. Each of the Ford boys had gotten their own cabin when they'd turned eighteen if they wanted to live and work on the ranch. This one had been Easton's.

Of course, this had to be the one he'd put her up in for the night.

Genevieve pressed the tape dispenser teeth into her thumb. No word from the police chief or the coroner who'd taken custody of the ear yet. They had no idea where the dismembered ear had come from, who'd sent it or if the Contractor had butchered another victim. She was still waiting for the report from the Alamosa medical examiner concerning Elisa Johnson's autopsy, but even then, Captain Morsey had banned her from looking into the case. Without access to updates concerning the most recent murder file, all she had was what she'd managed to bring with her. She focused on the spread of case files in front of her, but her gaze kept drifting out the window toward the cabin next door. It wasn't enough Easton had showed up at her motel room a few hours ago offering to help with the investigation, but he'd brought her to his family ranch. The epicenter of what her future would've looked like if she'd stayed.

The reverberation of footsteps echoed from the front door before two light knocks registered. Easton. Two steps and she'd crossed the kitchen and twisted the old ornate brass doorknob. Massive shoulders and a hint of soap consumed her senses as he filled the doorway, and her legs shook at the thought of collapsing into him. She wasn't exactly sure how much time had passed since she'd found Elisa strung up from her living room ceiling, but she hadn't slept. Hadn't eaten. None of which she could blame on anyone other than herself. "Hi."

"I brought you something." He held up a package of Scotch tape, unopened.

"You've been reading my mind." Genevieve buried her face in her palms, forgetting she still held the tape dispenser, and stabbed herself between the eyes. Stinging pain lightninged across her skin. She let go of the tape dispenser and pressed her hand to her head, coming away with a light streak of blood. "Ow, damn it."

His deep laugh grazed along her nerve endings and burrowed through sore muscle, straight into bone. It battled the fear undermining her thoughts and swept the doubt lodged in her chest clear. "Here. Let me."

Easton maneuvered around her, larger than life, and went straight for the cabinet under the sink to her left. He pulled out a first-aid kit and popped it open on the counter.

"It's fine." This was ridiculous. She didn't need a first-aid kit for a scratch of her own making. "You don't have to—"

"I know." His voice softened. "But we should at least clean it to prevent it from getting infected. Small wounds like this can turn into big problems if you're not careful." He ripped open an alcohol pad and centered himself in front of her. "Hold still. This is going to sting." Raising his hand in front of her face, he stroked the cold pad across her forehead. Sea-blue eyes steadied on the work in front of him.

"Did you learn that while you were deployed?" As much as she hated the thought of seeing him nearly break down in front of her at the motel, there was a deep need to know what he'd been through. What he'd survived. It wasn't enough a killer had used her assistant to punish her. She'd moved on to punishing herself by leaning into the temptation surrounding him.

"You learn a lot in a combat zone." His gaze lowered to hers, his movements more controlled, hesitant. As though he was preparing for another fight, but the last thing she wanted was to walk back into his life and mess everything up for him again. "Not sure I've ever had to clean a wound from a plastic tape dispenser though."

"Guess there's a first time for everything." Her laugh escaped past her lips, full and genuine. A first in a long time. She held still, cataloging the differences in his expression from over the years. He was older, of course, with lighter threads of hair at his temples. The cleft in his chin seemed more pronounced, but not in a bad way. He'd stopped using gel to style his hair, letting it lie where it fell. Thick bands of muscle roped his arms as he peeled a Band-Aid from the wrapper and gently pressed it to her forehead. Overall, he'd exemplified the best of his gene pool, but there was a weight—almost a shadow—in the way he concentrated on her that hadn't been there before. Experience. Wisdom. Trauma?

He smoothed the edges of the Band-Aid against her skin, rough calluses catching on the fabric. "There. Good as new."

"Thank you." She couldn't remember the last time someone had gone out of their way to take care of her like this. It was nice. It was…warm. Something she'd missed since turning her back on Battle Mountain. And him. Genevieve cleared her throat as he seemed to linger on setting the bandage. "Any word from Weston about the shipping warehouse?"

Reality penetrated the bubble they'd inadvertently created around themselves, and Easton set about cleaning up the wrapper pieces. "He interviewed everyone who'd been on shift this morning. No one remembers seeing anything or anyone out of the ordinary. Weston's running background checks on all of the employees to be thorough, but as of right now, it's looking like a dead end."

"What about the surveillance footage?" Such a simple question, but the entirety of this case hinged on them finding something they could use to identify the Contractor. Anything.

"Disabled about ten minutes before the first shift started loading the trucks," he said.

"Which means he knew their schedule, knew where the cameras were." Genevieve pressed one hand to her forehead, igniting the sting under the bandage he'd set. No matter which angle they looked at this—from the first murder, the last or the package she'd received—the killer was one step ahead of them. Maybe more. "And the 9-1-1 recording of Maria Gutierrez? Any chance Alamosa PD is willing to share with you?"

"I put in a call to Captain Morsey over there to get a copy, but once he learned one of his guys forwarded me the original case files, he severed contact. Seems there are unwritten rules that keep us from stepping into another department's investigation unless a body drops in our jurisdiction. He's holding any more information close to the chest." Easton tossed the bandage wrappers and settled himself against the arm of the couch, casual, at ease and home. "However, Chloe was able to get autopsy results for each of the victims from the medical examiner over there, and you were right. It's clear from the report on the fourth victim, Kayleigh Winters, that she was killed with a different size drill bit. The Contractor used a 5/16th, while whoever killed Winters used a 3/8th. That, combined with the wrong positioning of some of the steel eyelets the killer screwed into the victim's joints says we're very likely looking at two different killers."

"Corey Singleton killed Kayleigh Winters. He wanted her death to look like the work of the Contractor. He tried to put her murder on a serial killer to throw off suspicion. Only he didn't have the knowledge, the methodology or all the details that went into the kills." And she hadn't seen it. Not until it was too late for Elisa. Genevieve balanced against the kitchen table and stared out the window. "I knew there was something different about that case. I knew something wasn't right about Kayleigh's death, but I pushed ahead because I was so determined to stop the Contractor from killing again. Instead, I pissed off a serial killer, and Elisa Johnson ended up paying the price for my mistake."

"It wasn't your mistake, and this isn't your fault." Easton's boots reverberated off the hardwood floor and up through her heels as he closed the distance between them. "You're the prosecutor. You went to law school to protect the innocent and uphold the law. You aren't at the crime scenes. You aren't the one cutting into them to figure out how they died. You are not responsible for what happened to those women, Genevieve. The man who killed them is, and he'll pay for what he's done. You'll make sure of it."

She secured her arms around her midsection. Four victims. Four lives ended too early. "I've been trying to remember everything from when he was in my house. Anything that might tell us who he is, but all I can see is Elisa's face. I'd walked in the front door, and it looked as though she'd just been standing there, waiting for me. Every time I close my eyes, she's who I see." Genevieve swiped at her face to keep herself together, but it was no use. She hadn't been strong enough to fight off her attacker. What made her think she was strong enough not to fall apart? She raised her gaze to his. "It should've been me. Why wasn't it me?"

"I'm not sure I'm qualified to answer that for you. I've been asking myself that for over a year." The deep color of his eyes intensified the longer he stared at her, and in that moment, they seemed to reach a mutual understanding. One of loss, survival, guilt and pain. He'd lost his entire unit in a matter of seconds, walking away as the only survivor, and a killer had left her alive as punishment for not seeing his game for what it was. "We'll find him, Genevieve. Sooner or later, he's going to make a mistake. Killers like this get cocky believing they're out of reach. He's going to show his hand, and we'll be there to take him down."

"How? Alamosa PD isn't going to hand over that recording of the Contractor's first victim." She swiped the back of her hand under her eyes again and straightened, a fraction more stable than a few minutes ago. She wasn't sure why other than she wasn't alone. Despite what she'd done by leaving all those years ago, Easton was prepared to see this through to the end. "All we have is a theory about Maria Gutierrez knowing the killer, and detectives couldn't narrow down a suspect in the other three investigations. The only reason I was able to charge Corey Singleton with all four murders is because the MOs matched. The cases are closed. The evidence is in storage, and we don't have access to any of it."

A smirk tugged at the corner of his mouth. "Captain Morsey might not be willing to share evidence, but I think I know someone who can get us that recording."

BATTLE MOUNTAIN'S POLICE station wasn't anything much. Weathered red brick that'd seen better days stacked two stories high to match the roofline of Hopper's Hardware attached on the other side. A low-key sign reading Police in blue lettering had only recently started lighting up again in part because of the improvements Weston had been making. The wild shrubs and a small section of uncut grass out front would be next on his list, Easton was sure.

The pickup's brakes squealed as he maneuvered into the parking lot off the back. The alleyway along the side of the building fed directly onto Main Street, giving a once staffed department easy access to main roads. A lot had changed in five years. The town's former police chief had done what he could to ensure his officers had employment here in town, but after the mines had shut down and the money had dried up, reserve officers had to move elsewhere. Leaving Charlie Frasier to patrol Battle Mountain for close to two years alone. Until he'd had a heart attack in the middle of a call.

Now Weston held the reins and called the shots.

Well, Weston, Easton and their dispatcher, Macie. Together they'd served and protected this town against one of the most motivated killers he'd ever met, including the hostile forces he'd faced overseas.

Easton shouldered out of the truck and rounded the hood, waiting for Genevieve to meet him before going inside. "Welcome home. Is it everything you remembered?"

"Worse." Doubt settled into the fine lines branching from the corners of her eyes, but when it came to plugging into the lifeblood of nearby departments, Macie Barclay was their only shot.

Genevieve watched her step on the crumbling cement stairs leading up the back of the station. Swinging open the glass door emblazoned with the department's shield etched in gold, she stepped inside. "The last time I was here, we'd gotten picked up by Chief Frasier for parking up at the lake. Your mother picked us up. I'd never been so embarrassed in my life."

"Can't lie. Those were some good times." Easton let the door close behind them and motioned her down the long stretch of old industrial carpeting. Burnt coffee assaulted his senses as they passed the two cells—both empty—and followed the narrow hallway to the front of the station. Another glass door let in the waning light as the sun slowly dipped behind the mountains and highlighted the two-level desk serving as the first stop for townsfolk.

A waterfall of red hair and thick citrusy perfume introduced the woman behind the desk. Macie Barclay turned kohl-lined eyes on them and flashed one of the whitest and widest smiles in existence. "Well, look what the cat dragged in. Your brother's not here, if that's why you've decided to grace us with your grumpy presence." Her gaze cut to Genevieve a split second before she bounced out of her chair. The dispatcher stretched a freshly manicured hand—so fresh Easton could still smell the nail polish through her perfume—to introduce herself. "Oh, you brought a friend. You're not from here. I'm Macie. Let me guess." Macie leaned back slightly, extending one long index finger. "You're a Libra."

"I'm sorry?" Genevieve accepted Macie's hand, her smile faltering.

"She means your astrological sign." Easton swallowed the urge to roll his eyes. They were here to play nice, and to play nice with Macie meant buying into whatever new subject she was obsessed with that week. From the study of volcanoes, to viruses and…what had she talked about for nearly an hour a couple weeks ago? Right. Three-hundred-year-old flowers kept in the Natural History Museum in London. With photos. Today, it looked like they were going to get their signs read.

"Oh," Genevieve said. "To be honest, I'm not sure. My birthday is the beginning of October."

"I knew it. Libra it is." Macie slid her hand from Genevieve's and took her seat with her pen pointed straight at the prosecutor. "You're beautiful, like to see every side of a topic, prone to fantasies and hate being alone." She turned caramel-colored eyes onto Easton as though she intended to wish him away. "Guess that explains why you're with the inspiration behind the middle finger."

"Is this about what I said?" Easton asked. "I don't believe this. All I said was that three-hundred-year-old plants aren't my thing—" He stopped himself cold. "You know what, we don't have to like the same things to work together, and that's not why we're here." He took a deep breath. "Macie, I need a favor."

"Wouldn't imagine you were here for a social visit." The dispatcher lowered her voice in a mock whisper to Genevieve. "It's a miracle the staleness of his cabin hasn't killed him yet."

Genevieve's laugh intensified the heat rising up his neck.

This was going well. "Do you know who the dispatcher is over in Alamosa?"

Macie focused on him. "Sure. Can't say we're friends considering she's been trying to get me to let her and her boyfriend use my treehouse for one of these weekends, but we're on speaking terms. Why?"

"We need the recording of a 9-1-1 call placed by a woman named Maria Gutierrez. Dispatch received the call two weeks before she was found murdered in her home. We think that call might tell us who killed her." Genevieve handed off the call logs she'd pulled from her file with the highlighted line. "We've asked the captain for a copy, but he doesn't want any other departments involved in the case."

Macie sat a bit straighter, the humor draining from her expression. She centered her gaze on Easton. "You're asking me to break department regulations, Easton. Alamosa's dispatcher could lose her job if Captain Morsey realizes you're working one of his cases, and Weston would take the heat if this connected back to us. What's going on?"

"We believe Maria Gutierrez's killer has butchered three other women, including Genevieve's assistant three days ago." There was no other way to stress the importance of that phone call. All the forensics, the autopsy reports, all the crime scene analysis—none of it had pointed back to their killer. "He broke into Genevieve's home, Macie. He strung Elisa Johnson from the ceiling for her to find, and there's a possibility she's next. I'm not going to let that happen, but I can't find him if I don't know who I'm looking for. Please."

He settled his hand over Genevieve's, leaning into her warmth.

The dispatcher's maroon-lipsticked mouth twitched below the light birthmark on the right side. Macie's gaze slid to Genevieve then back. "All right, but if you get caught, I'll say you used your woman's voice to imitate me and asked for the recording yourself. Understand?"

"Thank you." Relief crushed through him, but he wasn't willing to let go of the woman at his side.

"Don't thank me yet." Macie turned back to her desk and set her headset. She rapidly pecked a series of numbers Easton didn't recognize with the end of her pen and leaned back in her chair. "Valerie, hey. It's Macie over in Battle Mountain. Were you still interested in my treehouse this weekend?"

In less than five minutes, Macie's email pinged with an incoming download from Alamosa's dispatcher. "This better be worth it. The last time I let someone stay in my treehouse, I had to throw away my sheets. If your victim doesn't say her killer's name on this recording, I'm going to make you listen to another two hours of what other kinds of anemones the Natural History Museum keeps in their drawers. By the time I'm done, you'll love them as much as I do."

"I'd rather go back to Afghanistan." Easton leaned down and anchored both hands on the edge of the dispatcher's desk.

Genevieve elbowed him in the ribs.

Macie hit the white triangle positioned under a linear countdown of the recording. "Here we go."

The countdown ticked down. Background static punctured through the silence. "9-1-1, what is your emergency?" Another few seconds slipped by. "Hello, is anyone there?"

"Yes. I'm here." The woman on the other end of the line sounded calm, collected. Nothing like Easton had imagined if their theory the victim had known her killer was valid. "My name is Maria Gutierrez. I'm calling because I think…" Maria inhaled sharply, lowering her voice. Because someone else was in the house? "I think my friend might hurt someone."

Easton raised his gaze to Genevieve's. She'd been right. Maria Gutierrez must've known her killer and paid the price for that knowledge.

"Where is your friend now, ma'am?" the dispatcher asked on the recording.

"He's… I don't know. I… I don't know what to do. I didn't know who else to call." Shuffling reached through the background of the call as the victim paused. "He's exhibiting all the signs I was trained to watch for. He's been lying to me. He's manipulative, and he's growing more hostile. The smallest things are setting him off, and I'm not sure I can do this."

"Ma'am, are you in danger?" The dispatcher's keyboard penetrated through the line. "Can you get somewhere safe until an officer arrives?"

Maria dropped her voice to a whisper. "I think he knows."

The call ended.

Tension intensified the ache at the base of Easton's skull as he stared at the screen. Prying his grip from the edge of the desk, he turned to face Genevieve. His heart threatened to beat out of his chest. He wasn't sure what he'd expected to hear, but the fear in the victim's voice had unnerved him more than being locked inside a freezer with his brother. "You were right. She knew him. She knew what he was capable of and called 9-1-1 because she was worried that he was going to hurt someone."

"Macie, are you able to see if an officer was dispatched to Maria Gutierrez's home or if there was report detailing what happened after the call?" Genevieve diverted her attention to the computer screen.

The dispatcher swung her legs out from under the desk. "No. The only system I have access to is Battle Mountain's. If you want to see any incident reports, you'll have to go through Alamosa's captain."

"She saw the signs." A hint of that same fear Maria exhibited on that call settled in Genevieve's voice and raised the hairs on the back of his neck. "He was there. He figured out what she suspected."

Easton straightened. "And he killed her for it."

Chapter Five

The tremble in Maria Gutierrez's voice echoed in her head.

Genevieve shuffled through the stack of case files she hadn't gotten around to taping on the walls. Night had fallen, closing in tighter than she wanted to admit, as she huddled near the cabin's fireplace. Every light in the room cast a haloed glow to counter the shadows, but it wasn't enough to erase Maria's voice from playing on an endless loop.

The victim's smiling face stared back at her from the murder board. No matter how many times she'd gone through the case, there wasn't anything new. Detectives had run down acquaintances, coworkers, family members, friends and neighbors even remotely connected to Maria Gutierrez. Men and women alike. No arrest records or priors. No sealed juvie records detailing childhood hostility or experimentation on animals. Not one of the victim's friends or family members reported any new men in Maria's life, no one she was dating at the time. Nothing that would make them think she was in danger. The man who'd killed Maria had slipped into her life unnoticed and slipped right back out. A ghost.

Genevieve closed the file and stared into the flames in the fireplace. Her fingers tingled with the urge to toss the case file and all the others into the fire, to forget. Alamosa PD had closed their case. A killer was behind bars. The families had gotten the closure they'd deserved. Why couldn't she? The Corey Singleton case had shot her career forward more so than any other she'd prosecuted. Only now she realized, it'd all been based on a lie. She closed her eyes, exhaustion increasing gravity's hold on her body. There wasn't anything more she could do tonight. They'd found proof Maria Gutierrez had known her killer, but that didn't give them a name or a connection to the man who'd broken into Genevieve's house three nights ago. They were back to square one.

It seemed as though the floor rose to embrace her. She wasn't sure how long she lay there, warmed by the fire, safe. It wasn't just the cabin. As much as she'd feared coming here would raise the past from the dead, there was no other place she'd rather be. Whispering Pines had been her second home for so long, she'd left a part of herself here. The missing piece of her identity was here. Easton was here, and an easiness she'd never achieved outside of Battle Mountain slid through her.

The jolt of steady footsteps kept her in that purgatory space between sleep and wakefulness, and then she was floating. The hardness of the floor slid out from under her, and a shiver crossed her shoulder from the loss of heat. Strong arms secured her against a broad chest. Her fingers dug into soft cotton. So familiar.

"Damn it, woman, you look like death. When was the last time you ate something?" His voice rumbled straight through her, soothing the rough edges of doubt and fear strangling her from the inside.

"*You* look like death." Her accusation elicited a delirious laugh she couldn't contain. Okay, it might've been a while since she'd let herself slow down, but she'd pulled all-nighters before. She just needed a power nap. Then she could get back to the case. Genevieve pried open her eyes, meeting the sharp angles of his jaw and the tendons in his neck. Easton. The cabin dissolved around the edges of her vision. Her feet touched down on the twin bed positioned into the corner of the room before he slid her onto the mattress. Flannel blankets and crisp sheets brushed against her skin, and she sank deeper into the hug of familiarity and comfort. "I couldn't find him, Easton. The man who hurt Elisa. I tried, but he's too careful. How am I supposed to stop him if I don't know who he is?"

"By remembering you don't have to do it alone." Callused fingers brushed through the hair at her temple. The intensity in Easton's expression drained as he studied her, and her heart squeezed in her chest. "Chloe's been through the autopsy reports of the victims you attributed to the Contractor. Killers like him are compelled to follow their own set of rules. Deviating from those rules is rare. If we can find the pattern, we can find the connection between the victims. He chose them for a reason, Genevieve. Just as he chose you. They weren't random. We know Maria Gutierrez suspected what he was. We know he inserted himself into her life before killing her. It's possible he did the same with the others."

But would it be easy to prove? Would it be enough to find their killer? And did that mean a killer had inserted himself into her life, too?

The three lines between his eyebrows deepened. Only this time, she didn't fight the need to smooth them from existence. Reaching out, she skimmed her thumb over his forehead. Rough lines eased from his face, his breathing slowing, and the image of him in pain outside her motel room infiltrated into the moment. All her life, Easton Ford had been a rebellious hero in her eyes, out of reach, elusive, strong. But in that moment, he'd been...human, and she'd wanted nothing more than to deny she'd played a part in it. "Why are you doing this, Easton? Why are you still here after what I did?"

Seconds distorted into minutes, into what seemed like an hour as he raised that piercing gaze to her. He lowered his hand away from her temple, securing his fingers around her wrist. He pressed her skin to his. "Because I don't have anyone else."

The grogginess of running off three days' worth of adrenaline and minimal calories evaporated. She didn't understand. Genevieve pressed her free hand into the mattress and sat up to balance on her left hip. "What do you mean? You have your family. Your brother, your mom. They'd do anything for you, if you asked."

"They're not you." He pushed to his feet, turning his back on her. "The minute I returned home after my discharge, I knew something had changed. They started treating me differently, as if I was something that could be fixed given enough time. They keep their distance to give me my space. They avoid talking to me about what happened, waiting for things to just go back to normal. But there is no more normal. Not for me. They look at me with nothing but pity in their eyes, but you…" His voice dipped lower. "You look at me as though I'm the man you said yes to when I asked you to marry me, like I'm still the center of your world. Like I'm…whole."

Whole. She didn't know what to say to that, what to think. Genevieve slid her legs from beneath the covers, instantly aware she didn't have the protection of her jeans and sweater anymore. Instead, she'd changed into her sleep shirt and shorts when they'd gotten back to the ranch, completely exposed as she stood there in front of him. "Can I tell you a secret?"

The muscles in his throat constricted on his swallow. "Okay."

"None of us are whole." She stepped into him, setting her hand over his heart. "None of us get to walk away from this life without a few scars. Yes, yours are deeper. They're more violent. They've changed you and changed the course you thought your life would take, but you're still you. Out of all the people I could've gone to when I needed help, I knew I could depend on you."

He didn't answer.

"I'm not going to pretend to know what you've been through or how it felt when you realized you were the only one who'd survived that ambush. But to me, you're still every bit the man I think about before I close my eyes at night." The steady beat of his heart against her palm settled something in her. She didn't know how else to describe it other than peace. "You're the one who stepped between me and Adan Robinson when he wouldn't take no for an answer that day in the lunchroom. The one who called to make sure I was okay after you found the engagement ring and I'd already left Battle Mountain. You protected our country until they wouldn't let you back into the field again and immediately chose to defend this town as one of its reserve officers, and no one gets to see you as anything less than the brave, sacrificing, loyal man you are. Not even you."

Easton pressed his thumb into her palm. "None of that was good enough for you. Why would it be good enough for anyone else?"

"It was. It is. The day I left…" Her mouth dried as her own confidence cracked under his scrutiny. No. This wasn't about her. This wasn't the time or the place. "What I'm saying is you've always been there for me. No matter the situation or had badly I hurt you all those years ago, you never gave up on me. Now let me be here for you. To listen, to be in the same room as you, to read you a bedtime story—whatever you need from me. I'm here. I owe you that much."

"Would you really read me a bedtime story?" he asked.

The pressure behind her sternum released, and she couldn't hide the curl at the corner of her mouth. He swept his hand down her forearm, igniting a trail of goose bumps, before settling it under her elbow and tugging her closer. "I mean, I'm not going to read you the articles from a dirty magazine, but I'm sure we could work out some kind of arrangement."

"Nobody reads the articles in dirty magazines. No matter what they try to tell you." His exhale brushed against her neck as he drew her closer. He threaded his fingers into her hair at the base of her neck, and her heartbeat ticked up a notch.

The heat she'd lost when he carried her from her position in front of the fireplace reignited under the weight of his study. The investigation, the package she'd received at the motel, the terror that'd become part of her—none of it seemed real in the circle of his arms.

Easton strengthened his grip on her and lowered his mouth to hers.

THERE HADN'T BEEN anyone else.

Easton penetrated the seam of her lips. Hints of toothpaste and something sweet burst across his tongue as he memorized her from the inside out. Her lips were smooth and warm. His heart seemed to seize in his chest. The guards he'd kept in place to keep him from hurting the people around him cracked under pressure. Passion built in a tornado of heated frenzy until every cell in his body begged him for release, and he drew back to catch his breath.

Color infused the tops of her cheeks and ringed her lips. "Wow, that was…"

"Not exactly the reason I came over here." His fingers dimpled the skin of her arms. Damn, she felt good. Familiar and warm. He couldn't remember the last time he'd let himself disappear into uncertainty like that, that he'd felt that at peace. His pulse pounded out of control, but he feared if he let himself fall back into her, he might never surface. Genevieve had left him once, and the only way he'd survived was drowning himself in service to his country. There were no guarantees he'd make it through a second time. Because she would leave. Once this case was finished, she'd go back to her life in Alamosa. She'd forget all about him. Flames crackled from the fireplace, ripping him back into the moment. The woman who had the ability to anchor him in the storm of his own mind had become a target. He couldn't afford to forget that. Easton peeled his hands from around her arms. He cleared his throat.

"I was going to say intense." Her coy smile ignited another knot of desire. But no matter how long they tried to convince themselves reality didn't exist, it would come back to bite them harder than before if they weren't careful.

"Yeah. I guess I had a few things I needed to work out," he said.

"With my mouth." She laughed, a light compelling note of music he'd fought to bury, but he'd only been kidding himself. "And you came over because…"

"Right. You've been running off of fumes since the attack. I thought I would take a look at your files while you rested. The ones I received from Alamosa PD aren't complete as far as I can tell, and the FBI is sandbagging me since I wasn't involved in the original case." He caught a whiff of the dinner he'd smuggled out of the main house. "Oh, and I brought you some of Mom's chili."

"I'm starving." She nearly lunged for the steaming bowl of hamburger, tomato, cheese and onions. Framing her fingers around the ceramic bowl, she inhaled the spicy aroma and raised curious green eyes to meet his. "You added pickles. I can't believe you remembered."

"I remember everything about you," he said.

She hauled a massive spoonful of chili into her mouth and closed her eyes, and damn, if that wasn't one of the most beautiful sights he'd ever seen. Despite the pain lodged under his rib cage, Genevieve had always captivated everyone around her like this. "I thought I'd made up how good her chili was, but it's heaven. Her homemade pickles are the best. Thank you."

"You're welcome." He circled the ring of papers she'd created in the center of the floor. Brightly colored sticky notes angled across multiple pages with handwritten notes. Witness statements had been highlighted, forensic test results compared between cases. She'd been at this for hours. "Anything new?"

"Not yet." Her spoon clinked against the side of the bowl as she maneuvered into his personal space. Pale skin warmed under the glow of the fire, but her gaze had lost the brightness he'd noted a few minutes before. "I've been through everything, including the victims' financials to try to connect them that way. There's a reason he chose these four women as a whole. I'm just not seeing it. They look nothing alike. Two of them visited the same restaurant the weeks they were killed, but that leaves two others who didn't. None of them were related or worked in the same fields. Apart from the fact they all lived in Alamosa or just outside city limits, there's nothing here to tell me why they were targeted."

"Well, the 9-1-1 recording told us Maria knew him. She was around him long enough to notice the signs something wasn't right. She called police because she feared he'd hurt someone." He bent to pick up the photo of Maria Gutierrez and straightened. "My guess, he killed her out of pure survival. She caught on to him before he could go after who he really wanted, so building a connection between her and the other three victims wouldn't get us far."

"You're saying she wasn't an intended target." Genevieve studied the arrangement of files around her feet. She set her bowl on the fireplace mantel and speared her fingers through her hair. "That would mean the FBI profilers based their initial assessments off of wrong information. They specifically built that profile based off of her when they took over after the second victim was found and tried to make the pieces fit when he killed the others."

"He told you Elisa Johnson was killed because of his disappointment in you," Easton said. "This isn't about finding a connection between the victims. We need to look at each case as its own crime. We need to find out what it was about each of these women that fascinated the killer."

"And we'll find him." Genevieve shifted her weight between both feet. "Okay. We know why Maria Gutierrez was killed. He didn't want her to expose him before he was ready. Friends and family don't know about any new men in her life, which means he made sure to keep a low profile. Elisa Johnson died because she had a connection to me. He didn't know her. He used her to get my attention." Her voice hitched on the last word, but she pushed on. She curled her index finger around her chin, and Easton caught a glimpse of the fire she'd lost since the attack, the intensity he'd always admired. "That leaves the other two victims. Annette Scofield was an Alamosa PD rookie. She'd only been on the job a few days when her partner arrived at her home to pick her up for their shift and discovered the body."

"The second victim was a police officer?" Instinct prickled at the back of his neck. Easton rifled through the victim's file. Annette Scofield had just graduated from the academy, but instead of taking on crime in a larger city as most officers were wont to do, she'd returned to her hometown. "An unofficial FBI profiler, an assistant in the district attorney's office and a rookie officer." It was a theory, but it might give them the break they needed. "Tell me about the third victim."

Genevieve collected the last file and handed it to him. "Um, Ruby Wagner. Twenty-eight years old, single…" Her mouth parted slightly. "She was an EMT for the city."

That was the connection.

"She was someone who had police connections and was familiar with human anatomy. When the killer broke into your house, you said he wanted you to become the opponent he deserves." Easton set the corner of the file in his hand in the center of her chest. "What if he put the same expectation on these victims as he put on you?"

"He's choosing them because he wants them to stop him." A combination of relief and exasperation unbalanced her, and she settled back onto the arm of the couch. "The first three victims were discovered in their own homes. As far as the crime scene units were able to tell, there were no signs of a break-in at any of the victims' residences, either. But the killer put Elisa Johnson in mine. He's rebelling against his own MO."

"It's possible he's escalating. He could be choosing targets that present a unique challenge. Maria because she could see him coming, Ruby as an EMT who would've known how to defend herself when it counted and Annette as an armed police officer. But they weren't able to stop him from killing, so he's moved on to the district attorney herself, but this time he wanted to announce himself. He went through your assistant. He broke into your home. He had chosen to confront you because of the challenge it presented then left her body to motivate you and to take the bait. He's upping the stakes for the pure joy of showing us his power." Which put Genevieve in more danger than they'd originally believed. If the killer was murdering the subjects of his experiments, how long did that give her?

There had to be more here they weren't seeing. The man who'd strung up Genevieve's assistant would've contacted each of his opponents to throw down the challenge to stop him. So why hadn't they gone to the police? Why hadn't they reported the incidents? Unless, they hadn't realized they'd been invited to his sick game.

"And the ear he sent to my motel room?" Her voice

shook. The rawness in her expression cut straight through him. She was exhausted, barely making it through the day. Even now, she tried to hide the tremor in her hand, but Genevieve couldn't hide from him. She'd never been able to. "What does that have to do with anything? Who did it come from?"

He didn't know, and a part of him didn't want to know the answer. Seemed after the first three murders, this killer was determined to prove the FBI profilers and Genevieve wrong on every account. Tears welled in her eyes as she stared into the flames, and he couldn't hold himself back anymore. Easton crossed to the couch and took a seat beside her. Sliding his arm around her hips, he tugged her into his lap. She buried her nose in the crook of his neck. Right where he needed her. "Chloe should have more information for us in the morning. Until then, you should sleep. There's nothing left for us to do tonight, but I can stay as long as you need."

"Thank you." She set her hand against his chest. "I promise to read you a bedtime story tomorrow."

"I'm going to hold you to that." His body turned heavy as the weight of the day infiltrated every muscle, tendon and bone, but he didn't dare move. Genevieve's breathing slowed after a few minutes as he studied the faces of the victims spread out in front of them. Clutching her closer, Easton set his head against the back of the couch and closed his eyes.

For the first time in years, he didn't have to imagine what it'd feel like to hold her again. He had the real thing. She was here, in his arms, alive.

Now all he had to do was keep it that way.

Chapter Six

Sweat built along her neck and arm.

Genevieve pried her head from the damp flannel beneath her. To find that damp flannel belonged to the man she'd never thought she'd see again. His mouth hung open, the deep rumble of his inhales burrowing through her. Sunlight pierced through the small window near the front door and sharpened the angle of his jawline.

He'd held her all night. Aside from the years of pain she'd caused and her promise to be there for him, he'd put her needs ahead of his own. Again. She skimmed the backs of fingers beneath his chin. How on earth had she walked away from a man like him?

A low sound caught in his throat as Easton stretched long legs in front of him. His jeans molded to powerful thighs beneath her, and he blinked a few times to sweep the night from his eyes. That mesmerizing gaze slowly slid to her, hesitation etched in his expression. "How long have you been watching me sleep?"

"Long enough to discover your secret." She liked this game, the one where she could make him squirm for a few minutes, and she got to see the unguarded and exposed ranch hand she'd fallen in love with all those years ago. "You talk in your sleep."

"No, I don't." He scrubbed his hand down his face. "And you can't prove it."

"You sure about that?" Genevieve reached down in front of the couch into her duffel bag. She curled her fingers around the phone she'd purchased on her way out of Alamosa and brought up the recording app. Hovering her thumb above the play button, she committed this moment to memory. "Would you care to amend your statement, Officer Ford?"

Pure panic washed across his face, and her heart shot into her throat. "Whatever I said, I was obviously asleep. It wouldn't be admissible in court, and I'll deny everything."

A burst of laugher rushed up her throat, and she tossed her head back. Genevieve hit Play. His sleep-addled voice ran through the exact location where he'd hidden his brother's favorite teddy bear as a kid between bursts of deep inhales. "If I go out there with a shovel and follow these directions, am I going to find Weston's Crunchy the Bear?"

Easton sat a bit straighter, which was harder to manage with her still in his lap. "I can explain. He stole my collection of superhero cards to trade them at school with his friends. Hiding his bear was payback. That's all, and then... I might've forgotten Crunchy was still out there."

"Easton." She wiggled the phone in front of him.

"Okay. I didn't forget, but I warned him what would

happen if he didn't get those cards back. I told him what I would do to that bear, and he didn't follow through. So, really, it's his fault," he said. "He's a grown man, a police chief, for crying out loud. I don't think he's still missing his bear."

His cell pinged with an incoming message.

She gripped the phone and set her feet to the cold hardwood floor. The fire had gone out hours ago, but she'd managed to sleep better than ever. Because of him. "You better hope not, or I'm going public."

"I'm going to get that recording." Easton lifted his hips off the cushion and retrieved his phone from his jeans. "Chloe has results on the ear that was sent to you at the motel room, but she's not comfortable talking about it unless it's face-to-face. I should get down there."

"I just need a few minutes to get ready." Genevieve collected a fresh set of clothes from her bag, but she was running out of clean outfits. Three days since leaving Alamosa, and all she had to show for it was unbridled fear threatening to rip her apart whenever she closed her eyes.

"I'm not sure that's a good idea, Genevieve." He'd lowered his voice, but every word registered as though he'd shouted across the room.

"It's not a good idea to get ready or that I come with you to see Chloe?" Halfway to the bathroom, clothes and toiletries in hand, she slowed. He didn't need to answer. It'd been clear in his tone. No. He didn't get to sideline her in the middle of the play. She turned to face him, her fingers aching from the grip on her belongings.

"I brought you this case. Don't you think I should be the one to make the call whether or not I'm involved?"

"This killer challenged his victims to stop him before he screwed eyelets into their knees and elbows and anywhere else he could before he hung them from the ceiling with fishing line." He pointed a strong index finger toward the floor to enunciate his point, but all she heard was that blood-curdling doubt in his voice. "He's already broken into your home. He's made it clear you're his next obsession, and I can't protect you if you're not trying to protect yourself."

"And I can't make sure he pays for what he's done if you lock me in my room," she said. "What are you doing, Easton? Do you think because you kissed me, and we spent the night on the couch together, that I'm going to let you do this without me? He might already have his next victim, and I'm not going to stand here and do nothing about it. You of all people should understand that."

"Do you want to end up like them?" The collapse of his defense took physical form as he stumbled back a step, and in that moment, she wasn't exactly sure which Easton she was talking to. The former fiancé, the soldier who'd survived Afghanistan or the Battle Mountain PD officer. "I can't…"

Seconds distorted between them.

They didn't have time for this. They'd made a connection between a killer and his prey, and they couldn't let that lead slip through their fingers. This was the first break in the case since Corey Singleton had copied the Contractor's MO, and she'd promised herself to see it through. The man who'd broken into her home wouldn't stop with her, but she had the chance to stop him. Here. Now. "You can't, what, Easton?"

"I can't lose you again!" He lunged forward, framing his hands on either side of her face. Fire burned in the depths of his eyes. His chest rose and fell in violent waves as he forced her back two steps. The hard length of his body pressed against hers. "I just got you back. Don't you understand that?"

She honed on the small muscles ticking below his jaw. Genevieve dropped her clothes at her feet, her toiletries spilling out of her cosmetics bag, but she didn't care. This moment. This was the one that had the potential to destroy the connection they'd started rebuilding, and she didn't want to lose that. She slid her fingers up his forearms, her senses at full attention. "The morning of our wedding, I was looking at myself in that dress in front of the mirror."

He moved to release her, but she kept his palms in place. "Genevieve—"

"No, you've been wondering what happened that day all these years. You deserve an answer." She forced herself to take a deep breath as the truth burned to the surface. "You were the reason we got together. You were the one always making sure I got to work okay and that I had everything I'd ever wanted for our wedding. You were this amazing, dedicated guy all the girls wanted, and I was nobody."

His mouth parted to argue, but she wouldn't let him.

"No one ever looked twice at me. Except you. I didn't understand why you'd stepped in between me and Adan

Robinson that day in the lunchroom, or why you asked me out on the way home. I didn't know why you'd want me at all. Then the longer we were together, I realized I'd gotten so wrapped up in you and your personality, in this idea of what we looked like to everybody else, that when I finally faced myself in the mirror, I didn't know who I was anymore. My parents, my brother— they all loved you. They pushed me to make the leap. To marry you, have your babies, to help you run this ranch and create this big family legacy, because that's what I was supposed to do. For them, Battle Mountain was it. There wasn't anything outside of this town, but when I was in that dress, all I saw myself as was… yours. I've spent the past fifteen years trying to prove I'm my own person." She shifted her weight between both feet and licked her lips. "Please don't try to unravel my hard work."

She'd never said the words out loud before, wasn't sure if they made sense, but it was too late to take them back now. Understanding melted the intensity from his gaze, and the pressure behind her rib cage subsided. "My leaving had nothing to do with you. Okay? I needed to create my own identity, away from you and this town. But the truth is, you can't lose me again because I'm not that woman you knew. Not anymore."

He smoothed his thumbs across her cheeks. A hint of acceptance filtered across his expression, and he backed away. "I believe you, and I have no right to decide if you're involved in this case, but I'm still your partner during the course of this investigation. If there is any doubt about your safety, I'll do whatever it takes to keep you alive. Understand?"

"I understand." Genevieve collected her clothes and toiletries from the floor and held them close to her chest. Her skin tingled under the remnants of his touch as she turned toward the bathroom. "I'm going to get ready. I'll be a few minutes."

"I'll meet you at the truck. There's something I have do to." Easton headed for the front door of her small cabin, and before she had a chance to take her next breath, he was gone.

Genevieve closed the door behind her and set her belongings on the small countertop. After twisting on the shower, she stripped free of her pajama shirt and shorts. She could still smell him on her, that combination of soap and man, as though he'd seamlessly worked under her skin all over again. A single day. That was all it'd taken to fall back into Easton's gravitational pull, but she wasn't nineteen anymore. She was stronger than her basic instincts, and she'd walk away from the investigation every ounce the woman she'd worked to become. Even if it meant never seeing him again.

She scrubbed from head to toe with the lavender-scented soap provided to tourists staying at the ranch and washed his influence down the drain.

THE JACOB FAMILY FUNERAL HOME had become a poor substitute for the coroner's office the past few years, but there wasn't anywhere or anyone else in Battle Mountain willing to work with the dead.

Easton shoved the shuddering truck into Park out

front. Residents took to Main Street on foot, coming and going through the old ma and pa shops that made up the heart of the town. Jagged cliffs and budding trees cast shadows along the street. But while a calm had settled over the town since a serial killer had claimed this area as his hunting grounds two months ago, a storm churned violently inside him.

He'd finally gotten the answer he'd been searching for since his wedding day. Genevieve had disappeared because she'd needed to figure out what she'd wanted to do with her life, to break away from the expectations of his family, hers, this town. She'd wanted more than he'd been able to offer at the time, more than him. Hell if he didn't blame her, but knowing the answer didn't lessen the loss he'd sustained or make it any less real.

"This is the coroner's office?" Genevieve pushed out of the truck, a few strands of hair sticking to the coat of intense red lipstick. She swiped at her face as she studied the two-story facade.

Easton followed and slammed the driver's side door behind him. A low whistle cut down the canyon. The official town anthem. "Chloe has an office set up in the back. Morbid, but it does its job." He motioned her ahead of him before ascending the three short steps inside.

Cool air tainted with a hint of cleaning chemicals dove into his lungs. Neutral walls and industrial carpet that'd once been littered with shattered glass from a bullet meant for Weston and Chloe had been replaced with a darker color. Images of the last time he'd stepped through this door threatened to pull him out of the moment, but he wasn't here to relive the past. It'd moved on without him. Easton led them through the sales room and deeper into the building.

Dr. Chloe Miles's office wasn't more than a single room with an exam table in the center, a drain underneath and an L-shaped formation of white cabinets stocked with medical supplies. No bodies today. Well, not entirely. He knocked on the open door, and the coroner turned with a wide smile. "You said you had some information on the ear sent to Genevieve yesterday morning?"

"Yes, come in. I don't…really have anywhere for you to sit though." Chloe's long dark hair had been pulled back in a tight bun at the nape of her neck. Her white lab coat accentuated sandalwood skin and the myriad of freckles across the bridge of her nose. Somehow, his soon-to-be sister-in-law maneuvered around the room on heels as though she'd been born in them. "Your brother borrowed my stool and never brought it back."

"The counter is fine." Easton took the edge of one cabinet, off guard as Genevieve settled next to him. Her fingers brushed against his, and his blood pressure skyrocketed. He forced himself to focus. "Did you find anything that can tell us who sent the package yesterday?"

"The tests I ran on the box itself produced one set of partial fingerprints. I compared them against the driver who delivered the package and was able to eliminate him based on his driving route and his phone's GPS at the time the truck was loaded. He's not your guy." Chloe rounded the head of the exam table. "But I found another partial print permanently sealed under the label the killer used to make the package blend in with the others. Unfortunately, the label's adhesive is making it impossible for me to run it through the federal database, so I need to send it to Unified Forensics in Denver. Even then it might not be enough to get an ID."

"That could be the killer." Genevieve stepped forward, her gaze locked on the spread of flattened cardboard inside of an evidence bag on the table. "What about all the other employees at the shipping warehouse?"

"According to their statements to Chief Ford, they were all wearing gloves when they loaded that truck yesterday morning. He alibied them out one by one, and I was able to compare the prints I found to each one of them," Chloe said. "No dice."

"What about the ear itself?" Easton sensed the defeat coursing through Genevieve's shoulders and stepped into her side. Securing his hand at her lower back, he intended to provide comfort, but she stepped around the far edge of the table. Out of reach. He forced himself to breathe through the slight chemical smell seemingly soaked into the drywall. "From the amount of blood coagulated around this edge, whoever he took it from was still alive when he cut it off."

"You're right." Chloe snapped latex gloves over long fingers and turned the ear on its side, incision side up. "I've determined the ear was severed two to four hours before it was delivered to your motel room yesterday morning. I've run DNA without any hits in the system, but I can tell you the victim is female, approximately thirty to thirty-five years old based on the age of skin, Caucasian and had detached lobes. Other than that, there's not much here for me to go off of. If I had a complete skull or even a sliver of bone, a forensic anthropologist would be able to pull a chemical signature about the area the victim grew up in. With what we have, there are no piercings, scars or other identifying characteristics. Not even any evidence of diseases in the cartilage or blood, but…" The coroner slid her pinky into the ear's canal. "If you look closely, you can see an abnormal structure of the outer ear, in the dip here right before the canal."

Easton maneuvered to get a closer look opposite Genevieve on the other side of the table. He leaned in. "It's not natural?"

"I don't think so, no." Chloe laid the ear on the layer of disposable drape. "It's possible the ear formed around an ill-fitting hearing aid. Something the victim would've worn when she was younger and still growing. Based on the density of the malformation, I'd say she wore the device for most of her childhood, and the cartilage grew around it the older she got."

"A female victim, early to midforties, Caucasian with a hearing aid." Genevieve focused on the evidence, but he could've sworn there'd been a hitch in her voice. She cleared her throat. "You should get a hold of Captain Morsey from Alamosa PD. Run the details by him to compare to missing persons reports in the area."

Easton retrieved his phone but hesitated sending the info. Something wasn't right. He wasn't sure how else to put it. "If there's another woman out there, what's her role in the killer's game?"

"What do you mean?" Genevieve asked.

"We determined the victims Alamosa PD and the FBI found strung up from their ceilings were women he was grooming to rise to his challenge. Like you." So why had the game suddenly changed? "Nothing in the previous files indicated he'd ever dismembered his victims or held them hostage. What makes this one so special?"

Genevieve slid her hands into her slacks. "You theorized he was escalating."

"Escalating usually means changes in frequency and violence. Not entire MO shifts." Although it wasn't unheard of, but that usually meant the killer was experimenting with his ritual and rarely followed a strict sequence of kills. No. This was a veteran killer. Organized, intelligent, careful. Easton messaged Alamosa PD's captain the details on their potential victim. There was more to this killer. An element they hadn't been able to uncover yet. Hell, even with Easton's up close and personal experience with the man who buried Chloe and Weston two months ago, he had a hard time cataloguing this killer. "This doesn't make sense."

"Well, until we get a positive ID from the partial print from Unified Forensics or a match to the ear's DNA, I've given you everything I have," Chloe said. "It's up to you to find him now."

"Thank you, Dr. Miles. You've been very helpful." Genevieve wound around the table and strode toward the door, faster than he expected. "Excuse me. I need to make a call."

One glance from his future sister-in-law told him

he'd better follow her out, and he nodded. "Thanks for your help."

He met a wall of fresh air as he shoved through the glass door and out onto Main Street. The chemical burn in his nose subsided, but the tension at the base of his skull refused to let up. He caught sight of Genevieve a few yards down the sidewalk, her back turned toward him. "Hey."

She turned at his approach, one hand pressed against her head. "Hey. I just had to get out of there."

"You're acting like severed body parts aren't part of your everyday routine." His sarcasm missed the mark. As a district attorney, she'd tried and prosecuted the worst criminals in southern Colorado, but studying the evidence from crime scenes and seeing it firsthand were entirely different things. The need to reach out to her, to settle the fear etched into her expression, tensed the muscles down his spine. But the way she'd pulled away from him in Chloe's office said no amount of comfort would wipe the agony swirling in her gaze. "Tell me what's going on."

"There's only one person I told I was leaving Alamosa three days ago, Easton, and now he has her." Genevieve jerked her arm down. "A woman in her early to midforties, Caucasian, hearing disorder."

His voice deadpanned. "You advised me to reach out to Alamosa PD's captain to run the details against any missing persons in the area. Because you knew."

"I tried calling her, but there's no answer. It keeps going to voicemail." Genevieve pressed the back of her hand holding her burner phone against her mouth, but a gut-wrenching sob still managed to escape. "I thought she'd be safe, but he must've followed me to her house. He must've seen me drive away in her car. He cut off her ear and sent it to me to let me know I wouldn't ever be able to escape him."

"The family member from one of your previous cases." Easton was already dialing. He pressed the phone to his ear as the line connected. "I need a name, Genevieve."

She swiped at her face. "Laila Ballard."

Chapter Seven

The truck protested the entire length of the drive.

Her fingers ached from gripping the edge of the old plastic seats until they hit Alamosa's town limits, but even then, she couldn't defuse the explosion of panic suffocating her from the inside. The three-hour drive stretched into days as they raced along the highway connecting Battle Mountain to the rest of the state, and still, it wasn't fast enough.

Patrol cars lined the street of the quiet neighborhood as they approached the house. Everything Genevieve remembered about the small rambler-style home looked the same as it had before she'd left town, but the entire world had changed. Beige stucco fractured along the base of the home where Laila Ballard had planted rose bushes of varying colors. Soggy leaves left over from winter overflowed from the gutters running the length of the roofline and fell to the wraparound porch styled with minimalistic outdoor furniture.

She and Laila had sat in those chairs and talked about her daughter's case countless times. How a drunk driver who'd been granted bail had once again gotten behind the wheel intoxicated. How he'd run a red light and plowed into the side of her daughter's car. Genevieve had kept her apprised of every development, and in the end, succeeded in making sure her child's killer had been punished. Now the mother who'd grieved her daughter's death had become a victim herself.

"Laila doesn't have any connection to law enforcement or experience with serial investigations. Her daughter was killed by a drunk driver last year. She's got nothing to do with this." Genevieve watched the police filter in and out of the home. EMTs had arrived on scene, but her gut told her Laila wasn't inside the house. There was no body because the killer still had her. Her stomach churned at the thought. First Elisa Johnson, now Laila Ballard. Seemed even the smallest connection put her associates and friends at risk. What did that mean for the man beside her? For her family? Colleagues?

"The crime scene unit is still going through the house. Captain Morsey won't let anyone near it until they're finished processing. If they find anything, we'll know. There's no way he can block us from getting involved now, not with the ear sent to you in Battle Mountain." Easton's voice penetrated through the wall of anxiety swelling in her throat, urging her to think logically and not emotionally. But this case was emotional. It was personal. "We're going to find him, Genevieve. I give you my word."

"How many other people will suffer before we do?" Storm clouds rolled over one another above, and within a few seconds rain hit the windshield and streaked down the passenger side window. Lightning shot across the sky, followed by the deep vibration of thunder. "How long until he turns his attention on everyone else I care about? What about you?"

"Hey." Warm hands coerced her to face him, and once she did, she met nothing but defiance in his expression. Easton tugged her across the seat, held her close, and she wanted nothing more than to stay in this moment of peace. "I've already got Weston moving your parents to a secure location and put word in with your office. Your brother should be fine now that he lives out of state. And you don't have to worry about me. Okay? I knew exactly what I was getting myself into when I showed up at your motel room yesterday. Just remember whatever happens, we do this together. Right?"

"Right." The promise in his voice, in his words, chased back the loneliness she'd tried denying ever existed since leaving Battle Mountain years ago. "But in case you die during this investigation, I want you to know I'm sorry."

His laugh drowned out the sound of the rain ticking in rhythm to her racing heartbeat. "I'll be sure to remember that."

"No." Genevieve sat up, locking her gaze on his. "I'm sorry. Whatever happens, I need you to know that."

Humor bled from his expression.

"You deserved better than me," she said.

He didn't move, didn't even seem to breathe. "Genevieve, I—"

Three loud raps on the passenger side window twisted her to confront the officer on the other side.

Captain Morsey holstered his baton and stepped away from the truck to allow her room to get out. Tension bunched in her shoulders as she moved to open the door. Stark blue eyes remained on her as she slid from the vehicle. The truck rocked on its shocks as Easton did the same. Defined lines deepened in an aged face as Captain Morsey shifted his attention from her to Easton and back. They'd only met a couple of times—not enough to form a professional or personal relationship—and from the way he stared them both down, she imagined that was as far as they would go. The captain's hand hovered over his baton as he sized up the Battle Mountain PD officer rounding the hood of the truck. "Counselor." He nodded before speaking to Easton. "I take it you're the other Ford, Weston's brother."

"Yes, sir." Easton extended his hand in introduction, but the captain ignored the offering. "Anything you can tell us about Laila Ballard?"

"I don't know how you and your brother do things in the middle of nowhere, Ford, but I told you from the beginning. This is my case." Captain Morsey hiked his hands to his hips as he surveyed the scene. "Now, I know you folks are new to homicide investigation, but we have rules about other departments stepping on our toes. You're not needed here. My department has this well under control."

He had to be joking. Genevieve took a single step forward. "With all due respect, Captain. The man you arrested for the deaths of Maria Gutierrez, Annette Scofield and Ruby Wagner isn't the Contractor. He's still out there—"

"Ms. Alexander, your assistant was murdered and discovered hanging from the ceiling in your home three days ago. As of right now, I have grounds to have you arrested for leaving Alamosa as a person of interest and interfering in the investigation." The captain's voice dropped into dangerous territory. "I don't care who either of you are. Come near this case again, I will throw you in jail. Do you understand?"

She didn't know what to say, what to think.

Easton acquiesced. "Yes, sir."

"Good. Now, I got a missing woman to find, and I'd appreciate if you let me do my job." Captain Morsey headed back toward the house, leaving them on the sidewalk as the storm protested overhead. He turned back. "Oh, and I'll be needing that ear your coroner examined. I'd rather have my medical examiner take a look. Until then, Lieutenant Parrish will make sure you get to wherever you're staying."

A younger version of the captain stepped into her peripheral vision, but Genevieve only had attention for the defeat coiling through her. They'd been barred from searching the scene of Laila Ballard's abduction, from examining any forensics the killer might've left behind and had officially lost the only piece of evidence linking Laila to their killer.

Strong fingers slipped beneath her arm as the lieutenant Captain Morsey had sicced on them tried to pry her away from the scene. "Let's go, Counselor."

Genevieve wrenched her arm out of the lieutenant's grip.

Before she had a chance to confront him herself,

Easton stepped between her and the officer. "I don't give a damn who you work for, you don't get to touch her. Understand?"

Lieutenant Parrish's mouth ticked higher at one side, as though looking for the opportunity to follow through with Captain Morsey's threat to have them both arrested and put behind bars. The lieutenant raised both hands in surrender. "Just following orders, sir. I didn't mean anything by it."

"Come on." Easton secured his hand at her lower back and maneuvered her toward the passenger side door of his truck. "The storm is getting worse. We need to find a room for the night."

The weight of the lieutenant's attention tightened the muscles down her spine as she climbed back into the truck. He watched them pull away from the curb then headed for his own patrol car parked behind them. The back half of the vehicle remained in her side-view mirror as they wound through the city.

Rooted in the heart of the San Luis Valley, Alamosa offered everything from natural wonders and outdoor activities, to culture and authentic eats. The city's close proximity to sights and attractions made it an ideal spot for tourists summiting the country's tallest sand dunes, wrestling local alligators, chasing waterfalls and relaxing in the hot springs. It was the place she'd called home the minute she'd run from Battle Mountain. Only now the familiarity of these streets grated against her sense of belonging.

Genevieve let the view blur in her vision. Not focusing on anything in particular. "I'd invite you to stay in my guest room, but, as far as I know, my house is still officially a crime scene."

"A motel is fine." He took a sharp right into the parking lot of the Riverside Inn, a one-level stretch of brown stucco and iconic hacienda architecture. A massive tree planted close to the main road broke up the number of cars parked in the lot, and her gut clenched. Limited availability.

Lieutenant Parrish parked behind them as she and Easton shouldered out of the truck but didn't move to follow. Genevieve studied him through the windshield with help from the dim lights outside each motel room door. She stuck her tongue out at him like a five-year-old just as he pulled out of the parking lot.

Easton motioned her ahead of him, as he always did. The growl of Lieutenant Parrish's engine reached her ears as the door swung closed behind them. "Guess he considers himself free from babysitting duty." He nodded as the front desk clerk rounded behind the counter. "Two rooms, please."

"Sorry, I've only got one left, single queen-sized bed. Minimum two-night stay. With the temperatures getting warmer around these parts, we're nearly booked solid for the next month." The clerk held up a single set of keys. "You won't find anything else tonight."

Easton pulled his wallet and tossed a card on the counter. "Book it."

One room. One bed. Pressure built behind her sternum as the clerk gave them directions to a room at the other side of the complex. Easton unlocked the door and kicked it open with his boot. It was exactly as she'd imagined. Dark wood paneling, ugly brown carpeting, a brown bed to match and an air-conditioning unit installed in the only window. She didn't even want to look at the bathroom, but driving back to Battle Mountain tonight was out of the question. Laila Ballard had fallen into the killer's hands, and no matter how many times Captain Morsey threatened to have her arrested, Genevieve was going to find her. Before it was too late.

Easton set his keys and wallet on top of the sixties-style television. "So do you want to be the big spoon or the little spoon?"

His ATTEMPT TO lighten the mood struck out.

Genevieve stared at the small room as though it were about to sprout mushrooms from the middle of the floor. Which, in all seriousness, was a possibility. She uncrossed her arms, turning to face him. She lengthened her neck away from her shoulders. "There isn't going to be any spooning because I'm going back to that crime scene."

"Genevieve, you know as well as I do Captain Morsey isn't going to give in. You're still a person of interest in the case. You might not have killed Elisa Johnson yourself, but your house was the stage for her murder." Easton closed the distance between them. "The crime scene unit will be there for hours, and even after they leave, Morsey will have at least two officers stationed for scene security. You're not getting in there on your own."

"I'm not going to be on my own. I have you." She moved around him, cracking the door to peer outside.

"Looks like Lieutenant Parrish is gone for now. Hopefully that means he returned to the scene. We can wait a couple of hours. They should be done searching the house by then."

"Oh, well, at least that's cleared up." Easton collapsed onto the edge of the bed. The downpour intensified in the seconds he watched her at the door. "We'll be breaking at least half a dozen laws if we cross that police tape. The district attorney I saw in all those interviews wouldn't even jaywalk let alone disobey a direct order from the police."

She remained poised at the door. "It's not my job I'm worried about."

"I know why you're doing this, Genevieve." The mattress shifted under him as he shoved to his feet. "You feel responsible for what's happened, for Elisa Johnson and for Laila, but putting your career at risk won't get us any closer to finding out who killed those women."

Seconds distorted into minutes the longer she didn't answer. The glow from the sconce outside the room cast angled shadows across her face. But the light, hell, the light highlighted the pain in her expression. Genevieve closed the door. "Do you know why I became a district attorney?"

"No." He shook his head.

"It wasn't to put the bad guys behind bars. I wasn't interested in name recognition or prestige or anything else that comes with this job. None of that matters to me." She set her thumbnail between her teeth and bit down. It was an old habit she hadn't been able to quit long before she'd left Battle Mountain, and he was instantly reminded of the woman he'd fallen in love with all those years ago. "I paid my way through law school and worked my way into Alamosa's good graces to give victims a voice, to make sure their loved ones and families got the justice they deserved. The police, Captain Morsey, they haven't considered the possibility Corey Singleton didn't commit all four of the original murders. Because of me. I saw the connection between Kayleigh Winters's murder and the first three deaths, and I created a narrative that made sense. I made a mistake, and I'm not going to let anyone else die because of it."

Damn. Putting aside the anger—the betrayal—he'd clung to since her arrival at his front doorstep, he couldn't deny his admiration right then. Goose bumps trailed up his arms as he crossed the room. One step. Two. The shag carpet threatened to trip him up along the way, but there was nothing that would stop him from getting to her. "We won't be able to take my truck. Captain Morsey most likely ran the plates to keep tabs on our movements, and the engine is loud as hell. Whichever officers he left as perimeter security will hear us coming from a mile away."

"My car is still parked in my garage a few blocks from here. The scene is a few days old. There shouldn't be any uniformed officers assigned security since the crime scene unit has already been through the house." Surprise infiltrated the soothing notes in her voice. "You're really willing to help me?"

"Yeah, I'm going to help you." As much as he hated the idea of pushing the limits between Alamosa PD and his department, it might be the only way to bring

Laila Ballard home before the killer finished the job he'd started with her ear. He skimmed his hands down Genevieve's bare arms and hooked his fingers under her wrists. "That's what partners are for."

"You're not just saying that because you're afraid I'd get myself arrested and rat you out?" she asked.

"That might have been a small part of my decision." He pinched his index finger and thumb together, raising his hand between them. "But a tiny part."

Genevieve used him for balance and rose on her toes. She pressed her mouth to his then lowered back down and set her forehead against his chest. "Thank you. For everything. I wouldn't have gotten this far if it weren't for you."

"I'll start thinking of ways you can pay me back." He kissed the crown of her head. "Until then, we should get some rest and order something in. You're dead on your feet. You look like you're about to fall over."

"Here I thought you might chalk it up to your charming good looks," she said.

"You think I'm charming?" Easton forced himself to release her.

"Don't push it." Her gut-wrenching smile nearly knocked him over as she stared up at him.

Within a few minutes, they'd ordered an unhealthy amount of Chinese food to last them at least three days before trying to distract themselves with something on the out-of-date television. It wasn't long before Genevieve was entering her garage door code into the keypad, and they'd parked a few houses down and across the street from Laila Ballard's home.

The rain had yet to let up, and the wipers worked overtime to keep the windshield clear. Two officers, just as Easton had predicted stood outside the house at the front door. From the look of things, the crime scene unit had cleared out. Captain Morsey had most likely warned his officers not to let the DA or him near the scene, but there was a chance his stunt having them followed to the motel eased his suspicions. Easton shouldered out the passenger side door of her too-small sedan. "I'll meet you at the back."

"Be careful." Genevieve cut the engine, fisted her keys and hit the sidewalk. In a matter of seconds, she disappeared into the shadows alongside the neighbor's side yard to cut through another property.

They'd been over the plan a dozen times. Get in. Get out. No mistakes.

Easton's boots echoed off the cracked sidewalk as he approached Laila Ballard's home and the crime scene tape strung up to keep nosey reserve officers out. He waved to the two officers descending the steps. He didn't recognize either of them from earlier. Perhaps their luck would hold. He flashed his Battle Mountain PD badge. "Evening, fellas. Captain Morsey thought I might be able to lend a hand to the investigation of the missing woman who lives here. I'm going to need to take a look at the scene."

"We weren't notified anyone outside of the department would be consulting on this case." The nearest officer set his hand against Easton's chest. "We're going to have to call the captain."

Easton studied the hand on his chest and recalled all

the different bones he could break in one move, but he wasn't here to start a war between their departments. All he had to do was get inside. "You go ahead and do that. You call him after he's been at this scene almost all day, after he's probably just sat down for dinner with his wife and turned on his favorite after-shift show. Let's see how that plays out for you."

Hesitation lined the officer's eyes as he slid his gaze to his partner. "Captain hates it when we interrupt his *Jeopardy* reruns."

"Yeah, all right." The second officer waved him past. "Make it quick though, will you? Our shift change is in twenty minutes."

"I'll do my best. Thank you, boys." Easton climbed the front steps of the rambler-style home. At the door, he pulled two sets of protective booties from the cardboard box and wrapped one over his boots. Fisting the other, he closed the door behind him. CSU had laid out a specific path for investigators to follow through the house with markers. A bedroom door stood open directly to his right, a small half bath directly after that before the hallway opened into a wide room. The open kitchen had been set off to his left with the living room opposite, and through the laundry room past that, he spotted a sliding glass door leading to the back patio.

The home wasn't large by any standard, but enough for the single mother Genevieve had described. Family photos decorated the mantel in the living room, staring him down, as he picked up the pace. Unlocking the sliding glass door, Easton whistled two short bursts into the darkness.

No answer. No sign of movement.

He waited another minute. "Genevieve."

Still nothing.

The hairs at the back of his neck stood on end as he stepped out onto the back patio. Rain pattered off the tall oaks lining the back of the property. Had she not been able to get into the backyard? They'd known there was a slim chance of the officers out front not recognizing her from the amount of face-to-face time she'd spent with the department and as a person of interest in the Elisa Johnson case. Going around through the back had been their only option. But now... "Genevieve?"

She should've been here by now. He walked to the north side of the house, but only met a row of bare rose bushes and thorns. It was too dark to see if there were any fresh tracks through the well-manicured grass. Genevieve most likely would've come over the neighbor's wood fence, and he put one foot in front of the other until he reached the end.

He kicked something solid. A metallic clink filtered through the constant tick of rain. A sprinkler head? No. He toed the object with his boot. Sprinkler heads didn't move unless they'd been decapitated by the lawnmower. Crouching low, Easton ran his hand through the grass. His fingers hit solid metal, and he clenched the object in his palm.

A set of keys.

The light from the back patio highlighted the vehicle key fob. Same manufacturer as Genevieve's. He hit the red panic button. An alarm blared from where they'd parked her car down the block, and it was then he knew.

She was gone.

Chapter Eight

"If you scream, I'll kill you, then I'll kill him." Movement—footsteps?—registered a few feet away. Twigs snapped under a heavy weight from nearby.

Genevieve dragged her chin away from her chest, but an unfamiliar heaviness forced her to overcorrect, and her head fell back. Pain ricocheted through her skull as rough bark scraped against her scalp. A tree. Damp earth soaked into her slacks, but she couldn't see much farther than maybe a foot to tell where she was. Cold spits of rain pelted her face, the soft rhythm bouncing off foliage and leaves. "Where…where am I?"

She was…supposed to meet Easton at the back of Laila Ballard's house. She'd gone through the side yard of one of the neighbor's properties, cutting in front of the tree line, and then… She couldn't remember. Why couldn't she remember? A shiver chased up her arms and down her spine. April had fooled them all, promising spring when there was nothing but bone-deep coldness in the dark.

"Someplace Officer Ford will never find you." Another shift of movement, closer than before. A ski mask and a white ring of eyes materialized to her left, and Genevieve pressed her heels into the ground to gain some semblance of distance. In vain. He kept his voice low, almost whispery. "Don't worry, I'm not going to hurt you, Genevieve. At least, not yet. You and I have a lot to talk about first."

Fractures of memory arced to the front of her mind. The neighbor's backyard, the feeling of being watched. The shadow that hadn't really been a shadow at all. She'd tried to scream, but he'd put an end to that before any sound had the chance to leave her mouth.

"You were waiting for me." It was the only possibility that made sense. But how would he have known she'd return to the crime scene? Genevieve blinked to clear the last of the dizziness. Had he followed her and Easton, or... "The ear. You sent it to me at the motel. You followed me from Alamosa to Battle Mountain. You knew I wouldn't be able to get involved in the case, but I would still try to find out who it came from. You used Laila Ballard to lure me here."

And she'd fallen straight into his trap.

"I have to tell you, I'm quite impressed you were able to discern who the ear belongs to, especially considering how careful I was not to leave any identifying markers." His voice—familiar and strange at the same time—grated against her nerves. "But if you'd just been a little faster, I wouldn't have needed to use her to motivate you at all."

"Laila." She tried to move her wrists from her lower back, but only met the sharp sting of plastic biting into her skin. Zip ties? He must've secured her wrists and ankles while she'd been unconscious. There was no give between the plastic and her skin. A tendril of fear combined with memories from the break-in at her home, and the air crushed from her lungs. Had he brought her here to show her Laila's body? Would her senses catch up with the darkness enough to outline her friend's remains nearby? Nausea churned hard and fast. "What did you do with her?"

"We'll get to that," he said. "First, I need to know what else you and Officer Ford have discovered over the course of this investigation."

Officer Ford. He knew. He knew about Easton. He hadn't just studied her. He'd wanted her to know how far his reach extended, but she wouldn't let him use the Ford family for whatever endgame he had in mind. Not what Dr. Miles had uncovered. Not the interviews Weston Ford conducted. And not the leads Easton had pulled from the victim files.

"Nothing." Genevieve pressed her head back into the tree. The pain intensified enough to keep her in the moment, to counteract whatever he'd done to her to knock her out. Blunt force trauma? A sedative? The memories were out of reach. She rolled her head from side to side. "I swear."

"You're lying to me, Genevieve. Do it again, and I'll have no use for you. You'll end up exactly as the others. Only I'll make sure your broken toy soldier is there when I screw the eyelets into your joints." The low slide of metal reached her ears a split second before cool steel pressed against her neck. Not the sharpness of a blade as before. Something duller. Stronger.

Thicker with a bite. The answer settled at the back of her throat. A drill bit. "I know Captain Morsey banned you from the investigation, but you didn't get to be a district attorney by giving up. Tell me about the 9-1-1 call made by Maria Gutierrez, the one you manipulated the dispatcher into sharing with you."

Every cell in her body caught fire. "How—"

"A true artist never reveals his secrets," he said.

"That's what you think you are? An artist?" This was nothing but a game to him, a way to stay close to the investigation, to stay ahead of police. No. She wasn't going to give him anything. She leaned away from the tree to gauge if he'd tied her to it. The drill bit nicked the side of her neck, but she didn't stop. Her knuckles grazed against soil and dead leaves. If she could break the zip ties, she'd have the chance to escape. She had to keep him talking. Distracted. "You murder innocent women. You string them up as though they're nothing but dolls, and I'm not telling you anything."

"That's too bad." Puffs of crystalized exhales escaped through the lower half of his ski mask. No identifying features. Nothing to tell her who'd terrorized and killed four women over the course of a year, one of which he'd staged in her own home. "I was hoping you'd last longer than the others. I thought you were different. You were supposed to be the strongest, but you're just like them, aren't you? Weak. Self-righteous. Emotionally compromised."

Genevieve set her jaw. She strained against the outer edge of the zip ties and increased the pressure between her wrists. "I tend to get emotional when someone kills the people I care about."

"You know, that's why I've always liked you. Even under the threat of physical harm, you don't deviate from your beliefs. We're the same in that regard." A low laugh rumbled into the small space between them. "But if you're not going to tell me what I want to know, I have to find someone who will, and you will be the reason they suffer. You see, just as you don't know who you are without your work, I can't live without mine. But to keep my edge, I have to make the game more challenging. So every woman who dies from here on out will be because of you. They will suffer more because you failed to stop me. Are you sure you're willing to live with that, Genevieve?"

"Go to hell." Genevieve hauled both feet into her chest and kicked out hard. Her heels rocketed into her attacker, and a vicious growl cut through the white noise of rain. She pushed to her feet as fast as she could, unbalanced, but still breathing. She dropped into a squat and severed the ties around her ankles. She didn't have time to claw through the zip ties at her wrists. She had to run. Shadows closed around her. Exertion burned down the backs of her thighs as she sprinted across uneven ground, but she wouldn't stop. She didn't know where she'd been held, where she was going. It didn't matter. "Help me!"

Her scream tore up the back of her throat, but she pushed herself harder. Cold settled at the bottom of her lungs. Rocks and fallen branches threatened to trip her up. She had to keep going. She had to find Easton.

The killer couldn't have taken her far during the few short minutes she'd been unconscious, which meant they were most likely still in Laila Ballard's neighborhood. "Help!"

Lightning arced across the sky and highlighted a section of thinning trees up ahead. A way out. Swinging her bound hands back and forth in front of her, Genevieve breathed a sigh of relief. She was almost there. She could see something on the other side of the tree line.

The cover of trees vanished as she burst through a growth of bushes lining the property, and she froze. No. Her breath left her in a rush. She didn't understand. Disbelief curdled in her stomach. It wasn't possible. She shook her head to rewind the past few minutes, but there was no denying the truth. They weren't in Laila Ballard's neighborhood anymore. He'd dragged her away from Alamosa altogether.

The Great Sand Dunes National Park stretched for miles out in front of her. Wet sand built up along the bottom of her shoes. Fourteen-thousand-foot peaks demanded attention along the Sangre de Cristo mountain range, the enormity of her situation draining the blood from her face. "Run."

The single word nearly ripped from her chest as she struggled through the quicksand terrain. Warm liquid combined with numbing rain between her wrists. Blood. She couldn't stop. No matter how much it hurt. Her breath sawed in and out of her chest as she dug her boots into the side of the nearest peak. If she could get to the other side, out of sight, there was a chance the killer wouldn't follow. Question was: Was she worth the trouble? The sick feeling in her gut intensified as she considered the answer.

A grittiness stung her face and neck as she rounded the first peak. Genevieve tried to block the onslaught with her bound hands, but it wasn't enough. A little farther. She could already make out the outline of the next peak. She might have a chance if she picked up the pace.

A wall of muscle slammed into her from behind.

She pitched forward and hit the ground. Sand filled her mouth and nose as she struggled to unpin her wrists from beneath her. Her lungs spasmed for oxygen, but the weight on her back refused to let up. Pain seared across her scalp as her attacker pulled her head back by her hair, exposing her throat from chin to her collar.

"Did you think I'd let you get away so easily?" He flipped her onto her back and grasped her throat. Pulling her closer, the killer leveled his crazed gaze with hers as she struggled for oxygen. He threw her back into the sand, grabbed hold of her ankles and dragged her back toward the trees. "I made you the woman you are, Genevieve. You don't get to walk away from me."

HE'D SEARCHED THE entire area.

The treads he'd matched to the bottom of Genevieve's boots had ended at the neighbor's back property line. There was no sign of her, but another set of prints—deeper, wider and longer than the district attorney's—had taken her place.

Someone had been out here. Someone had taken her, and Easton couldn't think of anyone else other than the killer who'd lured them here in the first place. None of the other victims had been dismembered, making Laila Ballard special. The killer had studied Genevieve well enough to know she wouldn't stop until they had an identification, and when she realized her friend had become a victim, he'd known she'd come running. The entire scene had become a trap, but Easton hadn't seen it in time.

He sped around to the front of the house and caught sight of the two officers assigned to secure the scene. "Call your captain. We've got a problem." He explained as much of the situation Alamosa PD needed to know then unpocketed his phone. He scrolled through the screen and hit the contact he needed. The line connected almost instantly, but he wouldn't waste time with politeness. "Genevieve's been taken. Ten to fifteen minutes ago, from Laila Ballard's home. Alamosa PD is on alert, but I need you here."

"I'm leaving now." The scrape of metal on wood pierced through the line as Weston set into action. "Listen to me, no matter what happens, remember he wants something from her. He won't kill her unless he has to, and we don't want to force his hand. Where would he take her?"

Easton scrubbed a hand down his face as the all too familiar sense of helplessness bubbled to the surface. Rain cascaded in lines along his neck. He stared out into the neighborhood. Pressure built behind his sternum as he ran through his limited knowledge of the area. "I don't know. All of his kills have been in Alamosa. This is his hunting grounds, but I'm in unfamiliar territory."

"It wouldn't be the first time, Easton. Think. He'll

have to take her somewhere private, isolated enough to give him the upper hand. Somewhere you'd never think to look for her. This killer is one of the rare types that wants to get caught, but he's not going to go down without a fight. He'll do whatever it takes to win." The distant rumbling of a truck engine filtered through the panic setting up residence in Easton's mind. Weston was already on his way, but it would take at least three hours for his brother to get here. Genevieve didn't have that kind of time. "Chloe's been through all of the autopsy reports for the victims. She didn't find anything out of the ordinary, but there's a chance we missed something. I'll have her run through them again."

"Guys like this don't kill where they sleep. He went out of his way to contain the forensics inside the victims' homes, including Genevieve's. He's not going to take the risk of evidence leading back to him. He's too careful for that." Damn it. They had nothing. Easton braced his weight against the vinyl fence of the wrap-around porch as a single truth penetrated through the haze of loss. He'd battled like hell to deny it, but the past forty-eight hours had obliterated his control when it came to that woman. "I can't lose her again, Weston."

"You won't," his brother said. "I'll be there as soon as I can. Until then, I'll call you if Chloe comes up with anything."

"Thanks." Easton ended the call.

"Captain isn't answering." The first officer stepped into his peripheral vision. "We've tried half a dozen times, but there's no response from him or Lieutenant Parrish."

Parrish. The officer who'd escorted him and Genevieve back to the hotel. The edgy smile Lieutenant Parrish had given Easton when they'd been removed from the scene had seared clearly into his memory. They'd been face-to-face with the officer for less than two minutes, but the man had left a hell of an impression. Without Captain Morsey or his right hand answering their phones, Easton was on his own. "You two come with me."

"With all due respect, Officer Ford, this isn't Battle Mountain," the second officer said. "Until Captain Morsey or Lieutenant Parrish tell us otherwise, we've been ordered to stay here to secure this scene."

He didn't have time for this. "Listen to me, the woman who lives here has been taken by a killer. He cut off her ear and sent it to the district attorney to lure her to this scene. Now, DA Alexander is missing, and I have reason to believe that same killer is behind her abduction. I'm not asking for permission. I'm telling you she's in trouble, and it's your duty to help me find her."

His heart threatened to beat straight out of his chest as both officers glanced to one another. "Yes, sir. Tell us what you need."

"Lieutenant Parrish. What do you know about him?" he asked. "Where does he live?"

"You're not suggesting the lieutenant is behind this." A scoff escaped the first officer's mouth.

"I don't know, but Genevieve Alexander and Laila Ballard are running out of time." Knowledge of forensics, seemingly familiar with the Alamosa PD playbook, constantly one step ahead—a law enforcement officer's involvement made sense. If the killer was involved in the case, he could lead the investigation any direction he wanted, but that didn't get them anywhere close to a location the bastard might be hiding two innocent women. As for Lieutenant Parrish, there was something in the officer's expression earlier that Easton couldn't get out of his mind. He thought back over what Weston had said. The killer would need somewhere isolated, private enough to keep uninvited guests from interrupting his playtime with his victims. "Does Parrish have experience with tools or own any properties outside of town?"

"Actually, yeah," the second officer said. "Parrish runs a construction company on his off hours. His cabin is just outside of the national park, along the southern end of the dunes."

Easton's gut twisted. A cabin was perfect. Out of the way, quiet. "Take me there."

Both officers raced for their patrol vehicle while Easton fisted the keys he'd found in the backyard and collapsed behind the wheel of Genevieve's sedan. Headlights cut through the darkness as he fell in behind Alamosa PD. They wound through the neighborhood then shot up the main streets of the growing city before the valley stretched out in front of him.

The low ringing vibrated in his ears, and he blinked to fight off the oncoming sensory overload, but it was too late. He'd lost control. The barrenness of the landscape transformed in front of him, night turning to day, temperatures rising in the too-small cab of the car. His pulse rocketed into his throat as the first of the flashbacks hit hard and fast. An echo of laughter replaced the constant tick of rain, and his mind urged him to relax. It was just a simple supply run. Sweat built in his hairline under his helmet as he scanned the faces of his unit. The thud of Watowski's weight against the side of the truck pulled Easton's attention from the road.

By the time he turned back, it'd been too late.

The explosion came out of nowhere.

Shouts replaced laughter. The entire vehicle was engulfed in flames and heat and pain. Until there was nothing but smoke and screams.

His vision wavered. Red and blue patrol lights distorted in his vision ahead. He hadn't been able to help them—any of them—but he wouldn't fail Genevieve. He'd find her in time. He'd keep her alive and bring down the killer terrorizing women in Alamosa.

Easton released the breath he hadn't realized he'd been holding. The memories were still there. Waiting. But, stronger than the past, was the woman he'd planned to marry. The windshield wipers worked overtime. High, smooth peaks of sand took shape outside the driver's side window as thick trees blacked out the Sangre de Cristo Mountains to his right. The tendons in his hands ached from his grip on the steering wheel, and he forced himself to focus. "Come on. Where are you, you bastard?"

The patrol vehicle less than twenty feet ahead skidded to a stop in the middle of the road. Dim lighting outlined a small angular cabin with a raised front porch, red-painted roof and what looked like a new set of handrails leading up the ten steps to the main door. Easton slammed on the brakes before the car's front grill met the back of the patrol vehicle's bumper and shoved the vehicle into Park. He hit the frozen ground still covered with patches of ice and unspoiled snow. She was here. He could feel it. He pointed to the two officers spilling out of their car. "Keep trying to get a hold of Captain Morsey!"

He hurried up the steep steps, the stairs shaking under his weight. Hauling his heel into the wood beside the untarnished dead bolt, Easton kicked open the front door. He scanned the small space, taking in the swell of cold and emptiness. No. Damn it, she had to be here. He searched the main living room, ran his hands over the stones of the fireplace and scoured for clues through the only bedroom in the back. Empty. Panic gripped him by the throat. "Where the hell are you?"

He stepped out onto the front porch. His exhales crystalized in front of his mouth. Temperatures had dipped below freezing. He squeezed his hand around the new guardrail. He'd been wrong. He'd taken the evidence and warped it to fit his own theory. Hell, he wasn't any better than the killer, only this mistake would cost Genevieve and Laila Ballard their lives.

Easton memorized a fresh pattern carved into the ground. Narrowing his gaze, he jogged down the stairs. He crouched a few feet from the corner of the cabin and traced a long length of tire tracks. Someone had been out here recently. Within the past few hours. His instincts pushed him to his feet. "I need a flashlight."

One of the officers handed him their light. "We're

still trying to get a hold of the captain. No answer from Lieutenant Parrish either."

Because the lieutenant was out here.

Easton didn't have proof. Nothing to connect Parrish to any of the murders. Nothing but a feeling. It would have to be enough. Easton followed the length of the tire treads, past the property line. Deeper. The rain had made a mess of everything and drew sand from the edge of the dunes into the woods. He swept the beam up ahead and landed on the distinct outline in the distance. He slowed. Denial lodged in his throat. "Genevieve?"

No answer. No movement.

Easton scanned the surrounding trees as he closed in on her. Her feet swayed above the ground. No. No, no, no, no. He lost his hold on the flashlight and sprinted through mud and loose rock. Circling his arm around her waist, he hoisted her higher to relieve the tension of the fishing line round her neck.

Her gasp filled the clearing.

Chapter Nine

"Are you experiencing any discomfort, Ms. Alexander?" The doctor pulled the curtain, cutting off Genevieve's view of the rest of the hospital. The screen of her tablet reflected a bright glare from overhead flourescent lights as the attending took a seat on the stool. She set the tablet onto the table beside the bed. "May I?"

Genevieve nodded. "I was…strung up from a tree with fishing line and left to die." Rawness prickled along the edges of her throat. It hurt to swallow, to talk, to move her head, but every streak of pain reminded her she was still alive. Somehow. "Yes, I'm experiencing discomfort."

"From what I've been able to tell from your scans, your jugular veins were compressed for at least a full minute, but the damage didn't extend to the carotid arteries." The physician kept her touch light as she prodded Genevieve's throat. "Seems Officer Ford pulled you down just in time. You're a very lucky woman. Thirty seconds more, and you'd be in a different room altogether."

She didn't remember that part. Easton pulling her

down. There was a lot she didn't remember, but her subconscious must've registered he'd been with her in the woods because her only thought had been of him. She traced her thumb along the gauze around her wrists. The lacerations underneath stung, but the ibuprofen the nurses had given her helped. Tears burned in her eyes, and Genevieve quickly swiped them from her face.

"Did that hurt?" Concern lightened the doctor's touch.

She tried to shake her head, reminded of the stiffness in the muscles along her neck and jaw. From what she'd been told, the killer had strung her up in the tree by the neck, but had positioned the zip ties around her wrists to take most of her weight. He hadn't been trying to kill her. At least, not quickly, but how much longer was she supposed to play this game? How much longer until Easton discovered her hanging from her ceiling with steel eyelets screwed into her joints and fishing line taking all of her weight? "No, I just…"

Just, what? Just wanted to go home? Her home had been broken into, turned into a crime scene and violated. Wanted to forget? There was nothing that could erase those terrifying hours from her memory.

Understanding swept across the physician's expression, and she pulled back slightly. "You've been through a trauma. Not just physically. It'll take some time for these bruises to heal, but more importantly… Ms. Alexander, is there anyone you can talk to?"

"Um." No. There wasn't. Laila Ballard had already suffered because of her connection to Genevieve. She wouldn't put anyone else in danger. "I'm fine."

"Okay." Suspicion replaced understanding as the doctor stood, but she knew as well as Genevieve did, if a patient wouldn't accept help, there was nothing she could do. "We'll keep you pain-free with the ibuprofen, but if the soreness gets worse, let me know. I don't think we'll need to keep you longer than tonight, if you're ready to go home. I recommend a liquid diet over the next few days to prevent any tearing. Be sure to stay hydrated and get plenty of rest."

"Thank you. Do you... Could you tell me where Officer Ford is?" she asked.

"I'll have one of the nurses track him down and send him your way." The scrape of the metal rings around the curtain grated against her senses as the attending enclosed her back into the circle of fabric and privacy.

Privacy was a misleading word. Because on the other side of that thin fabric was the low echo of dispatches from the PA system, squeaky wheels from long-past-their-prime gurneys, orders from physicians, steady footsteps of other nurses and staff. Yet, despite the number of people around her, Genevieve had never felt so alone. She smoothed her thumb over the call button of the remote attached to her bed. Closing her eyes, she tried to ignore the building agony behind her sternum. She could still feel the grittiness of the sand in her hair, smell the wet leaves on her skin. The crime scene unit had taken and bagged her clothes as evidence when she'd been brought in, but she was still living the nightmare with every inhale.

"You look like you could use one of these," a warm, familiar voice said.

Genevieve pried her eyes open when all she wanted to do was sink deeper into the pillows stacked behind her. She couldn't fight the slight tug of her mouth as she took in the mud still streaked across his face. Steam escaped from the small semicircle hole at the top of the large to-go cup he offered and curled between them. She stretched her free hand out, the other tied down with an IV and the blood pressure cuff. "That doesn't smell like coffee."

"Bone broth. Homemade. I keep a couple bottles in my truck for emergencies, and the nurses were nice enough to let me use one of their microwaves." Easton rolled the stool her doctor had occupied a few minutes ago between his legs and sat down, his own cup in hand. "Figured your throat might be sore for a bit. Considering you might not get to eat something for a while, this was the only thing I could think of that wouldn't make you feel like you were starving to death."

"Thank you." Scents of salt, carrots, celery, chicken and a few spices she didn't recognize filled her lungs. The heat bled into her hands and battled to chase back the cold that seemed to have permanently set up residence in her bones. She managed a sip and was instantly surrendered to the comfort she craved. Genevieve raised the cup. "This is really good. I take it your family knows I'm back in town."

Easton took a swig from his own serving. "I had Weston ready to run you off the property with his shotgun if I gave the signal, but my mother doesn't know you're here yet."

"The signal?" It hurt to laugh, but the simple act

relaxed the tendons down the back of her neck and between her shoulder blades. "Let me guess. Smoke signals from the chimney."

"Better. A secret Ford family whistle." He collected her cup from her and set it on the table beside the bed. "Every time we went out hunting when Weston and I were growing up, we would let each other know where we were on the property with this whistle. Made it so we were less likely to shoot each other."

She smoothed her palms over the invisible creases in the sheets. "I always admired your family, how happy you all were. I remember one time knocking on your family cabin front door to see you after school, but no one inside heard me because you were all laughing too hard. I stood there waiting for a few minutes until the laughter died down so I could knock again. My hands were frozen by the time I got the chance."

"Those were the good old days." Easton stared down at his cup, tracing the edge of the lid with the side of his knuckle. "Before…everything went to hell. Before the military sent me home and Weston became the police chief. Before dad died." He took another swig of his broth, but Genevieve had the feeling the action had more to do with distraction than any need for a drink.

"I heard about your dad through the grapevine. I'm sorry," she said.

"He died doing exactly what he'd taught us to do for others. Fight for and defend them until our last breath. The man who killed him was trying to get to Chloe, and Dad wasn't going to have that." Easton cleared his throat. "He's the one who got Weston through losing his wife a few years ago, managed to convince him to watch over this town when Chief Frasier couldn't do the job anymore to work through the grief. James Ford was a great man, I'll give you that. No matter how many times I slammed the door in his face those first few months I was home, he'd always come back. He'd hand me a shovel and tell me the land wasn't going to work itself, and that I had a lot of work ahead of me."

"You turned out all right." She'd missed this. Them just talking as though they'd picked up right where they'd left off all those years ago.

"Yeah." A lightness seemed to brighten the sea-blue color of his eyes for a moment. Something she hadn't seen since she'd showed her face in Battle Mountain. "Guess I did."

A thrill of being the center of this man's world raised goose bumps along her arms, and Genevieve ducked her chin to her chest. Falling back into old routines and patterns, falling for him and this town all over again, the familiarity and warmth, would only lead to one place: invisibility. She'd worked too hard to make an identity for herself, to prove she was more than that teenaged girl who knew nothing about the world or the people in it. She wasn't going to throw it all away now. She couldn't. She cleared her throat, but the pain was too much to do any good. "Was the crime scene unit able to find something from Laila Ballard's house that could lead them to her?"

Easton leaned back on the stool. Moment over. "Yeah. They recovered a set of footprints at the back of the property where yours disappeared, but the rain had washed a lot of the ridges away. From what Alamosa PD can tell, they're a match for a set recovered at the scene of your home. They managed to cast a partial print and compared it to those left near Lieutenant Parrish's cabin near the dunes where we found you. They were a perfect match. Captain Morsey was all too willing to give me and Weston access once the match was made. Turns out, Parrish is the one who responded to Maria Gutierrez's 9-1-1 call two weeks before she turned up dead in her home. He was the closest. The current theory is he suspected she was on to him and wanted to keep an eye on her. We're in the process of getting a search warrant for Parrish's main residence and access to his phone records and financials. With any luck, we'll find something there that will lead us to Laila."

Lieutenant Parrish. The officer who'd escorted them to the motel? "You think he might be the killer."

"He almost killed you, Genevieve. He would have if I hadn't gotten to you in time. The son of a bitch hung you from a tree with fishing line around your throat, but from what your doctor said, he ensured most of your weight was in your wrists. He wanted me to find you like that. He wanted me to know he could take you from me," he said. "This is nothing but a sick game he thinks he can win, but I won't let him. Okay? I give you my word, I won't stop until he's in cuffs or in the ground. So is there anything you remember that will help me find him?"

"He said…" Defiance coiled low in her belly. "He made me who I am."

EASTON CLEARED THE CABIN.

With Lieutenant Parrish still in the wind, he couldn't take any chances. Morsey's right-hand man had disconnected the GPS on his cruiser and turned off his phone, and the search of his home revealed he'd left his credit cards behind. They'd lost him.

CSU hadn't been able to come up with anything from the latest scene. Every surface capable of giving them a fingerprint had been wiped down. No DNA or fibers recovered from the tree Genevieve had been hung from or from the zip ties used to secure her wrists. The killer was covering his tracks, making it impossible for them to get a positive ID, and staying one step ahead. Alamosa's forensics unit had tried running the partial recovered from the package with Laila Ballard's ear inside a second time, but there still wasn't enough to match anyone in the system.

"Clear." He crossed back to the front door and reached for Genevieve to bring her inside. "I'll get a fire going. We'll have you warmed up and comfortable in no time." He tossed in a few logs from the basket beside the stone fireplace and set about feeding the kindling to start. Within a few minutes, heat sped through him and the rest of the cabin.

"Guess you lost out on your deposit for the motel room, huh?" Scanning the space, she looked as though she were stepping into it for the very first time. Cautious. Alert. Strung tight. She hadn't said a word since her discharge from the hospital or during the three-hour drive back to Battle Mountain. Exhaustion carved deep hollows into her cheeks, and right then, Easton wanted nothing more than to take her pain away. Mentally and physically. "You know you don't have to stay with me."

"The last time I left you alone, a killer dragged you out into the middle of the national park and strung you from a tree." He wrenched open the linen closet door and tugged a stack of pillows and blankets down from the top shelf. Tossing them onto the couch, he spread them out as any man who'd become accustomed to sleeping on the ground using a rock as a pillow would. "I'm not going anywhere."

He could protect her here. This was his territory. His gut said the killer would try for her again, but next time, Easton would be there. He would be ready.

Long fingers curled around his forearm, forcing him to slow down. "It wasn't your fault. The killer… He changed his MO. We had no reason to believe he'd use another victim to lure me to that scene, and blaming yourself for something you can't control will only eat at you until there's nothing left."

He memorized the ridges of her knuckles, the scrapes across the backs of her hands. He released his grip on the blankets and turned to face her. Sliding his hand beneath hers, he traced the edge of her bandaged wrists with his thumb. "I should've been there."

"You were," she said.

Confusion cut through him. "What do you—"

"I wasn't scared." Confidence registered in her voice, and the unsettled tremors he'd noted in her fingers a couple days ago had since vanished. "When he had me, when he tried to tell me every woman he'd kill in the future would suffer because of me, the only thing I could

think of was you. You were with me. I knew you'd realize I'd been taken. I knew you wouldn't stop until you
found me. I...knew you'd be there when I needed you
the most. At that point, there was nothing he could say
or do to hurt me."

He traced the patterns of fresh scabs and bruises left
by the fishing line across her neck with the tips of his
fingers, and she closed her eyes. As though she trusted
him. Dark splotches marred her perfect skin, but it was
the thin laceration across her throat that would scar,
that would announce to the world what she'd survived.
"Genevieve, I'm not who you think I am. I'm not some
knight in shining armor—"

"No, you're not." Genevieve secured her hands under
his ears and forced him to confront her head on. "You're
stronger. You fight for others harder than you fight for
yourself, and you'll go down with the ship to save the
relationships you've managed to hold on to. Just as you
did with us, like you did with your unit and your brother
when he and Chloe were in danger a few months ago.
You're loyal and committed to everyone who comes into
your life, no matter how strained the connection. You
see that dedication as a weakness and a vulnerability,
something your enemies can target because your brain
is still trying to process all that trauma. But the truth is,
it makes you one of the most admirable men I've ever
met. Despite what you think, I know you. Inside and
out, and I'm not saying any of this because if it weren't
for you, I wouldn't be standing here." Her voice softened as she lowered her hands to her sides. "Although,
that does have a small part to do with it."

Process trauma. Is that what his brain was trying to do? Make sense of what'd happened after all this time? Army shrinks had tried to help. His dad had tried to push him to open up. Weston did everything he could to force him back into the real world, but none of them were Genevieve. None of them had ever looked at him as anything more than a broken soldier, and it was only then he realized he loved her for it. After all these years, all the anger, he still loved her. Hell. Easton skimmed his hand down the back of her arm.

"When I was following those two Alamosa PD officers out to the dunes, I was back in that moment. In Afghanistan. Right before everything went to hell." He braced for the ringing in his ears, the first sign of another episode about to tear him apart. Only it never came. "We were assigned to make a simple supply run. Watowski had made a rotten joke and Ripper slugged him for it. She didn't appreciate the punch line, and she was a hell of a lot stronger than she looked. A few of the other guys were laughing. Watowski hit the side of the truck, and I turned around. Everyone was smiling, including me. We'd created a bubble of normalcy inside the terror we dealt with on a daily basis. In that moment, we were happy."

He'd never told anyone the details. Definitely not anyone in his family, but the weight of her attention, the feel of her skin against his, somehow settled the raging horror he'd lived with the past year. "After we hit the IED, I didn't know which way was up. I think I knew what'd happened. I remember I pulled every single one of them from the truck, but at the time it was like watching someone else do it from afar. I didn't realize a piece of shrapnel had penetrated my helmet until a sergeant from one of the other trucks pulled me away. I wanted to help them, but it was too late." The truth reverberated through him. "I didn't want to be too late for you, too."

"You weren't." Genevieve rose onto her toes and wrapped her arms around his neck. Her heart thumped hard against his chest. Strong, reliable. She buried her mouth between his neck and shoulder and pressed her mouth to his skin. Then again. Trailing her lips up the length of his neck, she craned her head back and skimmed her teeth along his jaw. "I told you. I'm here. However you need me. I'm here."

An explosion of desire lightninged through him, and Easton reached back to grip her hands in each of his. "Genevieve, don't." He shook his head, every nerve ending he owned on fire. Tension constricted the muscles down his spine. "Don't give me hope."

"Maybe I'm the one who needs hope tonight." Her mouth met his in a battle for dominance. Mint burst across his tongue as she penetrated the seam of his lips. Angling her head, she opened wider, surrendering.

Easton maneuvered her backward until she hit the frame of the couch. Heat that had nothing to do with the roaring fire worked under his collar. Her fingers speared through his hair, nails scratching against his scalp. Hiking her thighs around his hips, he balanced her with the help of the couch then hauled her into him. A soft moan escaped her control and shot a wave of desire into overdrive.

This. This was what he'd missed about her. This

connection. The invisible understanding they'd always shared. He'd felt it that first time he'd laid eyes on her in the high school cafeteria, and he felt it now. Maneuvering her around to the front of the couch, Easton settled her onto the pillows and blankets he'd intended to use as a makeshift bed. She'd always known how to talk to him, to handle him, when to back off and when to push him over the edge. It was a feat few had accomplished, and he admired the hell out of her for it.

Because she was right.

She did know him, inside and out, and he knew her. Every curve, every scar, every button to press and how far to push her before she pushed back. She was everything he remembered and everything he didn't want to live without. Contradictory to the danger surrounding her, she'd continually held her head high and given one of the most vicious killers he'd known the middle finger, and damn, if that wasn't the sexiest thing he'd ever seen.

"Tonight, you deserve not to have to hold yourself together. Tonight, you can let the cracks in that legendary armor show. I'll take care of you, Genevieve. I promise." He settled his weight over her and tucked a strand of hair behind her ear. "Tell me what you need."

Flames reflected in her gaze. She hesitated in the process of unbuttoning his shirt. Attention on him, Genevieve let her guard slip away. The district attorney he'd studied on TV over the years vanished, leaving the sensitive, isolated woman underneath. Pain reflected in her expression, and in that moment, his purpose, the one his father had been trying to get him to see long before now, became clear.

Everything he'd gone through—Genevieve leaving, the IED, the PTSD, losing his father two months ago— it'd led him right to this moment. It'd made him strong enough to help her and others still lost in that drowning darkness they couldn't escape. He had. Because of her.

She smoothed her thumb under his eye, and he leaned into her hand. "Make me forget. Please. Make me forget."

Chapter Ten

Heat chased across her skin.

Genevieve rolled deeper into the mountain of blankets they'd escaped under last night. A scraping sound reached her ears. Pressing her eyes together harder, she tried to fall back into the sweet release of unconsciousness, but the smell of coffee and eggs triggered hunger. Coffee, eggs and...something sweet. She stretched her toes to the bottom of the makeshift bed. Small muscles she'd forgotten existed protested at the slightest strain, and the flood of pleasure, whispers and a sense of safety charged forward.

She'd had boyfriends over the years. Nothing serious, but enough to satisfy her cravings. But last night, with Easton... She'd forgotten how reactive she could be under his touch. Genevieve peeled her eyes open. A couple more logs had been added to the fire. She brushed her hair back away from her face, all too aware of the feel of the blankets over her bare skin. She turned onto her stomach to watch him in the kitchen. She wedged her knuckles under her chin, captivated, but was quickly reminded of the soreness around her throat.

He kept his back to her, the muscles rippling and releasing across his shoulders as he worked. Larger than life. He'd adorned his jeans with a black apron tied at the back of his neck and around his lean hips. He didn't have to turn around for her to know the front read "Meat is murder! Tasty, tasty murder." The apron had been on their wedding registry, and his father had agreed with the slogan enough to buy it for them.

"I didn't realize you'd kept that." She secured the closest blanket under her arms and held on to the edges as she stood. Cold darted up her bare feet as she made her way into the kitchen. She tucked the corner of the blanket between her breasts, reached for a mug from the cabinet to his left and poured herself a cup of coffee. Leaning her hip against the counter, she faced him. "The apron. It looks good on you."

His laugh tendrilled through her and raised her awareness into heightened territory. His hair had taken on a life of its own through the night, revitalizing that boyhood charm she'd fallen for. "Figure as long as I look good, I could get away with cooking a pot of air, and no one would notice."

"I certainly wouldn't." Mug in one hand, she slid her hand along his lower back and hiked onto her toes. She pressed her mouth to his, a fraction of the desire she'd felt last night blistering her lips. She nearly dropped the mug as Easton left whatever concoction he was cooking in the pan and pulled her hips in line with his. Her mouth parted under his deepening assault. She dug the tips of her fingers into his spine as he memorized her from the inside out until she finally had to come up for oxygen. The sizzling from the pan didn't compare to the fire burning under her skin. Maybe she wasn't too hungry after all. Maybe they could wait another hour or two. "Your breakfast is going to burn."

"I don't care. I have everything I need right here." He kissed her again, claimed her and everything she'd feared the past three days. Easton had done exactly as he'd promised. He'd helped her forget, just for a little while, but it'd been enough.

A high-powered growl escaped her stomach at the thought of pushing off her body's needs any longer. She pulled back, nearly speechless at the smile coaxing his lips higher. She strengthened her grip on her mug for balance, but Genevieve had been in this man's orbit before. Balance wouldn't come easy. "On second thought, I'll take everything you've cooked so far as long as its soft enough." She eyed the pan as he got back to work flipping eggs. Wait. Not just eggs. "Is that... Is that chocolate in those eggs?"

"Yes, ma'am." He scraped the singed concoction from the pan and settled it onto a nearby plate. "I call it a s'morelet. I saw it on one of the cooking shows. It's your traditional omelet with salt and pepper, but there's marshmallow, chocolate and a bit of crumbled graham cracker inside." He handed her the plate. "Enjoy."

Genevieve accepted the plate. She could already imagine the taste, and it would be anything but a s'more or an omelet. "Okay. I'll take everything you've cooked so far. Except that."

"This is the only thing I've cooked." He handed her a fork, his eyes glittering with humor. "It's this or crossing the very public space between this cabin and the main cabin for breakfast with my mom, Weston and Chloe. In that blanket."

She used the side of her fork to cut into the semicircle shape. Spearing the almost solid bite, Genevieve brought it to her mouth. "Is there another option?"

"It can't be that bad. The chef who came up with it is on the biggest food network in the country." Easton grabbed the fork from her and shoved the entire bite in his mouth. The muscles along his jaw ticked as he chewed, but within a few seconds, his expression contorted into something unrecognizable. He groaned and spit the mouthful into the sink. Turning on the water, he rinsed over and over. Finished, he swiped at his mouth with the back of his hand. "Yeah, I don't recommend you eat that."

She calmly set the plate back onto the counter and secured the blanket around her chest. "In that case, I suggest you cross the very public space between this cabin and the main cabin to get my breakfast from your mom, Weston and Chloe. In that apron."

Defeat cascaded down his spine as he tossed a kitchen towel to the counter. "I'll be back in a few minutes."

"Thank you." Genevieve studied her rugged reserve officer through the small window over the kitchen sink. The phone she'd purchased before leaving Alamosa reported temperatures close to midtwenties. Served him right for trying to poison the name of s'more. Clinging to the bedspread she clutched around her, she made her way back to the couch and fell into the cushions. She could still smell him on her skin. That authentic blend of Easton and wild. Purely him. It was the same scent she'd breathe in every day he'd finished with his chores around the property. Dirt, pine and fresh air. It was the same scent she hadn't been able to get out of her mind after she'd left Battle Mountain. Her smile fell. How long would it take this time?

Because despite the connection they'd shared last night, nothing had changed between them. She'd go back to her life in Alamosa, and Easton would still be here. His mother needed him, Weston needed him, this town needed him. No matter how good it'd felt to have him—to counter the emotional loneliness she'd felt for so long—she'd fallen into the same pattern as she had at nineteen years old. She could feel herself getting swept off her feet by him all over again instead of standing on her own.

She bit down on her thumbnail, watching the flames dance back and forth in the fireplace. She'd given up everything to break ties with Battle Mountain. She'd left her family here, moved into a town she'd never visited, put herself through law school and made something of herself. Why then had it been so easy to let him under her skin? What did that say about her?

The front door swung open, and a burst of cold air followed him inside. Balancing two plates in his hands, he kicked the door behind him with his bare heel. "Breakfast—that I did not make—is served."

"Mmm, I'm starving." The heaviness of her thoughts instantly slipped to the back of her mind as Easton rounded the small kitchen table and offered her a plate.

Hash browns, scrambled eggs, bacon, sausage, pancakes. Everything she could want or need. He collapsed onto the couch beside her. "It's nearly twenty degrees out there, but you knew that, didn't you?"

"I had to make an example out of you. Don't mess with breakfast food." Genevieve forked a soft mound of hash browns with ketchup into her mouth and melted back against the couch.

"Could you at least share your blanket? All the other ones are cold," he said.

"I'm sure I could be persuaded, given the fact you had a taste of your own—what did you call it?— s'morelet." She set her plate on the arm of the couch and untucked the corner of the blanket from between her breasts. "And that you probably had to answer a whole lot of questions from your family about exactly who the other plate was for."

"I convinced them I was hungrier than usual," he said.

"How did that go over?" Her breathing turned shallow as he swept his gaze down the length of her neck and chest.

"I think my mom is on to us, but I have Weston's word he hasn't said anything. Can't say as much for Chloe." Easton tugged the blanket from around her and tucked himself inside. Pressing her flat onto the couch, he traced his nose along the shell of her ear. "Don't be surprised if my mother shows up at the front door demanding her dishes back to get a glimpse of the woman I'm hiding in my cabin."

Her heartbeat flooded between her ears. Their exhales combined between them, mixing until she wasn't sure where his began and hers ended. "I'd like to believe she wouldn't do that, but I've been around your family long enough now to know otherwise."

"It's only a matter of time really." He skimmed his teeth along her jaw, and an earthquake epicentered low in her belly. Easton followed the curve of her neck with his mouth, leaving her desperate and gasping. "So we shouldn't waste another minute. You know, to keep ourselves from being scarred for the rest of our natural lives."

Genevieve hauled the neck of his apron over his head. Her skin met his, and an explosion of need took control. She fanned her hands over his hips, trying to loosen the tie at his back, but the apron wouldn't budge. "I agree."

Two knocks was all the warning they had before the front door swung open. "I knew you weren't that hungry."

Genevieve froze as a different kind of heat flared up her neck and into her face.

Easton's forehead collapsed onto her collarbones. "Genevieve, you remember my mother, don't you?"

Craning her head back to center Karie Ford in her vision, Genevieve untucked her hand from around the woman's son and extended it in greeting. "Nice to see you again, Mrs. Ford."

"EASTON JAMES FORD. Here I thought your father and I had taught you better than to look for trouble." Karie Ford waited for them to get decent, her back to them.

The tendons in her neck protested under strain, but it was her tone that raised the hairs on the back of Easton's neck. He knew that tone well. Every time he and Weston had stepped out of line growing up. The voice of doom. That, combined with the use of his full name, clenched every muscle he owned. "Your father is probably rolling over in his grave, young man. Don't you have any respect for yourself?"

"I think you're about to get grounded." Genevieve buttoned her red silk blouse she'd worn a couple nights ago, the scrubs from the hospital crumpled near the fireplace. She tried to fight the smile curling the corners of her mouth but failed. The flush of pink coloring her cheeks stood stark against her pale skin. Absolutely beautiful.

"At least you knocked." Easton threaded his hands through his T-shirt and pulled it into place. He noted a black stretch of lace across the couch and handed Genevieve's bra off to her before his mother had a chance to turn around. "It could've been a lot worse."

"It could've been a lot worse? That's all you have to say about the fact you're sleeping with the woman who left you at the altar?" His mother turned sea-blue eyes—the same color as his—onto him. Most of his life, he'd been entranced by their warmth, but the past few months, there was a solidity to them he recognized in his own. Losing her spouse had changed Karie Ford from the strong matriarch he'd always known into little more than a husk of the woman she'd been all his life. She tried to hide it, the cracks in her armor, but in this instance, like recognized like.

Weston hiked up the two stairs and across the threshold, slightly out of breath. "Mom, the hash browns started burning. You set off the smoke detector. What are you—" His brother scanned the scene, from the discarded plates of food, to Genevieve buttoning her slacks and the pile of blankets in front of the fireplace. A deep laugh resonated through the small cabin as Chloe peered around her fiancé. "Oh, I get it. She lost her earring, and you were helping her find it."

Genevieve's hands shot to her ears. "I did lose an earring." She searched through the blanket on the couch then moved on to shoving her hands between the cushions.

"What's a single moment of privacy if it doesn't turn into a family affair." Easton ran one hand through his hair, but he wasn't about to be scolded for bringing a woman back to his place. He wasn't a teenager who'd only been thinking with his second brain. At least, not completely. He scooped one of the couch pillows off the floor and threw it at Weston's face. "You guys are the worst."

His brother caught it. "I'm not the one wearing an apron."

"You have a point." Easton tried to untie the strings around his waist but ended up ripping the apron clean off instead. "Problem fixed."

"It's all fun and games until someone gets hurt." Karie Ford's ear-length white-blond hair fell from its usual style into her face. She pushed it back, exasperation clear in her aged expression. Closing in on her early sixties, the woman was a tornado of authority and confidence. His mother's delicate jaw turned hard. In reality, there wasn't much else delicate about Karie Ford. Her dark jeans and a flannel shirt highlighted a strength Easton had relied on a lot over the years, the kind she got from working the land around them going on thirty-five years. Her laugh lines deepened around her eyes and mouth as she glared. Sobering him up faster than a straight black cup of coffee or a single touch from Genevieve ever could.

"Mom, it's not that big of a deal. Genevieve asked me to consult on one of her cases a few days ago." He wasn't sure why he felt the need to explain other than he needed them to see this was a good thing, that he'd let go of the anger and betrayal, and was attempting to move on with his life. "We got to talking. One thing led to another, and—"

"Yes, it looked like a good conversation from what I could see." Karie pointed to the floor. "By the way, dear, you can stop searching the couch. Your earring is over here by my foot."

Genevieve's gaze hit the floor a split second before she shot her head back up. She straightened, smoothing wrinkles from her slacks. A humorless laugh escaped past her kiss-stung lips. She pointed toward the door. "I'll tell you what, you can keep it, and I'll just—"

"You'll stay where you are," Karie said.

"Yep. That's exactly what I thought, too. I'll stay right here." Genevieve interlaced her fingers in front of her. "Great minds think alike."

"Easton, you're a grown man." Karie Ford's attention shifted to Genevieve and back. "Who you…talk to is none of my business. Hell, I'm glad you've found someone to converse with after you've spent the past year moping around, but you need to know what you're going to get yourself into this time. If this conversation is going to end the same as it did last time, I'm not going to stand here and let her hurt this family." His mother set her chin, and Easton braced for the wrath of that one look, the one that could strip him down to nothing. Instead, she turned that look onto Genevieve. "What you did was cowardly, Genevieve Alexander. You should be ashamed to show yourself in this town. You broke my son's heart, and because of you Easton felt the need to join the army. Because of you he was on that damn supply run in the first—"

"That's enough." Easton positioned himself in front of Genevieve. Blame wouldn't do them any good. "Mom, you have every right to be mad that I didn't tell you Genevieve was staying here, but you have no idea what she's been through. In fact, there's a lot you don't know, and going all mama bear is only making it worse. What happened fifteen years ago happened. Nothing you say or do will ever change that. If I'm able to let it go, so should you."

Weston and Chloe slowly backed out of the cabin as the tension physically solidified between him and his mother.

Karie Ford stepped back, the fine lines around her mouth deeper than he'd ever seen them before. Grief did that to a person, changed them from the inside out. There was no predicting it, no stopping it. The sufferer was at its mercy, and all they could do now was hold on for dear life until the weight lifted. "You want me to forget the look on your face when you found her engagement ring in that bridal room? How you disappeared into the woods for nearly two weeks without a word after you realized she wasn't coming back? How when you finally came home, you told us you'd be leaving for basic training the next morning?" A line of tears glittered in his mother's eyes. "Your superior officer had to call me and tell me what'd happened in Afghanistan because you were unconscious for a week after you pulled your unit from the wreckage, and now you're finally home. No. I'm not going to forget, Easton. Because of what she did, I lost my son, and I'm not going to lose you again."

Hell. Easton stepped toward her, his heart heavier than a moment before. The past year played on a black-and-white loop in his head, but the ones with Genevieve had color. Hope. "Mom, you know how hard it's been here for me. As much as I wanted to deny anything was wrong, I need help." Confidence held his head higher. "Genevieve helps me. Okay?"

One second. Two.

"You're right, Karie." Genevieve stepped around him, and it took everything in him not to pull her back. But this woman had never let anyone control her. Why would she start now? "I was a coward. I should've had the guts to tell Easton—to tell all of you—why I had to leave, but I was scared. I didn't think any of you would understand because I wasn't sure I did. I'm sorry. I know my leaving didn't only hurt Easton. It hurt you and your family as well, and there's not a day that goes by that I don't regret that choice. You were like a second mother to me. You were there to help me pick out a wedding dress and made sure I was taking care of myself during all the planning. I'll never be able to repay you for that, but most of all I'm grateful you raised such a strong son. Without him, I wouldn't be standing here."

"If you say she helps with what you're going through, I believe you." Karie nodded once. "Tell me what I can do to help, too."

"Forgetting you walked in on us would be a start," Easton said.

A quirk of a smile tugged at his mother's mouth. She folded her hands in front of her. "Lock the door next time, and bring the dishes back when you're through, for crying out loud. I didn't raise you in a barn." With that, Karie Ford turned and closed the front door behind her.

Genevieve's relieved exhale doubled her over beside him. She pressed her fingers into both eyes. "For the record, I don't think I've ever been more embarrassed in my entire life, and I've had everyone in Battle Mountain stare me down for leaving their golden boy at the altar. I didn't think it could get much worse than that."

"I warned you my conversation with them didn't go well when I was getting us breakfast." Easton pulled her into his side. He kissed her temple, resurrecting a hint of wood smoke and desire. If he was being honest, his mother walking in on him with a woman was probably one of the least embarrassing occurrences. "You might as well get used to it now. This is the first of many embarrassments for us in the future."

Genevieve straightened under his touch. "The future?"

His phone pinged with an incoming message. Releasing her, he crossed the small cabin and scooped it off the kitchen counter where the dying evidence of his attempt to be charming lay in shambles. He swallowed as his gag reflux kicked in. Eggs did not mix well with chocolate. He'd never make that mistake again. He tapped the new message.

"It's Weston." A spike of adrenaline lightninged through him. Tearing his gaze from the phone, he focused on Genevieve. "He got a call from Captain Morsey. Laila Ballard just walked into the medical center on her own two feet, claiming Lieutenant Parrish abducted her." His phone threatened to crack under his grip. "She's alive."

Chapter Eleven

Genevieve's fingers shook as she wrapped her hand around the door handle. Knocking, she shouldered inside and faced the woman she'd turned into a target. "Laila."

White gauze matted a halo of stringy brown hair. An oxygen tube strung across a weathered face. Dark eyes, the color of coal, quickly dried as Laila Ballard realized she wasn't alone. Two lacerations cut through a thin bottom lip, but the Contractor's latest victim still had enough strength to sit higher in the bed. Small stains of blood filtered through the wrapping around her left ear. Her low, slightly distorted voice barely carried across the private room. "Ms. Alexander, I wasn't expecting you."

"Genevieve." She closed the heavy door as quietly as possible so as not to alarm her friend, but firsthand experience warned her it'd take a lot more than a few niceties to help Laila process what she'd been through. Laila had been abducted because of her connection to Genevieve. There was no easy fix for something like that. No Hallmark card that expressed the guilt and sorrow raging inside. *Sorry you were abducted and dis-membered. Thinking of you.* She scanned the array of flowers and stuffed animals on the table beside Laila. "How are you?"

"Oh, you know. It's a little harder to hear nowadays, but what do you think of my new accessory?" Laila tugged at the wrap of gauze keeping infection at bay. Thin fingers picked at invisible specs in the sheets as Genevieve took her seat beside the bed. Flourescent lighting glinted off the spread of scalpels, tweezers and other surgical tools on a rolling tray a few feet away. "When I gave my statement to Captain Morsey, he told me the man who took me, who did this…" She motioned to her ear. "He's the same one who killed all those other women? The one who broke into your house before you borrowed my car?"

"Yes." She nodded, her chin wobbling. This woman had already been through so much. Losing her daughter so violently had nearly broken her. If it hadn't been for the trial giving her something to fight for, something to focus on, Genevieve wasn't sure the grieving mother would've made it. Now this. She reached for her friend's hand. For connection, for comfort, for a direct conduit to express everything she couldn't say. "Laila, I'm sorry. I thought I was being careful, but if it hadn't been for me, Lieutenant Parrish wouldn't have—"

"No sense in talking about things we can't change." Cool, papery skin countered the anger churning in her gut as Laila laid her hand over Genevieve's. Laila couldn't be much older than her late forties, early fifties, but she'd aged in a matter of days. Violence did that. It took the best parts of someone's being and wrung them out to dry, leaving nothing but emptiness and isolation. The ends of Laila's hair frayed around her face. Apart from the obvious damage to her ear, she had seemingly only suffered minor bruises and scrapes. Nurses had cleaned the blood from her skin, but Genevieve could still pick out debris in those dark curls. "Tell me about this police officer who's been helping you with the investigation."

"Easton?" How had she known about…? Captain Morsey must've told her. Genevieve tried to tamp the urge to fidget for a distraction, but the truth was plain to see. She cared about him. She squeezed Laila's hand. "He's a friend. We knew each other way back. In fact, we were engaged to be married before I came to Alamosa. I asked him to wait outside so we could talk alone."

A knowing smile thinned battered lips, and discomfort flared in Genevieve's chest. Laila pressed the oxygen tube harder against her nose and closed her eyes for a moment. "I appreciate that. As much as I'd love the chance to meet him for myself, I'm not dressed for company at the moment."

"You look great. Think of it this way. Now you can stop looking for all those single earrings you lost over the years." She shook her head at her own joke. "Too soon?"

"A little." A strangled breath pinned Laila to the bed for a series of seconds, and the woman clamped down on her hand. Hard. Exhaustion wrecked the once full cheeks and flawless skin under Laila's eyes. New lines carved between her eyebrows as she stared up at the ceiling. She'd been through a lot. It would take time to recover, but she would recover. One day her abduction wouldn't be the first thing she thought of in the morning, just as Genevieve hoped it wouldn't be for her.

"My friend I was telling you about, Easton, he was a soldier overseas up until about a year ago. His unit was on their way to make a supply run when they hit an IED. He was the only one who survived, but to this day, he still struggles with what happened." She hadn't meant to spill Easton's secret, but the buried terror in Laila's gaze, the vulnerability and unknown of what lay ahead, urged her to make this right any way she could. "He's only recently started talking about what he deals with on a daily basis, but it's changed him for the better. Do you want to tell me what happened?"

Laila closed her eyes again, turning her head away. "The police needed my statement, especially given one of their own was involved, but... I don't want to remember."

"I understand." Genevieve set her free hand over Laila's, sandwiching the woman's cool, onion-thin skin between hers. "You don't have to talk, but just know, I'm here. Okay? Whatever you need, I'll be here. I'll help you get through this. No matter what it takes."

The once stone-hardened mother Genevieve had studied in court during her daughter's killer's trial had vanished, and in her place, was a woman who'd never be the same again. Laila turned back, warm eyes locking on their intertwined hands on the edge of the bed. "You were always so kind to me. Always there when things got hard." Laila nodded. "It was dark in the house when he came in. I didn't hear him over the sound of the television. I have to turn it up so loud these days, but I felt a draft. I got up off the couch to make sure I hadn't left a window open, and there he was, standing there in the middle of the hallway. He stared at me like I was expecting him. Next thing I knew I was zip-tied by the wrists and ankles in some place I didn't recognize."

"You don't remember anything from when you were taken to when you woke up?" she asked.

"No." Laila shook her head. "But he was there. The same man. Lieutenant Parrish. He'd been waiting for me to wake up. He had a knife in one hand, told me he needed me to help him send a message." The woman's expression contorted in remembered pain, and Genevieve squeezed her hand again. "He took out my hearing aid and cut off my ear. I must've passed out because when I woke up again, he was gone. I don't know how long. I told myself the next time he came back I'd be ready, that I needed to stay strong for my baby."

Tears streaked down her hollow cheeks. "One of the floorboards was loose. I managed to pry it up and use one of the nails to cut through the zip ties around my wrists, but before I could get free, I heard his vehicle. I hid the nail in my hand and pretended I was still tied up, but when he got close to give me a drink of water, I stabbed him in the side of the neck. There was so much blood, but I couldn't stop. I cut through the ties around my ankles, and I ran as fast as I could until I got back to town."

Genevieve's pulse ticked harder behind her ears as

she tried to superimpose Parrish's face over the masked man who'd hung her from a tree in the middle of the woods.

"You were so brave. If you hadn't killed him, you might've ended up like those other women." Genevieve rubbed her hand along Laila's forearm, but a knot of hesitation clenched her gut. She didn't remember a whole lot about the minutes after the Contractor had caught up with her in the dunes, but there was one detail that stood out more than the others.

The killer had never showed her his face.

Her stomach soured. Why would Parrish have let Laila see his then? That didn't make sense. No. Something wasn't right about her story. She licked her lips to counter the physical signs Easton had always been able to pick up on when she lied and soothed her friend's hand again. "And Lieutenant Parrish wasn't wearing a mask, right? Just like he didn't when he took the other victims?"

Laila swiped at her face to catch the tears that'd escaped. "That's right. I recognized him immediately. I figured he'd planned on killing me, so why hide his face if I wasn't going to live long enough to identify him?"

Oxygen squeezed from her lungs. Genevieve struggled to keep her expression neutral. Laila was lying about the abduction. Why? She'd been through a physical trauma. Was she agreeing because she wanted this over with, or had Parrish forgone the mask specially for his latest victim? "I'm so glad you're okay now. Thank you for sharing with me. I think I'm going to let you rest for a bit. You've had a hard few days."

Another strangled breath filled the silence between them. Laila pointed toward the bathroom. "Could you fill up my mug with water first, please?"

"Of course." Genevieve patted her friend's hand, collected the empty oversized water mug with bendy straw from the bedside table and crossed to the other side of the room. Streaming water echoed in her ears inside the small bathroom, but the door had closed enough to block Laila's view of her. She let the water run a bit longer than necessary to sort through the details. Why would the Contractor reveal who he was to Laila when he'd gone out of his way to make sure Genevieve could never identify him at the dunes? They'd theorized he'd cut off Laila's ear to lure her to the woman's home and give him a chance to abduct Genevieve. But if he'd been using Laila to send a message as she'd said, why cut off her ear when Elisa Johnson's body had done the job?

She'd used up enough time. Turning off the water, she popped the lid back onto the mug labeled with the medical center's logo and returned to the main room. Laila hadn't moved as far as she could tell, but the way her friend studied her pooled dread at the base of her spine. Something was wrong. Genevieve set the mug on the bedside table. "Here you go. Anything else I can get for you?"

"It's getting hard to talk." Laila motioned her closer, her voice strained and weak. More so than a minute ago. "Come closer. There's something I forgot to tell you."

Genevieve took a single step closer. Only to realize the neatly organized surgical tools on the cart a few feet away had been disturbed.

One was missing.

A vivid awareness bled into Laila's gaze. She ripped her arm from beneath the sheets and arced the scalpel in her hand down.

A SHRILL RING filled his ears.

Easton checked the phone's caller ID as his candy bar from the clinic's waiting room vending machine fell. He answered on the third ring. "You find anything at the scene where Laila Ballard said she was being held?"

"Well, Lieutenant Parrish is dead. So that's something." Weston lowered his voice, most likely to contain information if he was still outside the crime scene. A search of the lieutenant's financials and property records hadn't produced a lead to narrow the manhunt, but one of the other victim's vacation cabin had served his purposes. The bastard had held Laila Ballard for three days with little sustenance or care for the damage he'd done to her ear. It was amazing she hadn't died from infection. "There's a rusted nail sticking out of his jugular. The medical examiner says he would've bled out in a matter of minutes. Would you like me to be more specific than that?"

"Damn it." He should've known. The proximity of Parrish's cabin to the scene where he'd found Genevieve hanging from a tree, the fact the lieutenant had disappeared off the radar after learning where he and Genevieve would be staying the night—it'd all been there. He and Genevieve had been closing in, and Parrish had upped the stakes. "What else?"

"The crime scene unit recovered two sets of severed zip ties lined with blood. Most likely your vic's, but Alamosa PD is having the DNA tested to confirm along with all the other samples of blood. Parrish's boots match the prints Alamosa cast from the abduction scene and Genevieve's home. Same size, same tread. I can tell you this is where he kept her for the past three days. I've got protein bar wrappers, empty water bottles, a bucket in the corner and a gag. We also recovered a blade that could've been used to cut her ear off. He was keeping her alive for some reason, and there are plenty more supplies here that makes me think he wasn't finished with her yet," Weston said. "From what I see here, she fought back. Hard. Aside from the arterial spray from the lieutenant here, there are clear signs of a struggle, but there's one thing I can't explain."

"What's that?" Easton asked.

"Laila Ballard told the captain she had to pry a floorboard free to access the nail she used to cut herself loose and kill Parrish." Heavy footsteps penetrated through the line. "I've been over every inch of this place. There aren't any loose floorboards."

"That doesn't make sense." Where else would the nail have come from?

A scream singed down every nerve ending he owed.

"Easton?" Weston's voice notched higher.

"I'll call you back." Easton sprinted down the hallway toward Laila Ballard's room and barged inside. The door slammed into the wall behind it as he faced off with both women, one wielding a scalpel. "Genevieve!"

She'd managed to catch Laila Ballard's wrist before the blade struck, but the fight in her shoulders said their victim was much stronger than she'd led police and hospital staff to believe. A growl escaped her throat as she threw Laila's arm out to the side, and she stumbled backward into the wall behind her.

A homicidal glaze had transformed the victim who'd walked into the emergency room just a few hours ago into an unrecognizable force. Rage contorted beaten features as Laila Ballard lunged. The scalpel curved downward toward Genevieve. "She's dead because of you!"

Easton threw her out of the way. The blade sliced down the length of his arm. Agony forced him to suck air between his teeth. Protest rumbled through his chest, but Laila wasn't stopping. He had to get control of the blade. Footsteps and shouts echoed down the hallway. Security must've heard the commotion and come running. Good. Because the woman on the other side of the blade wouldn't go down without a fight.

"Laila, stop! We can help you." Genevieve held her palms out in surrender. "You just have to tell us what really happened during your abduction."

Heavy inhales strained the victim's chest as she latched onto the end of the bed for balance. That dark gaze never left her target, but it was only a matter of time before Easton would be forced to take her down. Sweat beaded along the woman's temples and neck. "You. You were supposed to make sure that drunk never made bail. You are the reason my daughter is dead. If it wasn't for you, he never would've gotten behind that wheel again. My baby would still be here instead of the cemetery."

Genevieve's gasp filled the space between them. "I tried, Laila. You know that. The judge—"

"Will get what's coming to her." Spittle flew from thin, battered lips. "But first, you're going to pay for what you did to me. You all will."

Every muscle down Easton's back hardened in battle-ready defense. Awareness told him security had arrived, but he motioned for them to hold off. They could still get out of this without any casualties. He could still get Genevieve out of here. "Laila, put the scalpel down. You haven't hurt anybody. You can still walk away from this. We can help you."

"Shut up!" Laila Ballard angled the blade in his direction. Sobs wracked though her chest, hiking her shoulders up and down in short bursts. "Just shut up." She turned her drowning gaze back to Genevieve. "He wanted to help me. That's why he killed them. He did it for me, but you…you wouldn't die."

"The other victims, you mean. The Contractor killed them for you?" Genevieve's voice softened and understanding filled her expression. "Annette Scofield was the EMT on scene that day of the accident. She was the one who pulled your daughter from the car. In her report, your daughter was still breathing, but she died on her way to the hospital. You blame Annette for not being able to save her. And Ruby Wagner?"

"She was the responding officer." Laila's anger lessened as grief took its place. "My daughter was in the car. She was alive, but the police did nothing until the EMTs arrived. Officer Wagner let my baby suffer because she was too untrained to know how to get her out of the car. She could've saved her life!"

Genevieve lowered her hands to her sides, taking a single step forward. "And Elise Johnson was my assistant. She helped me file the charges against the man who got behind that wheel, but it didn't stop him from doing it again. From killing your daughter in the accident."

"Genevieve." Easton swallowed the urge to reach out for her, to pull her back to safety, but she took another step. His blood pressure skyrocketed into dangerous territory, and he lowered his hand from holding off security. One wrong move. That was all it would take. He'd grab Genevieve and let security do their jobs. All that mattered was her.

"You all failed her. Why should you get to live when she doesn't?" Laila asked. "Why do you get to go through the rest of your lives like nothing happened when I'm barely surviving mine?"

"I understand. All of it. You have every right to blame me, but the others? They didn't deserve what the Contractor did to them, Laila. They were good people. They had families and dreams and their entire lives ahead of them." Genevieve held her chin level with the floor, no trace of fear in her eyes. "You said he killed them for you. Do you mean Lieutenant Parrish? Why? What does he owe you?"

Laila shook her head. The scalpel wobbled in her hand as her arm grew tired, and Easton shifted his weight onto his toes. The next time she got distracted, he'd make his move. "It doesn't matter." The victim centered cold, dark eyes on Genevieve. "All that's left is for me to hold up my end of the deal."

Laila Ballard turned the blade on herself.

"No!" Genevieve lunged, but it was too late. The damage had already been done.

Easton threaded his hands between her ribs and arms and hauled her back into his chest as security and emergency personnel rushed into the room. Chaos filled the space as he maneuvered Genevieve through the door and down the hallway. She fought his hold, wanting to go back, but there was nothing she could do. Her sobs shook through him as he angled her into the waiting room. The image of the grieving mother slicing through her own jugular burned into his brain, and Easton closed his eyes against the violence of it all. He forced himself to concentrate on the curve of Genevieve's shoulder, the way she smelled, the rhythm of her heart beating against his. Her sobs quieted after a few minutes, but still, she didn't move.

"I could've helped her." She buried her nose in the crook of his neck.

The heaviness of that statement settled on his chest. "I'm not sure anyone could have, Genevieve. She was hurting. All she wanted was her daughter back, and you couldn't make that happen. No matter how hard you tried."

"Why didn't I know she was in so much pain? Why didn't I see the connection between the victims before now?" she asked.

"Alamosa's a small town. You, Elise, Annette, Ruby—you've all worked a number of cases together.

We were looking for a needle in a haystack that dated back years." He smoothed her hair back away from her face. "You did everything you could. You know that. Some people just don't want to be helped. They go through their lives lying to their loved ones, hanging on to the past like it's a lifeline. Hell, they even lie to themselves, but it only makes things worse. Until Laila was ready to accept help, her future looked exactly like this. She made the choice. Not you or anyone else. She chose this."

He knew that better than most, and Easton couldn't help but wonder if his future would've mirrored Laila Ballard's if Genevieve hadn't come back into his life. How much longer would he have suffered with nothing to believe in or show for it without her?

"She was going to kill me." Genevieve straightened. Tears dried in crusted lines down her face, streaking black mascara along the way. Some color had come back into her face, but it would take a while before the memories didn't hurt so much. "Guess that means I don't have to worry about getting her car back to her."

"Always looking for that silver lining." Easton swiped at her cheeks with the pad of his thumb, ignoring the pain down his arm. Damn, she was beautiful, and honest, and warm. Everything he wasn't. Everything he needed. He memorized the fullness of her lips, the flawlessness of her skin and wisdom in her eyes. Merely a little more than three decades on earth but more than a lifetime of understanding and perspective in the emerald depths. "That's why I love you."

Chapter Twelve

Love?

Genevieve angled away from his chest, and his touch slipped from her skin. Her heart rate ticked up a notch, blood draining from her face. No. That wasn't… That wasn't possible. "What do you mean you love me? We've only been working this case for three days."

"I mean exactly what I said," he said. "You might think it's only been three days, but I've loved you since the first moment I met you all those years go, Genevieve. I never stopped, even after you left. I knew. I knew I was going to spend the rest of my life with you."

She forced her legs to support her as she backed away. She didn't know what to say to that, what to think. Her decision to return to Battle Mountain had strictly been to ask Easton help in figuring out who'd broken into her home and murdered her assistant. Not to get involved with him all over again. They'd worked this case together, and while it'd been comforting and assuring to have him at her side, she wasn't ready for…this.

Her chest felt too tight. It was getting harder to breathe. Thank goodness she was still standing in the middle of the hospital. "What do you expect me to say to that, Easton? I've been running on nothing but adrenaline and fear since someone broke into my home. I just learned friend has been using a serial killer to exact her revenge on the people she blames for her daughter's death. I just watched her slice open her throat with a scalpel in front of me because she failed. Four women attributed to the Contractor are dead—possibly five if Laila doesn't survive—and you're telling me you want to spend the rest of your life with me. It's a little much to take."

Easton closed the distance between them, every ounce the ranch hand, the solider and the police officer she'd believed him to be. "I understand that, but I know exactly what Laila Ballard went through. I've spent the past fifteen years of my life denying anything that might've brought me pain. I was on the same path as she was, letting all that anger and betrayal build up. I ran as far and as fast as I could from the people who cared about me the most to make sure I couldn't be hurt again, and the only thing it got me was more pain."

Her gut clenched.

He trailed his fingers up her arms. "Then you came back, and you…you made me realize I'm more than what's happened to me. You made me realize I could take these experiences and use them for something good. I could help people. I wouldn't have considered the idea if it hadn't been for you. I would've finished this investigation, gone back into hiding and let you slip away again. But I don't want to be that man, Genevieve. I'm better when I'm with you. Stay. Please. Once this investigation is finished, we can get our own place on a ranch, in Battle Mountain or here—wherever you want. We can finally give this a shot."

She believed him. Sincerity laced every word, and there was no doubt about the changes she'd seen in him over the course of this investigation. He'd let his guard down, for her, but the knot of uncertainty, of having to make a choice right here, right now, tightened in her gut. Genevieve intertwined her fingers with his and held his hands to her chest. Despite the amount of crying she'd done in the course of forty-eight hours, tears burned in her eyes. "I'm glad you were able to find some healing during our time together, Easton. You have no idea how much it means to me, and I'm so honored I got to be here to watch it happen." She internally fortified herself. He'd finally found healing, and she was about to destroy it all. Again. "But I've already given this a shot."

"I don't understand." He slipped his fingers from hers, leaving her cold and alone as he stepped out of reach. Confusion deepened the lines between his brows and softened the sharp angles of his features. In that moment, he wasn't the soldier she'd envisioned or even the law enforcement officer who'd protected her. He was that barely-graduated teenager she'd lost herself in all those years ago.

"I came to Battle Mountain for your help, and I can't thank you enough for everything you've done. If it weren't for you, I wouldn't have made it out of those woods. I know that, and I'm not sure I'll ever be able to repay you for it, but..." She bit the inside of her mouth to keep herself from shutting down. "Falling into whatever this is between us, pretending we can pick up where we left off—I'm not ready for that. I thought I was, but I can feel myself getting completely wrapped up in you again, your way of life, your personality, your family, and I've fought too hard to be my own person to give it all up now."

"So, what? We go back to the way things were? Like nothing happened between us?" His voice broke, and her heart crumpled right along with it. "Once this case is finished, you'll come back to Alamosa, and I'll go back to Battle Mountain, and we just carry on with our lives?"

"I think it's better if we end it now." It was the only way. "I know you're invested in seeing this case through, but Alamosa PD has a connection between the victims now. It's over. Parrish is dead. If Laila survives, they can question her to sure up their case. You and Weston and Dr. Miles got us this far, but there's nothing more you can do here. You're officially off the hook."

"Off the hook." Easton scrubbed a hand down his face, turning his back to her. "It's that easy for you, isn't it? To walk away. I should've known you'd use me for what you needed and run. That's what you're good at, right?"

"No. That's not…" His words hit her as though she'd taken a physical punch to the gut. Oxygen crushed from her lungs, and she slid her palms over her midsection to somehow keep herself together. "Easton, I care about you. A lot, but that's not enough to drop everything and ride off into the sunset to live happily ever after. We have to consider each other's needs. I'm not a teenager anymore who will compromise what I want because that's what's expected of me."

"Then why are you still acting like one? You can't tell me this is all about your insecurity. You're the district attorney, for crying out loud." Shock at his own accusation smoothed his expression and parted his mouth, and the fight seemed to leave him right there in the middle of the hospital waiting room. "I don't just care about you, Genevieve. I love you, damn it. That has to be worth something to you."

Genevieve slipped her fingers into her slacks, all too aware of the eyes and ears of the hospital staff waiting for her next response. She directed her attention to the floor. Her insecurity. That was exactly what this was all about. Because no matter how many times she'd wished she could go back and change things between them, there would always be part of her that wouldn't feel worthy of him. A part of her that believed he'd worked out how to find that equal balance they needed that she couldn't, that she could be as casual and confident as he was.

Genevieve clamped her mouth shut, forcing herself to take a deep breath. The same feelings of doubt and self-consciousness that stereotyped her as a young woman still held weight. They still deserved to be respected, and so did she. She wasn't a teenager, and she didn't have to stand here and listen to him echo his own insecurities back at her. She had enough of her own. He was right about one thing. His love should've counted for something, but in her case, it wouldn't ever be enough.

She crossed one foot behind her, ready to flee before she shattered into a million pieces right there in the middle of the waiting room. "I think it's best if I leave. I'll get a ride from one of the Alamosa PD officers outside. Please, Easton, take care of yourself. Okay? Don't let this stop you from finding peace."

Shame broke through the last of her fortifications as she darted down the hallway. A flatline warning escaped the crack of Laila Ballard's room as doctors tried to bring her back. Genevieve slammed against the side exit door and shoved out into the blistering night. A chill ran up the length of her arms. She'd left her coat in Easton's truck, but she didn't have the courage to go back to face him for the keys. She ran her hands up and down her bare arms. She'd left her bag at his cabin too, but there wasn't anything in there that couldn't be replaced. Easton had returned her keys after her release from the hospital, and she'd luckily slipped them into her pocket instead of her overnight bag. All she needed was a ride to her house, and she could put the investigation behind her. Put Easton behind her.

She'd done it once. She could do it again.

Lieutenant Parrish was dead. The case was closed. She could move on with her life.

Genevieve rounded the side of the medical center and targeted one of the Alamosa patrol cruisers. She picked up the pace as she crossed the semicircle drive in front of the emergency room and flagged down the officer behind the wheel. Recognition flared as he stepped from the car, and a surge of relief chased back the pressure behind her sternum. "Mind if I catch a ride back to my house? That is, if it's been cleared as a crime scene by now?"

"Don't mind at all, Counselor." Chief Morsey collapsed back into his seat, a to-go coffee cup in his hand. He positioned it into the center console as she wrenched open the passenger side door and climbed inside. The heater was already running, filling the small space with a hint of cologne. "I've been out at the scene where Parrish was holding Laila Ballard all day. Just heard from her doctor about what happened with her. It's a damn shame. Ford decide to stick around to see if she recovers?"

"Something like that." Genevieve strapped into her seatbelt, attention honed through the windshield. It was stupid to fantasize about Easton running through the sliding glass double doors and stopping her from leaving, but she couldn't help herself. He'd always been her knight in shining armor when she'd needed him. Now it was time to be her own. She pressed back into the warm seat as they pulled away from the hospital. "Thank you, Captain. I'm sure you're just as glad this case is over as I am."

He moved so fast, she wasn't entirely sure what'd happened until pain lightninged across her neck. One hand steady on the wheel, Captain Morsey pinned her to the seat with a blade pressed angrily to her throat. "Who says it's over?"

GENEVIEVE WAS GONE.

He stood there in the middle of the waiting room, his reflection blurred in the window of the vending machine. The pressure building behind his sternum reached a crescendo. He'd given her everything these past few days, but it hadn't been enough. He would never be enough for her. She'd been the woman he'd relied on to help him heal. Now what was he supposed to do? Go back to his cabin, to his isolation?

Without her, he was losing his grip. The process was already starting. How long before the emptiness came for him? How long before he was completely alone? He studied the face staring back at him as failure consumed him from the inside. Numbness threatened to overtake his control. Easton leveraged his weight against the frame of the vending machine and set his head against the glass.

A soft ringing started in his ears. His breath fogged in front of him. Not enough to keep him anchored in the moment. Easton forced himself to take a deep breath, but the harder he reached for that control, the faster it slipped away. Images of pain, of fear and loss splintered his consciousness in two, but instead of sand and fire, there was only Genevieve. The desperation to find her after he realized she'd been taken from Laila Ballard's home, the lack of color in her skin when he'd found her hanging from a tree. Each memory twisted and folded into an unrecognizable torrent of emotion he couldn't regulate on his own. Not without her.

His fist penetrated the glass window.

It shattered around his hand and hit the industrial carpet. Pain rippled up through his forearm, and he squeezed his hand into a fist. Blood bloomed through the small lacerations across his skin. He'd survived his fiancée leaving, an ambush on his unit and the murder of his father. How much more was he supposed to take before it was okay to give up?

Easton stepped back from the vending machine. He tugged his cell phone free. Blood spread across the screen as he scrolled through his contacts. He hit the one he needed and brought the phone to his ear. Three rings. Four. The call went to voicemail, as he'd predicted it would, and he sank back into one of the chairs behind him. He closed his eyes to focus on the voice on the other end.

Hey, this is James Ford. I'm probably available right now, but I can't find my phone. Leave a message, and we'll see if I remember how to access voicemail when I find it.

The line beeped, and Easton didn't know what else to do other than to follow this through. "Hey, Dad. Guess I don't have to worry about showing you how to check your voicemail anymore. I lost count of how many times you'd shown up at my door asking for my help when we both knew you didn't need it. You were there to check on me, to see if I needed you, but I was an idiot who thought I could do this on my own. I need you now, Dad." His voice cracked as sorrow wrung him dry. "I need you to tell me what to do next."

He lowered the phone into his lap and hit End. James Ford wasn't going to call back. He wasn't ever going to hear the message. He wasn't ever going to show up on Easton's doorstep pretending he was too old to figure out technology on his own. Easton stared at the shattered remnants of the vending machine window. The man had taught him responsibility, reliance and loyalty, but in the end, his father had died for being selfless.

His phone rang.

Every nerve ending he owned caught fire at the name scrolling across his screen. James Ford (Dad). Impossible. Inhale shaky, he answered the call. "Yeah?"

"Easton." His mother's voice penetrated through the thick haze of betrayal and grief. Grief of losing his father, of not being strong enough to save his unit, of Genevieve walking out on him all over again.

"You didn't disconnect Dad's phone." He swiped at his face, realizing too late his hand was still bleeding from the vending machine and the other from the swipe of Laila Ballard's scalpel.

"No. I still call it when I need to hear his voice. I won't tell you how many times a day that's getting to be lately." The soft, familiar click of knitting needles hitting against one another filled the other side of the line. He recounted Sunday mornings in front of the television—he, Weston and his father glued to whatever mutant superhero episode had come on, while his mother knitted silently in the recliner behind them. Those mornings hadn't been exceptional, but they'd been everything to him. "Sounds like you needed to hear him, too."

A burst of pain and laughter shattered the last hold on his control, and Easton leveraged his elbows against his knees. He pinched his forehead between his index finger and thumb, trying to rub the shame away. "I don't know why. I know he's gone. There's no changing that."

"Honey, I don't call this number expecting your father to pick up the phone and start talking to me like nothing happened." The sound of his mother's knitting needles ceased. "I do it because hearing his voice makes me feel like I'm not alone. Sure, I have you and Weston and Chloe here from time to time, but you've each got your own lives, and there's no shame in searching for things that make us feel better. Even if no one else understands it."

His instincts gave him the distinct impression Karie Ford wasn't talking about calling a ghost anymore. The barriers that'd kept him from exposing his greatest weakness shattered as violently as the vending machine glass a few feet away. "Everyone I care about leaves. My unit, Dad, Genevieve. Weston and Chloe are starting their lives. They'll get married and want a place of their own, a family. As much as I hate to think about it, you're not going to be around forever. Soon enough, it'll just be me." There was no denying the truth as it exploded to the surface. "How am I going to get better if I don't have anyone left, Mom?"

Silence filtered through the line. One second. Two. "Maybe you don't—"

"Officer Ford, we managed to get Laila Ballard stable," an unfamiliar voice said.

He craned his head up. A physician caught sight of the vending machine and the bloody smears down Easton's arm. Bringing the phone back to his ear, Easton nodded. "Mom, I'm going to have to call you back."

"I'm going to hold you to that." His mother ended the call.

Easton cleared his throat, all too aware of the possible bill that could come with the damage he'd caused to the vending machine. "Sorry about the mess. I can leave my credit card information with the supply manager if I need."

"I'm more interested in your hand." The doctor motioned to him. "And your arm."

"Oh, no. It's fine. Thanks. Just a few scrapes. Nothing I haven't survived before." Easton pocketed his phone. "You said Laila Ballard is stable. Can I talk to her?"

"Not yet. The patient didn't just manage to cut through her carotid artery. She pressed hard enough to damage her vocal cords. It'll be a few months before she can speak verbally," the physician said. "We've managed to stop the bleeding but she's still unconscious. I can let you know when she's out of surgery."

"Thanks." Easton couldn't fight back the memory of what'd happened in that room, of Laila Ballard blaming Genevieve for what'd happened with her daughter. The woman had enlisted the help of a serial killer to carry out her revenge. Which meant she had to have known about Lieutenant Parrish's dark side. But why kill him before the job was done? Staging her abduction, he could understand. Laila Ballard had needed a way to lure her target out of hiding, but if Genevieve was the endgame, why dispose of the man who'd done her dirty work until now? To give her the honor of finishing the job only to end her own life next? To tie up loose ends? Easton called after the doctor already heading back down the hall. "All updates on Laila Ballard are supposed to go through Captain Morsey. Have you tried getting a hold of him?"

"Captain Morsey isn't answering pages or his phone," the attending said. "You may want to check with security."

"Will do. Thanks again." Easton followed the corridor past the waiting room and got the attention of an officer he recognized from Laila Ballard's crime scene. Hopefully there were no hard feelings about him lying to get past the perimeter tape. "Hey, man. I'm trying to track down Captain Morsey. Have you or your partner seen him around?"

"No. He radioed into dispatch about fifteen minutes ago, said he was end of watch." The officer accepted a cup of coffee from his partner and slugged it down. "After everything that happened today, I don't blame him. Parrish and the captain were close. Damn, I never would've pegged Parrish to be wrapped up in this. Abduction, killing. The guy was volunteering at La Puente every weekend. He'd pull over during shift to help folks get their groceries into their cars. Just doesn't make sense."

Alamosa PD had lost one of their own tonight, and the captain had gone home for the day? "Did Parrish and Laila Ballard know each other?"

"Nah, most of the time Ms. Ballard came around it was because she was looking for more information on her daughter's case." The second officer motioned toward Easton with his near-empty coffee cup. "She might've run into Parrish once in a while at the station, but Captain was the one who had her in his office week after week trying to keep her in the loop."

"Laila and the captain. Really? I didn't realize they

knew each other." Easton tried to recall when Laila Ballard's daughter had been hit and killed by the drunk driver from Genevieve's prosecution record. Two years? Three? If their abduction victim was coming into the captain's office for weeks on end, they might've struck up a friendship. Maybe a deal? He'd talked to Captain Morsey on the way in. He'd been concerned about Laila, worried even, but the look in his eyes hadn't matched his expression. Easton had dismissed it as stress. Stress from a serial killer stringing up Alamosa residents, stress from discovering one of his own responsible, stress from shouldering the safety of this town. Fifteen minutes ago. The same time Genevieve had run out the side door... "Excuse me."

Easton followed the signs to the security office and requested access to the video feeds from the side door. Within a minute, he pegged Genevieve escaping into the parking lot, but seconds later, she disappeared off the screen. He pointed to the monitor. "Can you track her?"

The head of security accessed the second feed, one positioned over the emergency room entrance. There. Two police vehicles had been parked in the semicircle wrapping the front drive. Genevieve headed straight for the one on the left. The driver stepped out from behind the wheel. Captain Morsey. She collapsed into the passenger side. Easton pulled his phone free and dialed the number of her burner. "Come on, come on. Pick up, damn it."

The line went straight to voicemail.

Chapter Thirteen

"I guess the gig is up," he said.

She felt as though déjà vu was playing a cruel game with her head.

Shadows crept across the hardwood floor, just as they did the last night she'd walked into her home. Moonlight filtered through the sheer curtains. She could even still see the outline of blood the crime scene unit hadn't been able to get out of the wood. Her neck burned from the previous sting of the blade as she tried to work her tongue around the gag. The fabric wicked moisture from her lips and mouth, making it that much harder to swallow. Blood and pain and steel was all she knew now. She struggled against unconsciousness. Sweat slid down her face and into the collar of her blouse. Her head sagged forward, but he was there. He wouldn't let her sleep.

The installation of the first steel eyelet had kept her from fighting back as he'd drilled into the side of her knee. It didn't matter if she escaped now. She wouldn't be able to get far.

The man who'd haunted her nightmares sat himself on one of her barstools a few feet away. His fingers moved over the drill bit as he cleaned away her blood. She should've known. She should've known it'd been him that night. Barring her from the investigation, pressing her to admit she'd been the one to kill Elisa Johnson, blocking Battle Mountain PD from getting involved. Captain Morsey had been inside the investigation all along, leading it wherever he needed it to go. He'd known where to find her, that she'd borrowed a car from Laila Ballard and had a connection to each of the victims. He'd been the Contractor all along.

"You're a fighter, Counselor. I guessed as much. The way you make your case in court… So compelling." Morsey finished wiping the blood from his drill. The lamp in the corner glinted off the gold-colored metal bit. Shoving to his feet, he faced her. Ready to place the next piece of his sick puzzle. "Usually by this time, women your size need a little help staying awake, but I've always underestimated you, haven't I? I certainly did when I left you in the woods. Didn't think you'd last long enough for Ford to find you alive."

Easton. His name settled at the front of her mind and took up as much space as it could. Their last conversation threatened to break her all over again, but she had to stay strong. Mentally, physically, emotionally. She wasn't going to let Morsey win.

"Why?" The single word died at the gag squeezing her head. She pulled at the ties hinged inside the hooks he'd installed into her ceiling stretching her arms over her head. Her left toes barely skimmed the floor, an ache bunching along her sides. He'd planned to kill her in those woods. She had no doubt about that now as he slowly prepared to hang her from the ceiling, but he must've been interrupted. Maybe heard the sirens as Easton and the two Alamosa officers arrived at Parrish's cabin. He'd lost his opportunity.

"Every week for three years, Laila Ballard was waiting for me at the station. Every week I sat her down. I patted her shoulder. I listened to her when she could speak through the sobs." His gaze distanced as he adjusted his grip around the drill. "The law had failed her. You and everyone else involved in her daughter's case had failed her, and there was nothing I could do but watch this beautiful women break over and over again every week. I'm not sure when it happened, when I swore I would do whatever it took to ease her pain. She's a magnificent woman who didn't deserve what she went through. It was my job to fix it."

Her heart shuttered. Captain Morsey had fallen in love with Laila Ballard. Over the course of those visits, he'd taken on the weight of her pain, her sorrow. He'd killed for her.

"By killing those women." Her lips barely met over the mouthful of the gag.

"To be honest, I wasn't sure I could do it." Morsey lowered the bright yellow power tool to his side, his aged index finger over the trigger. She'd managed to stay conscious through one eyelet in her joint. She wasn't sure she could through the second. "I had everything I needed. Profiles and surveillance on Elisa Johnson, Annette, Ruby Wagner and you. I learned your routines, tapped your phone lines, kept tabs on who you spoke to and cared about. I was ready to do this for Laila, but then Maria Gutierrez came along."

The hairs on the back of Genevieve's neck stood on end. The first victim. She pulled against the anchors he'd installed in her ceiling the night he'd killed Elisa Johnson, but they wouldn't budge. They'd held her assistant's weight for hours. They'd hold hers when he was finished with her. She rubbed the gag against her arm, dislodging it enough to breathe clearly for the first time in over an hour. "Maria wasn't a target."

Morsey stared down at the point where her toes skimmed the floor. Blood pooled beneath her, her slacks not thick enough to hold any more. "She was a good kid. I helped her apply to the Bureau, study for her exams. I gave her a reference and recommended for her to talk to some contacts I had."

"She must've seen something. Something she shouldn't have." Genevieve raised her gaze to the ceiling, all too aware Morsey held the upper hand here. She was hanging from the ceiling. The zip ties had cut into her wrists, and there was a steel eyelet screwed into her right knee. Still, there had to be something—anything—here that would help her get free.

"One night, Maria had come over to return one of my books. I invited her in out of habit. She saw the surveillance photos I'd taken of Annette Scofield on the table. I tried to tell her Scofield was the subject of an Internal Affairs investigation, but the look in her eyes... I could tell she didn't believe me." Morsey stepped into her, his dark eyes level with hers. He'd aged in a matter of hours. No longer the captain she'd worked with over the years, but someone she didn't recognize. "I didn't learn until later she'd called 9-1-1 when she got home that night, but accessing the recording—deleting it—would've raised too many flags. I had to wait so as not to spook her."

"You killed her to stop her from exposing you." Genevieve balled one fist and relaxed the muscles along her ribs as long as she could. One shot. That was all she had, but her toes barely swept across the hardwood. She wasn't strong enough to pull free. She'd have to jump in to unhook the zip tie from the ceiling, and her knee had been taken out of commission. "Is that what happened to Lieutenant Parrish, too? He got too close? Is that why you framed him for abducting Laila?"

"Parrish should've left well enough alone." Morsey shook his head as though in regret. "I was careful, but he followed me after the news of Laila's disappearance hit the news. I led him straight to where she was hiding when I went to check on her. He must've seen Laila through the window. I went to refresh her supplies, and he broke in, thinking I was holding her hostage. Laila had no choice but to kill him. He would've ruined everything."

"She cut off her own ear to lure me to the house." Genevieve's toes pressed into the hardwood. The muscles along her sides were lengthening with every exhale. "Why the pageantry? Why hang them from their ceilings? Why all of this?"

Sweat trickled into her eye and down her throat. Blood loss raised her pulse. Her nerves worked overtime to compensate for the pain in her knee, but there was only so much her body could do. Spidery lines crept into the edges of her vision.

"I wasn't going to let anything link back to Laila. If I made it look like a serial killer was on the loose, I could hide the connection between the victims. It worked for a while. Until you and Easton Ford insisted on getting involved." Morsey crouched, gripping her leg below her left knee. He stared up at her and pressed the drill bit into her. "Sorry, kid. I made a deal, and I'm a man of my word." He lifted the drill parallel to the floor.

No. This wasn't over. She wasn't going to die like this. "He won't stop. Easton will figure it out. He'll come for you, and you and Laila will never get to be together." It was the only play she had left. "That's what you want, isn't it? You love her. You killed for her. You can still walk away. You can disappear, but only if I make it out of this alive."

Her heart jerked in her chest at the thought of never seeing Easton Ford again. Those sea-blue eyes lighting up whenever she walked into the room, that smile that swept away violence and fear and loneliness. He'd always had that effect on her, as though he'd always been right there in the back of her mind. She'd battled long and hard for her independence, to prove she was more than his girl, his fiancée. His. But now… Now she understood. He hadn't just been at the back of her mind. He'd become part of her. He was hers, and no matter how many times she'd tried to deny it, she'd fallen in love with him all over again. Her friend, her protector, her everything. Hers.

Hesitation lightened the pressure of the drill bit

against her knee. Captain Morsey's eyes grew dazed, but not long enough. He readjusted his grip on the drill and leveled it off again. "It's too late for that."

"No!" Genevieve ripped her leg out of his clutch and jumped as high as she could. Her descending tug snapped the zip tie around her left wrist, and she swung off-center. Kicking out, she kicked Morsey back, but the pain in her right knee kept her from making contact with the floor. She was still hanging from the ceiling by one arm, and the tie sliced deeper. Blood slid down her forearm as her attacker regained his footing. A scream tore from her throat as she stretched her right toes for the edge of the brick fireplace, but she couldn't lift herself higher to break the second zip tie.

Morsey shot his hand out, securing her throat in a strong grip, and pulled her into him. "You're going to regret that."

THEY'D HAD THE wrong man.

Captain Morsey was the one who'd had a personal relationship with Laila Ballard. Not Parrish. He had a knowledge of forensics, access to each of the victims, inside information concerning the investigation—it all added up. He was the killer. He was behind this entire mind game.

Easton fled out the front emergency room doors, both officers on his heels. He had to think. Morsey couldn't have taken her far. Killers stuck to their hunting grounds unless forced to break habit. He ran through the parameters Weston had set from the beginning. Isolated, quiet, guarded. Morsey wouldn't go back to Parrish's cabin or the scene where Laila Ballard had been reportedly held. They were still crime scenes. "Damn it. He could be anywhere."

"Captain still isn't answering his phone," one of the officers reported. "Laila Ballard accused Lieutenant Parrish of abducting her. Now you think it's the captain? You've got a lot of nerve, Ford. Captain's a good man. He wouldn't do anything like this."

His exhales crystalized in front of his mouth. The spike in his heart rate beaded sweat in his hairline. The ringing started in his ears, too loud. Hell, he didn't have time for this. Genevieve didn't have time for this. He had to slow down, had to think. "Parrish must've gotten too close. He became a loose end. Laila killed him to keep us from exposing the truth. She's been working with Captain Morsey all along."

Genevieve. He closed his eyes against the oncoming attack of personal failures, but…they never came. The ringing blended in with the white noise of traffic outside the hospital's front doors. His pulse thudded hard behind his ears. He forced himself to take a deep breath and focus on nothing but her until the dull piercing in his ears vanished altogether. His senses evened out. He could do this. He could save her.

"Morsey took advantage when Genevieve came around that corner." Easton pointed back to the southeast corner of the building, where surveillance had lost her. "He'd come to the hospital because he'd heard what'd happened to Laila, but he couldn't pass up the opportunity to finish what he started. Not when she was too emotionally compromised to see him for who he really was. Laila was supposed to be the one to kill Genevieve, but she tried to take her own life instead. He wasn't prepared to abduct her, which means he didn't have a location set up to finish the job. If he wants to stick to his MO, he'll have to take her somewhere familiar. Somewhere he's already set up."

"You mean one of the crime scenes where the victims were found hanging from the ceilings," the second officer said. "They've all been processed by CSU. Everything the killer used at those scenes is in evidence."

Easton turned on them, his head clearer than it had been in months. "What about Genevieve Alexander's home? It hasn't officially been released by the crime scene techs. Have any officers been posted for security since Laila Ballard was taken?"

Shock filtered across the first uniform's expression. He looked to his partner. "Captain Morsey pulled uniforms off security once Ms. Ballard was reported missing. He wanted all available units working her abduction."

"Leaving the scene unsecure." Easton clenched his fist around his keys. "That's where he's taken her. We need to get over there now."

Neither officer argued this time as they ran to their cruiser. Easton sprinted across the parking lot and shoved his key in the old worn lock of his pickup, nearly breaking it in half in the process. He slid behind the peeling leather steering wheel and started the engine. The truck coughed, violent and exhausted, but he couldn't wait for it to warm up. Shoving it into gear, he fishtailed out of the parking lot.

A coat slid across the passenger seat at a hard right turn and bundled against his leg. Genevieve's. She'd been in such a rush to talk to Laila in the hospital, she must've left it behind. His lungs gave under the pressure of holding his breath. Their last conversation edged into his consciousness as the small town blurred through the windows. As much as it'd hurt to watch her walk out that door, she was right. All these years he'd tried fitting her into this…mold he'd needed in his life. A release, an emotional regulator, a lover, a listener, a companion. She was supposed to be the answer to his pain when he should've been the one to confront it head on, to take responsibility. Not hiding in the middle of his family's property, chasing away the only people willing to give him the time of day. The protest of leather in his hand kept him anchored into the moment, focused. Hell, she wasn't accountable for the hollowness in his chest, but he'd put the expectation on her to heal him anyway. No. The trauma he'd survived, the mental side effects of war and loss and grief, that was on him. How hadn't he been able to see it before now?

The answer was already there. Because he hadn't wanted to. Because it'd been easier to blame outside forces than to face his failure. But the truth was there, buried, but there. He hadn't seen her as anything more than someone to protect in that cafeteria back in high school, or his girlfriend when they'd started dating. His fiancée when he'd slid that ring onto her finger. The truth was, keeping his eyes on the road during his last supply run wouldn't have stopped that IED from taking out his unit. The truth was, his father had sacrificed himself doing the very thing he'd instilled in both of his sons, the ultimate example of selflessness and love.

He loved Genevieve. More than he'd loved anyone else in his life, but he'd been selfish since the moment she'd knocked on his door three days ago. In reality, he hadn't given her any other choice but to walk away. She'd held true to herself, and he'd discarded her for his own hubris.

Easton maneuvered onto her street and slammed on the brakes in front of her house. The rambler-style structure had been well-kept, the lawn perfectly manicured and welcoming. Genevieve hadn't just escaped to Alamosa. She'd made a career here, friends, a home. He didn't have any right to take that from her, even in the name of love.

He released his grip on the steering wheel as the Alamosa patrol cruiser pulled up behind him. This was it. The endgame.

The two officers from the hospital hit the sidewalk, each armed. The one closest to him nodded. "You strapped?"

"No." He'd sworn never to handle a firearm since his discharge with one exception: the night of his father's death. Adrenaline curled his fingers into fists as the second officer handed off a backup piece. He released the magazine, counted the rounds, and slammed it back into place before loading a bullet in the chamber. He faced the house, every muscle down his spine tightening with battle-ready tension. "Let's go."

Keeping low, they approached in a triangular formation. Easton signaled one officer off to the left, around

the back, and for the other to stick with him. No sign of
the captain's patrol vehicle parked out front or along the
block, but that didn't mean the bastard hadn't stashed
it out of sight.

He kept an eye on the windows for any sign of movement, but the night held still. Taking position on one
side of the front door, he waited as the Alamosa officer took the other. He'd trained for this. He was good
at this. He wouldn't fail Genevieve again.

Easton nodded then tested the doorknob.

It turned easily in his hand, and the painted wood
swung inward.

Shadows cut across the hardwood floor. He'd studied
the crime scene photos of Elisa Johnson's murder, but
he hadn't realized how…normal the house itself was.
A woven rug led them deeper into the home before the
space opened into the front living room where Genevieve had discovered the body of her assistant. Comfortable sofas and a warm wood coffee table had been
positioned for conversation while the massive stone fireplace—most likely original to the home—demanded
attention. Obvious care and an immaculate setting of
decor might've lured him into a false sense of security
if he hadn't noticed the corner of the hearth was missing. He stepped into the living room, his gaze automatically seeking the hooks the killer would've installed to
hang Elisa Johnson from the ceiling.

They were still there, but there was no sign of Genevieve.

Where else would Morsey have taken her? All of
the other crime scenes had been released, his equip-

ment logged into evidence. No. She had to be here. Easton twisted, his boot nearly slipping out from underneath him. He caught himself on the stone mantel. Blood. It'd almost blended in with the color of the dark wood, but there was no mistaking it now. It hadn't dried, and CSU wouldn't have left it behind, which meant... His grip slipped against the steel of his flashlight, and the resulting wound from his confrontation with Laila Ballard and the lacerations across his knuckles flared. "Genevieve."

"Clear!" The officers hadn't found anyone else in the house.

Easton studied the room before moving on to the kitchen then the guest bedroom and Genevieve's bedroom. A sleek black-and-white box stared back at him from the nightstand beside her bed. Chocolates. Where was she? He leveraged his weight against the door frame of her bedroom. The house was empty, and from the amount of blood he'd stepped in, Genevieve was running out of time. She'd been injured, but he had to believe Morsey would keep to his MO. All of the other victims had been kept conscious while he'd strung them up. It would've taken hours depending on how hard the women had struggled. Genevieve was a fighter. She wouldn't give up, and neither would he.

He stepped back into the hallway. If Genevieve had been moved as the evidence suggested, there had to be a trail. He retraced his steps back to the front room. "There's a fresh pool of blood by the fireplace. He must've moved her. Look for blood evidence. I need to know where he took her." If Morsey had moved her in a state of panic, the captain wouldn't have had time to clean up his mess. Both officers separated as Easton studied his own bloody footprints on the hard-wood. He'd compromised the scene in his search, but he couldn't worry about that right now. He heel-toed it slowly across the floor, each board vibrating under his weight, then froze. He stomped his foot harder and honed his flashlight beam on the floor.

He'd repaired enough floorboards over the years to know the sound difference between a foundation and a basement. Whispering Pines cabins didn't have base-ments. The reverberation under his foot here, however, was deeper, longer. He whistled as softly as he could manage, the same whistle that'd always let his fam-ily know where he was when they'd gone out hunting.

The Alamosa officers converged, following his mo-tion as he pointed to the floor.

Easton nodded. "She's in the basement."

Chapter Fourteen

Footsteps shook dust loose from the subfloor above her.

It filtered down through the light given off by the bare bulb, but she couldn't call out, couldn't scream. The pain and blood loss from the injury to her knees had stolen her voice. She tried to lift her head away from her chest, but the gravity on her skull was too much to fight. She had to stay awake, had to warn whoever was searching the house. She couldn't see Morsey anymore. He'd slipped into the shadows with a finger pressed to his mouth and the drill in his hand.

Genevieve tried to turn her wrist under the layered wrap of fishing line, but the chair he'd tied her to wouldn't budge under pressure. Not that she had much left to give anyway. A small whimper escaped up her throat. The gag had soaked through. Same as her clothing. Sweat, blood, tears—it all mixed to add to the weight on her body. Her spine stretched long. She'd managed to free herself from one hook upstairs, but it hadn't been enough. Morsey had ensured she'd never be able to walk again when he'd drilled the second eyelet into her opposite knee.

Silence burned in her ears.

No more footsteps. No more voices. No more help.

A deep sob replaced her low whimper. No one was coming for her.

Bare cement walls absorbed the frigidness of spring and filled the space with a chill. Her skin contracted in response. Insulation glittered under the exposed bulb from between bare-minimum framing. Cracks spread across the cement from the corners of the main room and branched off out of sight. The builder had wanted an arm and a leg to finish the space. Money she hadn't been able to afford at the time. Maybe that was a good thing. It was hard to get blood out of carpet and drywall. She'd never liked the basement in this house, using it for nothing more than Christmas decoration storage. Now she would die here.

The thought wedged through the lightheadedness. She didn't want to die. She'd worked too hard for the life she'd built. She'd survived loneliness and shame and self-consciousness and heartbreak, and she wasn't ready to stop feeling. She wanted to live, to love, to laugh. Nothing else mattered. She wanted Easton, and there was no way in hell she was going to give up now.

The layout of this floor mimicked the one above, only there were very few walls separating her from the stairs. Fifteen hundred square feet of inky blackness and angles she couldn't see around. Morsey would see her given the right angle. She had to move fast. She tugged against the fishing line. Blood bloomed in thin rivulets across her wrist. Rolling her head to one side, she struggled to catch something—anything—to give her an idea of where her killer had gone. Nothing. She'd wasted enough time walking through life afraid. It was time to take control. Genevieve pressed her teeth together as she strained against the fishing line. Pain exploded up her arm, but she couldn't stop. The groan lodged in her throat escaped as her skin broke under the pressure.

The fishing line snapped.

Momentum shot her arm up and tipped the chair to one side. Oxygen caught in her chest as the world threatened to rip straight out from under her, but she found balance. Scanning the shadows, she waited. Waited for Morsey to stop her, to end the insufferable pain in her knees. There was only silence. Genevieve threaded her fingers under the line securing her opposite arm to the chair and pulled as hard as she could. The second line broke with a soft split, and she unwound it slowly from around her wrist. Morsey hadn't taken the time to secure her legs. There'd been no need with the damage done. She was free.

Using the chair arms as leverage, she gritted against the agony ripping through her knees and slid to the glacial cement floor. Dust clung to her palms and clothing as she rolled onto her front. The eyelets Morsey had drilled into the outer edges of her knees brushed against the floor as she attempted to push off with her toes, and Genevieve slammed her hand against the floor to stay conscious. Lightning struck behind her eyes. She forced herself to keep breathing, to stay in the moment. She had to move, but the harder she pushed herself, the faster she'd bleed out.

The window behind her. It was the only escape Morsey couldn't cover if he was ensuring no one would interrupt him by the stairs. Or was this part of the game? Make her think she had a chance only to violently rip it away from her in the end? She didn't want to believe the captain she'd trusted had fallen prey to that evil part of him that'd given him the ability to kill innocent women, but maybe it was too late. The drowning pull of blood loss thickened, but she couldn't stop. Not yet. She set her weight in her elbows and dragged herself away from the chair. The eyelets scraped against the floor, too loud in her ears, but moving slower only increased her chances of getting caught all over again. Her muscles ached. It was getting harder to breathe, to keep her eyes open.

The light cut out, throwing her into utter darkness.

Her breath sawed in and out of her throat. She hadn't heard him enter the room. He couldn't have cut the power, which meant... Whoever'd been upstairs. They were still here. Tears of relief burned, but she couldn't relax yet. As long as Morsey held on to his power over her, she was still trapped. The only advantage she had was knowing the exact layout of her own house. The captain might be able to move faster, but he was in unfamiliar territory.

"Genevieve..." His voice pierced through the dizzying layer of fear gripping the muscles down her legs in remembered agony. The high-pitched whine of the drill filled her ears. "I can hear you breathing. You can't hide from me."

She forced herself to hold her breath. She stretched

her palms out in front of her, searching for something to use as a weapon. She hadn't been down here in months. She'd had no reason, but she wished she'd hidden an additional firearm down here as well as in her fireplace upstairs. The window couldn't be more than a few feet away, but at the same time it felt as though it were another mile ahead of her. Where were the people she'd heard upstairs? Had they given up? Had Morsey used his charm and authority to convince them there was nothing wrong? Genevieve forced herself to still, to buy herself more time.

No one was coming to save her.

She had to save herself.

Her fingers brushed over one of the larger cracks in the concrete from the house settling over the years. Movement registered a few feet off to her left, and she jammed her nails inside the small crack. She worked as fast as possible while trying not to give away her position in the dark. Morsey had been relying on her house electricity to keep the upper hand. He hadn't brought a flashlight or emergency supplies. Now she had the advantage.

"You can't escape, Genevieve. Those eyelets in your knees? It'll be impossible to walk, let alone run from me." His voice moved with him, farther away, possibly facing the opposite direction. "Even if you manage to get out of here, I'll find you. There's nowhere you can go I won't follow. One way or another, I'm going to keep my end of the deal I made with Laila. I'm not leaving until you pay for failing her."

A sliver of concert broke off in her hand. Genevieve

slowed, waiting. She pressed the edge of the shard into her palm. It wasn't much. It might not hold up against an attack, but she would do whatever it took to get out of this basement alive. Moving slower than she wanted to go, she swept her legs out to the side and balanced on one hip.

There was no making it to the window now. Not without drawing his attention. Who knew when the power might come back on. She had to make herself as small a target as possible until then, had to hide. The Christmas decorations. She'd stacked the boxes in the corner of this main room. There could be space behind the one she'd stored her tree in. A few seconds. That was all she needed. It might be enough until help arrived.

Easton would find her. She had to believe that. No matter how many times she'd hurt him, how strained their relationship, she'd always been able to count on him. He'd come through this time, too. He'd know she'd been taken. He'd figure out by who and where Morsey had brought her. He'd finish what they'd started and bring justice to the women Genevieve hadn't been able to protect.

Her hands shook as she rose to sit on her bottom. The concrete shard cut into her hand, but it was nothing compared to the agony burning through her knees. She set her weight into the base of her palms and tugged herself in the direction she believed the boxes would be. Her bare heels dragged against the cold floor, a whimper in the blackness.

"Marco…" The sound of the drill ticked off in rhythm to her racing heartbeat. Followed by three heavy footsteps. His boots scraped across the floor, accentuated by the layer of dust that'd accumulated over the years. "That's when you say Polo, Genevieve. Come on, play the game with me. Don't let the last moments of your life be made up of nothing but pain and desperation. Marco…"

She kept moving. She shot her hand out to get a feel for how far away she was from the boxes but met nothing but air. Ice infused her veins. She was still in the middle of the room, still exposed. Gravity and blood loss pulled her to the floor.

The single bare bulb in the room brightened.

Genevieve froze.

Morsey turned. He took a single step forward, his mouth stretching into an uneven smile as he advanced.

Another outline penetrated her peripheral vision as Easton raised his weapon. "Polo."

HIS GUN WARMED in his grip. It'd been months since he'd held a firearm, let alone pulled the trigger, but muscle memory had him taking aim between Morsey's eyes. "Put the weapon down, turn your back to me and interlace your hands behind your head. Now."

"She doesn't have much time, Ford." Morsey bent at the knees to set down the drill with one hand, the other raised in surrender. "Are you sure you want to waste the precious minutes you have left together on me?"

The only dry-walled wall framing the stairs blocked his view of Genevieve on the other side of the room. All he saw was blood. A long trail soaked into the concrete stretching the length of half the room, and his imagination was all too willing to fill in the blanks. Easton's mouth dried as he forced himself to step completely in the room. Genevieve. The source of the blood seemed to be coming from both of her knees where Morsey had screwed in the same type of steel eyelets he'd used on his previous victims. The captain had been getting ready to hang her from the ceiling. Just like all the others. "You son of a bitch."

"Let's leave the name calling at the door, Ford." Morsey lowered his hands to his sides. "You knew exactly what you were getting yourself into when you decided to intervene in my investigation. Now, you've got a choice to make. Save Ms. Alexander or take me into custody."

Numbness spread from his fingers down his arms as the seconds distorted into minutes. He moved deeper into the room. He studied her, unconscious, bleeding out, and his entire world shattered in the span of a single exhale. One moment, he was standing in the center of Genevieve's basement, and the next he'd been right back in that wreckage. Struggling to pull his unit from the carnage and flames.

"Time's up, Ford." Morsey lunged. The captain slammed his hand into Easton's forearm, and the gun slipped from his grasp. A solid kick crushed the air from his lungs, and Easton fell back. Morsey stood over him, fisting one hand in Easton's collar, and pulled his elbow back. The right hook shot Easton's head back into the concrete, followed quickly by Morsey's left. "You can't stop me."

The Afghanistan sun superimposed the bare light

bulb above then flickered back. Morsey himself dissolved into a soldier who'd caught up with the convoy, yelling at him through the ringing in his ears. Another strike from Morsey's left fist craned his head to one side, toward Genevieve. Her delicate features blended with those of Ripper's as the only female in his unit lay dead on the cracked asphalt. His heart thudded hard behind his ears. Hot sand and cold concrete twisted in an alternate reality he wasn't sure he could differentiate.

Morsey pulled him from the floor, the captain's outline blurring in front of him. "You can't help her, Ford. You can't even help yourself."

Easton blinked against the lightning streaking across his vision. Morsey was right. He couldn't help Genevieve. He couldn't help anyone. Not like this. Not with the past suffocating him from the inside. Not with pain and grief holding him back from moving on with his life. A glimmer of life opened Genevieve's eyes a fraction of an inch, and the buzz in his head quieted. For the first time in years, the hollowness in his chest didn't hurt. Because of her.

Morsey pulled back to strike again.

Easton caught the captain's fist in his palm. He clenched the killer's shirt in his other and slammed his head into Morsey's. The police captain fell back. Blood spewed down the man's face as Easton pushed to his feet. "She's not yours to claim, Morsey."

He launched his right hook straight into the bastard's temple. Pain rocketed down his hand and into his elbow, but he couldn't stop. He kicked Morsey's knee out from the back and forced the killer down.

The flash of metal was all the warning he got as the captain swung up. The blade hit into Easton's side. Pain arched through him, and Easton stumbled back into the nearest wall, holding his side. Morsey struggled for breath as he hauled himself to his feet. "Didn't that brother of yours teach you to always carry a backup weapon, Ford?"

"Didn't they teach you to always wear your body armor in the academy?" He straightened. Movement registered from behind the killer, and Easton straightened. It was over. The bastard who'd ripped his world in two had nowhere to go. He nodded over Morsey's shoulder. "Besides, why would I need a backup weapon when I have her?"

The captain turned to confront the threat, but he wasn't fast enough.

Two gunshots exploded in the small space as Genevieve pulled the trigger.

Morsey arched against the impact, eyes wide, jowls frozen with surprised creases. The killer dropped harder than the box of rocks Easton used to collect under his bed as a kid.

The thud of metal against concrete shot Easton forward. Genevieve collapsed onto her back, her eyes rolling up into her head. The gun slipped from her grasp as he threaded one hand behind her neck. "Stay with me, Genevieve. You're not allowed to die now."

No response.

Footsteps raced down the stairs. He'd left both Alamosa officers to wait for the ambulance, but they wouldn't have been able to ignore two gunshots. Identifying shouts pierced the high-pitched ringing in his ears from the shots as the officers rounded into the room, weapons up and aimed. Hesitation filtered across their expressions as they took in the scene. Their captain on the floor, the drill near the body, the bloody trail leading to Genevieve and the weapon beside her. It all added up.

But Easton didn't have time to catch them up. "Where the hell is that ambulance?"

"It just pulled up," one of the officers said. Another rumble of panicked footsteps bounced off the unfinished basement stairs. A pair of EMTs shoved both officers out of the way. One split toward the captain, the other toward Genevieve.

Easton's grip lightened on her as the EMT crouched to assess the damage. "Caucasian female, thirty-four years old, severe blood loss from the injuries in both knees."

"How long has she been unconscious?" The EMT set a stethoscope in his ears and listened for Genevieve's pulse. Tugging it down around his neck, he wrapped a blood pressure cuff around her arm then got to work on an IV.

"About a minute, maybe a little longer." The time that'd distorted a few minutes ago seemed to catch up with him all at once. Easton scrubbed a hand down his face, the other interlaced in Genevieve's. Her fingers were cold. She'd lost too much blood in too short of a time. "I'm not sure how much blood she's lost. There's what's down here and a puddle upstairs in the living room."

"The captain's dead on arrival over here. Detectives will be notified." The second EMT maneuvered to Genevieve's head and took over assessing her vital signs. "Sir, we need you to back away. Let us do our jobs."

"Please. Save her." He'd never been so desperate in his life. Shoving to his feet, Easton stumbled back against a collection of boxes packed with glittery balls and brightly colored ribbon. Christmas decorations. The cardboard nearly gave way under his weight, but he only had attention for Genevieve. For the perfect curve of her upper lip, the beauty mark he'd memorized so many times, the angle of her delicate jawline. She'd shared the greatest gift she ever could've given him during this investigation: healing. Now that gift would be taken from him.

"We're going to do everything in our power, sir, but we can't stop the bleeding until we get those screws out of her knees. We've got to move." Faster than he thought possible, EMTs hauled Genevieve onto a stretcher and had secured her for transport. They wound through the sharp angles of the basement layout and up the stairs. The oxygen mask placed over her mouth and nose cut off his view of most of her face. She'd survived the Contractor. That was all that mattered.

Police sirens and red and blue patrol lights converged outside the house as Easton followed emergency personnel out the front door. Alamosa PD officers sprinted past him, presumably at the call of their fellow brothers in blue still assessing the scene downstairs. EMTs loaded Genevieve into the back of the ambulance. The urge to climb in right behind her, to hold her hand in case she woke up midtransport to the hospital raged hard.

"Easton!" His brother's voice drowned out the controlled chaos around him. An officer tried to stop Weston from entering the scene as the crime scene tape was going up, but he flashed his badge with a don't-mess-with-me expression. "Considering your captain is the one behind these deaths, I recommend you let me by, Officer. You're going to need me."

Easton couldn't move, couldn't think. His gaze drifted back to the ambulance as the rig's sirens first chirped then screeched through the lightening morning. It pulled away from the curb and disappeared around the corner. Before he had a chance to make sense of what'd happened, Genevieve was gone.

"You've got blood on you." Weston settled dark brown eyes on him—the same color as their dad's—and fisted one sleeve of Easton's shirt. His brother scanned him from head to toe, presumably looking for an injury, but he wouldn't find any. Not any he could see anyway.

The pulsing in his ears intensified the longer he stood there. He licked dry lips, caught in the middle of considering climbing into his truck or staying to give his statement and help with the scene. Alamosa PD was hurting right now. Their lieutenant had been framed and murdered, and their captain had been behind a handful of murders in the name of love. They needed him. "It's not mine."

"Easton." Weston shook his arm, forcing him back into the moment. Understanding smoothed the harsh lines around his brother's mouth, the past couple years more evident in the creases around his eyes and mouth. But there was a warmth Easton hadn't seen since Weston had lost his wife all those years ago. Something that had to do with Chloe. "Go." His brother slapped him on the back. "You're no good here like this. Go. I've got this handled."

Easton ran toward the truck and his future.

Chapter Fifteen

She was tired of hospitals.

Tired of the incessant beeping of the monitors, of the dull ache in her knees not even pain medication could touch. Tired of the images her mind insisted on processing over and over when she closed her eyes. She'd lived through the worst trauma of her life, but had she survived? Captain Morsey had taken so many lives. Hers would be another tally on his belt.

The hospital room door clicked open, but she didn't have the inclination to greet one of the many doctors and nurses who'd bustled in and out of here. The surgeons had done what they could to repair the tears in her knees, but there would be permanent damage. The drill had severed the lateral collateral ligament on the outer sides of her knees. A complete separation. In a matter of minutes, Captain Morsey had ripped away her ability to walk away from this on her own two feet.

The wheelchair her physicians had showed her how to use earlier sat off to her right. Tears burned as she studied the black leather and chrome handles. Rawness scratched up her throat from her previous encounter with Morsey out at the dunes. "I'm too broke to buy anything, I know who I'm voting for and I've found Jesus. Unless you're here with a giant box of chocolate or another dose of morphine, I'm not interested."

"Then this is your lucky day." That voice. His voice. She'd dreamed about it while under the sedatives. It'd been the last thing she'd heard in that basement, and the first thing she'd craved when she'd woken up in this room, but he hadn't been here. "One giant box of chocolates for you, Counselor." Easton flashed that charming smile that'd forced her insides into a riot as he set down a sleek black-and-white box with the manufacturer's name standing out in the corner. Thirty-six pieces of Belgian chocolate truffles created to look like jewels of the most expensive kind. "These ones don't have any eggs, marshmallow or graham cracker in them. I checked."

She didn't understand. "How did you—"

"I noticed a box on your nightstand in your bedroom during our search of your house." His smile slipped, and she was thrown back into harsh reality instead of the few seconds of safety she'd found in their conversation. Bandages hid an array of injuries across his hand and up his forearm.

He'd been there. He'd been one of the officers she'd heard on the main level after Morsey had moved her to the basement. He'd come for her. Genevieve set the square box on her lap but didn't move to open it. "You knew he would bring me back there. Even after I told you I didn't want there to be more between us, you came for me."

"I wasn't going to let him hurt you, Genevieve." Those sea-blue eyes she'd equated with the loss of her identity studied the bulbous bandages wrapped around her knees beneath the thin sheets. "I'm sorry I wasn't fast enough."

Phantom pain prickled down her shins. After what they'd been through together, she didn't have much of a guard left anymore. "I'm in this bed recovering from surgery instead of lying to rest in the Alamosa Cemetery. This…didn't end like I thought it would, but I still owe you my life. I was hoping you'd be here when I woke up."

Easton hung his head, nodding only slightly. "I tried to be here when I heard you were out of surgery, but they wouldn't let me in the room. I may have made some threats after that. The administrators had one of their security guards sit with me until your doctors gave the okay for visitors once Weston vouched for me."

"Well, I appreciate the effort, and the chocolates. If you were hoping I'd share, you've got another thing coming." The bottom half of the box unsuctioned from the top, revealing a brightly colored array of gourmet chocolates. She chose a chocolate-and-pink-striped square of flavor and melted goodness and took a bite. Strawberry and dark cocoa burst across her tongue, urging her to forget everything that'd happened after the moment she'd knocked on Easton Ford's door. The bandages on her wrists punctuated how close she'd come to dying in her own house. Because despite the years she'd spent there, it could never be a home. Not anymore. "How is Laila Ballard doing?"

"She's alive, which is more than I can say for her partner. She'll spend the next few weeks recovering here, but once she's stable, your office will have Alamosa PD's full support in filing charges." He seemed to memorize the arrangement of truffles on her lap. Setting one hand against the guardrail alongside her bed, he tapped it with the base of his palm. Bruises darkened the circles under his eyes and marred the once perfect skin of his cheek. "She convinced Captain Morsey to kill those women, Genevieve. At the very least, she's looking at conspiracy to commit murder. She belongs behind bars."

"You think she's a monster." Genevieve handed off one of her favorites from the box.

"No, I think she's hurting." He bit into the circular truffle, chewing as though relishing every bite, and she didn't have the strength to look away. "But until she's ready to face that pain, she's going to keep hurting herself and others. Intentionally or not."

Genevieve set down the strawberry and chocolate combination. Her appetite for decadence vanished. The investigation, their interactions—they'd been playing in her mind since the moment she'd woken from surgery, and her insides somersaulted. "Before, when we were in the waiting room, you said you knew exactly what Laila Ballard went through. That your anger and betrayal made you run from the people who care about you, and you were on the same path as she was. What changed?"

"I had you." He said it so matter-of-factly, it was impossible to deny. Easton popped the rest of the truffle in his mouth. "As much as I blamed you for starting this… chain reaction in my life, you're the one who helped me see what was important. Showed me what I wanted and what I need to do to get better."

"What is it you want?" A tremor worked through her hands as she slipped them beneath her thighs. The movement caught his attention, and a rush of emotion lodged in her throat. Her nerves caught fire as he reached down and tugged one hand free, encasing it in both of his.

"You, Genevieve." Calluses scraped against her knuckles and heightened her senses into overdrive. "No matter how much time you want, how much space you need to figure out you and your independence, I'll wait. I'm in no rush."

Genevieve thwarted her expression's automatic response to contort into ugly-crying-face and set her free hand over his. "I want you, too. What I said before, about not wanting to get wrapped up in you and your personality and your family again—I didn't understand it at the time. You've been part of my life since I was sixteen. You've been a part of me since the moment you stood up for me in that cafeteria. If I lose you, I'll lose a piece of myself, and we've been apart long enough. I love you."

"I love you." Easton slipped his hands on either side of her face, careful of the bruises along her neck, and bent down. He pressed his mouth to hers, combining the aftertaste of his truffle mint with the strawberry still clinging to her tongue. The flavors danced alongside one another as he explored her mouth second by agonizing second. By the time he pulled away, she had a hard time remembering which chocolate she'd eaten and which one he'd finished. "Not sure I've ever mixed mint with strawberry." He swiped his thumb along the corner of his mouth. "I like it."

Her laugh shuddered through her, igniting another ache along the outer edges of her knees. She rolled her lips between her teeth and bit down to give her brain something else to focus on, but she couldn't ignore the truth. "It's not going to be the same, is it?"

"No." Easton interlaced his fingers with hers. "It won't, but I'm going to be there every step of the way. Follow-up appointments, physical therapy, the nightmares. Whatever happens, we'll get through it. Together. Here in Alamosa or back in Battle Mountain. Wherever you need me, I'll be there."

She pressed her palms into the tops of her thighs, but the pain medication had taken away even the sense of pressure. Why then did she still feel the weight of what Morsey had done to her? "I can't go back to that house. Every time I think about finding Elisa in the living room, what he was going to do to me…" She closed her eyes.

"Hey, look at me. You don't have to." He notched her chin higher with one finger. Easton unlatched the guardrail and lowered it. Maneuvering onto the edge of the bed, he leveled her gaze with his. "You know that. We can find you a new place. You could come stay with me until you get settled."

"That cabin can barely hold my investigative files." She pressed her free hand to her forehead. "How are we going to make that work with two of us and my wheel-chair in there? What about the commute?"

"We can find a place of our own," he said. "Here."

What? No. He'd already done so much for her, she couldn't ask for more. "Easton, I love my job. I ran for district attorney because I believed I could make a difference. I don't want to give that up, but I don't want you to have to give up the town you've felt safe in your whole life."

"I feel safe when I'm with you." Tucking his knuckle under her chin, he smiled. "If that means we're here in Alamosa and I'm not a Battle Mountain reserve officer anymore, so be it. I lost you once, Genevieve. I'm not willing to go through that again. Besides, there are more psychologists here who deal with PTSD."

Her heart squeezed in her chest, and she fell a little bit more in love with him right then. "Are you sure about this?"

"Who knows? Maybe Alamosa will be looking for a new officer given how they just lost two of their own." Easton eyed another one of her chocolates.

Her mouth stretched wide enough to tug on the split in her bottom lip, but she didn't care. Leaning in close, she kissed him, happier than she'd been in years. "I do like a man in uniform."

Three months later

WIND CUT THROUGH the pines around the cabin as he rounded the hood of the new truck. It wasn't anything he would've picked out for himself. Newer, less history, but it was perfect for allowing Genevieve to get in and out of easily and spacious enough to store her wheelchair in the back. He hauled the chair out of the truck bed and set it up a few feet away. Easton popped the passenger side door open and offered his hand.

Smooth skin brushed against calluses as Genevieve secured her hand in his. She maneuvered to the edge of the seat, her legs hanging over the side. Black leggings hid the scars originating around her knees and spreading up her thigh and down her shin on either side. The surgeries had gone as well as they ever could, but rehab was an entirely different beast altogether. Notwithstanding the immediate dive into physical therapy a day after her surgeries and her continued fight to make it through her exercises every day afterward, there were still no signs Genevieve would ever be able to walk on her own. She slid her arm over his shoulders as he positioned his under her knees. Just as they'd done a hundred times. "If this keeps up, you won't have to ever go back to the gym."

"One of the benefits of you not being able to run away." He set her in her seat and kicked down the footrests. Easton stepped to the back of the wheelchair and closed her passenger door before pushing her toward the main cabin.

Her smile overwhelmed the summer sun high overhead. She reached one hand back over her shoulder and settled it on top of his. "And the others?"

"We'll talk about those at home." Home. It'd had a different meaning up until Genevieve's discharge from the hospital. Whispering Pines had been the only place he'd found shelter from the world when it'd stopped making sense. Now he and Genevieve had a new place of their own. He, Weston and his mother had retrofitted the single-level house in Alamosa with wider doorways, a ramp leading up to the front door and even a massive tile shower large enough to fit her chair. It was perfect, but they made it a point to travel the three hours back here as often as possible. For his mom's sake. And his.

Karie Ford descended the main cabin's front steps, blocking the sun from her eyes. Her signature flannel shirt flapped with the breeze as she smiled at their approach. The new ramp addition to the cabin bled into the original design with dark wood and bright green trim, but that wasn't why he'd brought Genevieve here today. "Hey, you two. Hope you're hungry. Weston and Chloe might've eaten everything by now though."

Easton slowed, giving his mother a side hug. "Hey, Mom. The ramp looks great."

"Glad you like it. Felt good to keep my hands busy," Karie said. "Figured I can start making a few more adjustments this week based off that list you gave me."

"Wow, Karie. You didn't have to do that." Genevieve accepted the spine-cracking hug his mother was known for giving. Sunlight glittered off the line of tears in her eyes as Karie pulled away.

"Course I did, honey. You're family. It's my job to make sure you're taken care of. Besides, it makes the ranch a bit more accessible to those in wheelchairs who still want the benefits of the great outdoors." Karie patted Genevieve's hand but refused to let go, and Easton had never felt lighter. His mother pushed at his chest so she could take over driving, leaving him in the dust. "Well, come on now, let's test this sucker out."

Genevieve and his mother climbed the ramp to the front door, but Easton could only marvel at the expanse of wilderness and beauty around him. In the distance, he caught sight of the project he and Weston had been building these past few months. It was hard work constructing something that big from scratch, but their father had taught them right, and he and his brother had worked well together after he'd dug up Weston's childhood bear. He shook his head. The things he did for the woman he loved.

Weston was in the process of recruiting more reserve officers, but they'd managed to make Easton's new part-time schedule work. Three days a week, he was here in Battle Mountain with Genevieve working her cases remotely, and the rest of the time they spent in Alamosa for her court proceedings and in-office administration. Judges, clerks and assistants alike had been all too willing to accommodate her needs. Their new routine was about to change through.

Easton jogged up the cabin's front steps and into the house where he'd always felt welcome. Heat wrapped around him the moment he stepped over the threshold. A massive stone fireplace climbed two stories up the open main living space. Builder-grade wood, lighter than the exterior of the cabin, absorbed the sunlight penetrating through floor-to-ceiling windows on one end of the structure. His grandmother's frayed multicolored crocheted rug took up a majority of the hardwood floor in the front room. A small carved bear holding a bowl of fruit he and Weston had always been too rough with greeted him from the table stretching along the back of the dark leather sofa. Similar carvings had been strategically positioned around the open kitchen and against the grand staircase leading to the bedroom level. Handcrafted lamps, varying shades of animal fur and muted nature paintings finished the space in old-style hunter decor, and peace tendrilled through him. Every time.

The spice of cooking sausage, and the comforting aroma of biscuits with a hint of heavy cream dove into his lungs. Biscuits and gravy. His favorite. Karie maneuvered Genevieve and her chair to one end of the table as Weston and Chloe took up the other. Small talk filled the room as Easton gripped the back of the head chair. His father's chair. He scanned the smiles and relaxed into the warmth filling the house, memorizing everything he could about this moment. A year ago, he'd isolated himself in one of the satellite cabins, content to live with his demons. Now, after a few months of therapy and taking care of Genevieve's needs, he couldn't imagine living the rest of his life alone.

"Your father would've loved this. Having all of you here for breakfast. Any meal really. The man loved his food, but he loved this family more." His mother pulled out the chair and nodded. "Take a seat, Easton. It's yours now."

A knot of hesitation twisted in his gut, but the rest of the family kept about as though nothing had changed. They exchanged plates, their silverware clinking against glass. They filled their cups with juice and mugs with coffee and caught up with their weeks and went on about their lives. Easton took his seat at the head of the table. Grasping his spoon, he tapped it against the side of his juice glass as his mother sat at the other end. He cleared his throat, nerves shot to hell and back. "I, uh, have an announcement for you all."

Genevieve's smile slipped from her mouth as she eyed him. The realization the ramp out front wasn't why he'd brought her here this morning widened her eyes. She lowered her voice. "What are you doing?"

"Genevieve, these past three months, building a life with you and confronting the demons in my head have changed my life. I never imagined I could ever be this happy, and it's because of you I was finally able to find the purpose my father always wished for me." He set down his juice, his grip too tight. "The past few weekends when I told you I was coming out here to work, Weston and I were building a recovery facility for returning soldiers and trauma survivors. Whispering Pines played a key role in protecting me since my discharge, gave me someplace I felt safe. And with Mom's and the town's permission, now it'll help others like you and me."

Genevieve tossed her napkin onto the table as though she intended to stand. Instead, she leaned over the side of her chair and reached for him. Her fingers slipped along his jaw, and he met her the rest of the way. "Easton, that's amazing. You've been working on the facility this whole time, and you didn't tell me?"

"I wanted it to be a surprise." He pressed his mouth to hers, and a feeling of completeness, of wholeness, filled his chest. "There's still the matter of a few permits, and we're on the hunt for certified psychologists and physical therapists specializing in trauma, but we should have everything up and running within the year. Even have a couple potential patients in line. I know you love your job, and we want to stay in Alamosa, but this way, you'll have somewhere to do your physical therapy without breaking your routine when we come to Battle Mountain."

Clapping and hollers echoed off the walls.

"I'm so proud of you." Genevieve set her forehead against his, her smile destroying the last reservations he'd carried since their wedding day all those years ago.

Another round of clinking glass dragged his attention from the loving depths of her eyes. Weston stood, his juice glass raised, and his arm latched around his fiancée. "Turns out, we've got some good news, too. Chloe and I are pregnant."

As delirious happiness shot through Easton, he started a second round of applause and hoots. Hell, he was going to be an uncle. Who would've thought?

"Oh!" Karie Ford jumped from her seat and raced around the table. Enveloping Weston and Chloe in one of her bone-crushing hugs, his mother nearly started jumping up and down. "I knew it. Congratulations!"

"Congratulations!" both he and Genevieve said. He intertwined his fingers with hers on the surface of the table then brought the back of her hand to his mouth. The past three months had been filled with the unknown, a desperation for normalcy and finding their pace, but Easton didn't have any doubt in his mind he and Genevieve would be making an announcement of their own soon.

The diamond engagement ring he'd worked two jobs to afford fifteen years ago weighed heavy in his pocket. He'd kept it on him since the day he'd found it in the church's bridal room, through his escape into the wilderness and war. Not waiting for the right moment or the right woman. Waiting for her. And when the time was right, Easton would get down on one knee and make them partners. Forever. "Here's to the future, Counselor."

"The future." Genevieve pressed his hand against her check. "Whatever it may hold."

Epilogue

She set a timer. Two minutes.

That was all the time she had to get out of the house.

Alma Majors slid her feet into the shoes she kept under the bed as quietly as possible. Her husband didn't take long to go to the restroom in the middle of the night, but this was her only chance of escape. Her wrist protested as she twisted the doorknob to their shared bedroom open.

One minute.

She was down the stairs and pulling her go bag from the top of the linen closet.

The kitchen lights flicked on. "What are you doing?"

Fear skittered up her spine. She curled her uninjured hand into the thick fabric of the duffel bag. Six years. They were supposed to be happy. They were supposed to be in love, but something had changed. Alma turned to face him. "I couldn't sleep. Figured I'd head to the treadmill downstairs for a quick run to see if that helped."

She slid the hand he'd slammed in the car door into

the bag, felt for the solid weight she'd never thought she'd need.

He maneuvered around the kitchen island, setting down the glass of water. He'd tricked her. He'd made it sound as though he'd been using the bathroom and come down here instead. She wasn't sure how. It didn't matter. "You and I both know that's not where you were thinking of going, Alma. Come on. We've talked about this. You have nowhere else to go. No one who will believe you."

"You're right about one of those things." Three hard knocks echoed from the front door, and every nerve ending in her body flinched at the overly loud sound.

"Who is that? Who did you call?" He stepped toward her, his eyes nothing but pools of fire.

She secured her grip around the weapon she'd hid in the bag, pulled it free and took aim. "Don't come any closer. I'm warning you." Alma sidestepped toward the door. If she didn't answer it, the officer on the other side would kick it in. "I'm leaving, and you can't stop me."

Another three knocks from the front door. This time harder.

"It wasn't supposed to be like this." He was supposed to be in the bathroom. Her hands shook as she clung to the unfamiliar weapon. This wasn't her. She didn't handle guns. She extracted artifacts of the rarest kind and showed them to the world. Alma fumbled for the doorknob, the gun heavier than she imagined it would be. The dead bolt. She had to unlock the dead bolt. "Don't come looking for me. I don't ever want to see you again. Understand?"

"You're making the biggest mistake of your life, Alma." The warning was there in his voice, and the muscles down her spine tightened in preparation for what came next.

"No." She swung the front door open. "I'm saving my life."

The man on the other side stepped over the threshold, so much bigger than she remembered in the emergency room that day he'd come looking for the district attorney from Alamosa. Reserve officer Easton Ford stared down her husband as she recalled their conversation, how he'd known exactly what'd happened to her and who had inflicted the damage to her hand. "Ms. Majors, I'm here to escort you from the house. Is that going to be a problem?"

Alma lowered the weapon and handed it over to Officer Ford. She didn't know where she'd go now, what would happen next, but it couldn't be worse than this. She was ready to take back her life, to learn how to protect herself, and she'd start right now. "No. I'm ready."

* * * * *

SNOWED IN
WITH A COLTON

LISA CHILDS

With great appreciation for the
Mills & Boon Heroes editorial team:
Patience Bloom, Carly Silver and Megan Broderick.

Prologue

The heat of the fire warmed his skin, making the hairs on his forearms tingle. The acrid smoke filled his nostrils, and his lungs began to burn.

The building's windows were all aglow from the flames burning within, and he was standing too close to it, in an alley behind, which hadn't been blocked off by the emergency crews already on-site. The firefighters were working to extinguish the fire and to make sure everybody got out.

He, too, had to make sure that everybody was safe, that nobody suffered because of him. Because this was his fault.

He hadn't set this fire, hadn't started the hotel burning, but every place he'd stayed had had some malfunction—something that led to a fire. To devastation...

But not to what it was supposed to have led to...

His death.

That was what this fire was meant to have caused. When was the Camorra going to give up its quest for revenge? His exposé had led to several arrests—of people within their organization as well as of people in governments and legal authorities that had helped them conduct their business.

Those arrests should have weakened the Camorra in Naples, but enough of them must have remained free. Or maybe they were conducting their business yet from behind bars.

He knew they would not be done with him until he was dead. They would keep trying, keep tracking him down, as they had at every place he'd hidden.

Was there any place he could go where he'd finally be safe—where other people's lives wouldn't be put at risk just for being near him?

Chapter One

The Truth Foundation.

Because the truth was very important to her family, Aubrey Colton loved its name. After all, her dad had used his power as a judge to send innocent people to jail and take kickbacks—and she was determined to be nothing like that. To atone for his misdeeds, her siblings had formed the organization to help wrongly convicted people fight for exoneration or get reduced sentences for criminals who had gotten overly harsh ones because of the not-so-honorable Benjamin Colton. While she supported the idea that no innocent person should be left in prison, she worried about accidentally freeing someone who was actually culpable, though. Too many of the guilty claimed innocence.

Like her slimy ex-boyfriend...

Her cell phone, in the pocket of her flannel shirt, vibrated against her breast. She'd shut off the ringer while she and her twin, Jasper, had been at a meeting held in the downtown Blue Larkspur offices of Colton & Colton. That was where the law practice of her oldest siblings, twins Caleb and Morgan, was situated. She was glad now that she hadn't turned her ringer back on, as she was able to ignore her cell and focus on driving.

She and Jasper had peaced out of the meeting early, using the excuse that they had work to do at Gemini Ranch, the dude ranch they co-owned. Usually they were too busy with work to help out much with the foundation. But fortunately there were twelve of them, including her, so the workload was spread around.

"Are you okay?" Jasper asked.

Aubrey glanced away from the road to her twin, who sat in the passenger seat of the truck she drove. They didn't look exactly like each other. His hair was more strawberry blond than her lighter locks, but they had the same dark blue eyes. He didn't have to wear glasses like she did, though. "Why do you ask?"

"Well, for someone who cares so much about being truthful, you didn't mind stretching it to get out of that meeting." He grinned. "We're *so busy* at the ranch right now..." He mimicked her voice, repeating what she'd told their siblings just moments ago.

"Well, we are," she insisted self-righteously, her face heating a little over being called out. That was why their partnership worked so well: they never had hesitated to call each other on their crap. Jasper knew her so well; he was aware she wasn't as interested in the foundation as their siblings were. While she appreciated its intent, she was too worried that someone guilty might get set free and hurt someone else. She didn't want to be even partially responsible for that happening.

He snorted. "It's March. The cattle drives aren't

happening right now, so we only have a handful of rooms booked."

Their working dude ranch was of course busier in the warmer months. But in the winter, guests could still enjoy horseback riding—either outside or in the indoor ring—and there was snowshoeing, skiing and snowmobiling to do as well. And when they came in from the cold, they especially appreciated the spa facilities and hot tubs and the mammoth fireplace in the main lodge.

The ranch was her main concern; they'd dreamed about starting it for so long and had worked so hard to have their dream realized that she wanted to make sure it thrived. "More guests are checking in, so of course, we need to make sure everything's ready. And," she reminded him, "you've been yammering on about some snowstorm in the long-range forecast that's going to hit the area hard."

But she wasn't so sure. The streets of Blue Larkspur, Colorado, were clear and dry now. And the grass was beginning to turn from brown to green as it bathed in the sunlight. That sunlight glinted off the Colorado River that bordered town and made the roads twist and wind as she headed toward the nearby mountains. Snow clung yet to the peaks, the temperature still too low at those elevations to melt it away. Gemini Ranch was located between the city and those mountains.

"A storm is coming," Jasper insisted. "It's going to hit later this week, so we do need to get the cattle moved in closer."

They were drawing closer now, driving along the fence that marked the roadside of their one-hundred-acre property. Sometime over the next few days, she and Jasper would move the cattle to these pastures to make sure they got food and water in case the storm raged on for as long as Jasper seemed to believe it would.

"See, then we do have a lot of work to do at the ranch," she said in her defense. "I wasn't stretching the truth at all—which is probably more than Ronald Spence can say…"

"You don't think the Truth Foundation should take his case?" Jasper asked.

Ronald Spence was currently serving several life sentences for the crimes he'd committed as the head of a drug smuggling ring. But six months ago he'd started claiming that he was wrongly convicted, that there was evidence out there to clear him and prove that he had been the operation's fall guy.

Aubrey didn't easily believe anyone anymore, so she just shrugged. "I don't know…"

"This could be the last one, you know…" Jasper murmured.

"The last one of the rulings that Dad was paid to deliver…" She cringed at the knowledge of what their dad had done, how he'd forfeited justice for money. As a judge, he'd accepted bribes from private prisons and juvenile detention centers to deliver tougher sentences to offenders.

But would he have let someone guilty go free while knowingly sending someone else to jail for that person's crimes?

She shuddered at the thought. Usually, she tried not to think about the Colton family's past and their father's legacy of corruption. She focused on Gemini Ranch and making that her legacy. Hers and her twin's. That was why it was so important to her—to them. She wanted to provide wonderful memories for her guests to carry home with them from their stay at the working dude ranch. She wanted families to bond there and couples to reconnect or for singles to find the solace and comfort they sought.

Jasper uttered a weary-sounding sigh. "It's sad…"

It was more than sad. It was *tragic*.

Just like their dad's death in a car accident before he'd gone on trial for his corruption. His victims had never gotten true justice. So if Ronald Spence was being honest…

She sighed, too, as she slowed the truck for the turn into the long driveway. "I know the foundation needs to investigate, needs to make certain…" *that Ronald Spence had not been another victim of their father's greed and corruption.*

"Caleb and Morgan will figure out if Spence is innocent," Jasper assured her.

But she shook her head. "How does anyone really know if someone's actually telling the truth?" she wondered. "Look at how Dad fooled Mom all those years, making her think that his money beyond his salary came from a family inheritance."

"Is it just Dad who's made you distrust everyone?" Jasper asked. "Or is it that idiot Warren Parker?"

She nearly shuddered again at her twin's mention of her ex-boyfriend. But she didn't know if she blamed Warren for lying to her or herself for falling for those lies.

She should have known better, especially after what her father had done to her mother—to all of them. How had she missed all the red flags of another man's falsehoods?

Or had she seen and just ignored them because she'd wanted to believe that someone loved her after she'd finally opened up to a man?

As it turned out, the only thing Warren had been attracted to was the money he'd thought she made as half owner of the ranch, and he'd needed that money for his gambling debts. He hadn't gotten anything out of Aubrey. Even though she'd fallen for some of his lies, she hadn't fallen irretrievably head over heels for him. When he'd verbally lashed out at her after she refused to pay his debts and had admitted that he was only after money, she'd been hurt but nothing like Dad had hurt Mom. Nothing like that...

And she would make certain that she was never hurt like that. Even all these years after Ben Colton's death, Isadora Colton was still struggling with the devastation of his lies. They all were, in their own ways—even her, with her reluctance to trust or fall in love. All Warren Parker had done was confirm what she already knew; she was better off single than being with someone she couldn't trust. No. She wasn't just better off. She was better—happier.

"Aubrey," Jasper prodded her, "you're not going to let that loser Warren keep you from dating anyone else, are you?"

She snorted. "Of course not." And she wouldn't let Warren or even her father keep her from falling for a good man. That is, if one, besides her brothers, actually existed. "But the next person I date will have to be so transparent that I can see right through him. No lies. No deceptions. No secrets."

LUCA ROSSI KNEW his life had become a complete lie. He wasn't sure when he would ever be able to tell the truth again. Or *if* he would ever be able to tell the truth again…

If he was honest with anyone, he would be putting them in danger, too. The same threat that had followed him to nearly every place he had hidden since he had reported the crimes of the Camorra in his native Naples.

Maybe it just wasn't possible to hide from the Camorra since the gangsters kept finding him everywhere he'd gone.

Or at least that was what he believed, but maybe he was just paranoid. Maybe all those things that had happened were just accidents…

And not the Italian criminal organization's attempts on his life. First there had been that fire at the B and B in Toronto and then another fire at the hotel in Wisconsin, and that car that had nearly run him down in the street in Iowa…

Those could have been accidents, coincidences. But he doubted it and because he didn't want anyone else to get hurt, he couldn't risk it. He couldn't risk staying in one place for too long or getting too close to anyone.

Constantly moving, constantly traveling, was how Luca had wound up here in Blue Larkspur, Colorado, on Gemini Ranch. But here he wasn't Luca Rossi; now he was Luke Bishop.

Luke Bishop had checked into a private cabin at Gemini Ranch—one far enough away from the main lodge and the other cabins that nobody else would get hurt if he was found yet again. On a travel blog, he'd read about the working dude ranch and had figured since it was the off season, there would be few other guests or even employees for him to endanger if the Camorra tracked him down.

In the week since Luke Bishop had arrived there, nobody had seemed to notice him much at all. He hadn't felt as he had in other places, as if he was being watched. Maybe he'd finally lost whoever had tailed him from his home in Naples.

Maybe he was finally safe.

But as safe as he was, he was getting bored. His restlessness must have affected the horse he was riding, which lurched forward. Enjoying the exhilaration of the sudden rush of speed, Luca urged the dark bay gelding to go faster.

They raced against the wind, which riffled through Luca's hair and chafed his skin. He didn't care; he raised his face to it, breathing in the fresh air and the sunshine.

Colorado—and the Gemini Ranch especially—were beautiful. Luca should have been at peace there, but that restlessness persisted. Boredom…

He'd never done well with it. As a boy, he'd gotten in trouble in school whenever he was bored. And as a man, he'd found that it compelled him to take risks that other people didn't dare to take…

Like going undercover as a Camorrista to find incriminating evidence against the gangsters to write that exposé about the Camorra for a local political newspaper—an article that had gone viral and led to numerous convictions and arrests. But apparently not enough. Not enough that he was safe yet. Still, he didn't regret what he'd done. He hadn't been able to do what everyone else had been doing, turning a blind eye to crime, to the cold-blooded murders, to the terror with which the Camorra had ruled and ruined so many lives. Instead of living in fear, like so many others in his hometown, he'd taken action. And just as he'd learned as a bored, little kid, there were consequences for actions. His had been living under protection, locked up in windowless rooms, or going on the run. He'd chosen to take his chances on his own—like he always had.

As they neared the barn, the gelding automatically slowed his pace—as if the horse was as reluctant to end their ride as Luca was. Maybe he would go back out and explore the beautiful property some more...

But then he noticed the truck, with the name Gemini Ranch imprinted on the passenger-side door, pulling up near the barn. If new people had been arriving, he would have turned around then, but the name on the door assured him that the vehicle's occupants were workers or the ranch owners. A man pushed open the passenger door. Jasper Colton. The tall blond man was one of the owners of the property; Luca had met him when he'd checked in and then he'd run into him at the barn a few times. Luca hadn't actually met the other owner yet.

He was curious about her because Luca was curious about everyone. He slowed the horse and watched, as he was always people-watching, wondering about their lives...

His curiosity and desire to help people was what had led to all his revelations and all the evidence he'd unearthed about the Camorra. He'd wanted to end the reign of terror, had wanted to save lives and have people feel secure again in their own homes and on the streets of their city. But surely his interest in the ranch and its owners wouldn't put him or anyone else in danger?

Then she stepped out of the driver's side and came around to the box of the truck. Aubrey Colton, he'd learned her name from the travel blog.

The wind blew through her long blond hair, swirling it around her face and shoulders. She was so beautiful and so strong. She lowered the tailgate of the pickup and pulled out a big bag of something, slinging it over her shoulder as effortlessly as her brother did.

Aubrey wasn't as tall as her brother, but she was probably five eight or nine, tall for a woman. And she was definitely all woman, with voluptuous curves Luca couldn't help but notice. As she leaned into the bed of the pickup truck, her jeans stretched taut across her butt.

That restlessness coursed through Luca again, making him want things he had no business wanting. Making him want...

Aubrey.

The horse must have sensed his restlessness again, because the gelding pawed at the ground and whinnied. Aubrey glanced back at him and something jolted his body—a sudden awareness, an attraction—that passed between them. But then she turned away again, as if she hadn't been affected at all. Luca realized that in his boredom he must have been letting his imagination run as wild as the horse had just run on their return to the barn.

Aubrey continued working with her brother, unloading the truck as if she hadn't even noticed him. And she probably hadn't...

She was a busy woman, according to the blog. A no-nonsense businesswoman who probably had no time for dalliances—not with a ranch to run.

Not that Luca wanted to dally with her. He knew he couldn't act on any attraction. Because there was a hit on his life, with people trying to track him down, being anywhere near him would put her in danger, too. Most of his own family had had to flee Naples and live under assumed names, too, for their own safety. And he'd rather sacrifice his own life before he put anyone else in peril.

WHERE THE HELL was Luca?

And how the hell did he keep escaping death? Over and over, city after city, he slipped safely away—completely unscathed.

Unlike those he'd left behind in Naples...

Unlike *him*...

If Luca didn't call...

Just then his cell vibrated against the mahogany surface of his desk. The screen lit up with private caller. He tensed as fear and dread gripped him. Was it them?

Were they calling to threaten him again?

Or was it him? Luca kept switching phones just as he kept switching hiding places.

He accepted the call with a hopeful "Ciao?"

"Paolo," a deep voice greeted him.

"Luca?"

"Yes…"

"I've been so worried about you," Paolo said. "Everyone has…"

Luca sighed. "I know. I hate this. I don't want Mama and the others to worry."

Paolo knew that was why his cousin called to check in despite the danger—because he loved his family, but his love for them was going to cost him his life. Paolo ignored the pang of guilt that struck his heart.

He <u>had</u> no choice.

He had to…

Luca could go on the run, could hide out with the money he'd made on all his exposés, on the book he'd been contracted to write.

The only money Paolo had he'd borrowed from the very people who were using those debts and threats to get him to turn his cousin over to them.

"Let me assure her that you're okay," Paolo said. "Where are you? Are you safe? Can she call you on this number?"

Luca chuckled. "Slow down, *cugino*. I cannot tell you where I am—for your safety."

Paolo nearly snorted at the irony of Luca thinking that, which was exactly the opposite. But he couldn't explain that to Luca; the man was too honorable and selfless to understand.

"And Mama cannot call me. I will discard this phone as I've done all the others I've called you from, in case someone's tracking your phone line."

Paolo swallowed a curse. He was the someone tracking his phone line, with an app on his own phone that was trying right now to narrow down Luca's location. He glanced at his screen, at the little light flickering in North America. It needed more time. *He* needed more time.

"At least assure me that you're well," Paolo said. "So that I can tell Aunt Teresa. Are you really all right? You don't sound quite like yourself."

The line went silent, so silent that Paolo was worried that his cousin had hung up, but the light still flickered on the app on his cell screen. Luca hadn't hung up. Why was he so quiet? "Is everything all right?"

"Yes, yes," Luca said. "I'm just bored, I guess. Restless…"

"You want to come home," his cousin surmised.

Luca's weary sigh rattled the phone. "We both know that's not possible."

It was, but Luca would be coming home in a casket. That twinge of guilt struck Paolo again, but he had no choice. He had to…

"So what have you been doing to keep busy?" Paolo asked and hoped like hell that it wasn't writing that book. Luca had done enough damage.

Luca chuckled. "I've been riding."

"Horses?" Paolo asked. But he shouldn't have been surprised; his cousin had once wanted to be a cowboy and had taken riding lessons and had even worked some summers on a cattle ranch. "Are you working on a ranch again?"

Luca sighed again. "I wish. It's a dude ranch that only offers cattle drives when the weather's warm."

"It's not warm there?"

"Not yet," Luca said. "But I better not tell you any more."

"Is that why you don't sound like yourself?" Paolo asked. "Or is it possible that you've met someone?"

There was that hesitation again, and then a repeat of Luca's sigh rattling the cell phone. "No. I haven't met her..."

But there was someone who'd caught his attention, hopefully enough to keep Luca wherever he was until the Camorra could take care of him. And maybe this time, Luca would be too distracted to escape.

The app pinged, and Luca asked, "What was that? I bet someone is tapping the line. I better go. Ciao."

The line clicked off. But it was too late. Paulo had his location, or at least the location of the cell tower through which Luca's call had been placed. That tower was somewhere called Blue Larkspur, Colorado. Now it would be up to the Camorra to find the dude ranch where Luca was hiding. It wouldn't be long now. It would all be over. Paulo rubbed his chest, which ached from the twinge of guilt and loss that *had* struck him. But he had no choice. His cousin had crossed the Camorra; his cousin had to die.

Chapter Two

The morning after the meeting of the Truth Foundation, Aubrey knew where to find Jasper: in the barn. It was where she preferred to be herself, but she'd been busy helping the staff give guests riding lessons in the indoor ring. Not that she minded. This time of year was usually easy for them, more relaxing than the summers, when they were fully booked without a moment to themselves, especially during the cattle drives.

Unfortunately, Jasper was right and that storm was coming. She hopped out of the driver's side of the truck and headed into the barn. After her busy morning with the guests, many of them being young and very loud children, Aubrey took a moment to appreciate the relative silence of the barn and to breathe in the scent of fresh hay.

The barn wasn't entirely silent. The horses shifted and nickered in their stalls, and the blades of shovels scraped against cement as piles of shavings were mucked out.

Jasper worked in one stall while their one female ranch hand, Kayla St. James, worked in the next. Despite their proximity, they didn't acknowledge each other, didn't speak, which reminded Aubrey of her own strange encounter the day before with their mysterious guest, Luke Bishop.

She shivered now as she remembered how their gazes had locked across the distance between the back of the truck and where he'd ridden up close but not entirely to the barn, as if he'd been holding himself back.

Keeping his distance...

But for that moment, when their eyes had met, that distance had disappeared. She'd felt like she was in his arms, clasped against him.

And her heart had raced, and her breath had caught in her throat. For a minute, she'd wanted things she'd had no business wanting.

Him...

And she didn't even know him. She only knew that he was good-looking. Tall and lean, black hair with a tiny bit of gray in the temples and on the scruff that clung to his angular jaw. His whole face consisted of interesting angles and planes, making him look rugged and yet...

There was more to him than that—something smart and sexy and secretive. She suspected there was more depth to Luke Bishop than he wanted anyone to know.

Because despite all the open rooms in the main lodge, the receptionist had told her that he'd specifically requested a private cabin—the farthest one from the main lodge and from the other guests. He really wanted to be alone. He didn't come to the lodge for meals or social events like the wine tastings or live music. And while Jasper had mentioned meeting and talking with him over the past week that Bishop had been staying at the ranch, Aubrey herself had yet to exchange a word with him.

All she'd exchanged was that *look*…

She shivered again as she remembered and relived the intensity of it, of *him*…and of what she'd felt in that moment. Such a powerful attraction…

"Is it getting cold out?" Jasper asked—with that twin thing where it was almost as if he'd felt the same shiver she had. He stepped out with another shovelful, and when he dumped it into the wheelbarrow between the stalls, Kayla dumped in her load and their shovels clanged.

They didn't even exchange a glance, though. Kayla offered Aubrey a small smile before she stepped back into the stall she'd been cleaning and resumed her work.

Jasper leaned against the open door of the stall he was cleaning. "The first sign the storm's coming is the drop in temperature. That's the cold front moving in."

Aubrey sighed. "You were right. I've heard the reports, too. It sounds like it's going to be bad."

Jasper nodded. "I know. We need to move the cattle from the pastures that are too close to the mountains."

That was for the safety of the livestock and of the hands responsible for taking care of them. If the ranch got the snow and wind that were being predicted, there could be whiteout conditions and even avalanches in the nearby mountains.

She shivered again.

"Must be getting cold," Jasper remarked.

One of the barn doors had opened, but it wasn't so much the cold wind that blew through it but the man who stepped inside the barn that had Aubrey shivering again.

Luke Bishop…

He walked in, leading the gelding he'd been riding yesterday. Wearing a black cowboy hat, a sheepskin-lined denim jacket, jeans and battered-seeming boots, he looked like one of the ranch hands. But guests often dressed as if they were cowboys, too, especially for the cattle drives.

Cattle drives were only scheduled for warmer months of the year, not the colder ones. They ran the ranch with less help in the winter, and usually it wasn't a problem.

Before she could meet his gaze again, Aubrey quickly looked away from their guest and turned back toward her brother. "Do you think we can get any of the family to help us out?" she wondered aloud. "Since we lost one of our best ranch hands when Bruce retired, we're going to need more hands to bring in the cattle, especially since some have just given birth." They would have to go slow, make sure that the mamas and babies didn't get separated.

Jasper shook his head. "I don't know. Everybody's so damn busy—with their own careers and now with this latest Truth Foundation case for Ronald Spence."

"The storm's still a couple of days away from hitting us," Aubrey said. "So we have time to call them, see if we can recruit them or any of our summer staff if they happen to be home—"

"I will help," a deep voice murmured.

Just the sound of his voice had something stirring inside Aubrey, fluttering through her stomach. It was Luke Bishop. His accent must be French, or maybe Italian...

She glanced back at where he'd walked up behind her. He was closer now so she could see his eyes. They were a pale blue with such a riveting gaze that she caught herself staring just like she'd stared at him yesterday. Those eyes shone with intelligence, but he had a toughness to him as well. With his skin chafed from the cold and his lean muscles taut against his jeans and the sleeves of his jacket, he looked like he was capable of physical work. Like an artist forced into manual labor so that he didn't starve...

Aubrey shook her head, clearing away her fanciful thoughts. She wasn't like that; she didn't romanticize men. She knew them too well, knew that they lied and let down the people who loved them most.

"No," she said shortly, before turning back to her brother.

"But the storm is coming," Jasper said. "We need help."

Aubrey felt as if the storm was inside her with her tension building. The pressure between two fronts, warm and cold, shifting everything...

Bringing with it something bad and not just snow and cold. Something even more unsettling.

Something like their mysterious guest, Luke Bishop.

LUCA WASN'T USED to being so summarily dismissed as Aubrey Colton had just done, with a glance and a single word.

No.

As a journalist, he was accustomed to hearing that word, of course. People often turned down requests for interviews or for more information. But women didn't often turn him down, not that he'd often asked them for anything. He'd been so busy with work over the years that he hadn't had much time to pursue relationships. He was usually pursuing a story instead.

Even as bored as he currently was, he didn't have time for a relationship now, either. Because this would be the worst possible time for him to get involved with anyone.

But he couldn't help thinking about Paolo's question the night before, asking if he'd met someone. Not that he'd actually met Aubrey Colton. They hadn't been introduced. He only knew, from his research before checking in, that she was one of the two owners of Gemini Ranch.

Her brother was the other, so Luca appealed to Jasper Colton. "I would like to help move the cattle," he said. "I have worked on other ranches before. I know what I'm doing." But he wasn't entirely sure about that now. He was supposed to be keeping his distance; that was why he'd wanted the private cabin far from the main lodge and every other cabin. His intention was to not get too close to anyone, so that he didn't put anyone else in the danger he was in.

"No," Aubrey repeated, answering before her brother could. "It's too much of a liability to have a guest help out."

"But you advertise cattle drives—"

"In the warmer months," she said, interrupting him. "The storm that's coming in will make the conditions too dangerous." She spared him another brief, dismissive glance.

And he couldn't help but wonder if she was talking about the storm or him.

Did she somehow sense the threat his very existence posed?

But did it?

How would anyone find him here?

How would they think to look?

How had they thought to find him in any of those other places, though? It was almost as if…

He shook his head now, dismissing that thought before he even allowed it to form. "I've seen the weather reports as well." There was Wi-Fi in the cabin, and he was often online. He didn't have much else to occupy his time…besides the book. "The storm is still a couple of days away. If we move quickly," he said, "we can beat the worst of the snow and win. There will be no danger."

"There is always danger," Aubrey insisted. "Unforeseen threats. Coyotes. Mountain lions. Rattlesnakes…" Her eyes, such a dark and fathomless blue, narrowed behind the lenses of her black-framed glasses as she stared at him.

Did she consider him a snake? Or all men?

"These are the same threats that would be here in the summer," he said. "They are probably bigger threats in the summer, but yet you let guests participate in the cattle drives. In fact, you even charge them more." A grin tugged at his lips, but he only allowed them to curve slightly. "I will pay more if you insist…"

Jasper chuckled. "He's got you, Aub."

She glared at her brother now. "You're the one who's been harping about this storm," she reminded him. "You know it's too dangerous. We need experienced ranch hands—"

As she had interrupted him, he interrupted her now. "I am experienced…" He lowered his voice on that last word. He couldn't resist teasing her, flirting with her, especially because she was so clearly uninterested.

But she shivered slightly, and he wondered…maybe she was more interested than she wanted to be.

Maybe that was the danger of which she spoke.

She shook her head. "You're not experienced here, at Gemini Ranch. I'm going to bring in hands who know the property, who won't get lost in whiteout conditions, whom we won't have to look for if they go missing."

Thinking of how easily he'd been tracked down over the past several months, Luca murmured, "I am surprisingly easy to find…"

And now he was the one who nearly shivered with fear. Not just for himself, for his safety, but for anyone to whom he got close.

No. Aubrey was right to turn him down. She was smart, smarter than he had been when he'd made the offer to help.

"But I respect your decision," he said, and he respected her more for making it. He touched the brim of his hat, tipping it toward her, before continuing to lead the horse to its empty stall.

The gelding pulled slightly on its reins, as if reluctant to go back. He was restless like Luca, or maybe he only sensed his rider's disquiet.

Luca was more than restless, though. He was intrigued with Aubrey Colton. And he couldn't ever remember a woman arousing his curiosity so much before. A story, certainly, but he suspected that Aubrey had a story of her own, one that had made her smarter and stronger and certainly more distrustful because of it, of whatever had happened in her past.

JASPER WATCHED AUBREY walk off in one direction and Luke Bishop in another, and frustration tugged at him. She was never going to trust anyone again. Not after what Dad had done and certainly not after that loser Warren Parker.

Did she even trust him anymore?

He'd been telling her about the storm, but she hadn't believed him until more reports had come out warning about the danger. She'd certainly had no problem spouting off about that danger and others to Luke Bishop when she'd shot down his offer.

When she'd shot him down as if the guy had been hitting on her. Jasper glanced back at the guest, who disappeared into a stall with Ebony, the gelding. Had he been hitting on Aubrey?

Hell, maybe Jasper had been out of the dating game so long himself that he had missed the signs of flirting, of attraction.

Kayla stepped out of the stall she'd been cleaning then. She didn't even glance at him as she dumped her shovelful of soiled shavings and straw into the wheelbarrow before stepping back inside the stall.

With a sigh, Jasper headed after his sister. She stopped outside the barn, standing next to the pickup as she glanced down at her cell phone.

Had she already sent out the text to their siblings to request their help? But when he peered over her shoulder at her phone, he noticed it was an incoming text—from Warren Parker.

Give me another chance...

"You haven't blocked that creep?" Jasper asked, appalled that she would have any contact with the man after what he'd done, after how he'd tried to manipulate her into paying off his gambling debts.

Aubrey's face flushed, but that could have been as much from the cold wind blowing as embarrassment. "Reading over my shoulder like when we were kids?" she asked him with exasperation.

He grinned. "It's easier now that I'm taller than you," he said. "And we're twins. We're not supposed to have any secrets."

"We don't," she said. And she swiped her finger across the screen of her cell, deleting Warren's text.

"Then what's your beef with Bishop?" he asked.

She shrugged. "I don't know what you mean. I don't have a beef with him. It's exactly what I said. We can't risk losing a guest during a snowstorm with possible whiteout conditions."

"We won't lose him," Jasper said. "He's been out riding every day since he checked in. He knows the property, and he's a natural in the saddle. I believe that he has experience working some other ranches."

Her face flushed a little deeper red. And Jasper wondered if the two had been flirting in front of him and he'd missed it. No. It would have been Bishop flirting and Aubrey ignoring him.

If only she had ignored Warren when the guy had lavished compliments on her, then maybe she wouldn't be struggling so hard to trust anyone right now. Even him...

"Come on, Aubrey," he urged her. "Give the guy a chance."

"Wh-what do you mean?" she sputtered, and her face definitely got a darker red.

And Jasper wondered...

Was his sister interested in their solitary guest?

"I mean that we have more guests checking in, some couples and another family," he reminded her. "We can't spare any of our already lean crew of staff to help bring in the cattle from—"

"I know," she agreed. "As great as Kayla is as a ranch hand, she's better at giving riding lessons to the guests."

Jasper didn't want Kayla out in the storm anyway, even if she wasn't going to be busy with the guests. He didn't want her getting hurt any more than she already had been. He and Aubrey weren't the only ones at Gemini Ranch who struggled to deal with the sins of their father...

"That's why I'm going to reach out to family," Aubrey said. With as much time as their siblings spent at the ranch, they knew it well.

But Jasper persisted, "Bishop is here. He can help right away."

"He's not leaving?" she asked, with some odd note in her voice.

Like she hoped that he was...

Jasper shook his head. "His stay is open-ended right now. I think he intends to be here for a while."

"Why?" Aubrey asked.

Jasper shrugged. "I don't know. I don't interrogate our guests."

"Maybe we should," she murmured.

"He offered to help," Jasper said. "And thanks to you, he knows every possible danger. He won't be a liability."

Aubrey sighed. "Maybe he won't be a liability..."

"But?" he prodded.

She shrugged now. "I don't know. I just get an odd feeling from the guy..."

Maybe Aubrey hadn't recognized his flirting, either. "Like what?" Jasper asked.

"Like something's going on with him, like he might *be* the danger..." She shivered, and Jasper suspected it had nothing to do with the cold.

"How? Why?" he asked. And he was glad that he wasn't so cynical, that he didn't struggle as hard as she did to trust anyone.

She shook her head. "I don't know..."

"Then give him a chance," Jasper urged.

"I have a feeling that if I do, we'll both come to regret it," Aubrey warned him.

Both—did she mean her and Jasper? Or her and Luke Bishop?

Before he could ask, she was pulling open the driver's door of the truck and hopping inside, and for once the twin intuition didn't work. He didn't know what she meant.

Or why she was so damn suspicious of their guest?

Bishop stepped out of the barn then and stared after the pickup as Aubrey drove away. And there was some odd expression on his face, one almost of longing.

And Jasper had to acknowledge that maybe his sister was right not to trust this guy. Maybe there was something off about him, something not quite what it seemed...

But what?

What could Luke Bishop possibly be hiding?

Chapter Three

What was Luke Bishop hiding?

Using the computer at the reception desk in the main lodge, Aubrey scrolled through the guest's records. He'd paid with cash. No credit card on file, even for extra charges. Not that there had been any of those...

He'd eaten no meals in the main lodge. And he hadn't even made any phone calls on the landline in his cabin. Of course he probably had a cell phone, but the reception was so spotty out at the ranch that most guests used the landline.

Hell, he hadn't even rented a movie. What was he doing at his solitary cabin for entertainment, for companionship? He'd checked in alone.

That didn't mean that he hadn't met someone, though. But where?

He had to be going to town, buying his food or supplies there.

If she was going to give their guest the chance Jasper had asked her to give him, she needed to know more.

And she could think of only one way how...especially if he was dangerous, as she was now beginning to suspect.

Along with the guest records on file, there were also the codes for the automatic locks on every room and for every cabin. She made a mental note of his before grabbing the keys and heading back out to the pickup truck.

Not that she was going to search his place or invade his privacy…if he was there. And he probably was, since he'd been returning his horse to the barn instead of saddling up.

But if he was gone…

Maybe on one of those trips to town…

His cabin was the farthest from the main lodge and the barn. It was closer to the distant pastures, the ones where the cattle were that needed to be moved, closer to her house and to Jasper's. She loved sitting on her deck, staring at the snowy peaks in the distance as she sipped her coffee in the morning and an occasional glass of wine at night.

Alone…

Or so she'd thought, but Luke Bishop had been just a short walk away. Well, a short walk on the ranch; it was still a distance if they were in the city. If there had been other buildings and people between them…

But there were only pine trees and boulders and, out here where it was colder than in town, snow-covered grass.

And all her suspicions. She needed to know more about him and not just because she was entertaining the thought of his helping move the cattle but because he was so close.

Closer than she'd let anyone get in a while and not just physically. He was on her mind. And she didn't like it—and something about him worried her.

She didn't like that she'd been thinking of him ever since she'd gotten caught up in his gaze yesterday. That she'd wondered about that jolt of attraction she'd felt for him, had wondered if he'd felt it, too.

But he was probably married or involved with someone. Or worse yet, up to some kind of scam, like Warren had been.

She needed to know if he posed a threat to herself or anyone else on the property. So, instead of continuing down the road that led to Jasper's ranch house and then hers, she stopped at the cabin. There was no vehicle parked outside, so he must have gone into Blue Larkspur.

She could check out the cabin, but she hesitated, reluctant to invade a guest's privacy. But as a good hostess, she should make sure that he had everything he needed, that the cabin's small furnace was functioning properly, that none of the pipes were freezing. Or so she told herself.

She shut off the truck and pushed open the driver's door. Reciting the code to the lock beneath her breath, she walked up to the door. Before touching the buttons, she leaned close and listened.

But the wind picked up, whipping around the cabin. The sound of it was all she heard, that and the howl of coyotes in the distance.

She quickly punched in the numbers. The lock clicked, and she pushed open the door and stepped out of the cold. The cabin wasn't much warmer inside or brighter. It was afternoon yet, but clouds blocked the sun, casting shadows everywhere—especially within the small log house.

Maybe Luke hadn't even returned here after going to the barn. He certainly hadn't turned on any lights or turned up the heat.

The place was tidy, so tidy that she wondered now if he'd checked out. If he'd left…

So much for his open-ended plans to stay.

But then her eyes adjusted to the dimness, and she noticed the boots at the door. Her pulse quickened with nerves. It was possible that he had more than one pair. Jasper certainly did, and her other brothers probably had as well.

But…

She hesitated about moving away from the door. And she cocked her head to listen, but even inside, all she heard was the wind, rushing around the cabin, hurtling against the windows. The storm was coming.

She needed to get to the cattle. It was too late to leave today. But tomorrow the livestock would have to be moved closer.

Just as she needed to move.

She stepped away from the door and noticed that other things, besides the boots, were inside the cabin. A laptop and some notebooks lay on the table next to the kitchenette. She opened one of the notebooks, but she couldn't read what was written inside. While the handwriting was bold and clear, the language was not. It definitely wasn't English.

But it looked beautiful, just like Luke Bishop's slight accent and his pale blue eyes.

Next to the laptop lay a battery, too small to have come from the computer but it had come from some electronic device. A phone?

She didn't see any...until she glanced into the trash bin next to the table. There were wadded up notes in there and not one but two disposable cells and the little chips that had come from them. The phones were broken, and those little chips looked mangled or burned.

"What the hell..." she murmured.

"Exactly," a deep voice said. "What the hell are you doing?"

She jumped and whirled around to the open door to the bedroom of the one-bedroom cabin. Luke stood, framed in the doorjamb, partially concealed in the shadows. For a moment, she thought he was naked, until she skimmed her gaze over his bare chest to where he'd knotted a towel at his lean waist. Her heart had been pounding fast and hard already, but now it pounded harder and faster.

"Damn..." she muttered.

Damn that she'd been caught snooping. But most of all, damn was he hot! So hot that heat rushed through her—the heat of attraction and the heat of embarrassment.

LUCA FOUGHT TO keep from grinning at her. He should have been furious that she'd let herself into the cabin, but the look on her face, the way she kept staring at him had male pride rushing through him, along with a hot wave of desire. He wanted to reach for her, wanted to pull her into his arms against his naked chest, wanted to lower his head to hers, brush his mouth across...

He cleared his throat of the desire choking him and repeated his question, albeit without the expletive. "What are you doing?"

When he stepped out of the shower, he'd realized that he was no longer alone—even though he'd been able to hear nothing but the wind.

There'd been a shift in the air, an awareness, an electricity.

At first he'd thought it was danger, but then he'd glanced out the window and noticed the truck parked out front. The Gemini Ranch truck...

And even though it could have been her brother who'd driven it here, he'd known it was her—because of that heightened energy in the cabin, in him.

But that didn't mean he wasn't in peril. Because he had a feeling that he was in uncharted territory with Aubrey Colton.

"You offered to help move the cattle," she said.

He glanced around the small cabin. "I don't see any of them in here. Why did you let yourself inside?"

"The door wasn't locked," she said, but she didn't meet his gaze when she made the claim.

The lie...

He always made sure to lock doors and windows and to double-check that they were secure, to make sure nobody could sneak in while he was sleeping. Not that he slept all that much or that soundly.

"So you just let yourself inside?" he asked.

"It's going to get cold tonight—"

"So you're here to keep me warm?" he interrupted to tease her.

Her face flushed, and she met his gaze now, her eyes narrowed in a glare. "No. I came to check the furnace."

"But the furnace isn't on the table or in the trash can," he pointed out.

She'd found the broken burner phones. She had to be curious about those, about his notes, but hopefully she wasn't able to read Italian.

She gestured toward the door next to the kitchen cabinets. "It's in that closet. I was just about to check on—"

"—when I caught you looking in my trash can," he finished for her. "But you first said that you came here about my offer to help move the cattle."

Her head bobbed in a quick nod that had her golden blond hair bouncing around her shoulders. "Yes, that's why I'm here." A few pieces of her long bangs fell across her glasses. Instead of pushing them away, she blew out a breath that chased them back into place.

He wished he'd been close enough to feel that breath, to taste it, so he stepped out of the bedroom doorway and moved closer to her. The cabin was small. In two strides, he was standing right in front of her, right in front of his laptop. Even if she'd opened it, it was protected with a special, encrypted password and facial identification. She wouldn't have been able to access anything on it. His book.

His life...

"Moving the cattle or checking the furnace?" he asked with the same abruptness he used when interviewing reluctant subjects or witnesses. "Which is your real reason for breaking into my cabin?"

"I—I didn't break in," she said even as her face flushed, and her gaze dropped from his eyes to his chest.

"Or do you have some other reason for seeking me out, Ms. Colton?" he asked less abruptly, but he still wanted an answer.

She took a step back so quickly that she nearly stumbled. He reached out and caught her shoulders, steadying her. But she quickly tugged away from him. "I came here to talk to you about the cattle and then it occurred to me that I should check the furnace."

"So you just let yourself in?"

"I didn't think you were home." She gestured toward the window. "There was no vehicle outside."

"I don't have one..." He'd taken the bus from Boulder to Blue Larkspur, paying cash for the bus ticket and the fare for the cab that had brought him out to the ranch from town.

"Why not?"

He shrugged. "Does it matter? Surely we're going to use horses to move the cattle?"

"Sometimes we use trucks," she said. Or they made sure trucks were close by, in case they needed medical assistance for hands or veterinarian services for the livestock. "But these pastures aren't accessible by vehicle."

"Which is one of the reasons I assume you need the cattle moved closer," he concluded.

She nodded. "The snow could make it too hard to get feed to them."

He glanced toward the window, where the sky had gone dark. "Do we need to leave now?"

"You're a little underdressed," she said and smiled. "Especially with the storm coming, you might get cold."

He should have been cold now; he hadn't turned up the furnace when he'd returned from his ride. But after his long walk from the barn, the cabin had felt much warmer than it had been outside. And now with the way she kept looking at him, his blood was pumping hot and fast through him—heating him up from the inside out. He couldn't resist teasing her some more and said, "You won't keep me warm?"

"You would have better luck with the cattle," she told him, and even though her lips were still curved into that smile, her voice was serious as she clearly offered him the warning that he wasn't going to get close to her.

"So I better get dressed, then," he said.

She nodded and released a quiet breath. But then she added, "We won't ride out until tomorrow morning, though. We'll have time before the storm hits to move them."

He nodded now. "If that's the case, you could have called and let me know." On the wall next to the cabinets of the kitchenette hung a landline telephone with a direct connection to the main lodge.

"I pass this cabin on my way home," she said.

"The big house at the end of the road—that's yours?" he asked, his pulse quickening at the thought of how close he was to her and she was to him...

Maybe too close, if he was found again.

But he couldn't be found again. He had to be safe

somewhere, and for some reason, he hoped that Gemini Ranch was that somewhere.

She nodded. "Yes. That's mine." And there was pride and satisfaction in her voice. This was a woman who worked hard and took care of herself—a strong, independent woman.

But she could still be hurt. Just like his family and friends back in Naples.

"This is dangerous, you know," she murmured.

And he wondered if she was talking about the cattle or about this attraction that sizzled between them. She had to feel it, too, he could tell from the way she kept looking at him.

"I have worked as a ranch hand before," he assured her. "I know what I'm doing."

"What do you do now?" she asked, and she looked away from him to the laptop.

"I—I…" Didn't want to lie to her. But he didn't want her in danger, either, and anyone who knew the truth about him, who knew his true identity, could be in danger. "I'm writing a book. Or at least I'm trying…"

"Writer's block?" she asked.

"I am struggling," he admitted. With as often as he'd had to move to stay ahead of the Camorra, he hadn't been able to focus on his writing. Only on the danger.

"Is that why you smashed the phones?" she asked. "Editor or agent bothering you for the finished product?"

"Something like that."

"My brother Gavin is a writer," she said. "Well,

maybe he's more of a journalist. He has a podcast called *Crime Time*."

A gasp slipped between Luca's lips.

"You know him?" she asked, and now she beamed with pride in her sibling.

Luca nodded even as his stomach knotted with apprehension. Gavin had reached out to interview him before Luca had learned about that hit taken out on him. "I've streamed an episode or two. I thought he was based out of New York City or Chicago." And he hoped like hell he was still there and not here, where he might recognize Luca.

"He lives in New York, but he was born and raised in Blue Larkspur just like the rest of us," she said with a smile of affection for her family.

"How many of you are there?" he wondered.

Her smile widened. "Twelve."

And Luca inhaled sharply. "Your parents were very busy."

Her smile slipped away. "Well, there were several multiple births like me and Jasper."

"You're twins?"

She nodded. "Gemini…"

"Oh, of course…" That explained the origin of the name of the ranch.

"We're the second set," she said. "My oldest siblings, Caleb and Morgan, were the first set. Followed by triplets, Oliver, Ezra and Dominic…"

"Wow," he murmured. "Your poor mother,"

"You have no idea," she said, and there was something in her voice, something poignant about her tone.

"After the triplets, there were two single births, Rachel and Gideon, then Jasper and I came along, and next was Gavin. Maybe that's why he's such a loner."

Luca could relate: he was an only child. But his extended family was big with many aunts and uncles and cousins. He'd been closest to Paolo. Maybe too close... for Paolo's safety. Unlike Luca's mother and aunt, his cousin had refused to go into hiding. He believed he was safe, even after all the murders the Camorra had committed to intimidate and punish.

"But Gavin wasn't the youngest for very long before the last set of twins were born," she continued. "Alexa and Naomi." She heaved a heavy sigh, as if reciting her family tree had exhausted her.

The affection on her beautiful face and in her voice when she spoke of her big family took his breath away. Family was important to her. He understood because he would do anything—even stay away—to keep his family safe.

"Will any of your siblings be helping us move the cattle?" he asked.

"Jasper, of course," she said. "And hopefully we'll be able to recruit some of the others, if they're not too busy." She pointed at his laptop. "Are you sure you're not too busy? Don't you have a deadline you need to meet?"

His shoulders stooped slightly. "Yes."

"If you're struggling, I can see if Gavin could talk to you, offer some pointers. I know journalism is probably quite different from writing a book, unless..." She narrowed her eyes behind her lenses and studied him. "Are you writing about something true?"

Too true.

He shook his head. "No. Fiction. Entirely made-up." *I wish.* And he wished even more that he didn't have to lie to her. But just in case she'd recognized any of the words in his notes, it was better that she thought anything about the Camorra was just from his imagination and not the frightening reality of the murderous gangs.

"Then I don't know if Gavin can help..."

"I appreciate the offer," he assured her—though he had no intention of speaking to her brother and was glad he was far away from Blue Larkspur. Since Gavin Colton had heard enough about him to reach out for an interview, he probably would have been able to recognize him.

At thirty-eight, Luca had been a journalist for a long time, nearly a decade longer than Gavin Colton, but he wasn't often recognized outside Europe, despite all the high-profile exposés he'd done. The Camorra had been just one of many, but they were certainly the most dangerous—since they'd put out the official hit on him.

"And I appreciate you offering to help with the cattle," she said. "But not if it's going to be any trouble to you..."

The deadline wasn't the problem. Yet. But Aubrey Colton might be.

Even if the Camorra didn't find him.

"I think the fresh air helps clear my head," he said. "That is why I go riding so often." And because he felt so restless, so on edge...

Would he ever be safe anywhere?

Would he ever get his life back?

Or would the Camorra keep coming for him until his life was over?

"You will get plenty of fresh air tomorrow," she said, as she turned and headed toward the door. "But I suggest that you dress a little warmer..." Her gaze slid over his chest again and down further...

His body began to tighten, to react...

He could almost imagine that she was touching him, her hands sliding over his bare skin...

His breath caught in his throat, nearly choking him.

And she chuckled, a sexy little chuckle. She knew that she was getting to him. "I will be sticking close to you tomorrow," she said, her voice just above a husky whisper. "Really close..."

His chest moved with the force of his pounding heart. "I thought you weren't going to keep me warm?" he reminded her of her warning.

"I'm not," she said. "I just want to keep you alive..." Then she opened the door and stepped out.

So she missed what Luca murmured in response. She missed him saying, "I wish you could..."

PAOLO'S PHONE VIBRATED against his desk again, and he hastened to answer it. He knew it wasn't going to be Luca. His calls were never this close together. So it had to be...

"You better be right this time," the caller warned him before even making certain it was him.

"I am," Paolo said. "A dude ranch in Blue Larkspur. The tracker I had on my phone revealed his location in Colorado, and that's the only ranch that takes guests through the winter. Luca has to be at the Gemini Ranch."

"So are the assassins," he was assured. "As long as this is really where Rossi is, he will be eliminated."

"He was at all the other places," Paolo said in his own defense. "He's just smart, observant. He caught on to the 'accidents' that were supposed to befall him."

"These assassins will eliminate Rossi by whatever means necessary, and they don't care about collateral damage. This has gone on long enough—the man has lived too long with his betrayal. He is beginning to make even more of a mockery of us. He has to die. Soon, or…"

Paolo would die. He'd been given that ultimatum a while ago; he knew the expiration date was running out on it. He'd already been in deep to the Camorra, for the money they'd loaned him for his car dealership, for the exorbitant interest that compiled on that "loan" and for the other debts he'd compiled for their "help" in eliminating his competition.

The Camorra was calling in his debts now, and he had to pay up with his cousin's life.

If Luca wasn't dead soon, Paolo would be. So Luca had to die…

Chapter Four

I wish you could...

Just as Aubrey was pulling the cabin door shut, she heard what Luke Bishop had whispered. *I wish you could...*

She probably should have stepped back inside and asked why he'd said that, what he meant, but she didn't expect him to answer her truthfully. So she walked out to her truck and, her hand shaking a bit in reaction to their encounter, jammed the key in the ignition and started it. Then she drove the too-short distance down the road to her house.

After parking, she pushed open her door and hurried toward her house. It was a hybrid between a log home and an A-frame, with tall windows that looked over the front deck and the property. Thanks to the glass French doors, it was always bathed in light. But for now...

Now the sky was growing dark, casting long shadows into her home. She unlocked the doors and stepped inside, but instead of starting a fire, she reached instead for her phone.

She needed to call in those reinforcements, and not just for moving the cattle…

As her hand closed around it, her phone vibrated with an incoming text. Maybe Jasper had already called their siblings with requests for help. But he would have asked just for assistance with the cattle, not with what she wanted done…

She needed help getting some information.

She swiped her cell screen to read the text and found that it wasn't from a Colton at all.

Please, Aubrey, give me a chance to prove to you how much I care…

She snorted in derision at Warren's message. The only thing he cared about was himself and his gambling debts. His creditors must have been getting impatient for their money.

Aubrey was getting impatient as well. Maybe she should have blocked him, like Jasper had said. But getting these texts reminded Aubrey of how she'd nearly been duped. Of how she shouldn't trust her judgment when it came to men.

Not that Warren was much of a man, not when he wanted someone else to clean up the mess he'd made. He was more like a child in his personality—and especially in comparison to Luke Bishop.

Now, *there* was a man. Heat flushed Aubrey's entire body when she thought of him. His chest bare but for a smattering of black hair on his lean body, washboard abs and the hip bones that had jutted over the top of that low-hanging towel.

That towel hadn't hidden much from her imagination. Yet, she suspected that Luke was hiding something. Why smash those phones and destroy the chips inside? Or was he in hiding?

Was that why he'd made that cryptic comment? Or had she just imagined that?

It had been windy outside; it howled around her house now. The heat of her desire for her guest faded away, leaving her chilled and oddly frightened.

She'd accepted his offer to help move the cattle, but that didn't mean she trusted him. In fact, she trusted him even less now than she had before. Everything she'd seen had only reinforced her uneasiness around him, that sense of danger she'd picked up on the very first time their gazes had locked.

Ignoring Warren's text as she had all of his other ones, she swiped through her contacts to the C's. And in the long list of Coltons, she chose Dominic.

He was an FBI agent—he would know if Luke Bishop was on a most-wanted list.

Standing in that small cabin, with him barely dressed, she'd wanted him. Too much. Wanted him still, even knowing that she shouldn't trust him. But maybe she didn't have to trust him as long as she knew not to let her heart get involved.

If she knew exactly what and whom she was dealing with…

"Hey, Aub," Dominic answered. "Jasper sent out the

text already. I'd love to help, but I can't get away from Denver right now."

"I don't need your help with the cattle," she said. Though she could have used it. "I have another favor to ask you."

"Shoot," he said, getting right to the point in his usual no-nonsense manner.

Aubrey smiled, imagining him running a hand through his shaggy dark blond hair as he waited for her request. "I want you to find out everything you can about one of our guests."

She waited for the why and wondered how she would explain this gut feeling she had. This...

"What's his name?" Dominic asked instead.

"Luke Bishop," she replied. But remembering that notebook filled with writing in some other language, she wondered. Bishop didn't sound very European, unlike Luke's subtle and sexy accent.

"Do you have a date of birth?" he asked. "Driver's license number? Social security?"

"No."

"What about his credit card?"

"No, he paid cash."

"Thought you had to have a credit card on file for additional room charges," Dominic said. "Or damages..."

"He made an additional cash deposit for incidentals and damages." But nothing had been credited to it. No meals. No calls...

"What do you know about this guy?" Dominic asked.

That he looked damn good in nothing but a towel. But she definitely wasn't going to admit that to her older brother. "He's probably late thirties. Claims to be a writer..."

"You don't think he is?"

"I don't know." She sighed. "But maybe he is." He'd certainly seemed to recognize Gavin's name.

"Are you interviewing the guy for a job?" Dominic asked. "Are you just looking for a background check on him?"

"If he'd filled out an application, we can do that ourselves," she said. Then she would have had his social security number and his date of birth. "I think he's probably mid-thirties." She remembered the gray at his temples and in his stubble; there had even been a few silver strands in the hair on his sculpted chest. "Maybe late thirties..."

"Anything else?"

She swallowed hard as she remembered and wondered...

"I found some things in his trash can. Some notes that weren't written in English and some broken up cell phones."

"Are you cleaning rooms now?" Dominic asked. "Or searching them? What's the deal with this guy, Aub? What's made you so suspicious of him?"

There it was: the why.

And she wasn't sure she could honestly answer. She wasn't sure what it was about Luke Bishop that just didn't feel right.

Or maybe it was that he felt too right, too handsome, too charming, too intriguing...

"I don't know," she admitted. "I just have this feeling…" Too much feeling for a stranger—a very strange stranger at that. Maybe that was what fascinated her so much about him, that he seemed unlike anyone else she'd ever met. And she'd met a lot of people over the years that she and Jasper had been running their business.

Aubrey held her breath as she waited, wondering if her vague answer would be good enough for Dominic to check out her mysterious guest.

"You didn't give me a whole hell of a lot to go on," he told her. "But I'll see if I can find out anything."

"Thank you," she said.

"Just…" Dominic began, "since you have this feeling, keep your distance from Luke Bishop until I can check him out."

She couldn't promise that, not when she intended to do exactly the opposite. "Don't worry," she told him instead.

"I do," he said, "especially after that loser you dated last…"

She flinched just as her phone dinged with another text.

Warren: Please…

He could beg all he wanted, but she was never letting him get close to her again.

Now Luke Bishop.

She wanted to be close to him, curled up in his strong arms, tight against his bare chest, but she couldn't. Not when she didn't trust him.

I wish you could...

Maybe she'd just imagined that; maybe he hadn't said anything like that. Or maybe that feeling she had was right, and Luke Bishop was trouble. Hopefully, Dominic would be able to find out more about her enigmatic guest.

And in the meantime, she would stick close enough to Luke that he might reveal some of his secrets—because she had no doubt that the man had some.

But what kind of secrets? Secrets like her father had kept from his family?

THE WALK TO the barn the morning after Luca had found Aubrey Colton in his cabin was a long one. The temperature had definitely dropped, and the wind was fierce, but only a few flurries swirled around the ground. The storm wasn't here yet, but it was coming.

Luca felt it, and he shivered more in anticipation than from the cold. He could have gotten a ride from Aubrey; she'd driven past his cabin. But whenever he heard a vehicle, his first instinct was to slip out of sight, to watch and wait and hope like hell that it wasn't someone coming for him.

So when he'd heard the rumble of her pickup, he'd slipped into the pines around his cabin and waited. He could have come out when Aubrey had stopped. But then he would have had to explain...

No, he would have had to lie to her again, and he hadn't wanted to do that. So he'd waited while she stalled for several long moments before driving off again.

She hadn't gone up to the door. She hadn't knocked.

Or let herself in as she had the day before. She hadn't even tooted her horn. Maybe she was hoping he'd changed his mind about helping.

Or maybe she just hadn't wanted to catch him as she had yesterday. Half-naked...

He'd barely been able to sleep for thinking about how she'd looked at him. How flushed she'd been, despite the chilly air in the cabin.

She had to feel this, too—this attraction between them. But it couldn't go anywhere, couldn't lead to anything but danger for her and heartache for him.

Luca couldn't act on that attraction. But he could help her with the cattle. Surely, nobody had found him yet. The only people he'd encountered since coming to Gemini Ranch were the receptionist at the check-in desk, Jasper, Aubrey and a few of the ranch hands.

Kayla was the one he found first in the barn when he stepped inside it. She was saddling a horse, her arms rippling with her lean muscles. Like Aubrey, she was a strong woman.

"Are you going with us?" he asked.

She shook her head, and her dark brown ponytail swished across her back. "No, I'm needed here," she remarked with a trace of resentment. "New guests arrived yesterday and have signed up for riding lessons at the indoor ring."

"You don't like giving lessons?" he asked. As a journalist his first instinct was always to question everything and everyone—often to his family's annoyance. A pang of longing over missing them struck his heart.

She shrugged. "It's fine. I just prefer ranching."

"What about your bosses?" he asked.

"What about them? They probably make more money off having guests than they do off the livestock and the land."

"I meant, how are they as bosses?" he wondered. Especially about Aubrey...

"They're great," she said but without a whole lot of enthusiasm. Then, almost as if speaking to herself, she added beneath her breath, "Their dad ruined my life, but they're great."

"What?" he asked, shocked.

She sighed and shook her head. "I'm sorry. I shouldn't have said that. You're a guest—"

"I'm helping out with moving the cattle today," he said. "I'd like to know more about the people I'm working for."

"You're not working for their dad," she said. "He's been dead for twenty years."

And Kayla couldn't be a whole lot older than twenty—maybe five or six years—so how had their father ruined her life?

"I'd like to know more," he told her. He would like to know everything about Aubrey Colton, like how her skin felt, how her lips tasted...

Another pang struck him—this one of lust. He closed his eyes for a moment and willed it away before focusing on Kayla again.

"What did her—*their*—father do?" he prodded the female ranch hand.

But she just shook her head again. "I'm not dredging all that up again. It's too late now anyways."

He wasn't sure what she meant by that. If it was too late because what had happened had already happened, or if there just wasn't enough time for her to tell him about it without anyone else overhearing them. Because he heard other voices now, and he turned to see Aubrey walking toward him from another area of the mammoth barn.

She wasn't alone. A tall man with medium brown hair walked beside her, so close that their shoulders bumped. And something churned inside Luca, twisting his stomach with dread and…

Jealousy?

Was that what this nauseous feeling was? He'd never experienced it before. Had never gotten attached enough to anyone to ever feel possessive of them…

Not that he was attached to Aubrey Colton. He barely knew her. But what he knew intrigued him. She was strong and smart and so incredibly sexy with her curvy body.

And something about the way she looked at him, through the lenses of those black-framed glasses, stirred something deep and almost primal inside him. He wanted her. Too much…

And when she turned her head and laughed at something the man said, he sucked in a breath at what felt like a blow to his stomach.

Or maybe to his pride.

He'd thought she'd been interested in him. Attracted to him.

But he must have just imagined it all. Because clearly, she had a close relationship with whoever this guy was. And for some reason that made Luca hate him before he even met the guy.

So THIS WAS the guy?

The one that had Aubrey all unsettled and edgy? Since Gideon had showed up that morning, his younger sister had been acting odd. Distracted. Moody.

Gideon studied the older man with curiosity and some amusement. The guy stared back at him, his pale blue eyes icy cold. As a social worker, Gideon had dealt with a lot of animosity. Parents were rarely happy to see him—unless he was reuniting a family. Unfortunately, he wasn't able to do that as often as he would like. But the children were always his first priority.

Children. Then family...

He'd hoped by now to have one of his own. But at least he had his siblings and his mom. He'd thought once that he'd had someone else—*the* someone else— that special person with whom he could start that family he wanted.

"Gideon," Aubrey said.

And he realized he was the one who was distracted now. "Yes?"

"This is Luke Bishop," Aubrey introduced him to the tall stranger. "And, Luke, this is my brother Gideon."

The stranger's eyes immediately warmed, and he offered Gideon a grin along with his hand. Gideon shook it, marveling at the strength and the calluses. Maybe the guy would be able to handle himself with the ranch work.

But what about Aubrey?

She was tough. But not nearly as tough as she thought she was. Despite what she'd claimed, that idiot Warren Parker had dealt quite a blow to her ego—if not her heart.

"So she roped you into helping move the cattle," Luke remarked, his voice deep with a curious accent. Gideon wondered where he was from but refrained from asking.

"He just stopped by to visit the horses, like he often does, and I enlisted him. I am very good at roping," Aubrey said with pride.

Gideon nodded. "She is. She and Jasper played cowgirl and cowboy all the time growing up. And they lassoed everything in the house—the newel post on the stairwell, the trash can, the family dog and even the rest of us if we didn't move fast enough."

Aubrey nudged his shoulder with hers. "*You* never moved fast enough."

He chuckled.

So did Luke. "So you didn't move fast enough this time, either."

"No, but I actually enjoy coming out to the ranch," Gideon admitted. Any time spent doing the physical labor in the fresh air was a welcome respite from the emotional demands of his job. "It's not often she ropes a guest into working, though, unless they've signed up for the cattle drives."

"I offered," Luke admitted. "But I think she's going to charge me extra for this *experience*."

"That depends on how much extra work you make

this," Aubrey said. She glanced at her watch. "You're already late. We need to get saddled up and get going."

Luke touched his fingers to the brim of his hat in a mocking salute. "Yes, boss. I'll be ready in just a few moments." With a grin he headed past them to one of the stalls, like he already had a horse here and he knew where everything was.

For a guest, he seemed awfully comfortable at the ranch and with Aubrey. Gideon studied him for a moment before turning to study his sister.

"So where do you want me, *boss*?" Gideon asked her. "With you or with Luke?"

"You're riding with Jasper. Luke's riding with me," she said, almost possessively.

"What's going on with you two?" he asked with some curiosity.

Aubrey was usually very adamant that guests were off-limits for dating—for her and Jasper and for their siblings. Their brother Oliver was the only one she'd really needed to be concerned about, though. He'd always been a heartbreaker.

She shook her head. "Nothing. He's a guest."

"A guest who seems really comfortable with you," Gideon remarked.

She shrugged. "That's just his personality."

She didn't seem too upset about it, but Gideon wondered if that was why she was so edgy. The guy was getting to her. "Is that all it is? Is he something more to you than a guest?"

"No, absolutely not," she replied a little too vehemently.

"That's too bad," Gideon said. "You deserve to have

someone special in your life." Especially after how Warren Parker had tried to use her.

"I don't have time," she said. "Not with the ranch and now the new case that the Truth Foundation has taken on." She uttered a ragged sigh. "I feel bad that I don't help out more with the foundation."

He reached out and squeezed her shoulder. "You carry a lot of responsibility already. Don't worry about it. Focus on yourself and…" He grinned and glanced over at the stall Luke had slipped into. "…maybe on finding that certain someone…"

She smiled at him. "You're the one who deserves someone special."

He'd had someone like that. Once. But he'd come on too strong and lost her. He forced a smile. "I'm fine."

At least he was better than Aubrey seemed at the moment. She kept glancing toward that stall where Luke had gone. In anticipation or trepidation?

He was usually pretty empathetic and could pick up on the emotions of others, which served him well when kids were so often reluctant to share their feelings. Or afraid to…

Was that Aubrey's problem? Was she afraid to fall again? Afraid to risk her heart, only to have it broken?

Or was there another reason she was afraid of Luke Bishop?

Chapter Five

He was good. Really good…

As comfortable as he seemed to be in the saddle, he was equally comfortable with the cattle—directing them through the open gates in the fence from one pasture to the next.

But Aubrey wasn't convinced yet that he hadn't told her other lies. Like Warren had…

Like their father had told their mother and them. So many.

Wondering how truthful Luke Bishop had been with her, Aubrey glanced over at him now as they rode side by side back to the barn from the pastures that were close to the riding ring. They'd moved a lot of livestock today but not all of them.

And while the wind continued to blow, the snow wasn't falling hard yet. Just big, soft flakes that floated down on them, sticking to their hats and onto their coats.

"Are you sure you don't want to return for the rest of them?" Luke asked even as he huddled in his jacket and turned his face from the wind that had already chafed his skin.

His work ethic impressed her, too. He'd been tireless the entire day, not even stopping for the lunch she'd brought, even eating his sandwich in the saddle.

He was nothing like the many guests who'd dropped out of the cattle drives over the years because it hadn't been as glamorous as they'd thought it was going to be. Who'd been surprised that it had actually been work.

Luke had already done more than she'd expected of him, so she shook her head. "No. We'll go back out early tomorrow morning. We'll have time before it gets bad. The worst of the storm isn't coming for a day or so. And hopefully, it's not going to be as bad as they're predicting." But if it was, they needed to be prepared.

Luke nodded. "You're the boss."

"One of them," she said. "Jasper and I are equal partners."

"You started this together?" he asked.

She nodded. "Yes. It was our dream since we were little kids."

"When you played cowgirl and cowboy all the time," he said.

She smiled at the memory Gideon had shared that morning. They were drawing closer to the barn, so she looked for Gideon's vehicle, but it was gone. He and Jasper must have returned already. Or Gideon had been called out on a case. Her smile slipped away at the thought. She didn't know how her older brother handled his heartbreaking job, especially given how empathetic he was.

She was glad she and her twin had chosen another

path. "Yes," she replied to Luke. "Jasper and I always had our plan. What about you?"

"Did I play cowboy and cowgirl?" he asked. "I don't have a sister or a brother."

She sucked in a breath at the thought of not having her siblings. "That must have been very lonely for you."

He shook his head. "I have many cousins that lived close by, so I was never alone unless I wanted to be."

"Is that why you're here now?" she asked. "Because you want to be alone to write your book? Was it your plan to always be an author?"

"So many questions," he said, his body suddenly tense in the saddle.

Clearly her questions unsettled him. But he'd shared some information about his life, so she'd thought he was willing to open up. She persisted. "Do you have a problem with questions?"

He murmured, almost beneath his breath. "No. Just that I'm usually the one asking them..."

"What?" she asked, uncertain if she'd heard him correctly, like the other night.

"I—I just prefer to ask the questions," he admitted. "I was a curious kid, probably why I'm a writer."

"Seems like that inquisitive nature would have led you to be a reporter," she remarked, "since you like asking questions."

He swung out of the saddle—on the side away from her, as if he suddenly wanted to hide, as if he'd revealed too much.

But she hadn't even asked all the questions she had

for him. "Where did you grow up?" she asked. "I can't quite place your accent…"

"What accent?" he asked, and he grinned at her over the back of her horse.

"Exactly," she said. "What kind of accent is it?"

"The kind that usually makes the ladies swoon," he said, his smile widening as he flirted with her.

Aubrey swung down from the saddle, too, and led her horse through the barn doors Luke held open for her. "I'm not the swooning type." If she had been, she would have swooned last night when she'd seen him in nothing but that towel. She and Luke took off the bridles and hitched their mounts to crossties.

"I know," he said, watching as she removed the saddle from her horse and hefted it onto her shoulder. "Fortunately I prefer strong women."

She appreciated that he didn't try to help her as she carried the saddle to the tack room. He'd removed and carried his, their shoulders nearly brushing as he walked close beside her.

She'd strolled that way with Gideon that morning, but being next to Luke was entirely different. She felt tense and edgy and totally aware of him, of every brush of the sleeve of his jacket against her clothing. To take her mind off his proximity, she murmured, "I learned how to be strong from my mother."

Isadora Colton was the strongest woman Aubrey knew; she'd survived so much loss and humiliation. "She raised twelve kids, most of them on her own after my father died."

"I'm sorry," he said. "I heard that he passed away twenty years ago. You must have been young."

She tensed now. "What did you hear about him?" Despite how long he'd been gone, people had yet to forget or forgive everything he'd done—herself included. She couldn't forgive him for how he'd hurt and humiliated her mother, for how he'd lied to them and for how many other people he'd unjustly sentenced as a judge.

He shrugged. "Someone just mentioned in passing that he was dead."

"Yes, he died in a car accident."

"I'm sorry," he repeated. "That must have been difficult."

"It might have been more difficult if he had lived," she murmured.

"What?" he asked, obviously shocked—his blue eyes wide as he stared down at her.

"It's just…" she sighed "…he had some major legal issues. There was going to be a trial…" She shook her head. "I'd rather not dredge it all up again."

"I've heard that recently, too," he remarked.

"Is that why you don't answer questions?" she wondered. "You don't want to dredge up painful subjects?"

"I definitely don't want to cause pain," he said, and while his choice of words was odd, it was clear he was sincere.

"Your pain or someone else's?" she asked.

"Neither," he said, but then he emitted a soft sigh and added, "Unfortunately that's not always possible."

"Why not?" she asked. "Why can't we all just be

open and honest? That would save everyone a lot of heartache."

"Or cause even more," he said. "Sometimes the truth hurts."

Finding out the truth about her father certainly had, so Aubrey couldn't argue with him. But if only the Honorable Ben Colton hadn't done the things he had in the first place, then there would have been nothing to hide, no dishonor or disgrace...

No pain for any of the people his dishonesty had affected.

Tears stung her eyes, but she blinked them away. She was strong—too strong to dwell in the past over things she couldn't change. That was why her family had started the Truth Foundation—to change the things that they could.

And while Aubrey knew she couldn't change others' decisions, she could change herself. She could make sure she never fell for anyone she didn't fully trust.

And she certainly didn't trust Luke.

Not at all. Even though she was so incredibly attracted to him. That was why moments later, when she stopped outside his cabin, she shook her head when he asked if she wanted to come inside with him.

Just being this close to him—in the small cab of the pickup truck—had her skin hot and tingling with awareness, with attraction...

"No," she said. "That wouldn't be a good idea."

He didn't argue with her—didn't try to convince her. He just nodded in agreement. "You're right."

But why was she right? Because he was a guest who was just passing through, or was there another reason?

Like he was married?

Or a criminal?

Either way, Luke Bishop was a risk Aubrey wasn't willing to take. So she held her breath until he stepped out of the truck cab and closed the door.

Then she released it in a ragged sigh. And she tried to release the temptation to follow him as well. She was entirely too eager to do that.

Luke Bishop wasn't just physically attractive; he was intriguing as well. She wanted to know more about him, but she had a feeling that no matter how much she tried, she was never going to get out of him any answers for her questions. At least not any answers she could trust...

STEPPING OUT OF her truck, shutting the door and walking away from Aubrey Colton had been hard for Luca. He'd had such an enjoyable day with her, working beside her. Seeing how strong and capable she was had attracted him to her even more.

Maybe that was why he'd issued that ridiculous invitation for her to come inside with him. He hadn't wanted the day to end; he'd wanted to spend more time with her, talk to her more, look at her longer...

With no makeup, and her skin chafed from the cold, she was incredibly beautiful, natural and vibrant, and that was so damn sexy to him.

So it was good that she'd turned down his offer, that she'd remained in the truck while he walked to his cabin. She didn't stay in the driveway, though; she backed out and peeled away as if anxious to escape him. Hopefully, he hadn't made her uncomfortable— because even though he knew he couldn't offer her a future or even the present, he wanted to spend more time with her.

Working with her.

Talking with her.

But if he was found again, that would only put her in danger. No. It was better that she'd left. So Luca shook off his disappointment and proceeded to the door.

He wasn't sure why he checked, but before touching the buttons on the electronic lock, he tried the door and found it opened easily. It was not locked now. But he knew he'd locked it that morning, just as he had every time he left the cabin. Just like he had when he'd come out of his shower to find Aubrey inside, looking in his trash.

He'd spent the entire day with her, so she couldn't have been the one to unlock it. And he'd declined maid service when he'd checked in a little over a week ago, so nobody had come in to clean the place.

So who had been inside? Or was the person still there—waiting for him?

If only he had a gun or something he could use as a weapon...

Luca had always used his mind and his words to fight his battles in the past and to protect himself and those he cared about, but he doubted the Camorra had sent someone with whom he could reason his way out of danger.

Not danger. Murder. If the Camorra had sent someone for him, that person had come with Luca's death warrant. He glanced back toward the road, but Aubrey and her truck were gone.

That was good, though; he didn't want her in peril. But was she?

Was *he*?

The person he'd found in his cabin yesterday had been her, and while she'd been with him today, many staff members and her siblings lived in the area as well. Gideon and Jasper had returned before they had, leaving them time to search his cabin before he got back. Aubrey obviously had issues with trust. Because of her father? He resolved to research Aubrey's dad later, when he had time.

Whatever had happened hadn't ruined Aubrey's life; she'd achieved the dream she and her twin had had when they were children. But it might have been the reason she was so distrustful.

Or had another man broken her trust as well?

Or maybe she was just so smart that she knew Luca was hiding something and that he was lying about who he was.

Luca would rather believe that she was the one who had had his place searched. Then that meant that whoever had searched it posed no threat to him, or at least not the same threat the Camorra did. Because Luca was beginning to believe Aubrey posed a threat of another kind.

The kind he'd never encountered before, the kind where he might get attached...where he might fall for her. And that would only wind up hurting when he had to leave.

And he would have to leave...

Even if the Camorra hadn't found him yet, they might if he stayed in one place for too long. If he didn't keep moving around...

He needed to move now. Before pushing open the door, to see if anyone was still there, he looked around the immediate area. The tire tracks from her truck were the only ones in the fluffy, light snow. Luca inspected the steps, but there were no discernible prints from whoever had unlocked the door.

Whoever had gotten inside his place had likely done so a while ago; more than likely they had given up waiting for him and were already gone.

He raised his hand to the door again and pushed it open the rest of the way. The only way he would know was to go inside and check. He drew in a deep breath, just in case he was wrong...in case his intruder had stayed. But when he stepped inside, the cabin was cold and quiet and empty but for his belongings, which had been strewn around the small space. Fortunately, he'd hidden the things she'd found the other day—his laptop, the notebooks, the phones. But someone must have been searching for them, or perhaps for something else.

The doors of the kitchen cabinets had been left open, the drawers overturned. And through the doorway to the bedroom, he could see his clothes strewn around. What had they been looking for?

HE STARED AT the phone, willing it to ring or vibrate with a text…to do anything but remain so damn stubbornly silent.

The assassins were there—more than one—at that dude ranch in Colorado. Surely, Luca wouldn't be able to escape this time. He wasn't that lucky, and he couldn't be as smart as he thought he was, either.

Or he would have figured it out by now…

He would have realized Paolo was betraying him, was helping the Camorra find him.

But he had no choice.

Would Luca realize that as well if he figured it out before he died? Would Luca understand that Paolo couldn't give up his life, even for Luca's?

Paolo had a wife. Well, an ex-wife now…

But he had kids. They were teenagers, and he barely saw them since they lived with their mother. But he had family. He had people who cared about him.

He had Luca.

Except for his mother, Luca had no immediate family of his own; his dad had died when he was just a child. So all he had was his career. His damn career that had caused so many problems, so many arrests and convictions…

And now—soon—it would cause Luca's own death…

Chapter Six

Aubrey had had to speed away from Luke's cabin so she wasn't tempted any more than she already was to stay with him. Or to turn around and go back to him.

When she'd left, the truck tires had spun on the snow-covered road. There wasn't much accumulation yet, just that light dusting—just enough to make the asphalt slick.

So she had to slow down for the rest of the trip to her house. But when she pulled into her driveway, she found another vehicle already parked there, and she wished she'd driven even slower.

Or better yet, that she'd stayed with Luke.

No. This—Warren Parker—was a good reminder of why she'd been smart not to stay with Luke Bishop. Warren was a good reminder that Aubrey shouldn't trust too early or too easily. Or maybe not at all…

Especially when someone avoided answering questions as much as Luke Bishop did. He had to be hiding something. But what?

Warren certainly wasn't hiding anything—because the minute she stepped out of her truck, he threw open the driver's door of his vehicle and ran up to her, reeking of desperation. His brown hair was disheveled, as if he'd been running his hands through it, and dark circles rimmed his brown eyes. "Aubrey, I've been texting you over and over, and you never reply. I've been so worried."

She didn't doubt that he'd been worried, but it hadn't been about her. "There's a reason I don't reply. I don't want to talk to you. So get back in your car and drive out of here."

He widened his eyes as if shocked at her words. "But we meant so much to each other..."

She laughed. "All I meant to you was a way to pay off your debts."

"I didn't take any money from you," he said.

"Because I refused to give you any," she reminded him. She was not a fool. Once he'd asked her to help him out, she'd figured out why he'd been so interested in her and had been so charming—because he'd wanted something from her. And then he'd been so angry that she hadn't fallen in with his plans that he'd actually admitted it.

"I'm not going to lie," he said—which probably indicated that he was. "It would have been nice if you'd given me a loan, if you could have helped me out. But that wasn't why I was with you, Aubrey. I only said that it was because I was upset. I felt rejected by you, and unlike other guys, I think you're beautiful."

"Unlike other guys..." she murmured. This was what he'd started doing with her, gaslighting her into thinking that if she wasn't with him, she would spend the rest of her life alone. Hell, she'd rather spend the rest of her life alone than with a creep like him. She definitely should have blocked his number.

"You know that other guys don't see what I see when I look at you," he said. "I find you attractive just the way you are." He smiled smugly—condescendingly—as if he was doing her a favor.

Her fingers curled into her palm, and she thought about throwing her gloved fist into his face. But from the fading yellow bruises around one of his eyes, it was clear someone else had beat her to beating up him. She shook her head, pitying him now. "You obviously owe someone a lot of money, Warren, but you're not going to manipulate me into giving it to you. So get the hell off my property."

He lurched forward then and gripped her arms. "Aubrey, you know we had something special. You know that you're important to me. Please, give me another chance. Nobody will ever treat you as well as I have. Nobody will ever give you the time and attention that I did."

She snorted. He'd always been busy with a game—playing poker—or watching a game, some sport on which he'd placed bets, that they'd actually spent very little time together over the months they'd dated.

How the hell had he thought she'd fallen for him so hard that she'd pay off his debts? Did he really believe she was as desperate as he was?

That she was so undesirable she'd let him mess with her head and her self-esteem?

She nearly flinched as she felt a twinge of pain over

some of the insults that had been hurled at her in the past. Kids had teased and picked on her in school. Her siblings had stepped in—had tried to protect her—but Aubrey had insisted that the petty remarks didn't bother her. And that she could take care of herself...

And she could and she had. Then and now. She knew better than to let anyone mess with her head or with her heart—like Warren was trying.

"Please, Aubrey," he implored her. "If you gave me another chance, we could have something real here—something lasting..."

She snorted again and shook her head. "Give it up, Warren. You're not fooling me again."

His hands tightened around her arms then, pinching her muscles, even through the thickness of her jacket. She could fight him off. While he was taller than she was, she was stronger—physically as well as mentally. She worked hard, whereas Warren only played hard and not too well.

But then she heard a sound behind her, bootheels crunching over the gravel drive as someone joined them. Had Warren been accompanied by someone else?

Or had someone followed him here?

She could get rid of her ex, but she wasn't sure she could fend off two people. And for the first time, real fear surged through Aubrey when she realized how alone and vulnerable she was.

Even if she screamed, Jasper's house was too far from hers for him to hear her. And Luke's cabin was nearly as far...

Not that Aubrey was looking for anyone to rescue her; she was no damsel in distress.

ANGER COURSED THROUGH LUCA. He'd walked over to Aubrey's house to confront her over his searched cabin, but he'd quickened his pace as soon as he saw her in the distance with another man. He didn't like the way that man was holding Aubrey, his hands wrapped so tight around her arms. And his face was red—either from the cold or from struggling with her. Not that Aubrey appeared to be struggling much.

Was this man her boyfriend?

He certainly wasn't one of her brothers—not with the predatory way he was acting. Then the stranger suddenly released her and doubled over, gasping in pain.

Aubrey whirled around to him, her fists raised and ready to swing.

He held up his hands. "Don't hit me."

Though with the way the other man coughed and sputtered, Luca suspected she hadn't hit him with her fists but with her knee. Between gasps of pain, the man whined, "Aubrey, sweetheart, why did you do that…"

"Sweetheart…"

Who the hell was this simpering fool?

"You know why, Warren. Get in your car, get off my property and leave me the hell alone!"

"It was all a misunderstanding," the guy insisted. "You and I have too much going for us to give up so easily."

Clearly this person wasn't willing to give up easily, no matter how emphatically Aubrey told him she wanted nothing to do with him. Luca's heart lifted at the thought of that, and that sick feeling churning in his stomach when he'd seen her in the arms of another man was gone.

"Darling," Luca said to her. "Who is this man? And why is he bothering you?"

She arched a blond brow above the rim of her glasses. *"Darling?"*

"Yes," Luca said, infusing his tone with affection along with confusion. "Doesn't he realize that you're seeing me now, that you've moved on?"

Finally the man turned toward Luca, and his dark eyes widened as he stared him up and down. "You're— you're her boyfriend?" he asked, skepticism in his voice and in his beady eyes.

With all his traveling and riding, Luca knew he had lost some weight; he probably looked skinny, and with the silver creeping in at his temples and in his scruff, he probably appeared a whole lot older than Aubrey. But she hadn't looked at him last night, when he'd been wearing nothing but a towel, like she'd found him undesirable. While she might not feel the attraction for him that Luca felt for her, she hadn't been completely unaffected.

Was she still hung up on this guy—despite her rejection of his appeals for another chance?

That feeling was back, that sick jealousy swirling inside him. Luca closed the distance between himself and Aubrey. He slid his arm around her shoulders and pulled her against his side. "Yes, I am her boyfriend," he lied. "So do as the lady told you and get the hell off her property."

"Don't make me call security, Warren," she warned.

"That won't be necessary," Luca said, and he dropped his arm from her shoulders. He stepped closer to the other man, who still couldn't stand up straight after she'd kneed him in the groin. "I will get rid of him..."

Already injured, Warren must not have been spoiling for another fight, because he finally moved toward his car, his hand shaking as he reached for the door handle. But then he turned back to say, "Aubrey, you can't be serious about this guy. You and I haven't been broken up long enough for you to have gotten to know him well. Obviously he's just after your money."

"Like you were, Warren?" she asked. "Give it up. You're not getting a dime out of me. You're going to need to find another way to pay off your debts."

His jaw clenched as if he was grinding his teeth, but he didn't argue with her. He only glared at Luca before pulling open his door and sliding behind the wheel.

Not trusting Warren to not try to run him down, Luca reached out and tugged Aubrey with him toward the porch on the front of her house. Then he kept his arm wrapped around her while the guy drove off, feeling her body tremble slightly against his.

"Are you all right?" he asked with concern. "Did he hurt you?"

She snorted dismissively. "He's the one hurting right now."

But Luca wasn't so sure that she hadn't been harmed as well. "You're shaking."

"I'm just cold," she said. But instead of snuggling into him—into his warmth—she pulled away and opened the door to her house.

When Luca had found that someone had searched his cabin again, he'd been so hot with anger toward her that he hadn't felt the cold on his fast walk from his place to hers. And when he'd seen how that man was holding her, his temperature had gone up even higher. So he didn't mind standing outside on the porch even with the wind picking up. "Who the hell is that man?"

"A mistake," she murmured. Even though she'd opened the door, she had yet to step inside what looked like a big, open room. Instead she turned back to look at him. "And a reminder to be very careful about who I trust..."

"Is that why you had someone search my place again?" he asked.

Above the rims of her glasses, her brow furrowed. "What are you talking about?"

"While we were out moving the cattle, someone broke into my cabin again. They must have been looking for something."

"Again?" she asked.

"Have you already forgotten that I caught you searching it yesterday?"

Her gaze slid away from his and she turned to step inside her house. In case she was going to shut him out, he stepped forward—making sure he got his foot in the door before she could close it on him. Not that he suspected that would stop her if she really wanted to get rid of him...

Remembering what she'd done to her ex-boyfriend, Luca braced himself for a blow or a well-placed knee. But instead she opened the door wider and said, "Get inside. It's freezing."

The snowflakes were still fat and light, but they were starting to fall harder now. The storm that was forecast was intensifying, along with Luca's attraction to Aubrey Colton. He wasn't certain he should join her inside, just as she'd been reluctant to be alone with him in his cabin.

But if she really hadn't been the one who'd searched his place, he needed to know—because he needed to leave Gemini Ranch before anyone got hurt. So he followed her into her house. With its wood beams and rustic furnishings, it reflected her earthy, no-nonsense style.

She headed toward the stone hearth in the center of the great room and started a fire. Then she held out her hands to the flickering flames that reminded him of other blazes.

That B and B in Toronto…that hotel in Wisconsin.

Nobody had been hurt in either fire. But it could have been bad. Innocent people could have died because Camorra assassins had committed arsons to kill him.

"I shouldn't be here," he said as a sudden pressure settled on his chest, on his lungs, making it hard to breathe.

"You invited me to come into your cabin earlier," she reminded him.

"And you were smart to turn me down," he admitted.

She sighed. "I'm not always smart, or I never would

have dated such a loser. You didn't have to act like that…"

He cocked his head. "Like what?" Like a jealous idiot?

"Like you're my boyfriend," she said. "He didn't believe it, anyway."

"Why not?" he asked. "Am I not your type?"

She tilted her head and studied him. "Unfortunately, you probably are…"

"Tall, dark and handsome?" he teased her.

"Not entirely open or honest," she corrected him.

And he flinched but he couldn't deny it.

"That's not what he meant, though," she said. "He's always been disparaging about my appearance."

Luca's jaw dropped. "What? That man is definitely a liar. How dare he insult you!" And now he wished he had hit Warren. Hard.

She shrugged, but it was as if a burden still remained on her shoulders. "He just tries to mess with my mind, tries to make me think that nobody else will want me but him. And he only wants my money—"

"Then he's an idiot as well as a liar," Luca said, his outrage boiling over. "How can he not see how beautiful you are? How amazing?"

Her eyes narrowed behind her lenses. "Aren't you laying it on a bit thick?"

He stepped forward then and tipped up her face to his. "You are so beautiful. Your eyes such a deep blue and so full of intelligence. Your body…" his mouth dried out just thinking about it, about her curves "…is strong and sexy…"

Her eyes widened with surprise, as her pupils dilated. She leaned forward a bit, as if waiting for him to kiss her. He wanted to, so badly, but when he began to lower his head toward hers, she pulled back and dislodged his hand from her chin. "You don't have to say this…"

"I don't have to," he agreed. "But it's true, and I hope you know it and that you would never let a creep like Warren affect your self-esteem."

She shook her head. "Of course not. I wouldn't…"

"But what?" he asked because he heard the *but* in her voice, the reluctance to let the man's awful comments go.

"When I was growing up, I got picked on sometimes," she admitted. "Girls can be cruel…" She shrugged again. "It's nothing. I didn't let it get to me then, and I certainly won't let Warren Parker get to me now."

"I'm so glad you kneed him," he said. "I wish you had done it so hard that he couldn't have walked, though."

"But then he wouldn't have been able to leave," she pointed out. And she clearly had wanted him gone as badly as Luca had.

"And he'd better stay away," Luca said.

Her lips curved into a slight smile. "You know you're not really my boyfriend, right? You don't have to act like you're jealous."

Luca released a shaky sigh. "The sad part is that I'm not acting…" And he couldn't remember the last time— if ever—that he'd felt jealousy like this.

The smile slid away from her mouth. "But you're

not my boyfriend," she repeated. "Remember—I want someone that I can trust completely."

His heart ached that he couldn't be that man, but there was so much that he couldn't tell her, that he couldn't share with her, without putting her in danger. He glanced toward the door now, wondering if her life was in peril just because of him coming here to Gemini Ranch and now to her house.

What if whoever had been in his place had hung around and followed him here? But if the Camorra had sent someone, they wouldn't have been hired to just follow him. They would've been hired to kill him.

"You really didn't have my cabin searched while we were out today?" he asked.

She shook her head but then slowly added, "At least not intentionally..."

"But?"

"I might have asked one of my brothers to check into you," she said. "And they can be overly protective."

Alarm struck his heart. But his new identity was solid; Italian authorities had helped him with all the documentation. "Gideon?" He'd had time to search the cabin; he and Jasper had returned earlier than they had.

She shook her head. "I didn't ask Gideon to check into you. He's a social worker. I have other brothers. One of them is an FBI agent."

He shrugged as if it didn't matter. But it did...

How much could the FBI find out about him? Would just an inquiry alert the Camorra to where he was? He needed to leave the ranch, he knew—for his sake and most especially for hers. But there was something he needed to do first, a temptation he could no longer resist.

So he leaned down again and brushed his mouth across Aubrey's soft lips. And he braced himself for her to hurt him the way she had her ex-boyfriend.

But instead, she kissed him back, her lips moving over and clinging to his. And Luca knew he was going to get hurt even worse than if she'd kneed him.

DOMINIC'S PHONE RANG—the cell for which only a select few people had the number. He had that device because he was about to go undercover again, and he couldn't take the other one, which might lead someone back to all the important contacts in his life: his family.

"Yeah?" he answered with his usual caution. He hadn't been given the new assignment yet. He was still doing the paperwork and interviews to wrap up the last one.

"Agent Colton?"

He recognized the voice of the supervisory special agent. "Yes, this is Colton."

"You've been asking around about someone…"

Around? He'd asked a couple of other agents, his international connections. "I made some inquiries about a Luke Bishop," he admitted. "I know I didn't have much to go on…" So he hadn't expected much, certainly not a call back from a bureau supervisor.

"There's one strong possibility for the Luke Bishop you're inquiring about," the supervisor said. "One guy who seems to have just materialized less than a year ago."

Dominic sucked in a breath, surprised that Aubrey's *feeling* about her mysterious guest had been right.

"What's your interest in this, Colton? Did you suspect that he could be on the wanted list?"

Dominic's pulse quickened. He sure as hell hoped Bishop wasn't on any such list, not when the man was staying at Gemini Ranch, and especially not when his sister seemed very curious about him. "Just checking him out over someone else's suspicions."

Maybe Aubrey should have gone into law enforcement—she obviously had good instincts. She had been hurt before, though, by that idiot Warren Parker. After that unfortunate experience, she was obviously being more cautious.

"Is he on the wanted listed?" Dominic asked.

"We won't know unless we figure out who he really is," the supervisor said. "It feels like this is a new identity. There's the possibility, I guess, that he could be in witness protection, but the US Marshals aren't usually very forthcoming with information about WITSEC."

Dominic knew one marshal who would be, especially when she learned that the information was for their sister. But he wasn't going to give up that connection to his supervisor.

"Can you forward me what you found?" Dominic asked. "I'll make some more queries."

"Let me know what you turn up."

"Of course," Dominic said. But his supervisor wouldn't be the first person he notified; his sister would be. Or maybe Jasper...

Because Aubrey would confront this Luke Bishop

with whatever she learned—no matter how dangerous he might be—while Jasper would be cautious.

After disconnecting that call, Dominic picked up his other phone and called one of those personal contacts.

"Dominic, are you okay?" Alexa Colton answered, her voice full of concern. As a marshal, she knew how dangerous his job could be—which unsettled Dominic as much as it did her.

He didn't like that his baby sister had gone into a dangerous profession as well. "I'm fine," he assured her. "You?"

"Of course. I can take care of myself," Alexa replied, her voice sharp with defensiveness.

He hoped that she was right, that she could.

"Is that why you called?" she asked. "To check up on me?"

"No," he said. "I want you to check up on a man called Luke Bishop."

"Who's he?"

"That's what I would like to know. I'm going to forward you what's been dug up about him so far," he said. "I want to know if he's in WITSEC."

"I can't tell you if he is—"

"It's for Aubrey," he interrupted her protest. "She asked me to check him out."

"Why?"

"He's a guest at the ranch."

"Has she ever had you check out a guest before?" Alexa asked.

"No."

They both knew what that meant—that Aubrey was interested in this guy. Something was going on.

"Okay, send me what you have, and I'll let you know what I find out," she told him. "In the meantime, tell Aubrey to stay away from him. Even if he's in WIT-SEC, that doesn't mean he's one of the good guys. He could have just made a deal to flip on his partners to save himself some prison time."

"I know…" No matter who Luke Bishop was, his curiously new identity made him too dangerous for Aubrey to be around him.

Chapter Seven

What the hell had she done?

Aubrey flopped around again on her bed, her body aching with longing. How had she sent Luke away after that kiss? How had she found the willpower to push him back and tell him it was time for him to leave?

She'd offered him the truck to drive back to his cabin, but he'd insisted he needed the cold air. And she had been able to imagine why—for the same reason she'd taken a cool shower after he left.

But still her skin had been hot with desire, her body tense with need. How had just a kiss affected her so much?

Because it hadn't been just a kiss. It had been like an explosion. The minute his mouth brushed across hers, the attraction that simmered between them had burst into a passion so hot and fierce that it had felt like a flashfire.

And she would have let it burn her alive in that moment…if she hadn't felt the vibration of her phone. Somebody had been calling or texting her, and that interruption had brought her back to her senses.

She'd suspected it was Warren, trying to whine and manipulate her into giving him that second chance and probably a significant loan. And that had reminded her of her poor judgment, that for some reason she was only attracted to men that she couldn't—or shouldn't—trust.

Maybe she had more daddy issues than she'd realized after what her father had done, the double life Ben Colton had led. All those thoughts had tumbled through her mind and doused that conflagration of desire like a bucket of ice water.

But even though she'd found the strength to send Luke away, she hadn't been able to stop thinking about him or to stop wanting him, and so she'd spent a restless night flopping around on her bed while outside the wind howled.

The storm was beginning to intensify. There wouldn't be much time to move the rest of the cattle. So at the first light of dawn, she gave up trying to sleep and jumped out of bed. She dressed quickly and skipped breakfast, her stomach still too unsettled to eat. But she packed some food, leftovers from the kitchen at the main lodge, into a backpack. She didn't need to worry about keeping any of it cold, not with how much the temperature had dropped. She slung the backpack over her shoulder and headed out to her truck. Once she'd brushed off the snow and warmed it up, she reached for her cell phone to let Jasper know she was heading to the barn. When she glanced at the screen, she saw that the call she'd missed the night before hadn't been from Warren but from Dominic.

Her pulse accelerated. Had the FBI agent found out

something already about Luke? Had he been the one who'd searched her guest's cabin the day before? She'd thought he was in Denver, though, so maybe he'd enlisted Jasper or Gideon to carry out his orders.

Jasper would have been able to access the code for the lock on Luke's cabin as easily as she had. Or maybe the receptionist, knowing Gideon was her brother, had given him the code.

The woman also often stepped away from her desk without locking her computer, so anyone in the main lodge might have been able to access it—if they'd found her away from her desk.

Not that it mattered who'd searched it. Dominic must have found out something that he wanted to share with her. And she was stalling instead of calling him back...

She didn't want to know because she had a horrible feeling—like she'd had when her gaze had first locked with Luke's—that it wasn't going to be good. Otherwise, she doubted that Dominic would have sent a text reading:

Need to talk to you ASAP.

Cursing beneath her breath, Aubrey punched in Dominic's number. But she put the cell on speaker so that she could shift the truck into Reverse and back out of her driveway.

Despite the early hour, Dominic answered immediately and with obvious concern in his deep voice. "Where have you been?"

"Sleeping," she replied—even though it was a lie.

She wished she'd been able to doze because today was going to be a long day. "Why'd you call so late?"

"Because you asked me to do you a favor," he reminded her.

"And you found out something about Luke…" He wouldn't have called had he not. Dread settled heavily in the pit of her empty stomach.

"Not really," he said. "There isn't much to find out about a man who just came into existence less than a year ago."

"What do you mean?" she asked. Luke had to be close to forty.

"That's as far back as he can be traced. Born in Naples to American parents, per his birth certificate and social security card, but…"

"So that means you've traced him back to his birth," she pointed out.

"Nope. No activity on that social security number with his date of birth until less than a year ago," Dominic said. "Your instincts were right. There's a whole lot to mistrust about this guy. He's obviously hiding something."

"Or maybe *he's* the one who's hiding," she murmured. That would explain his requesting the cabin farthest away from the main lodge, how he used all cash and made no calls but for maybe the ones on the cell phones he'd destroyed. She slowed the truck as she neared where Luke was staying.

"From what?" Dominic asked her. "From the authorities or from bad guys?"

She thought of how Luke had offered to help with

the cattle, how hard he'd worked the day before, how he'd jumped to her defense last night with Warren and how when she'd pushed him away, he hadn't pressed her for more.

He'd respected her wish for him to leave. Unlike Warren, who kept trying to manipulate her into doing what he wanted.

I wish you could...

Maybe she had heard that correctly, what he'd replied when she'd assured him she would keep him alive while they moved the cattle.

"I would say he's hiding from bad guys," she said as she stopped beside his cabin.

"Why? Because he might have turned against them to save himself a prison sentence? Even if he's in witness relocation, that doesn't make him a good person," Dominic warned her. "You need to stay far away from him. Far, far away from him, Aubrey."

But just then the door to the cabin opened and Luke stepped out and walked toward the truck, getting closer and closer until he touched the handle. She hadn't unlocked it.

Yet. But she intended to. She intended to ignore her brother's advice because she suspected the only way to find out the truth about Luke Bishop was to stick close to him.

Very close...

"Thanks, Dominic," she said. And she clicked off the cell just as he was starting to speak again. Then as she unlocked the passenger door, she powered off the phone.

She didn't want Dominic calling again or texting

while she was with Luke. While her mysterious guest already knew she had her brother checking him out, she didn't want him to know what he'd found, or, actually, what he hadn't found.

A past…

Luke Bishop didn't have one. So who was he really?

WHILE SHE'D UNLOCKED the truck door for him that morning, Aubrey had locked Luca out in other ways. She'd barely spoken to him since she picked him up, and whenever he glanced at her, either in the barn or while riding, she wouldn't meet his gaze. It was as if she couldn't stand to look at him.

Maybe she was just intent on herding in the cattle. Or maybe she was embarrassed about what had happened the night before or could have happened had she not come to her senses. He should have been relieved that she had—because he'd been so overcome with desire that he hadn't been able to think at all, let alone rationally.

Realistically, he knew that he should leave—just in case that hadn't been one of her siblings who'd searched his cabin. Just in case the Camorra had somehow tracked him down once again…

And if one of its killers had…

Well, he wasn't willing to face that suspicion yet although it niggled at the edge of his consciousness, just as his desire for Aubrey niggled inside him, making him tense and edgy. Or maybe that was because he hadn't slept at all the night before.

He hadn't been able to stop tasting her on his lips,

the sweetness of her mouth. He hadn't been able to stop feeling the heat and softness of her body pressed against his.

Despite the wind whipping around them, hurling sharp chunks of snow at their faces, heat flashed through Luca. Even though he knew she'd done the right thing last night when she pushed him away, he wished that she hadn't—that he could at least be with her once before he had to leave.

But that wouldn't be fair to her. Or to him—because it would make it even harder for him to say goodbye to her.

And the ranch...

He wasn't bored anymore. Moving cattle was hard work, especially with the storm coming at them full force now, but it was satisfying in a way nothing had satisfied him since filing his last exposé.

"Luke!" Aubrey called out, shouting over the roar of the wind.

And he tensed in his saddle at the alarm in her voice. "What is it?"

"Listen," she said.

They were moving the last of the livestock from a pasture near the mountains, its peaks now hidden by white. Only a few cows remained between him and Aubrey; he urged the last of them through the open fence.

She turned back, her head cocked as she listened. He couldn't hear anything over the wind. But she headed back, urging her horse in the wrong direction—into the swirling snow and the wind.

"Aubrey!" he yelled back at her. But she kept going. So he nudged his horse with his knees and followed her.

She stopped her horse and dismounted. The minute her boots hit the ground; she was crouching down—digging through a snowdrift.

He slid off his horse and squatted down next to her. "What are you doing?"

Then he heard it, too, the pitiful cry, so weak and soft…

How had Aubrey heard it? She used her gloves to wipe the ice off what he quickly realized was a small body: a calf.

There had been a few other calves, born early but healthy, among the cattle they'd moved, but not one like this, separated from the others.

Luca glanced around. "Where is its mother?"

She shrugged. "I don't know. Maybe we moved it yesterday…" Her voice cracked with emotion, with concern that they'd separated the baby from the dam. It was small, smaller than the other ones they'd found with their mothers in the herd yesterday. Maybe it had been born prematurely.

Many of the cows they were moving were about to give birth, which was yet another reason Aubrey had wanted them closer. So that if there were complications, she would be able to get a veterinarian to aid them.

Maybe there had been a complication with this birth and the dam had passed. He glanced around, looking for the mother while Aubrey moved her hands over the calf, trying to warm it. "We need to get it to the barn," she said.

He nodded. "We can head back now, keep the cattle moving that direction…"

He stood up then and turned toward his horse. He intended to climb into the saddle and have Aubrey hand him the calf. But when he closed his hands over the saddle horn, gunshots rang out.

THE CAMORRA MUST have sent amateurs before him. Because Luca Rossi hadn't been nearly as hard to kill as he'd been warned that he was.

The only thing that was hard about this hit was the elements.

That damn snow fell so fast and hard now that he couldn't be entirely sure if Rossi was really dead or just injured and unable to move. But Rossi and that woman weren't the only ones in this area, so he couldn't risk getting close enough to check his body.

Somebody might see him. Like maybe that woman. He hadn't aimed at her. She'd been crouched on the ground, looking at something, so he hadn't worried about her seeing him. But if he got closer, she might.

Hell, she could even be armed because she was one of the property owners. The other one was out here somewhere, too, with other hands. The gunshots could bring them all riding over here.

So he had to leave now—before someone saw him. But he took one more look through the scope, to make sure, and he saw not one but two bodies, lying prostrate on the ground, not moving. Maybe he'd hit them both…

Chapter Eight

Last night Aubrey had longed for this, to feel the weight of Luke Bishop's body lying atop hers. But she hadn't imagined those circumstances, that he would have knocked her flat onto her back on the cold, snow-covered ground.

"What the hell are you doing…" she murmured into his shoulder. She'd heard the shot, too. But it sounded like it had been a distance away, probably another ranch away.

But then she remembered Dominic's call and warning. Was someone after Luke Bishop? Had they killed him?

His body was heavy on hers, hard and unmoving. "Luke!" she exclaimed, gripping his shoulders now with her gloved hands, like she'd gripped the calf. It lay next to them, crying out weakly for its mother. "Are you all right?"

His hair brushed her cheek when he nodded. At least she hoped he nodded.

"Luke?" she asked again. "Are you sure?"

"Yes, I'm fine. Are you?" he asked, his breath warm against her cheek.

Her heart was beating fast and hard, and it was hard to breathe—either because of his weight pressed on top of her or because he'd knocked the wind out of her when he'd slammed her down so abruptly.

He braced his gloved hands beside her and levered himself up, but he remained crouched, glancing around as if he expected more shots to be fired.

She wasn't sure what to expect. Had someone purposely fired at them? And was that person out there yet? Then she heard the rumble of an engine. This far out from passable roads, it couldn't have been a vehicle; it must have been a snowmobile.

Luke must have heard it, too, because he stood up straight and peered around—as if trying to see through the snow. But the rumble was growing fainter as it drove away from them.

"Whoever it was who fired those shots must be leaving," she said, and she jumped up from the ground before the snow got her any colder. Like the poor calf…

She reached for it next, gathering it up in her arms again. "We need to get this little guy back to the barn before he freezes to death." And he probably wasn't going to be the only one.

"Are you really okay?" Luke asked, and from the gruffness of his voice, clearly he was not. The gunshots had shaken him up.

She was trembling, but she didn't know if that was from the cold or in reaction to those shots. "I don't think the bullets came anywhere near us," she said. "It must have been another rancher shooting at a coyote or a mountain lion." Her arms tightened around the calf. "Maybe that's what happened to this one's mama…"

Or, hopefully, they would find the dam already back at the ranch, in the pasture close to the indoor ring.

"We need to get back," Luke agreed as he swung his long body back onto his horse. Used to gunshots from hunters, their horses hadn't moved—hadn't reacted the way Luke had.

"Why did you react like that?" she asked. "Why would you assume someone was shooting at us? At you?" Who was he really?

He shrugged. "I think anyone who's lived in a big city knows to duck when you hear gunshots. It's instinct."

He hadn't just ducked, though. He'd knocked her flat and then covered her body with his, protecting her. Thinking first of her safety before his own.

He couldn't be the bad man her brother Dominic was worried that he was. No matter Luke Bishop's real identity, she doubted that he was a danger to her physically.

Now, emotionally…

He held out his arms. "Hand the calf up to me," he said. "I'll carry him back."

As Aubrey lifted the cold little animal, Luke opened his jacket and pulled the calf tight against his body— to keep it warm.

Her blood raced and she felt her face flush. And then Aubrey knew that Luke might just be a very serious threat to her heart.

Luca wasn't sure if Aubrey really believed that had just been another rancher firing at some threat to his livestock. He just knew that he didn't believe it. Those shots had sounded too close, too purposeful for him to think there had been anything innocent about them.

At least the snowmobile sounded as if it had driven away from them, not toward them. But that didn't mean that the shooter wasn't somewhere out there yet, between them and the barn—waiting to try for them again.

So Luke made certain to stick close to Aubrey as they drove the last of the livestock back toward the pastures closer to the barn. But with his arms wrapped around the weak calf, Luke wasn't sure how he would be able to protect Aubrey.

Or himself...

His arms strained from carrying the animal. Calves weren't born little: he knew that from his days of working on ranches, during his university breaks, in the Province of Isernia, not far from Naples. This one had to be close to eighty pounds, but Aubrey had managed to lift it up to him without much effort.

She was strong. He'd already known that. She was also fearless because she didn't seem as shaken as he was by their close call.

Or was it just that she hadn't realized how close it was?

With the wind blowing and the snow whipping around them, it was hard to hear—hard to see...

Yet she'd heard the calf and had found it in the snow. She was sharp, so sharp that he wondered maybe if

he had overreacted. Maybe the shots hadn't been anywhere near them.

Maybe he hadn't endangered her life with his presence. Yet…

But he worried that the Camorra would find him,
just as they had in the past. Someone had to be giving
him up, betraying him.

"Luke!" Aubrey yelled.

And he tensed, worried that she'd heard something
he hadn't again. Like the snowmobile…

"What?" he called back to her.

"Are you all right?"

He nodded.

"The calf isn't getting too heavy?"

He shook his head.

"We have a distance to go yet," she said, "and the
weather is getting worse…"

The storm was definitely as bad as had been predicted. With his jacket open, he would have frozen,
if not for the relative warmth of the animal cradled in
his arms.

"Stick close," she told him. "It's getting to near
whiteout conditions, and I don't want you to get lost."

While night was a few hours off, there wasn't much
light shining through the sheets of snow falling on them.
Maybe the shooter wasn't the worst danger right now.

Maybe the storm was…

THE CHANDELIERS, DANGLING from the rafters of the two-
story great room, flickered as the power threatened
to go out. If it did, the backup generators would kick

on. They wouldn't be without electricity or heat at the main lodge.

Which was good since Jasper was still freezing. With the help of some ranch hands, he'd moved the last of the cattle from the pastures near the mountains. Aubrey and Luke had been working nearby, but the only people he'd seen, besides the other ranch hands, were some snowmobilers. A group of guests had gone on a guided excursion. But Jasper had been worried, with the storm intensifying, that the guests might get separated and into some trouble out there. So after putting away his horse, he'd hurried up to the main lodge to make sure they'd all returned safely.

Trisha, the snowmobiling guide, nodded, but then sheepishly admitted, "Several of them got separated from the main group for a while, but I made sure they all returned to the equipment shed. It was hard to see out there, and the snowmobiles just seemed to whip up the precipitation even more."

The young woman, a recent college grad with a degree in hospitality, stood beside Jasper in front of the giant stone fireplace. Her face was chafed from the cold like Jasper's probably was. His skin felt raw—at least what he could feel; he'd gotten so cold that he'd gone numb in some places.

"Did you hear the gunshots?" she asked.

Jasper tensed with concern. "Gunshots?" he echoed.

She nodded. "A few of the guests mentioned them. I thought I heard something, but with as loud as the machines are and then the wind…" She shrugged. "I'm not sure what it was…"

Gunshots?

Hunters weren't likely to be out during a blizzard, unless they weren't tracking animals…

He shook his head at the leap his imagination had taken to the worst-case scenario. The storm must have been getting to him.

The lights flickered again before going out. Some of the guests sitting in the great room gasped, while some chuckled. It was early evening yet, but night was close, so thick shadows darkened the lodge until the generators fired up.

He glanced around the room. Aubrey wasn't here. But then, she hadn't come up to the main lodge after getting back yesterday, either.

Maybe she had safely returned. But he needed to know for certain, so he grabbed his cell and tried calling her. But his phone stayed dead, the screen blank.

Either he'd run down the battery or lost a signal.

Probably both. So he walked over to the reception area and used a landline to call her house. The phone rang a few times before her voice mail picked up. He hung up before leaving a message, and then he called the extension in the barn.

"Gemini Ranch," Kayla answered the phone.

He recognized her voice, and his pulse quickened. But he was sure it was just with concern—for his twin. "Kayla, have you seen Aubrey?"

"No. I was going to wait for her to get back—"

"She's not back yet?"

"No." And now there was concern in her voice. "She and that guest—Luke Bishop—are both still out there."

He cursed. He should have checked on them while they were out in the storm, made sure they got back safely. If something had happened to her...

But he couldn't let his mind go there, either. Aubrey knew how to handle herself in any conditions.

"Do you want me to go out and look for them?" she asked.

"No!" he replied emphatically. "I don't want you getting lost out there."

"I would not get lost," Kayla replied, just as emphatically.

Maybe she wouldn't—she knew the ranch well. "I haven't been back that long, so I know how nasty it is out there," he said. "Don't go looking for them. I'm sure they're on their way back."

But what was taking them so long? Of course Aubrey had insisted that she would move the cattle from the pastures that were the farthest out. Jasper should have stood his ground, but he knew all too well that his twin usually won their arguments.

"Then I'll just wait and make sure they return safely," she said.

He looked out the windows at the snow swirling around the lodge in a thick white cloud. "No," he said. "You should get back to the bunkhouse or come up here to the main lodge. You don't want to get stranded out in the barn."

There was enough heat to keep the animals comfortable, but it wasn't warm enough for humans, except maybe in the tack room. But the small heater wasn't likely to warm the entire long room that was filled with saddles and other equipment.

"I'll go to my room in the bunkhouse," Kayla said.

"And be careful getting there," he advised. "It's pretty much whiteout conditions right now." Even the lights of the pickup truck wouldn't do much to help her see in this weather.

"I'll be fine," she said, her voice terse with defensiveness.

That was how his sister got, too, as if worrying about them meant that you didn't think they were as strong or tough as they were when all it really meant was that you cared...

Not that he cared about Kayla as anything other than an employee, but still he didn't want anything to happen to her.

She must have thought their conversation was over because she hung up on him. While he suspected Kayla could make it safely to the bunkhouse, he was worried about Aubrey and Luke, who'd been so far from the main buildings of the ranch.

Had they gotten lost out in the blizzard?

But Aubrey knew the ranch so well that she would have been able to make it back to the barn blindfolded.

But then another thought occurred to him...

What if the guests had been right? What if shots had been fired? And what if one of the bullets had struck Luke or Aubrey?

Then they could be out there, hurt and freezing.

Or worse...

Chapter Nine

The wind hurled snow and ice against the barn as Aubrey fought to close the doors. Since Luke had been holding on to the calf, she was the one who'd jumped down from her horse to open the doors and to hold them open for him to enter with his burden. But when she'd jumped down, her body frozen from the cold, she'd nearly collapsed into the snow. But she'd managed and Luke had led her horse inside while he rode his and carried the calf. They were both in the barn now.

She continued her battle, the snow swirling through the doors and adding to the accumulation already on her hat and in her hair and scarf. But she couldn't quite get the doors shut. Then another body was there, pressing against the door beside her. With Luke's help, they shut and barred the entrance, and the wind outside seemed to howl even louder in protest.

Shaking with cold, she turned toward Luke and saw that he was shaking, too, his arms jerking even as they dangled at his sides.

"Are you okay?" she asked with concern, her voice hoarse from the cold.

He didn't reply, just nodded, and snow fell from the brim of his hat.

"Your arms…"

Because he'd held the calf all the way from the pasture to the barn, he must have been having muscles spasms in his arms now. He'd carried the animal the entire trip back without complaint, even refusing when Aubrey had offered to take a turn. She'd thought at the time that he might not have heard her—with the way the wind had been shrieking and how hard the snow had been falling. If they hadn't stayed close to each other, they all might have been lost. She wanted to throw her arms around him and hug him close and not just for warmth. But she resisted the temptation, knowing they had to take care of the animals.

"I'm okay," he insisted, then he turned away and headed down the wide aisle. He stepped around the saddles he'd taken from the horses while she'd been struggling to close the doors. The animals were in their stalls, where Kayla must have left them fresh food and hay. The blankets spread over them must have been Luke's doing. He continued past to the stall where he'd left the calf, lying on fresh hay. He dropped to his knees beside it and reached out, using his gloved hands to rub its snow-covered coat.

"I…" She had no words for how impressed she was, for how he'd gone above and beyond what she could have expected of a paid ranch hand, let alone one of their guests. "I…"

He turned toward her. "Are you okay?" he asked.

No. She wasn't. She was in trouble—real trouble

with Luke Bishop. But she couldn't admit that to him, so she focused instead on the calf. "Just worried about this little guy…" And herself.

She bustled around, gathering supplies. Within minutes she had a bottle ready for the calf and a warm blanket and some feed. "Now that I see him in here, out of the blizzard, I think he's a little older than I initially did," she said with some relief.

"That's good," Luke murmured.

She continued talking, more to reassure herself than to explain anything he probably already knew. "I think his mother must have nursed him for at least a week or so. He's had his colostrum, so his immune system will have started. He's more likely to survive…"

But he wasn't moving yet. His eyes were closed now, maybe in deference to the snow earlier. Luke had rubbed the ice from the calf's face and from his coat while she was fixing the bottle and gathering the other supplies. She pressed the nipple of the bottle to the baby animal's lips. At first he didn't react, didn't move, and she worried that they might already be too late to save the little guy. But then he latched on and suckled, albeit weakly, on the bottle.

"He's definitely nursed before," Luke agreed, and his breath shuddered out in a sigh of relief.

The calf tried to nuzzle then against the bottle, knocking it from Aubrey's hand. She picked it up and held it again, and Luke's big hand wrapped around hers, helping her hold it.

They both wore gloves, so they weren't really touching—at least not skin to skin—but she was still affected.

Still so incredibly attracted to him…

Hell, after today, after he'd thrown his body across hers to protect her and then been so gentle with the calf…

She was *more* than attracted to him.

But she couldn't be. She shouldn't be…

Not after Dominic had warned her. With the limited activity under the Luke Bishop that Dom had found with her guest's approximate age and description, that was probably not even his real name. So who was he?

And why had he automatically assumed that those gunshots were meant for him?

Was someone trying to end his life? And why?

Because of what they'd done or because of what he'd done?

She couldn't believe that this man who'd protected her, who'd carried the calf through a blizzard, was a bad person. Even now, as he watched the calf nurse, his light blue eyes brimmed with concern and tenderness.

The animal slurped the last of the milk from the bottle and continued tugging at the nipple, making it squeak.

And Luke chuckled, a deep, throaty sound that made Aubrey's pulse quicken.

"I brought some calf starter, too," she said, and she pulled out the mixture of minerals and vitamins and ground oats, soybean meal, molasses and cracked corn. She poured some into her glove and held it out.

The calf must not have had any of the starter yet because he didn't sniff at it, didn't try to eat it, just swung his head back and forth as he searched around for more milk.

"You need this, too, little guy," she said, and she pressed her hand against his mouth.

His tongue swiped out and across her glove, taking some of the mixture into his mouth. Then he swiped at it again and again. And as he nibbled at the mixture and her glove, she giggled.

Then he began to push his hooves against the stall floor until his legs straightened and he stood up and stumbled toward her, nuzzling against her. And she laughed with relief.

Luke's chuckle echoed hers. "Look at him! He's going to be okay!"

Since she was sitting on the ground, the calf was in her face, so she couldn't see anything but the animal. But she wanted to look at Luke instead, so she poured more starter mix onto the floor. Then she turned toward Luke and threw her arms around his shoulders.

"Thank you! Thank you!" she exclaimed. "You saved him. You're amazing..." And he was—whoever the hell he was—he had to be a good man because he'd done this.

Luca closed his arms around her, his gloved hands clutching the back of her jacket. He wanted to hold on to her forever. But he knew that he couldn't.

That he would have to let her go. That he would have to leave her.

He wanted to believe, like she seemed to, that the shots that had been fired had been just another rancher protecting his cattle. He wanted to believe that so badly, so that he could stay, so that he could think he was safe yet and so was she.

He wanted to stay at Gemini Ranch with her as long as he could, wanted to spend time with her no matter where they were or what they were doing—even moving cattle during a blizzard.

And rescuing a calf...

His arms ached from carrying it all the way back, but his efforts had been worth it. To see the little guy start moving like he was...

And to witness Aubrey's joy over the success of their rescue...

And to feel it. Her happiness warmed him as if the sun was shining brightly on him, but instead of warming him from the outside in, she warmed him from the inside out. He'd been frozen for so long—even before they'd been out in that storm. He'd been emotionally reserved for years, not allowing himself to feel anything for anyone because he'd been too busy, too focused or in entirely too much danger.

That hadn't changed. The threat to his life had just increased.

So he forced himself to relax his fingers, to release the back of her jacket, and to ease away from her. She held on to his shoulders yet, and the way she stared at him, her eyes dilated, her face flushed...

He wanted to kiss her so badly, and he suspected she wanted the same. But it wasn't fair to get any more involved with her—not when he couldn't be as open and honest as she wanted him to be.

So he pulled away from her and stood up, saying, "We should make sure the horses are okay now."

"Yes, of course," she hastily agreed, and she stood up now, too. "They must be cold and wet yet." Her face was still flushed, but he suspected it was with embarrassment now.

She probably thought he was rejecting her when it was entirely the opposite. He wanted her so damn badly. But even more than he desired her, he didn't want to hurt her. And if those shots hadn't been just a rancher firing at a coyote or mountain lion, then the Camorra might have found him again.

He felt a sickening lurch of dread in his stomach that had as much to do with fear as with acceptance. He couldn't deny it any longer. He couldn't pass off being tracked down in every city as just a coincidence anymore.

He knew who had betrayed him.

He's missing…

That was the text that Paolo had received just moments ago. What did that mean?

That Luca had once again escaped before the Camorra had caught up with him? Or that he was missing and presumed dead?

He needed to know. So he called the number that had texted him. "So he's gone?" he asked.

"Presumably…"

"What does that mean? He left the dude ranch? Or that…?"

"I cannot say..."

Because they didn't trust Paolo? Did they think he was recording this call? That he was as reckless as his journalist cousin had been when he'd accumulated enough evidence to take down nearly the entire organization?

Unfortunately he hadn't taken down all of them. Some remained—like the man who spoke to Paolo now.

"A winter storm has moved into the area," the man said. "People are missing..."

People.

Luca...

"But even if there is survival, for now, because of the severity of the storm, there will be no escape..."

No escape this time. An ache spread through his chest. He knew what that meant.

If Luca wasn't already dead, he would be soon.

Chapter Ten

Aubrey's face burned and not just because it was so chafed from the wind and the cold. It burned with humiliation. She had pretty much thrown herself at Luke, and he hadn't reacted—beyond that first hug where he'd clutched her so tightly as if he hadn't intended to let her go.

But he hadn't kissed her.

In fact, he seemed intent now on getting away from her. Maybe he was just tired and cold, though. Like the horses. They quickly tended to Ebony and her mare. Since Luke had already taken off their saddles, they rubbed down the animals' coats, then groomed their mounts and picked their hooves. The horses already had clean stalls with fresh water, feed and hay.

Kayla must have done this before she'd left for the evening. The barn was empty but for the animals and her and Luke, which made it feel eerie—like they were the only two people in the world.

A world Luke apparently didn't want to share with her, because once the animals were tended and the tack put away, he headed right for a side door. When he turned the handle, the wind propelled the door back into him, nearly knocking him to the ground. Snow blasted into the barn with all the force and fury of a tornado, and even though on this side of the barn there were exterior lights, it wasn't possible to see outside. Not through the snow.

She couldn't even see her truck. It had to be there. Kayla had her own vehicle; she wouldn't have taken Aubrey's. It was either buried under snow or the falling precipitation was just too thick, too impenetrable to see through.

Kind of like Luke…

She couldn't see through him to the secrets he was carrying like he'd carried that calf, his arms straining from the effort.

The snow blasted his face, knocking his hat from his head while it clung to his hair and lashes. He blinked, trying to see, then he pushed his shoulder against the door and shut and locked it.

Was he worried about someone forcing their way inside?

He'd been on edge even before those gunshots; he'd been on edge from someone searching his cabin. What had he been worried that they would find?

"It has to let up," Luke said between gasps for breath from his battle with the door.

"Seems like it's getting worse," she murmured. And she wasn't talking just about the storm.

She was thinking about her attraction to him. Even though she knew better, knew that she couldn't trust him, she wanted him.

"If it had been like this earlier..." She shuddered to think that they might not have made it back. She'd been worried about the animals, about the calf, but their lives had been in danger as well.

Had Jasper and his crew made it back? She pulled her cell phone from her pocket as she peered around the barn. The horse Jasper usually rode was warm in its stall. A small sigh of relief shuddered out of her lips.

Her twin must be safe. He was probably worried about her, though. She hadn't checked in with him yet, like they usually checked in with each other. Her phone was dead, the screen black. She didn't know if the lack of signal had completely run down the battery or if the cold had broken the cell.

"I don't suppose you have a phone," she murmured to Luke.

He shook his head.

Fortunately there was a landline in the tack room, so she hurried toward it. Before she stepped inside, she glanced back at Luke. He was still by the door, staring at it as if he was tempted to try again—to go out into that storm.

"It's not safe to leave," she said.

He was still turned toward the door, but she heard what he murmured beneath his breath. "It might not be safe to stay, either..."

Unlike last time, she wasn't going to let his cryptic comment go without questioning it. "What did you say?" she asked. Because it had been a mutter, just a rasp of his deep voice, so maybe she had misunderstood.

He turned toward her and shook his head. "Nothing..."

She narrowed her eyes and studied his face. The skin that wasn't covered with salt-and-pepper stubble was chafed red but for the dark circles beneath his eyes. He didn't look as if he'd slept any better than she had the night before. Or maybe he was just exhausted from the day. "You said something," she persisted. "Something about it not being safe to stay here…"

Instead of denying it again, he nodded. "I just meant that while the barn is warm enough for animals, it's probably too cold for humans."

"The tack room has a small wall heater," she said. And like the main lodge, there was a generator in case the power went out. She pushed open the door to the tack room and waited for him.

But Luke was clearly hesitant to join her. "I'll check on the calf again," he said.

"Thanks," she said. She stepped inside the tack room and reached for the phone on the wall. First she dialed Jasper's cell, but an automated message proclaimed that exchange unavailable. The blizzard was so fierce that it must have blocked reception from the cell tower.

She dialed the number for the main lodge. She suspected Jasper would be there, keeping the guests calm in case any of them were worried about the storm. "Gemini Ranch."

"Jasper," she said, recognizing his voice and surprised that he'd answered instead of one of the staff. He must have been waiting for a call.

"Aubrey, you're all right? You made it?" he asked.

"To the barn," she said. "We found an abandoned calf, so it took us longer to ride back."

"Is it okay?" he asked. "Are you okay?"

"Yes."

"I heard there were shots fired earlier."

She nearly groaned over his bringing them up. She'd wanted to forget about them. Mostly she'd wanted to forget Luke's reaction. "I'm sure it was nothing."

But she wasn't sure of anything or anyone…

"Just another rancher," she said. "Something must have happened to the mother of the calf we found, so maybe there's a mountain lion on the prowl or a coyote…"

Jasper released a shaky breath. "You're damn lucky you made it back. Are you really all right?"

"I'm fine," she assured him. Now she was the one lying, though, because she wasn't fine. She was rattled, but it had less to do with the storm and more to do with the man with whom she would have to ride out the bad weather.

"What about Luke Bishop?" he asked.

"He's fine, too," she said. "Just sore from carrying the calf in on his mount."

"We'll have to comp his stay," Jasper remarked. "He's worked hard."

"Yes, he has," she agreed.

"Though maybe we should wait and see how long he intends to stay before we give him the cabin for free," Jasper said with a chuckle.

How long *did* he intend to stay? Aubrey wondered. "I'll ask him," she said.

"Are you still together? He's in the tack room with you?"

"He's checking on the calf," she said. "But I'm not

sure we'll be able to leave the barn. It's coming down even harder now."

"Whiteout conditions," he said. "Weather reports are saying to shelter in place."

"For how long?"

"At least until morning. There won't be a break until then," he said. "Do you want me to come out to get you?"

"If I can't see to drive away from here, how will you be able to see to drive to get here?" she asked him.

"I just don't like that you're out there alone," he said.

"I'm not alone," she reminded him.

"That's what I don't like about it most," he admitted.

Maybe Dominic had talked to him, had shared with him what he'd learned—or actually hadn't been able to learn—about Luke Bishop.

"Don't worry," she told him. "I will be fine." Just a short while ago, Luke had been the one who'd pulled away from her.

He hadn't kissed her like she'd wanted him to, like he had the night before when he'd come to her house. He'd left then, when she'd pulled away. He would respect her wishes.

She didn't need to worry about unwanted attention from Luke Bishop She needed to worry about how much of himself he was holding back from her.

Like his real identity…

THE CALF WAS ASLEEP, peacefully, and warm in its bed of straw, a barn cat—a tiger-striped gray tabby—curled up at its side. Luca petted them both and considered staying there, in the straw with them. But his stomach rumbled; he wasn't just cold but also hungry.

He and Aubrey hadn't stopped once that day to eat. It had been too important to round up the cattle. But now he was a little light-headed and shaky from low blood sugar. He needed something. So he left the animals in the stall and headed to the tack room where Aubrey was.

He heard the soft sound of her voice and hesitated a moment. She was talking to someone. Had another person returned to the barn?

But he didn't hear anyone else speaking. So he pushed open the door, wondering if she'd been talking to herself. She cradled a phone against her shoulder while she foraged in the backpack she'd placed on one of the tables in the long room. The air was warmer in here and rich with the scent of leather and polish.

"I'm fine," Aubrey said, her voice sharp with frustration. "Stop worrying about me, Jasper, and tend to the guests. You need to make sure the generator stays running. We can't have any guests freezing to death." Then she pulled the receiver away from her ear, her brother's voice still emanating from the speaker, and hung it up on the cradle.

"What about starving?" Luca asked. "Are you going to let any guests starve to death?"

She gestured at the containers she'd spread out on the table. "I intended to share," she told him.

He should have packed something for himself, but the supplies he'd ordered from town had gotten low. He was going to need to order more if he intended to stay.

But he didn't, he couldn't...

Even as longing pulled at him, at his heart, at his stomach...

It growled, and Aubrey giggled, like she had over the cattle. And something kicked his heart, making it beat harder. And suddenly he wasn't hungry just for food but for her as well.

So damn hungry...

She leaned toward him...with one of the containers. "Think it might be a little frozen yet from being outside with us," she said. "But there's a microwave in the corner over there." She gestured past boot-filled cubbies toward a small refrigerator with a microwave sitting on top of it.

Luca took the container from her, picked up a couple of other ones and carried them toward the microwave.

"You're going to share, too?" she asked.

He chuckled. "I'll bring them back." Then he teased, "Empty..."

"I have the silverware," she said.

"Who needs silverware?"

She chuckled again.

And some of the tension inside Luca eased. He heated up the dishes and brought them back to the table. They pulled up chairs on either side of it and feasted on their dinner of beef stew, roasted vegetables, a cheesy noodle dish and some kind of breaded meat.

Even as he filled his stomach, it rumbled. This time in appreciation. "You're an excellent cook," he complimented her.

She shook her head. "I can't claim credit for this meal. This is all the work of the brilliant chef we have at the main lodge. I don't cook. I know my limitations, unlike my mom, who keeps trying." Her lips curved into a warm smile at the mention of her mother.

"You're close to your mom," he said.

She nodded, but her smile was a bit more wistful now. "As close as you can be when you're one of a dozen kids that she basically raised on her own. I admire her, but I've always had to share her. That's one perk you had, being an only child. You never had to share."

"No, I didn't have to," he agreed. His heart ached with missing his mother. When he'd left her, he'd explained why he'd had to stay away. He'd even sent her off on her own adventure, on a cruise with her sister, Paolo's mother.

"She must miss you," Aubrey said.

And that pang in his chest intensified. He dropped the spoon he'd been holding into one of the empty containers. "Maybe while we were eating, the storm let up..."

Her smile slipped completely away, and she shook her head. "No, Jasper said there's not going to be a break until morning."

"A break?"

"A cold air system that's going to hover for a bit," she said. "Authorities are advising no travel for a few days yet."

A few days.

So if an assassin hired by the Camorra had fired those shots, Luca was stuck on the ranch with them. The tension was back inside him, gripping him so tightly that he struggled to breathe.

She must have noticed his reaction to her news because she asked, "Were you intending to travel?"

He shook his head.

"How long will you stay at the ranch?" she asked.

He shrugged. "I haven't made any plans." His only plan was to stay alive, and to do that, he had to stay at least one step ahead of the Camorra.

"What about your book?" she asked. "Are you really writing one?"

"You think I've lied about that?" he asked.

"I think you're not being completely honest with me," she said.

"Do you ever think anyone's being completely honest with you? Or did your dad and Warren destroy your ability to trust?"

She sucked in a breath, and Luca worried that he'd gone too far.

"I'm not criticizing you," he assured her. Then he uttered a heavy sigh. "In fact, I should be commending you. You're smart not to trust anyone." And maybe if he'd been that smart, he wouldn't have to be worried that he'd been found again.

But if he had…

Then there was no denying that only one person could have given him up—someone he had believed he could trust. Someone he loved like a brother.

"Sounds like you might have trusted someone you shouldn't have as well," she surmised. "Is that why you're hiding out here? Why you're traveling under an assumed name?"

He sucked in the breath now. "Assumed name? Is that

what your brother told you?" he asked, and his heart pounded fast and hard with nerves.

He'd thought his new identity had been so well established. Maybe he shouldn't have trusted the people who'd helped him create it, either. After discovering how many people the Camorra had corrupted in the government and law enforcement, Luca hadn't entirely trusted them before he wrote his exposé. And he definitely didn't trust them not to betray his true identity now. That was why he always paid with cash instead of using credit cards.

Instead of answering her, Aubrey just silently studied his face, her blue eyes narrowed with suspicion.

"Your FBI agent brother thinks he's found something," Luca surmised now.

"No," she said. "He wasn't able to find out much of anything about you. That's why he's worried."

"Are you?" Luca wondered. What did she think he was—a criminal on the run? He wanted to tell her everything, but if the Camorra had already sent someone here...

Then that person might hurt her, too, if they figured she knew too much. It was safer for her to know nothing or as little as possible about him. Unfortunately he'd probably already revealed too much about himself, but he'd never felt as comfortable with anyone else as he did her. As connected to anyone else...

They were so different, but yet he felt as if he knew her on some other level. Was this connection what people were feeling when they spoke of soul mates? He'd always thought that was overly romantic drivel, something to explain the way friends had dropped him to spend all their time with their new significant other.

"I should be worried," she said.

"I am," he admitted. He was worried about these feelings. But most of all he was worried about leaving her without learning more about her: like how she would feel when they made love, how she would make him feel…

He suspected that because of the connection they shared, it would be an experience beyond anything he'd ever felt before.

He didn't dare share those thoughts with her, though, just as he didn't dare share anything else. But he couldn't help grinning and teasing her, "You should be worried…"

"Are you dangerous?" she asked.

He didn't want her to be afraid of him, to think that he was a bad person, and the urge to tell her everything overwhelmed him. But he just shook his head and said, "Maybe dangerous to be around…"

"Why?" she asked.

Wanting to keep her safe but also share more with her, he began, "Let's just say in doing research…"

"For your book?" she asked when he trailed off.

Maybe he could be honest about that, although he hadn't intended to write a book when he'd first started investigating. But then he'd uncovered so much…

"Yes," he replied, "the research I did for the book has brought me to some dangerous places with some dangerous people."

"But you said you're writing fiction," she said. "Did you lie to me?"

"Calling it fiction protects me," he said. And believing it was fiction might have kept her safe, had she been able to read any of his notes.

After he'd caught her snooping around his kitchen, he'd hidden his laptop, notebook and those destroyed phones. And it hadn't appeared that the intruder had found his hiding spot in the empty space beneath the bottom drawer of the chest of drawers in the bedroom. He'd already been hiding the documents for his new identity there—the passport and credit cards.

"What does calling it fiction protect you from? Lawsuits or from these dangerous people hurting you?" she asked. "Is that why you're hiding out?"

He wondered now if she was the journalist and he was the rancher. She was a natural at interviewing, but he just smiled at her instead of answering her question. Then he leaned across the table, until his face was close to hers, and said, "I think I'm in more danger here—with you—than I've been anywhere else…"

And not just because the Camorra might have found him.

"Why?" she asked.

"Because you are a dangerous woman, Aubrey Colton," he said. A woman who tempted him to share all his secrets, to share everything with her—even his heart.

If only it was safe for him to stay, then maybe he'd follow his heart when it fell…for her.

THE CELL PHONE vibrated across the nightstand next to Dominic's bed. He swiped to accept the call and answered with a gruff hello.

"Did I wake you up?" Alexa asked.

He sighed, wishing she had. "No..."

He needed to get some rest before his next assignment started. When he was undercover, he could never completely relax. Never let his guard down...

Sometimes his life depended on staying awake and aware. So he saved his sleeping for when he was between assignments.

But now he was so on edge about Aubrey's mysterious guest that he couldn't sleep.

"What did you find out?" Dominic asked his US marshal sister.

Alexa exhaled a sigh, a ragged one of pure frustration. "I wasn't able to find him in WITSEC, so he's not with the US Marshals."

"Or with Federal," Dominic said. "Aubrey said he has some kind of European accent. He might be Italian, since his documents, doctored or not, claim that's where he was born."

Alexa sighed. "I don't have any overseas connections."

"I already checked with mine," Dominic said. "Maybe Ezra can check with his."

Their brother Ezra, one of Dominic's fellow triplets, was a US Army sergeant, but sometimes Dominic suspected he was something more. He was harder than hell to reach, though.

"Good luck getting a hold of him," Alexa said. "In the meantime, you need to tell Aubrey to steer clear of the guy."

"I already have. Maybe you should talk to her," Dominic suggested. Aubrey was strong and stubborn. Too stubborn to admit that she wasn't that tough when it came to matters of her heart.

Alexa chuckled. "Ah, no. I'm your baby sister," she reminded him, even though she and her twin, Naomi, actually shared that title.

"Afraid of Aubrey?" he teased her.

"I respect her," she said. "And I know what it's like when people don't think you can take care of yourself."

It hadn't been easy for Alexa to become a US marshal, and the hardest part for her had probably been her family trying to discourage her from joining the organization, out of their concern that she would be hurt.

"Okay," he said with a weary groan. "Point taken. I'll call Jasper."

Alexa groaned, too. "You guys just don't get it," she complained. "Your sisters, including me, can take care of ourselves."

In his head he knew that; he knew they were all so strong and smart—like Mom. But in his heart he loved them too much to do nothing when he thought one of them might be in danger.

Alexa willingly put herself in the line of fire for her job—so he usually worried about her the most. But Aubrey...

She wouldn't have asked Dominic to check out her guest if she wasn't interested and concerned about the mysterious Luke Bishop. And she'd already had her heart and ego hurt once by a man she shouldn't have trusted...

Twice, if you counted Dad. And Dominic tried not to think about him, about any of that. He focused only on the things he could change or help. And he was too far away to help Aubrey right now, especially with the storm that had struck Denver and the surrounding areas. So, after hanging up from Alexa, he called Jasper.

Or he tried. The first call—to his cell—didn't go through, so he called the main number for Gemini Ranch and asked for him.

He must have been at the lodge because within seconds, Jasper was on the line. "What's up, Dom?" Jasper asked.

"Everything okay there?" Dominic asked.

"You heard about the storm?"

"It hit here, too," Dominic said. "I'm just calling to make sure everyone's all right."

"I'm fine..." Jasper murmured.

"What about Aubrey? Is she with you?"

"She's spending the night in the barn," Jasper said. "Got stuck out there after bringing back the cattle."

Dominic sucked in a breath from a jab of concern. "Won't she freeze?"

"There's a heater in the tack room and a generator to keep it running if the power goes out again."

"Again?"

A ripple of noise emanated from Dom's cell; it must have been the collective gasp of the guests.

"Again," Jasper confirmed. "It keeps blinking on

and off and off..." He sighed. "But the generator kicks in, so we're good. How's everyone else?"

"Everyone else?" Dominic asked. Even though he was one of the triplets, he felt like a loner most of the time. He and his brothers stayed connected, aware of where each other was or what was going on, but they each lived pretty solitary lives.

"You said you were checking on everyone," Jasper reminded him. Then he added, "Or are you just checking on Aubrey? What's up?"

"She asked me to look into a guest for her," Dominic admitted. "You didn't know?" If she hadn't shared her suspicions with her twin, something was definitely up.

"Luke Bishop?" Jasper asked.

"Yes." So maybe he had known.

Jasper cursed.

"What? What is it?"

"Did you find out anything bad?" Jasper asked. "What did you learn?"

"Just that she was smart to be suspicious," Dominic admitted. "There's something not right about the guy. Why? What do you know about him?"

"That he's with her in the barn right now," Jasper said. "He got stuck out there with her."

So Aubrey was trapped alone with a man she didn't trust.

A man who shouldn't be trusted...

Dominic cursed now.

"He doesn't seem like a bad guy, though," Jasper said.

But he tended to see the positive in life instead of the reality.

"He's been helping us move the cattle," Jasper said. "He's a hard worker."

That didn't make him a good person. Dominic had known some really hardworking criminals through the years he'd been a federal agent. And then there was another criminal he'd known well… That he and his siblings had all known well. A seemingly hardworking judge who'd turned out to be a criminal.

"Just keep checking on her," Dominic urged him. "Make sure that she's safe."

"Aubrey is tough," Jasper said. "She got through the blizzard. And earlier…"

"What?" Dominic asked when his brother trailed off.

"Earlier there were some shots fired."

"At Aubrey?"

"She didn't think so. A cow is missing. A calf abandoned. She thinks someone was probably shooting at a mountain lion or coyotes…"

Or Luke Bishop and whoever was unfortunate enough to be too close to him.

Like Aubrey…

Panic gripped him. He didn't want his sister getting caught in the crossfire between Luke Bishop and whoever might have tracked him down. Dominic didn't know yet who the man really was, but maybe someone else had figured it out, someone who might have wanted him dead.

Dominic wedged his fingers between the blinds on his bedroom window and peered out. The streetlamp was only a faint glow through the heavily falling snow, and he couldn't even see the road. It hadn't been plowed;

interstates were getting shut down. He was trapped here—unable to help his sister—while she was trapped with Luke Bishop.

Whoever the hell he was…

Chapter Eleven

More than the table between them separated Aubrey and Luke.

She didn't believe for a moment that the book he was writing was fiction—if he was even writing anything at all. She doubted that Luke Bishop—or whoever he really was—had been honest with her about anything. Yet she still wanted him...

What was wrong with her?

Why was she only attracted to men that she couldn't—that she *shouldn't*—trust?

"We should check on the calf again," Luke said. "Maybe bring him in here with us if he's not warm enough."

Aubrey was warm now, the warmth spreading from her heart. He'd been so sweet with that calf, so protective and as determined to rescue it as she had been.

"I'll bring it another bottle," she said. While Luke cleaned up the containers from their belated dinner, she retrieved the milk from the small refrigerator.

He opened the door and held it for her, and as she passed him, her pulse quickened. She drew in a deep breath of his scent. He smelled like hay and horses and fresh snow and man. She was hesitant to release the breath, wanting to hold the smell inside her for just a bit...until she found the strength to come to her senses.

To avoid temptation...

But that was beginning to prove harder and harder, especially when she knew they were trapped in the barn. The snow was still blowing so hard outside that some of it had filtered through the small crack beneath the big double doors, forming a drift just inside the barn.

She shivered as the cold swirled around them, and Luke's arm moved over her shoulders, pulling her tight against his side.

"Are the animals going to be warm enough?" he asked.

She nodded. "The bigger animals like cattle and horses can survive frigid temperatures, and despite the ferocity of this storm, it's just a little below freezing. The barn is warmer than that, though, and has a ventilation system that keeps warmth circulating with drier air."

"So they'll all be okay?" he asked. "Even the little guy and the cat?"

"Cat?" Aubrey asked.

Luke pulled open the door of the stall where they'd settled the calf, and she saw the gray tabby curled up against the calf. "Isn't it sweet?" Luke asked, and he stepped away from her to kneel next to the animals. "The cat is taking care of our new friend."

She chuckled. "More like taking advantage of his body heat."

"You're so cynical," Luke remarked, but he grinned at her when he said it.

Aubrey felt the pang of regret nonetheless. "How are you not?" she asked as she knelt down next to him.

He stared down at her, deep into her eyes, and said, "Because I've met some pretty amazing people over the years."

Was he talking about her?

"That's why you think someone's searching your cabin and that those shots today were meant for you? Because you've met *amazing* people?" she asked, reminding him of the things he'd said.

His grin slipped away, and he sighed. "I've met some amazingly bad people, sure. I've also met some amazingly good people." And his hand covered hers over the bottle of milk. They'd removed their gloves in the tack room and must have left them there. His skin wasn't cold, though, and the touch of it—his touch—warmed hers. Just being close to him had heat streaking inside her as her blood pumped fast and hard.

She pressed the bottle into his hand and said, "You can feed him."

The calf nuzzled the bottle, then slurped greedily from it. The cat lapped up the drips that fell from the calf's chin.

Luke chuckled. "You might be right. She is a little opportunist."

Aubrey stroked her hand over the cat's head. "She looks well-fed. Somebody's been taking care of her here." Aubrey hadn't seen her before, but the feline must have belonged to one of the ranch hands.

"And she's not the least bit skittish," Luke said as the cat pushed its head against Aubrey's hand and purred.

The calf greedily finished the bottle, then settled back into the pile of straw. The cat burrowed in next to it, and they closed their eyes, warm and content with each other's companionship.

"I guess they're fine," Luke mused.

"Yes," Aubrey agreed.

Luke shivered and said, "Now, I, on the other hand, would appreciate a little more heat. Unless…" He turned toward her and arched a brow. "I think you once offered to keep me warm…"

Aubrey snorted. "I was just making sure your furnace was working," she said, hanging on to the excuse she'd given him when he'd caught her in his cabin.

And she'd caught him fresh from the shower, his chest bare, the towel knotted just below his waist. Her heart was pounding so hard now, as she remembered seeing him like that, that she was surprised that he couldn't hear it, too.

Embarrassed and so very tempted to reach out to him, she jumped to her feet and hurried out of the close confines of the stall. "I—I should make sure the heater is working in the tack room," she said. "Or it's going to be a cold night."

Even though she hurried back to the tack room, Luke, with his long strides, easily caught up to her at the door. His hand covered hers on the knob as she reached out to turn it.

"I'll keep you warm," he offered, his voice a deep rumble near her ear.

Just the sound of it, and the heat of his breath in her hair, had her tingling everywhere. "Luke…" she murmured. She wanted him so badly.

Would it matter if she couldn't trust him as long as she knew not to fall for him? Could she just take tonight to appreciate and celebrate that they'd made it through a blizzard, that they were alive?

Especially if those shots hadn't been meant for wildlife but for…

Luke.

Could his life be in danger?

And if it was, she knew he wasn't staying. Hell, he was just a guest. And if he left without her knowing how it could have been between them, she would always wonder…

She turned toward him then and studied his face— his impossibly handsome face with its salt-and-pepper stubble clinging to the strong line of his jaw. "Are you married?"

His eyes widened in shock.

And she laughed at his expression of horror. "I'm not proposing," she assured him. "I just need to know." While it was bad enough that he was a guest, she couldn't break her personal rule and bend her moral principles—no matter how attracted she was to Luke.

He shook his head. "I've never even been close," he admitted as if he'd just realized that himself.

Men lied about being married all the time; she knew that, but something about the way he'd said it made her trust that it was the truth—probably more than anything else he'd told her.

So she turned the knob and pushed open the door. After she stepped inside, she reached back for him, grabbed the front of his jacket and tugged him toward her.

He reached for her, but his hands just cupped her shoulders and he stared down at her as he asked, "Are you sure?"

He knew then what she wanted, that she wanted him. She smiled and nodded. "Yes..."

"But—"

She reached up and pressed her fingers over his mouth. "You said you're not married. Were you lying?"

He shook his head.

Then she rose up on tiptoe and replaced her fingers with her mouth, sliding her lips over his. He stepped farther into the room then, his body pressing against hers, and he kicked the door shut with the heel of his boot.

He kissed her with a passion that equaled, if not surpassed, the desire she felt for him. His mouth moved hungrily over hers, his lips nibbling at hers, and then he deepened the contact even more, his tongue sliding over hers.

He kissed her as if he couldn't get enough of her until they finally broke apart, panting for breath. Her lungs burned with the need for air as her body burned with desire for his.

She couldn't remember ever wanting anyone this much. The passion coursing through her overwhelmed her. But even with him breathing heavy, too, she wondered if he wanted her as much...

She blinked away the haze of desire and focused

on his face, which was flushed. His eyes were dilated. She'd been worried earlier, after Luke had pulled away when she hugged him out of gratitude over rescuing the calf, that he might not be as attracted to her as she was to him. Maybe she'd let Warren's manipulations affect her self-esteem, or maybe how much she was drawn to Luke had made her vulnerable, reminding her of the teased kid she'd once been.

She had survived school, though, and her regretful dating experience with Warren, and she would survive, too, when Luke checked out of Gemini Ranch, as he inevitably would.

But in the meantime...

She intended to make the most of this night with him. She pushed his sheepskin-lined coat from his shoulders and reached for the buttons of his blue flannel shirt. But his hands gently gripped hers, stopping her. "Too cold?" she asked.

"Too hot," he said, his voice gruff with passion. "I need to slow down. I need to take care of you first."

"Luke..." She was ready for him now.

But her hands clasped yet in his, he led her to one of the benches across from the boot cubbies, and he gently pushed her onto it before kneeling in front of it.

Nerves fluttered in her stomach now. It was almost as if he was proposing...and she knew that would never happen, but her heart...

She drew in a shaky breath and then murmured, "What are you doing?"

"Undressing you," he replied. First he tugged off one

of her boots. Her sock came with it, leaving her foot bare and cold. He rubbed it in his hands, warming it.

Warming her...

Heat trailed up from the arch of her foot his hand was massaging to her very core. "Luke..."

He tugged off the other boot and warmed that foot, too, until her toes curled in anticipation of what was to come. Of how he would make her feel when he touched her other places...

She looped her arms around his neck and pulled him toward her for another kiss. Lips nibbled on lips, tongues stroked and mated...

Then he broke away again with a low groan. "Aubrey..."

"I'm ready," she assured him. And she reached for the buttons of his shirt again.

But he ignored her efforts as he pushed her coat from her shoulders. It dropped onto the bench behind her. Then, as she clumsily fumbled with the buttons on his shirt, he deftly undid hers. His fingers brushed over every inch of skin he exposed.

She could barely breathe again and it wasn't from his kisses; it was from anticipation. She was so affected by just the sight of him, the taste of him on her lips...

Then his lips brushed across her mouth and slid down her throat and over her cleavage. He released the hook of her bra, and her full breasts burst out of the cups.

He groaned. "You are so beautiful, so incredibly beautiful..."

And the way he stared at her, as if in awe, made her

feel more beautiful than she'd ever felt. She felt more powerful than she'd ever felt.

Then his tongue swiped across one of her nipples, and she felt powerless, unable to stop the pleasure rushing through her. Not that she wanted it to stop; she never wanted it to stop. And that was the problem, that she was never going to want this feeling to go away.

His lips tugged at her nipple now, and she moaned as desire wound through her, twisting her stomach, making her ache for a release. "Luke..." Her hands slipped away from his shirt, from the buttons her fingers had been shaking too hard to undo.

His weren't shaking because he had no problem unbuttoning her jeans. Once he unzipped them, he tugged the worn denim down her legs along with her panties. Then with his mouth and those steady fingers, he took care of her like he'd promised, finally releasing that unbearable pressure he'd built inside her.

Clutching his shoulders, she screamed his name as the power of the orgasm overwhelmed her. "Luke!"

She couldn't remember any other lover being as generous, as unselfish. Hell, in that moment, she couldn't remember any other lover but Luke.

Her body pulsating yet with the pleasure he'd just given her, she should have been satiated. And she was, but she was also greedy for more. For all of Luke...

Desperate to see him again as she had that day in his cabin, when she'd been caught snooping, she returned her attention to his buttons again. She quickly undid them and then tugged up the thermal shirt he wore beneath his flannel. His abdominal muscles rippled as he helped shuck the shirt over his head.

She leaned forward and kissed his chest, swirling her tongue around one of his nipples. He groaned and then bucked as he rid himself of his jeans and underwear, as desperate now as she had been. Beneath her lips, his heart pounded hard. Then she skimmed her lips down his stomach, and those muscles rippled again. But then something else caught her attention…

He was so big. So engorged.

When she wrapped her fingers around his pulsating shaft, he groaned as if in pain. Then his hand covered hers, stilling it. With his other hand, he rifled through their discarded clothes until he found a condom packet. His hands were shaking too badly now, so she took the packet from him and tore it open. Then she rolled the condom over him. He pulsated within her hand and groaned again.

"Aubrey…"

Despite the cool air in the tack room, sweat beaded on his brow, on his lip. "I'm so on edge… I can't…"

She pushed him back on the floor, on top of the clothes they'd discarded there. And she straddled him, guiding him inside her. She could only take so much of him—he was that big. But she moved her hips, arching, taking him as deep as she could.

He moved within her, thrusting, as he gripped her hips, guiding her up and down. They found a rhythm together, as if they were dancing, as if it was a step they'd done many times.

She bit her lip and moaned as the pressure built

again. Then he drove deeper inside her, and that pressure snapped. She screamed again as an orgasm shuddered through her.

Then he shouted her name, as his body convulsed beneath her with the power of his release. She collapsed onto his chest, which heaved with his deep breaths and the mad pounding of his heart.

Her heart pounded, too—from the exertion and from panic. Because she'd thought she could just enjoy the moment, just appreciate being with him this once…

But it was too good. He was too good, and she knew she would want more, probably more than he was able to give.

His honesty and his love.

THE STORM HAD struck hard—in the tack room. And it had raged all night. Luca lay limp in the aftermath of it.

Clothes were strewn all around the room. At one point they'd managed to pull out some blankets and they'd made a makeshift bed. They lay in it now, Aubrey curled against his side, her head on his chest.

She was so warm, so soft and comfortable in his arms, like she belonged there. Like Luca belonged here…

If only that was possible, if only he could stay.

But he couldn't risk that the Camorra wouldn't find him, if they hadn't already. He couldn't risk Aubrey getting hurt because of him.

But would she get hurt anyway? Was she getting as attached to him as he was to her?

Luca had never felt so close to anyone before. He

hadn't lied when he'd told her he'd never even come close to getting married.

He'd always thought he was too busy before, but now he realized it was because he'd never found someone like her, someone who engaged him on every level. Someone who fascinated him as much as an interesting story had. Or maybe more…

Maybe that was because Aubrey had an interesting story of her own, with her father's betrayal, with her running a ranch.

She was a strong, incredible woman.

He'd thought he was satiated moments ago, but now his body began to stir again from the closeness of hers. Her hand was on his chest, over his heart, and maybe she'd felt it, felt the sudden increase in the beat because she chuckled—a low, sexy chuckle.

"Luke…" she murmured—so much quieter than when she'd screamed his name a short while ago.

He wanted to tell her his real name. Wanted her to scream "Luca" with all the wonder and pleasure that she'd screamed "Luke."

But he didn't dare share his real identity with her, especially if the Camorra was here. If she slipped up, if she called him Luca…

Then she might become the target he was.

He didn't want anyone getting hurt because of him, but most especially not her. He wanted to give her only pleasure.

Not pain…

He rolled then, onto his side, so she flopped onto her back. And he set about giving her more pleasure…

FROM A DEEP, drunken slumber, he was jerked awake—literally—as two men dragged him from his bed. His body struck the hardwood floor, pain shooting from his elbow down to his fingers. He didn't fight back. Did nothing to protect himself...

Just as he'd done nothing to protect Luca. He should have warned him. Instead, he'd betrayed him. But the Camorra had given him no choice. It was his life or Luca's.

And now he was going to die anyways. He'd been a fool—such a damn fool for getting involved with them in the first place. "What—what's going on?" he asked in Italian.

"That is what you need to find out," he was told. "There has been no confirmation from the assassins. You need to find out if your cousin is alive or dead."

"Uh, how?" he asked in confusion as he lay on the floor where they'd dumped him.

"You are going to America, to that dude ranch. You will find out," he was told. "And if Luca Rossi is alive, you will make sure he dies."

He shuddered then at the thought of pulling the trigger himself, of ending Luca's life.

"It's him or you..."

And that was why he had no choice. He had to do what they wanted. He had to live, even though that meant Luca had to die.

Chapter Twelve

The break in the storm that Jasper had mentioned came with daybreak. Kayla had made it to the barn. Fortunately Aubrey and Luke were dressed by then and in the stall with the calf. Or she might have known for certain what she probably only suspected.

For she'd cast them a strange glance when she found them in the stall, crouching close together over the calf. Or maybe Aubrey was just paranoid that everyone else could see how much she was affected from her night with Luke.

She was worried most of all that he would see it, that he would see how much she wanted from him. And she knew the thing she wanted most, he couldn't give her: honesty.

So none of the rest of it mattered.

"Jasper said you made it back last night," Kayla said. "And I saw, as I drove here, that the rest of the cattle were in the pasture by the indoor ring. But who's this little guy?"

"An orphan," Aubrey replied. "Luke carried him all the way back."

Kayla looked at him then and nodded. "That's not the easiest thing to do when it isn't a blizzard. These calves weigh more than you think."

Luke was strong. Aubrey knew that because he'd lifted her a few times last night as if she hadn't weighed much more than the calf.

Luke gently patted the animal's head. "He was worth it."

That was how Aubrey had decided to look at last night. That all the pleasure he'd given her would be worth the pain that would surely follow when he left. And as if he was eager to leave now, he asked Kayla, "How are the roads?"

"Jasper has the grounds crew clearing the roads on the ranch," she said. "I'm not sure about the main streets. Why are you asking? Are you leaving?"

He hesitated just long enough for Aubrey to know that he was. And a pang struck her heart so sharply that she nearly gasped.

"I was just curious," he replied.

Just curious if he could leave or if he was trapped here with her?

Aubrey didn't ask.

"I doubt the street coming out here from Blue Larkspur is clear yet," Kayla said. "The road crews will focus on the city first."

He nodded. "Of course."

"Jasper does want you to head up to the main lodge right away," Kayla told Aubrey. "He's anxious to talk to you."

"He could have called me," Aubrey said. "I know

cell reception isn't the best right now, but there's the landline in the tack room."

Kayla shrugged. "He must have tried—said you weren't picking up."

Had the phone rung? Aubrey had been so preoccupied with Luke that she might not have noticed. Heat flushed her face, and she looked away from Kayla, who was studying her a little intently.

Was she judging Aubrey for crossing a line with a guest? Maybe that was why Jasper was so anxious to talk to her—to remind her that Luke was a guest. And she was one of the owners, responsible for the ranch and everyone on it.

And with the blizzard hitting, there was probably a lot to attend to—which Jasper had been doing on his own. Now she felt a pang of guilt.

"Can you call the vet and see if she can make it out here on her snowmobile or at least advise you on how to check out the calf?" Aubrey asked her.

Kayla nodded.

"Then I better get up to the main lodge and see what Jasper needs," Aubrey said and she stepped out of the stall.

Luke followed her out. "I'll go with you."

She waited until they were walking out the side barn door to her snow-covered truck before she asked, "Why?"

"You probably have a lot you need to do with the storm hitting," he said. "I can help."

"You've already done so much..." And not just in moving the cattle.

Even now he was using his arm to knock the snow from the hood of her truck.

She unlocked the door and reached inside for the snow brush. Then she started the engine to warm it up. Not that she was cold...

Just being close to Luke had her body heating up, as thoughts of the night before, of all the places he'd touched her, kissed her, played through her mind. He had already done so much.

He'd made her feel beautiful and desirable in a way nobody else ever had. But she couldn't allow herself to get used to being with him, especially like they'd been last night or even like the past couple of days that they'd moved the cattle, working together—instinctively anticipating what the other needed. Just like when they'd made love...

She couldn't remember ever having a connection like that with another human being. And feeling overwhelmed by it, she offered, "I can drop you at your cabin."

He shook his head. "I don't think I have any food left. I'd like to check out the dining room at the main lodge. For some reason I'm starving." He patted his flat stomach, and she remembered what he looked like beneath the heavy coat and his shirt, how his washboard abs had rippled when he moved, when she...

Her breath caught at the image, at the memory, at the burning desire to do it again, to make love with him over and over.

He must have noticed her reaction because his eyes dilated until the blue of his irises was just a thin circle around the black. "Or maybe we should go back to my cabin. Or your house…"

She wanted to—so badly, but she forced herself to shake her head. "I better talk to Jasper before he sends out a search party."

"I'm kind of surprised he didn't do that last night," Luke said.

"He trusts that I can take care of myself," Aubrey said with pride.

"He knows you well," Luke remarked.

"It's the twin intuition thing," she said. But even that didn't compare to her connection with Luke.

Luke had cleared the snow from the truck, and now hopped into the passenger seat. She could have tried to drop him at his cabin, but she had a feeling he might not get out of the pickup. So she drove him up to the main lodge like he wanted.

But when they walked into the great room together, Aubrey felt as if everyone turned and stared at them. She probably looked a mess since she hadn't showered or changed her clothes. She probably had straw in her hair and scrapes on her skin from Luke's stubble—dead giveaways to how they'd spent the night. So she felt as if she was doing the walk of shame with everyone watching her and judging her.

Which made no sense. She was probably just paranoid because she knew what she'd done wasn't smart—for so many reasons. She'd broken her own rule of never getting involved with another man she couldn't trust.

Now Luca remembered why he hadn't come up to the main lodge before. There were too many people. Too many people who could be hurt if someone tried to take him out here like they had at that B and B in Toronto and that hotel in Wisconsin.

Unless those had just been strange coincidences. But he doubted that, just as he doubted those gunshots had been for a mountain lion or a coyote. They'd been meant for him.

And if someone tried again to take him out on the ranch, there were more people who could be hurt. More people than just Aubrey—although her being in harm's way would affect him the most.

In the enormous great room, there were a few families with kids, some couples, and they were all staring at him and Aubrey now. Maybe they were just curious about him because he hadn't come up to the main lodge before, and he was a stranger to them. A stranger who'd showed up during a storm when the roads were supposedly impassable…

Despite the grounds crew working on the roads on the ranch, they had still been snow-covered and slippery. But just as she was good at everything else, Aubrey was a skilled driver.

There were some things that she was better than good at, things at which she excelled, like making love. He'd never had a more responsive, more generous partner than Aubrey Colton. And he suspected that he never would.

Leaving this place, leaving her, was going to be the

hardest thing he'd ever had to do. Maybe harder even than leaving his country and his family.

And yet they barely knew each other. Hell, she didn't even know his real name. Because of that, because of the lies he'd had to tell her, they had no future.

Luca suspected that if he didn't get off the ranch soon, he would have no future on his own, either. Because it didn't feel like everyone was watching them with just mild curiosity.

Someone was staring at him intently, almost malevolently—Aubrey's twin. Jasper asked, "Where the hell have you been?" He might have been addressing Aubrey, but he was staring at Luca.

"What?" Luca asked in confusion. "You were expecting me?"

"No," Jasper said. "I wasn't." He turned toward his sister. "I was trying to call you back last night in the barn, but you didn't pick up."

"I was fine," she said.

Jasper stared intently at her for a long moment before glancing back at Luca. "Dominic called me to check on you."

Was he still talking to her? Or to Luca?

Aubrey must have been confused as well, because she asked, "Check on me?"

Jasper narrowed his eyes and gave her a pointed stare, as if he was silently communicating with her.

Aubrey must not have picked up on his silent message because she shrugged off his concern. "He had no reason to check up on me. I'm fine."

Apparently the FBI agent had found just enough to

raise his suspicions and apparently Jasper's even more. Was Jasper the one who'd searched Luca's cabin? And had it been on his other brother's orders or because of his own suspicions?

"He has concerns," Jasper said. "Especially when I told him about those gunshots."

"And I told you that those gunshots were probably from another rancher who was firing at a wild animal."

"I talked to the other guests who heard the shots," Jasper said. "It sounds like they came from the direction of the Sutherlands'."

Some of the tightness in Luca's chest eased; that was good, then. Another rancher had fired those shots just like Aubrey had thought.

But she was tense now and her face pale. "How could anyone even be staying out there since the fire?" she asked.

Jasper shrugged. "Mr. Sutherland sure isn't. Nadine isn't going to let her dad come back out until the place is rebuilt. So who would have fired those shots, Aubrey?"

She shook her head. "I don't know. Caleb is getting a contract ready for us to sign a lease on the pastures. There hasn't been any livestock out there in years. So what would anyone be doing on that property?"

Jasper's brow furrowed. "Could it have anything to do with that oil company that was trying to take Al Sutherland's fracking rights before Caleb and Nadine stopped them?"

Luca narrowed his eyes at the other man's tone. "There were issues with this company?"

Jasper nodded. "There were some dangerous people working for it."

"Maybe somebody from that place came back," Aubrey suggested.

"Where is the Sutherland property?" Luca asked. "I can ride over and check it out." If someone pointed him in the right direction…

"The roads are impassable outside the ranch," Jasper said.

Luca nodded. "But surely a horse could get through."

"With the snow and drifting it wouldn't be safe on horseback," Jasper said. "The snowmobiles would be an easier and faster way to get there."

"I need to check out the ranch," Luca said. Even though he'd never ridden a snowmobile, he was determined to find out what those gunshots had really been about, if someone had found him…or if it was safe—especially with Aubrey in mind—for him to stay awhile longer.

"Why?" Jasper asked him. "What's your interest in all this?"

Aubrey's twin was definitely suspicious of Luca, and rightfully so.

"Those gunshots seemed like they were close to us," Luca admitted. Much too close. "I just want to make sure that it wasn't personal."

"Why would it be personal?" Jasper persisted.

Luca shrugged. "I wasn't the only one in that area where the shots were fired," he pointed out. And he glanced at Aubrey.

"I was the one who pushed for us to lease the Sutherland property," she said. "Maybe the oil company is trying to scare us away from it."

Jasper shook his head. "Caleb got the company's henchmen to turn on the executives. If they were going to go after anyone, it would probably be him. I can't imagine who would want to hurt you, Aubrey."

Neither could Luca but then he remembered the ugly encounter she'd had in her driveway. "Warren Parker wasn't happy the other night with the way she got rid of him."

"Warren..." Aubrey gasped. "I forgot all about him..."

Luca's heart swelled with relief. He was ridiculously happy that she'd forgotten all about her ex-boyfriend. Unfortunately, so had Luca. Was it possible that Warren Parker had been trying to eliminate his competition for Aubrey's heart? No. Warren didn't want her heart; he wanted her money. He was a desperate man, and Luca shouldn't have forgotten that.

If it was Warren who'd tried for him, he was safe. He could stay, but even then, he wasn't sure that he should—because then he would definitely fall for Aubrey Colton if he hadn't already.

"Come with me, then," Luca said to Jasper. "Let's check out the Sutherland property and see if anyone is staying there."

"I'm going, too," Aubrey said.

"Neither one of you needs to go," Jasper said—to them both. "I can take a fast ride out there and see if it's as deserted as I think it is."

Luca shook his head. "No. The weather is still bad.

Nobody should go alone." If Warren Parker was willing to shoot at them, he might go after Jasper, too.

And if it hadn't been Warren or someone from that oil company...

Then he'd been right, and somehow the Camorra had figured out where he was, and they had no problem with collateral damage in their quest for revenge against him. They could have killed other guests at the hotel or B and B fires. Luca didn't want anyone else to become collateral damage in the hit on his life.

LUCA ROSSI. SURE, he was calling himself Luke Bishop now, but the assassin recognized him from the picture he'd been given with the envelope of cash. The cash had been enough to pay for two killers, but he'd already cut his partner out of this deal before they'd left for the ranch.

He hadn't wanted to share that money. The initial down payment, or the payoff he would receive when they had proof that Luca Rossi was dead. And he needed the proof—not just to receive the payout but so that he himself wasn't eliminated.

Like those other guys had been by the Camorra for their failures.

His predecessors had failed to take out Luca Rossi in any of those other cities where they'd been tipped off he was staying. The target wasn't a master spy; he was just a journalist.

Rossi should have been easy to kill.

He should have died yesterday. But the guy didn't

have a scratch on him. How the hell had he missed? Had he been too far away?

The next time he would have to make sure he was very close, so that Rossi didn't escape death yet again. And, from eavesdropping on the conversation Rossi had had with the owners of the dude ranch, he knew where Luca was going to be. And he intended to be there, too.

If the Coltons got in his way, then Luca Rossi wouldn't be the only one dying today.

Chapter Thirteen

Warren...

Why hadn't Aubrey considered that he might have had something to do with those gunshots? Probably because she didn't want to admit she'd once dated such a loser. It was bad enough that he'd lied and manipulated her. But to have fired those shots...

Then she remembered the yellowed bruise around his eyes. Maybe he was so desperate to pay off his debts that he'd become dangerous.

Aubrey shivered and it had nothing to do with the cold. She wore a heavy snowmobile suit, gloves and a helmet. So, despite the cold air rushing over her as she sped along, she felt warm. Probably because Luke was pressed against her back, his arms wrapped around her waist.

While he had experience riding horses, he'd admitted to never driving a snowmobile before. She'd tried to get him to remain behind at the ranch and not just because she didn't have the time to give him the lessons that they gave their other guests before they allowed them to use the snowmobiles. She hadn't wanted Luke riding along with her and Jasper. She'd wanted to talk to her twin alone and find out what was wrong exactly.

What had Dominic said to him? Because it was clear that he didn't trust Luke now. In her head, she knew that she shouldn't, either, but in her heart...

She just couldn't believe that he was a bad man. But maybe that was because she was already falling for him.

Why had Luke been so intent on checking out those gunshots? Because of the dangerous people he'd admitted to meeting in his research? Were those people after him now?

He must have thought so, or he wouldn't have been so concerned. He'd tried talking her out of going to the Sutherlands', like he wanted to protect her, like he didn't want to put her in harm's way.

But if Warren was the one who'd fired those shots, then she was the one who'd put Luke in peril.

And if the blizzard had forced Warren to hole up on the Sutherland property, then Jasper could be in danger now as well. But her twin had also been insistent on going along, almost as if he didn't trust her to be alone with Luke.

Maybe it was twin intuition, and he somehow knew that even she didn't trust herself to be alone with Luke. Not because of what he would do but because of what she would do—fall so completely for him that she would get her heart broken for certain. Maybe it was already too late for that.

Jasper had stared most intently at them when they'd entered the great room earlier, like he'd been trying to figure out what was going on between them. He wasn't the only one...

But she'd known what she was doing last night, known that last night might be the only chance she had to be with Luke, to find out if the attraction between them was as powerful as she'd suspected.

It had been more...

So much more.

But that one night would have to be enough—just as she'd determined it was going to be the night before. Maybe, so that she didn't risk falling for him, she would have even been more comfortable if she'd dropped Luke off at his cabin and had never seen him again.

Not that she could see him now but she could feel him. Even through their heavy snowsuits, she could feel the heat and hardness of his body. She wanted to lean into him, but somehow, even with his helmet on, she knew that Jasper was watching them, wondering...

And Aubrey suddenly wondered if he was the only one watching them. Despite the warmth of Luke's body, a sudden chill rushed over her. It wasn't the wind; that had subsided during this break in the storm. The sun was shining, glistening off the snow-covered ground. No. The weather was calm; the storm was inside Aubrey, making her uneasy.

Maybe it was because they were fast approaching the Sutherland property. What if Warren was here? If he was the one who'd fired the shots the day before, then he was armed.

They slowed as they neared the Sutherlands' barn. It was one of just a few structures standing yet on the property. The house had burned, but now even the charred remains of it were gone. People had been working on rebuilding, and maybe someone still was, because despite the storm, another snowmobile was already parked near the barn.

Luke leaned close to her, his helmet bumping against hers, and he advised her, "Kill the engine." Then with a chopping signal with his gloved hand, he gestured for Jasper to do the same.

If it was Warren's snowmobile—and Aubrey knew he had one unless he'd sold it to pay off some of his mounting debts—then he would have already heard them driving up. There wasn't any escaping now…unless they turned around and fled.

But Luke seemed determined to face the danger head-on; he jumped off and rushed toward the barn, pulling his helmet off as he ran. Jasper pulled off his helmet, dropped it onto the seat of his snowmobile, and followed closely behind Luke. Aubrey then tried to catch them, but their legs were longer and the snow was so deep. When she started toward the barn, she sank into a drift up to her thighs.

If that was Warren's snowmobile, if he was holed up in the barn with that weapon, and he hurt either of them…

She would never forgive herself for bringing that man into their lives. "Wait!" she called out to them. "Remember, he has a gun."

"How do you know?" a deep voice asked, and a man stepped out of the open door of the barn. He held a long gun in his gloved hand, but his fingers were nowhere near the trigger. "And do any of you know what the hell this gun was doing here?"

Luke stopped in front of her, turning toward her as if trying to shield her with his body. As if he expected this man to shoot her.

She smiled reassuringly at him and said, "This is my oldest brother, Caleb. His fiancée, Nadine Sutherland, owns the property—but we're going to lease it for grazing."

Nadine stepped out of the barn behind Caleb. Like the rest of them, she was bundled up in a snowmobile suit, the hood covering most of her shoulder-length brown hair but for a few auburn-kissed strands that had slipped out to frame her beautiful face.

"And this is Nadine," she said.

"What are you guys doing out here?" Jasper asked. "How did you even get out of town?"

Caleb pointed to the snowmobile. "Same way you did," he said.

"But you don't own one," Jasper said.

"I borrowed one from a client," Caleb replied. "Nadine got a call yesterday that there was someone shooting around here, and we wanted to check the place out. Make sure nobody from Rutledge Oil was causing trouble again. And we found this…" He held up the gun. Then he focused his lawyerly gaze on Luke like he was on the witness stand. "Who's this?"

Aubrey wasn't sure how to introduce Luke. He was more than a guest but less than a boyfriend. A one-night stand?

Luke saved her the trouble when he stepped forward

to extend his hand to Caleb. "Luke Bishop. I'm staying at the Gemini Ranch."

Caleb shook Luke's hand, but his brow furrowed beneath the fall of brown hair that stuck out beneath his hat. He glanced from Luke to Aubrey and back. "A guest?"

"He's been helping out during the storm," Aubrey explained.

"We heard those shots yesterday while we were moving the cattle. They sounded like they came close to us," Luke explained, "so we wanted to check it out."

Caleb was checking him out now, his eyes narrowed in speculation.

"When you were driving up on your snowmobile, did you see anyone around here?" Luke asked.

Caleb shook his head.

"Does anyone come around to check on the place besides you? A caretaker?" Luke asked, and now *he* sounded like a lawyer. Or an investigator...

Caleb shook his head again. "No. Do you have any ideas about why someone might have been shooting at you?"

"I don't think they were shooting at us," Aubrey said. At least she hoped not. "You know how sounds echo around the mountains."

Jasper pointed at the gun. "Well, the other guests were right when they indicated the sound of shots came from this direction. Any idea who might have been out here?" he asked Nadine.

She shook her head. "I don't know. Maybe one of the

other neighbors. They feel bad that they didn't know what was going on with my dad..."

Al Sutherland was in the early stages of dementia, but he was so proud he hadn't admitted to anyone that he was having trouble remembering things. And that oil company had taken advantage of his age and his pride until Nadine had gotten Caleb involved.

"One of the neighbors called me about the gunshots they heard," Nadine continued, "asking if I was letting anyone hunt on the property."

"Have you given anyone permission?" Luke asked.

Nadine shook her head again. "I haven't, but my father probably has. I will ask him, but I doubt he'll remember who he told..."

Caleb slid his free arm around Nadine's shoulders, pulling her close to his side to comfort her. Al Sutherland had been a difficult man without the dementia. So very proud. Too proud to ask for help when he'd needed it.

If not for Nadine and Caleb's intervention, Rutledge Oil would have gotten away with their horrible plans.

Aubrey gazed around the beautiful property and shuddered over what it might have become. She was thrilled Gemini Ranch would be leasing the pastures for their own livestock.

"Maybe that's all it was, then," Jasper said. "Somebody hunting..."

Her twin didn't sound any more convinced of that than Aubrey was now, since Luke had mentioned Warren. Her ex-boyfriend had been unusually persistent lately with the texts and the calls and then showing up as he had at her house. No, not just persistent. He was clearly desperate.

"Why would a hunter leave their gun behind?" Aubrey asked.

Caleb shrugged. "Maybe they intend to come back."

"Do you mind if I look around?" Luke asked.

Caleb shrugged. "Suit yourself..."

Nadine gestured toward Aubrey. "Come in here and see our plans for the house. We've tacked them up on the barn wall."

Aubrey glanced at Luke, who was walking around the area near the barn, as if looking for tracks. But after last night's storm, she doubted he would be able to find anything that would lead to the location of the shooter. And since Caleb had the gun, she wasn't worried about him getting shot at again, so she followed Nadine inside.

"What's with your guest?" Caleb asked Jasper, as her twin passed their oldest brother.

"Ask Aubrey," Jasper said. "Or better yet, Dominic."

"Dominic?" Caleb asked, his voice sharp with concern. "What's going on?"

Aubrey shook her head. "Nothing." Then she glared at Jasper. "Just my brothers overreacting. That's all that's going on—the usual."

Nadine chuckled and linked her arm through Aubrey's, tugging her farther inside the barn. "He's good-looking," she remarked.

Clearly she'd picked up on Aubrey's attraction to

their guest. Unable to deny the truth, she just nodded and agreed, "Yes, he is…"

And Nadine hadn't even seen him without those clothes.

The image of Luke's long, leanly muscled body flashed through Aubrey's mind and heat flashed through her body, despite the coldness of the empty building.

Nadine chuckled again and pulled Aubrey over to the wall where the construction plans hung. "We're going to completely rebuild the house. It's going to have a private wing for my dad," Nadine said, pointing to the print. "And a lot of bedrooms for all the kids we want to have…"

Caleb and Jasper had joined them, and Caleb slid his arm around his fiancée again. Pulling her back against his body, he kissed the side of her face. "It's going to be perfect," Caleb agreed. "Just like you…"

Aubrey's heart swelled with love and happiness for them, but a pang of envy struck her as well. She wanted that for herself. She wanted what they had.

But would she ever find it when she kept falling only for men she couldn't trust?

MAYBE THEY INTEND to come back…

Caleb Colton's words echoed in Luca's head. That was his fear. That whoever had left that weapon behind planned to return for it. To use it again if they'd not been successful the first time.

Had that person been Warren Parker—intent on

eliminating the competition? Or had it been someone carrying out the Camorra's hit on Luca Rossi?

Too much snow had fallen to see any tracks beyond the ones from Caleb and Nadine's snowmobile and Aubrey's and Jasper's. But someone had been out here, someone had left the gun in the barn.

Luca stepped inside, where everyone had gathered around the plans hanging on one of the barn walls. The four of them laughed and teased each other, and there was so much love that longing struck Luca's heart. And he saw that emotion on Aubrey's face as well.

She wanted this—the kind of future her oldest brother was planning with his fiancée. The house. The kids...

Luca had never considered that kind of future for himself. Had never imagined himself a husband or a father.

He'd always seen himself chasing the next story. But now that last story kept chasing him, trying to kill him. And if he died, what would he leave behind? Who would mourn him besides his mother and some relatives?

And he wondered now about some of those relatives...

At least one.

Or had he been wrong to suspect his cousin of betraying him? Maybe it was that idiot Warren Parker who'd fired those shots. He really hoped it was, even though he could tell that the thought upset Aubrey, undermining her self-confidence even more than Warren's manipulative, backhanded remarks already had.

Aubrey doubted her desirability because of Warren. But she also doubted her own judgment because of Warren and because of Luca. His heart ached that he couldn't be honest with her, that he couldn't tell her everything.

While everyone else studied those plans, he studied her face, watching every emotion play across it. She was so expressive, so genuine…

She deserved someone who could be as sincere as she was. She deserved someone better than a man with a price on his head.

He dragged his gaze away from her and found that someone was watching him. Nadine. The woman studied his face like he'd been studying Aubrey's. What had she seen?

A small smile curved her lips as if she knew or had realized something that no one else knew. Even Luca?

A shiver chased down his spine. The wind returned, a gust of it pushing open the door Luca had closed behind himself. The cold breeze rattled the papers on the wall.

"Oh no," Aubrey said. "Do you want to take them down?"

"We have more than one copy," Caleb said.

He seemed like the kind of guy who would be thorough, who would make sure all the bases were covered. Every one of Aubrey's siblings that Luca had met had impressed him. But what impressed him most was how much they seemed to love each other.

"We should head back to the lodge," Jasper said. "I don't think this break is going to last much longer before the snow starts up again. Why don't you two come back with us?"

"Yes," Aubrey said. "We need to talk about your wedding. Summer will be here before we know it. We want to make sure we have everything ready at the ranch for it."

Nadine shivered inside her snowsuit. "Doesn't feel like summer is coming, and it can't get here fast enough for me."

"Or me," Caleb agreed. "But we'll have to talk wedding plans another time. I have too much to do in town, with work and the Truth Foundation."

"Have you found out anything about Ronald Spence's claims of innocence?" Aubrey asked, and she sounded suspicious.

"Not yet," Caleb said. "But Rebekah is busy working on it."

"Rebekah is Caleb and Morgan's brilliant assistant," Nadine informed Luca. "If there's evidence to be found, she'll find it."

Too bad Rebekah hadn't come out to the ranch with them; maybe she would have found a clue Luca had missed. Because he had no way of knowing for certain who'd fired those shots or why.

They all left the barn together, walking out to their snowmobiles. Caleb held on to the gun he'd found.

"What are you going to do with that?" Luca wondered.

Caleb glanced at it like he'd forgotten that he had it. "It might belong to one of my future father-in-law's friends, so I'm going to hang on to it. See if anyone claims it."

Luca nodded because he couldn't argue with the man. And it wasn't as if he had any connections in Blue Larkspur like he'd had in Naples. He couldn't ask someone to check the registration on it or run a ballistics test.

"Turn it over to Chief Lawson," Jasper recommended. "He should be able to find out who it belongs to. We should know who was firing that thing up here and why." He was staring at Luca now, and his interest drew the oldest brother's gaze to him, too.

Their scrutiny unsettled him, but he suspected they weren't the only ones staring at him. When he glanced at Nadine, though, she wasn't studying him like she had earlier, in the barn. She was engaged in a quiet conversation with Aubrey.

But beyond them, in the fringe of trees around what must have been the foundation of the burned-down farmhouse, Luca noticed something. Between some of those fire-blackened branches, he caught a movement of some sort, a shadow…

Was somebody out there, watching him or all of them?

CALEB STARED AFTER the snowmobiles as they headed away from the Sutherlands'—from his future home— toward Gemini Ranch. Luke Bishop had his arms wrapped around his sister, and Caleb didn't much care for it. And it wasn't just because Aubrey was his younger sibling. A man she shouldn't have trusted had already hurt her, and Caleb was worried that it was about to happen again.

"What do you think about Luke Bishop?" he asked his fiancée. Nadine was a good judge of character.

She smiled. "I think that he's at least halfway in love with your sister, if not all the way," she said.

And Caleb groaned.

"She's not just your little sister," Nadine said, and now her smile was a teasing one. "She's also a beautiful woman."

"I know that," Caleb said.

"Do you know that she's also smart and strong and can take care of herself?"

Caleb narrowed his eyes as if glaring at her even as a grin tugged up his lips. "Yes. But I worry about her. That last guy she dated was a loser."

"And from what I've heard about that situation, Aubrey figured out quickly what the creep was really after, and she didn't fall for him," Nadine said. Her smile slipped away then. "But it might already be too late for her now. Not that I think Luke Bishop is a creep..."

But clearly, she didn't know quite what to make of the man, either.

"When we get back to town, I'm going to call Dominic," Caleb said. "See what he knows about Luke Bishop."

Nadine cocked her head. "Hear that?" she asked.

"What?" he asked. All he could hear was the sound of the snowmobile engines echoing around them. Sounds did carry out here.

"I thought I heard a third snowmobile starting up," Nadine replied.

Caleb's pulse quickened. "You think someone else is hanging around here." He gripped the gun more tightly in his hand. "Coming back for this…"

And when he'd seen them, instead of walking up to talk to them, he'd taken off so he wouldn't be seen. Caleb released a shaky sigh. He'd thought it was all over; that no more bad things were going to happen at Nadine's father's ranch.

"It's going to be fine," his fiancée said, as if she'd read his mind. "We're going to build our beautiful home here and start our family."

She was right. They were going to be fine. It was his siblings whom Caleb was worried about now. Specifically Aubrey…

Chapter Fourteen

Luke's arms tightened around Aubrey, and he leaned over her, his helmet bumping against hers. "There's another snowmobile behind us," he yelled. "And it's not Jasper."

Her pulse quickened, but that was from his closeness, from his breath against her neck. She wasn't worried about the other snowmobiler.

"Caleb and Nadine probably changed their minds," she shouted back at him. She hadn't been exaggerating when she said that summer would be here before they knew it. It was already March, and there was a lot of planning to do for the wedding yet.

Next to her, Jasper turned and glanced over his shoulder. He'd seen it, too.

They weren't far from the ranch now. The sled was the same color as theirs, and as close as it was drawing to them, it was possible that there might have been the Gemini Ranch symbol on the hood of it. If it was one of their sleds, then it was probably a guest out for a solo ride. Or one of the staff coming to get her and Jasper.

Maybe the generators had stopped working or there was an issue with the livestock. The calf...

Jasper must have been having the same thoughts and concerns because he stopped his snowmobile just as she stopped hers.

"What are you doing?" Luke asked, his voice gruff with concern. "You should keep driving. Wait until we get back to the ranch."

"It might be Kayla or one of the other hands," Jasper said.

Interesting that his first thought was of Kayla. Aubrey had begun to wonder about her brother's interest in her. Not that he ever acted interested in her or she in him whenever they were together.

It was almost as if they made an effort to ignore each other. She doubted it was Kayla. For one, the rider was obviously bigger than Kayla. Bigger than Aubrey, too.

This wasn't a woman driving the other snowmobile. But the rider's helmet had a tinted mask on it, hiding their face. Before Aubrey could take another look at the rider, Luke jumped off the back of her sled and stepped between her and the other snowmobile. She tensed, waiting for it to pass them, but it drew to a stop, the driver's gloved hand on the brake. The engine still ran, as if the driver wanted to make a quick escape.

Jasper jumped off his sled, too, and gestured for the person to kill his engine. But the rider revved it instead before finally lifting the shield on his helmet.

Leaning around Luke, she could see the man's face, and anger had her heart slamming against her ribs. She jumped off the sled. "Warren! What the hell are you doing out here?"

She'd tossed him off the ranch two nights ago.

"I want to talk to you," he said, his tone petulant.

"So you stole one of our snowmobiles?" Jasper asked.

Heat flushed Aubrey's face with embarrassment that she'd shown Warren where everything was on the ranch. Apparently she'd shown him too much.

"I'm just borrowing it," Warren said. Probably because he'd sold his, just as she'd wondered if he'd had to, to pay off his debts.

"How'd you get out here from town?" Luke asked. "The roads are impassable."

"Not that it's any of your damn business but I didn't stay in town," he said. He turned back to Aubrey now, his face flushed with his own anger. "Where were you last night?"

She gasped. "You were at my house? How did you get inside?"

"He must've broken in," Luke answered for him, "after he shot at us."

"Shot at you!" Warren exclaimed. "What the hell are you talking about?"

"You know," Luke insisted.

"I'm going to call the police chief," Jasper said. But when he pulled out his cell phone, he grimaced slightly. And Aubrey knew that his phone must be dead or at least without service. Hers had to be the same; she hadn't charged it last night.

And Luke...

His cell phones were in his trash. But he wasn't

reaching for his phone, he was reaching for Warren. Before he could pull the other man from the snowmobile, though, Warren released the brake and headed toward him. One of the skis struck Luke, knocking him back. Since he'd been so intent on staying between her and Warren, he fell into her.

She grabbed at him, trying to hold him up. But he jerked away and started after Warren. Her ex-boyfriend revved the engine and took off, sending a spray of snow back at them—into their faces.

Jasper sputtered, too, then jumped back on his sled. "Don't!" she yelled before he could start it. "Don't chase him! Just let him go."

Luke turned toward her now. "Let him go?"

"He's dangerous," she said. "If he was the one who fired those shots yesterday——"

"Then he left his gun behind," Jasper interrupted her.

"He might have another," Luke admitted. "And if he broke into her place and took the snowmobile, you need to call the police chief like you said you were going to."

Shame rushed over Aubrey, churning in her stomach. For some reason she didn't want the chief—didn't want anyone else—to know how stupid she'd been to get involved with a man like Warren Parker.

"Wait," she said.

"You don't want to call the police on him?" Jasper asked.

"Call Caleb," she said. "Make sure he brings that gun to the chief. If it's Warren's or can be traced to him, then yes, we need to call the police. But right now we don't know that it's his weapon. We don't know that he broke into my place or the snowmobile shed." He could have paid attention when she'd entered the code for the door lock—which was an electronic one like the ones on all the cabins and rooms in the lodge. He could have remembered how to get inside.

But if he knew the code, he could claim that she'd given it to him. And all of this would just be a messy case of "he said, she said," with no proof to support their suspicions about Warren Parker.

"He stole that snowmobile. Even if you don't believe he fired those shots yesterday, he should be arrested for theft."

Jasper nodded in agreement. "He will be. I'm going back to the lodge. I'm going to call the police."

Aubrey figured the chief would come out—even though it wasn't a big theft. He seemed to have some kind of personal interest in their family—maybe because of what their father had done. Or maybe because of their mother...

Isa Colton was a beautiful woman; Aubrey had been told that she looked like her. Sometimes when she looked at older photos of Isa she could see it, and she certainly hoped she aged as well as her mother had. Mama was a beautiful seventy-two with her blond hair cut to shoulder length and a full figure that still made men turn their heads when she entered a room. Along with her looks, she had talent—as an artist. She also had a strength that Aubrey envied—the strength to survive her husband's betrayal and raise twelve kids on her own.

Mama had been fooled, so maybe Aubrey shouldn't feel so bad about Warren having momentarily fooled her. Unlike Aubrey her mother had made certain to never trust another man. Not that Aubrey trusted Luke...

But she hadn't been able to resist her attraction to him, either.

She continued to resist his and her brother's insistence on calling the police, though. "It's going to be a waste of time investigating a snowmobile theft." For an officer and especially for the chief. "I'm sure it will soon be found somewhere on the property."

And when Warren was questioned, he would swear that she'd told him he could use them anytime. And nearly a year ago, she probably had—before she'd learned about his gambling and that getting her to pay off his debts was his real reason for dating her.

"He's dangerous," Jasper said. "You need to come back to the lodge with me."

Aubrey shook her head. "I can handle Warren," she insisted. She wasn't sure she could handle the humiliation of being involved with a loser like him, though.

She could barely look at Luke. If Warren had fired those shots, and it certainly looked like he had, then Luke could have been killed because of her. Because of the mistakes she'd made...

LUCA WASN'T SURE what was going on, why Aubrey didn't want her brother calling the police. But Jasper had insisted on doing it and had ridden off on his snowmobile toward the main lodge.

"You should have gone with him," she said.

He shook his head. "I'm not leaving you alone. Jasper's right. You should go back there, too."

"I'm going to check on my house," she said.

He'd known she was going to stubbornly insist on it; that was another reason he hadn't gone with Jasper— though the man had offered. Warren Parker showing up when he had, on a stolen snowmobile, must have allayed whatever suspicions Jasper had had about Luca.

About Luke Bishop...

A pang of regret struck Luca that he had to lie to all of them. But most especially to Aubrey.

She deserved better, especially after being involved with a guy like Warren Parker.

"I'm going with you," Luca insisted, but as he started toward the snowmobile, pain shot up his leg, and he stumbled and nearly fell.

"Oh my God, are you all right?" she asked.

He glanced down at the snowmobile suit he wore— the material on one of the legs was torn.

"You're bleeding," she said.

If he was, it was too cold for him to feel it; and now that his suit was torn, he could feel the cold. The wind was beginning to whip up again—just a gust here and there, not yet the sustained fury of the night before.

And only a few random snowflakes drifted down from the dark clouds hanging overhead. It seemed as if the storm was hovering just out of reach for now, but it wasn't done with them yet.

Kind of like the Camorra...

Even if they hadn't found Luca yet, they would. And

they certainly weren't done with him yet. They wouldn't be until he was dead.

Just as Warren didn't seem done with Aubrey yet. What was he going to do to her, though? How did he think he was going to change her mind about giving him money?

"I'm fine," Luca insisted, and he managed to suppress the grimace of pain that threatened to cross his face when he hobbled the couple of feet through the deep snow to the machine.

Aubrey had already jumped on it, and he swung his leg over the seat and climbed onto it. "I'm taking you back to the lodge," she said as she turned back toward him. The face shield was up on her helmet, so that he could see the furrows on her brow, the concern for him. "And maybe the roads will be clear enough to get you to town."

"I'm fine," he insisted. "It's not broken." Or he would have fallen on his face. "It's just a scrape. Let's get back to your house and make sure that it's secure."

"But if Warren's there…"

"You'll protect me," he said with a smile.

She didn't smile back, and her blue eyes darkened more with concern. "I'm sorry," she murmured.

"For what?" he asked.

"That you were hurt—"

"I'm fine," he insisted.

"You could have been hurt worse," she said. "With the snowmobile and with those gunshots. If that is Warren's gun, he probably was firing at you, trying to get you out of his way."

"We don't know that it is Warren's gun," he reminded her. And he had a niggling doubt that it wasn't, that Luca was instead the one who'd put her in danger.

But he didn't know for certain…

It could have been Warren. The man was certainly acting desperate enough that he might have shot at him.

"Let's go to your house," he said. "Let's check it out."

She nodded in agreement. "And we can look at your leg. See how bad it is, if you'll need stitches…"

He grimaced now.

"Not a fan of hospitals?"

He shook his head. But it wasn't just his injury that concerned him. He had that sensation again, that feeling he'd had earlier when he'd noticed someone around the Sutherland barn. Someone was still watching them.

AT LAST THEY were alone…

Just Rossi and that woman, Aubrey Colton. Earlier there had been the other man, Jasper Colton, and then the other one.

The one who'd been skulking around the ranch, sticking close to them but not close enough that he would have been able to kill them all. Somebody could have served as a witness to the assassination.

He *would* leave no witnesses behind to identify him. He waited a few moments until he started up his snowmobile again, wanting to make sure that anyone else was far enough away that they wouldn't hear it.

It didn't matter, though. He'd heard them. He knew where they were going, back to her house, which was perfect. It was near Rossi's little cabin, and far enough away from the rest of the ranch that nobody would see or hear the murders.

Because now he had no choice. With the woman sticking as close as she was to Luca Rossi, she had sealed her fate.

Or Luca had sealed it for her.

She was going to die. Just as—*finally*—Luca Rossi was going to die.

Chapter Fifteen

Aubrey knew someone had been in her home the moment she opened the door, and a shudder of revulsion rippled down her spine. Luke must have noticed, too, because he caught her arm and held her back from stepping over the threshold.

"Wait," he said. "He could still be in here."

She shook her head. "No. We didn't see any fresh tracks." But there had definitely been tracks from another snowmobile outside and footprints from someone walking out of the French doors and across the deck that spanned the front of it. She shuddered again at the invasion of her privacy, of her space, and suddenly she realized how Luke must have felt when he'd found her in his cabin.

"I'm sorry," she said, guilt weighing so heavily on her for that and for his getting injured. "Let's get you inside and take a look at that leg."

She would deal with Warren later, or better yet, she would let the police deal with him. Jasper had been right to insist on calling them.

"I'm fine," Luke assured her again, but he wobbled a bit in the doorway.

She slid her arm around his back and helped him over the threshold. Then she closed and locked the door. Not that that would keep out Warren.

He knew the code.

How had she been so stupid?

And was she being that stupid all over again with Luke Bishop? She turned toward him then and found him staring at her.

"Please, stop beating yourself up," he implored her. "It's not your fault. None of this is your fault."

She nodded as if she agreed. But she didn't.

Luke pulled off his gloves and reached for her face, cupping it in his hands. "You are a smart woman, Aubrey Colton. You didn't fall for him…" He waited then as if he was afraid that she had; maybe he thought that was why she'd been reluctant to call the cops.

"No, I didn't," she said. "But I shouldn't have even gone out with him. I was a fool."

"Why?" he asked. "You didn't give him any money…"

"No, I didn't," she said. "When he started asking for it, I broke things off. I realized then that was his only interest in me."

"He's an idiot," Luke said. "You're so damn desirable. And you know you deserve better than Warren Parker." Then in almost a whisper he added, "I know that, too."

Was he implying that he wasn't better? Because he was…

He was so good that he was making her heart ache for him. And he was right there in front of her, his balance unsteady as he shifted all his weight to one leg. He swayed as if he'd been drinking, but she wasn't sure he'd even had a cup of coffee yet that morning.

"Come in here," she said, and she helped him over to the hearth. A fire had been lit there last night; it must have been how Warren had kept warm the night before. That and the blankets he'd left piled on the couch.

At least her ex apparently hadn't used her bed. She had never invited him to share it, and she certainly never wanted him to be there.

Not like she wanted Luke...

But he was hurt. She needed to focus on that now and not her attraction to him. "I'll start a fire while you get out of your snowsuit."

Fortunately Warren hadn't used all the wood that she had chopped and piled in a large crate next to the hearth. She was able to start a fire quickly, the flickering flames casting a warmth and a glow into the room and onto Luke. He'd unzipped and pushed his suit down, revealing his second layer of jeans and flannel shirt beneath them. The jeans were torn, just like the suit had been.

With the heat of the fire warming her, she shucked off her boots and suit as well. But she suspected it wasn't just the flames that warmed her but the memories that flitted through her mind from the night before, of what Luke had done to her, how he'd made her feel...

"You need to take off your jeans, too," she said. "We need to see how bad the wound is."

He wriggled his dark eyebrows at her. "You sure you're not just trying to get me out of my pants?"

She wouldn't mind; she definitely wouldn't mind. "We need to evaluate whether or not you'll need stitches."

"It doesn't matter if I do," he said. "We're not going to risk the roads and storm to drive to town, and you're not a doctor. Not that I'm opposed to playing doctor with you..." He wriggled his brows again.

And a smile tugged at her lips. "You're..."

"Incorrigible," he supplied when she trailed off.

That hadn't been the word she'd been about to use— she was going to say *wonderful*. But she didn't know if that was true; she didn't know if anything was true anymore. Her smile slid away, and she narrowed her eyes. "We need to at least clean up the wound," she said. "So drop your jeans."

"If you insist..." he murmured as he undid the button. Then he slowly—so very slowly—lowered the zipper.

The rasp of the metal echoed the rasp of the shaky breath Aubrey took. He pushed down the jeans, revealing the boxers he wore beneath them. As the denim caught on his lower leg, he grimaced.

Aubrey stepped closer and crouched down to inspect his wound. The snowmobile ski had ripped the material of his suit and jeans and some of his skin. But the scratches weren't deep; they'd already stopped bleeding, the dried blood sticking his jeans to the wound.

"I need to get your jeans off so I can clean your scratches," she said.

"Then do it fast like you're ripping off a Band-Aid," Luke agreed, and his jaw clenched as if he was gritting his teeth.

She couldn't bring herself to pull it hard, though; she didn't want to hurt him. So she started easing the denim away from his scratches, but he reached down and jerked it, then let out a low groan.

Blood started oozing again, streaking down his leg through the hair on his shin. "We need to clean this up," she said. "And get some bandages on it."

"Can I use your shower?" Luke asked.

And she remembered that day he'd been fresh from the shower when he'd caught her in his cabin. Desire choking her, she could only nod.

"It would be more fun if you joined me," he said but almost hesitantly as if he wasn't sure he should make the offer.

Or that she would welcome it?

She shouldn't, because she couldn't completely trust him. But then she might never be able to feel that way with anyone, not fully. She did trust, though, that Luke was a good man—one who pitched in and helped out, who cared about animals and people.

One who cared about her...

And she cared about him. Even if they had no future, even if he didn't intend to stay on in Blue Larkspur, she would always remember him. And she wanted more memories with him.

"The bathroom is this way," she said and started up the stairs that led to the second story of her home, which encompassed her master suite. As she'd hoped, the bed was made—the space untouched—and she was grateful that Warren hadn't been in her room.

She doubted, too, that he'd stuck around the ranch. If he believed they were going to call the police on him, he would have definitely found a way to get off the property—even if he had to drive the snowmobile to town.

"Are you okay?" Luke asked, as his hands settled on her shoulders.

She leaned back against him for a second before remembering that he was the one who was hurt—because of Warren Parker and because of her. And she jerked away from him. "Yes," she said. "Are you? How badly is your leg hurting?"

"Not so bad that I can't do this..." He leaned down then, scooped her up his arms and carried her into the adjoining bathroom.

"Luke!" she protested. She was too heavy for him—even if he wasn't injured.

But he didn't betray any weakness. All he betrayed, as he stared down at her so intensely, was desire. For her...

In the bathroom, he moved his hand from beneath her legs, so that she slid down his body. And through the thin material of his boxers and her jeans, she could feel his reaction to her closeness.

She was reacting as well—with a quickening of her pulse, with a pull from her nipples to her core. She'd never desired anyone the way she did Luke Bishop.

"We should shower," he said. "Clean up. Warm up..."

But instead of reaching for the faucet in the large walk-in shower, he reached for the buttons on her shirt and her jeans. He undressed her quickly; just as quickly she undressed him.

Then, naked and vulnerable before him, she shivered. And finally he reached inside the shower and turned on the faucet. While they waited for the water to warm up, he heated her with his gaze, running it hungrily over her.

"You are so beautiful..." he murmured. Then he leaned down and kissed her, and his mouth moved hungrily over hers.

Locked in each other's arms, they stumbled into the shower and under the warm spray of water. They bathed each other—with soap and caresses and then kisses.

There was a bench in her shower, and Luke settled her onto it before settling between her legs. He made love to her with his mouth, and as she screamed his name, he entered her. Then he tensed and groaned. "Condom..." he murmured.

Before he could pull out, Aubrey clutched him against her. "It's fine. I have an IUD and I've been tested."

"Me, too," he said then chuckled. "Well, not the IUD. But I've been tested." All soap and water, his skin was slick, her body wet as he slid in and out of her. And as he moved inside her, he kissed her and stroked her nipples, rousing her desire again, building that pressure inside her.

Until it broke and she screamed his name...

Then he tensed again, and his body shuddered as he found his release.

"Aubrey!" He uttered her name with awe and wonder.

And she felt the same—that what they shared, what they felt with each other was awe-inspiring. And even if it didn't last, that would be enough.

These memories would be enough—she hoped.

HE SHOULDN'T BE HERE. Not in her bed after sex in the shower. Not in her home. But Luca couldn't bring himself to leave her even though he knew he should.

If the Camorra found him...

But maybe it was safer for her if he stayed—in case Warren Parker came back. What the hell was the man up to? And how the hell had he had the nerve to let himself into her house?

Luca could understand her ex not wanting to let her go, but the man wasn't going to win her back by manipulating and threatening her.

Even if Aubrey could be won back...

Once her trust had been broken, it was clear that Aubrey wouldn't offer it again. Which was yet another reason Luca knew he needed to leave.

He had been concerned earlier, when she hadn't wanted her brother to call the police, that she still had feelings for her ex. But it was clear that she'd been more worried about looking like an idiot than about the police arresting Warren Parker.

Warren deserved to be arrested, though. He needed to be locked up for threatening her.

"What's the matter?" Aubrey asked, her head on his chest. She must have heard the fast beating of his heart, or maybe he'd tensed with the anger coursing through him.

"I'm worried about you," he said.

She uttered a soft sigh that whispered across his bare skin as she murmured, "Me, too…"

He wondered if she was worried because of Parker or because of him. And he was afraid to ask.

A sound saved him from asking, though—the low rumble of an engine. It wasn't a car or truck, but a snowmobile.

Was it Warren?

Had he come after them? Luca released Aubrey and slid out of the bed.

"Where are you going?" she asked.

Hadn't she heard it?

"Someone's coming," he said. And he intended to be ready for whomever it was.

JASPER UNDERSTOOD WHY Aubrey didn't want him to call the police on Warren. She was embarrassed, and more than that, she was probably concerned about the ranch as well.

How would a police report about a theft and a break-in affect their reputation? Would word get out? Jasper really didn't care about any of that; he cared instead about protecting his sister, his partner.

And once he'd left her alone with Luke Bishop, he had a strange feeling. Not so much about Luke but about Warren.

Where had he gone?

Had he left the ranch? Or was he just out there some-where? And what did the man intend to do?

Had Warren fired those shots from the Sutherland

property? Had he been trying to scare Aubrey or Luke? Or worse?

While Jasper had understood Aubrey's qualms about calling the police, he'd returned to the main lodge and done it anyway. If Warren had fired those shots, he was even more dangerous than Jasper had once thought he was. Then he'd considered the guy to just be a gambler and grifter. Now he realized that the man was capable of even more. Of theft.

Of attempted murder?

Unfortunately Jasper hadn't been able to convince the dispatcher that Warren posed an immediate danger, and with the storm having shut down the city, they hadn't been willing to spare an officer to come all the way out to the ranch to investigate someone taking a joyride on one of their snowmobiles. So, after making the call, Jasper had climbed back onto his machine to do a little investigating of his own.

Knowing that Aubrey and Luke had intended to return to her house to see if Warren had broken into it the night before, he'd headed in that direction. He hadn't gone far when he'd seen their tracks. At least sets that might have been theirs...

Theirs weren't the only ones, though.

Somebody had followed them. Had Aubrey and Luke noticed that they were being tailed?

Jasper couldn't tell. He could only speed up and follow the tracks to where they'd stopped—on the edge of the road that led to Aubrey's house. One snowmobile was parked in that area, and Jasper pulled his sled up next to it and killed the engine. Then he pulled off his helmet, so that he had better peripheral vision. And he peered around him.

Where had the rider gone? He studied the ground and found the bootprints deep in the snow that led from the abandoned snowmobile toward a stand of pines along the edge of Aubrey's yard.

A dark figure crouched beneath the boughs of one of the big pines, staring at the house.

Warren...

It had to be.

Jasper moved more quietly, more slowly—intent on sneaking up on the man, on catching him...

But he only made it a few feet before something struck him, knocking him into that deep snow, and everything went black.

Chapter Sixteen

Where the hell had he gone? One minute Luke was in bed with her. The next he was nowhere to be found.

Would it be like that when he left for good? Aubrey had no time to ponder that. She quickly dressed and headed down the stairs just as the side door flew open, bouncing back against the mudroom wall. Two men stumbled through it, blood dripping from one of them.

She gasped at the sight of Jasper, leaning heavily on Luke, who had his arm wrapped around him. "Oh my God!" Her heart pounded hard with fear. "Are you all right?" she asked her twin.

Jasper squinted at her, as if his head was pounding as well as bleeding. Or as if he was struggling to focus...

How badly was he injured?

"Are you all right?" she asked again. "What happened?"

He grunted but nodded. "Yeah. Somebody hit me over the head..."

She turned on Luke. "Did you hit him?"

"Of course not!" he exclaimed. Then he half dragged, half carried her brother through the mudroom down the hall to the great room and the couch. "I found him lying in the snow like this..."

Bleeding. Injured.

With a grimace of pain, Jasper sank into the blankets Warren had left piled on the couch.

Her heart ached with pain and concern for her twin. "I'll call an ambulance."

"If I've got a pulse, they're not coming out—not with the mess the snowstorm caused," Jasper said. "The police wouldn't send anyone out to take a report about Warren stealing the snowmobile."

"But now that he hit you, they have to send someone out," Luke said, and he handed Jasper a towel he must have retrieved from the kitchen.

As Jasper pressed the towel to his head, he stared at Luke, his eyes narrowed now with suspicion, as if he doubted what Luke had said. Did he think that Luke was the one who'd struck him?

Luke shook his head. "It wasn't me. It had to be Warren."

"How?" Jasper asked. "He's the one I was sneaking up behind when someone whacked me over the head."

Aubrey gasped again. "What?" She looked at Luke hard, wondering, too, but then she shook her head. "No." No matter what his secrets were, Luke Bishop had no reason to hurt her brother.

Warren did, though, especially if he'd been worried Jasper was going to hold him until the police arrived to arrest him.

"Are you sure it was Warren you were sneaking up behind?" she asked.

"Who else would it have been?" Jasper asked. "I saw

a snowmobile from the ranch parked along the road and followed tracks up to your yard. Someone was crouching down by the pine trees, watching the house."

She shivered at the thought of someone being out there while she and Luke…

Her face got hot as embarrassment rushed over her. She and Luke had come here to see if Warren had broken into her house and to check his wound and then they'd wound up in the shower and then in bed.

Just as last night in the barn, they'd made a bed of blankets in the tack room. And she hadn't wanted to leave his arms then or now.

But Luke had had no such qualms of his own when he'd jumped up and rushed out of the bedroom. To strike her brother?

She shook head. "It doesn't make sense…"

"You said Warren has gambling debts," Luke reminded her.

And her embarrassment increased so much that she could only nod.

"Maybe someone is after him, trying to collect them," Luke suggested.

"And I got in the way?" Jasper asked and shrugged. "Makes about as much sense as any of this does." Then he turned toward Aubrey and asked, "Why does Warren think he's going to get money out of you?"

Because he thought she was so undesirable to any other man that he could manipulate her…

She wasn't about to admit that aloud, so she just shrugged.

"Because he's a fool," Luke answered for her. "Because he never really knew or appreciated you at all."

Was that how Luke really felt or was he the one who was trying to manipulate her now? Aubrey wasn't certain if she should believe him, but then she remembered how they'd just made love.

And she doubted that anyone could fake the passion that Luke seemingly felt for her.

The passion she felt in turn for him—so much so that she'd forgotten Warren was running around out there somewhere, desperate and dangerous, and apparently he was not alone.

But Jasper had been alone out there and could have died. "We need to get you to the ER," she insisted. "You need to have a CT scan, make sure that you don't have a concussion."

"I've got a hard head," Jasper said. "And you can't deny it since you tell me that all the time."

"You're the one who tells me that," she reminded him.

"That's because we're so much alike," he said and his lips curved into a slight, weak smile.

She wasn't so sure about that; Jasper certainly had had better judgment than she did when it came to relationships. Not that he'd had many, either, since they had always been so busy with the ranch. All their hard work had paid off, though. The place was a success; unfortunately, that had made her a target for Warren. And he just couldn't accept that he had failed to charm her.

"We need to get back up to the main lodge," Jasper said, "and make sure our guests are all safe."

Of course he would be worried about the business, just as he always had.

"My first concern is for you," she said.

"Same," he replied with a glance at Luke Bishop. Was Warren or Luke the reason he'd come out to her house to check on her?

"Let's get you up to the main lodge and we'll find out how the roads are and if we can get you into town," she said.

Jasper stood but wobbled slightly before Luke reached out and caught his shoulder to steady him. "Careful," he murmured.

"You're going to have to drive his snowmobile," she told Luke.

Luke nodded. "Fine. And we need to be extra careful on our way back to the lodge because he's still out there somewhere."

Jasper had already been hurt. Clearly, they were all in danger. Aubrey's shoulders drooped with the burden that it was her fault—because she'd had the bad judgment to date Warren Parker in the first place.

Had she fallen victim to her own bad judgment again over getting involved with a guest—with a man she barely knew?

Was Warren Parker the only danger? Or was Luke Bishop dangerous, too?

LUCA DIDN'T KNOW what might have caused more damage to Jasper Colton—the blow to his head or clinging to Luca as he'd learned how to drive the snowmobile. The man had been lucid enough to direct him with how to use the controls and where to go.

Aubrey had been following them, probably to make sure that she'd be able to notice if Jasper fell off. Luca hadn't liked her being back there; he'd worried that if someone shot at them again, she would be hit.

And she couldn't really be the target, could she? Warren wouldn't be able to get any money out of her if she was dead. The same of whomever Warren owed that money to...

They couldn't collect their debts from a dead man, either. So why would they try to shoot or kill people? Maybe that was why Jasper had been just knocked out, and why he wasn't dead.

When Jasper slid off the snowmobile back at the main lodge, he was steadier despite the way he flinched.

"You okay?" Luca asked him.

Jasper flinched again. "Yeah, now that that ride's over."

"Sorry." And not just about the ride...

Luca wasn't convinced that Warren was the one who'd hit Jasper or shot at them. Jasper had been sneaking up behind someone, so who had snuck up behind him? Who'd struck him hard enough to knock him out?

It made no sense for it to be someone Warren owed money to...

What made sense was that the Camorra had found Luca again and that this time they'd sent a couple of assassins after him. After the previous attempts on his life had failed, they probably weren't taking any more chances on his slipping away unscathed yet again.

But until they knew how bad the roads were, Luca wasn't sure he would be able to go anywhere. He was trapped here...maybe with his would-be killers.

When he and Jasper and Aubrey walked into the

lodge, everybody once again turned to stare. It probably wasn't because of Jasper—not with the way his blood had dried and blended into the strawberry blond color of his hair. Nobody had probably noticed that he was hurt…unless they were the one who'd struck him.

Luca peered around the room now, automatically dismissing the families. There were several of those in the great room, using tables to play games or put together puzzles while outside the snow began to fall again.

The wind wasn't hurling the precipitation at the glass with the velocity it had come down last night. The sparkly white flakes just drifted softly to the ground now, falling atop all that had already accumulated.

Just how long was this break in the storm supposed to last? Long enough for him to leave Gemini Ranch and Blue Larkspur?

But that meant getting someone from town to come out to pick him up. Unless he could drive Jasper to town in one of the ranch trucks. Surely they were four-wheel drive?

"You really should have a CT scan," he said. "Make sure that you don't have a concussion."

"I'm fine," Jasper insisted. "I just have a little headache. I'll take something for that and be back at it."

Aubrey studied her twin through eyes narrowed behind the lenses of her glasses. "Luke's right. You really should get checked out. I can drive you to town."

Jasper shook his head and flinched again. "We shouldn't both leave the ranch," he said. "Not with the storm starting up again. We don't want to get stuck in town."

"I can take you," Luca offered.

And Jasper narrowed his eyes now with suspicion. "No. I'm not leaving."

"Then at least let me get you the painkillers," Luca offered. "Where are they? Behind the desk?" He started toward the reception area at the front of the lodge. The computers were back there, the ones with all the guest records. He could find out who'd checked in recently, like after he'd made that call to Paolo.

Maybe Paolo hadn't given him up to the Camorra. Maybe he wasn't even aware that his phone had been tapped or his line recorded or…

Luca thought about his last conversation with Paolo, wondering if his cousin purposely kept it going, getting details out of him about where he was staying just as he had done every time Luca had called him before. He understood Aubrey's embarrassment and frustration over trusting Warren Parker.

Luca knew how it felt to trust someone you shouldn't have. He even understood her situation with her dad, now that someone he loved might have betrayed his trust, too.

"They're not back there," Jasper told Luca, stopping him from going any further.

"We have a small medical office in the lodge," Aubrey explained. "Usually it's staffed with a nurse, but since it's technically the off-season, she only comes in a few days a week."

"Is she here today?" he asked.

She shook her head.

But Jasper hesitated. "She might be here. She was

here yesterday, and if the weather got too bad for her to leave…"

Like it had for Warren? Was that why he'd stayed in Aubrey's house? Because he hadn't been able to leave? Or was he hiding out from the people to whom he owed money?

No doubt the man was desperate; Luca understood that better than anyone. But was he dangerous?

Luca suspected there was someone far more lethal hanging around the ranch. Someone who'd been sent here specifically for him.

"Why don't you two see if the nurse is here?" he suggested. "Maybe a medical professional can talk him into going to the ER."

And even if she didn't, maybe Luca would have enough time to search through those guest records, to find viable suspects for the roles of Camorra hitmen…

Aubrey stared at him with suspicion, as if she knew he was up to something. "What are you going to do?" she asked.

He shrugged. "See what the chef has available to eat." His stomach grumbled at the thought of food, and he realized he hadn't eaten in a while.

But when she and her brother walked off, Luca didn't head to the kitchen. He headed instead to that reception desk. Whoever had been working it must have stepped away, and she'd left her computer unlocked. He didn't even have to figure out a password to pull up guest records. That could have been how someone had been able to search his cabin without breaking into it. Aubrey and whoever had searched his cabin the next day could have easily obtained the codes.

He scanned through the ones who'd checked into Gemini Ranch after Luca had placed that ill-advised call to his cousin. Even then he had already begun to suspect...

To wonder how the Camorra had tracked him down, despite the haphazard route he'd taken from Italy through Canada and then the northern United States to Colorado now. He knew all too well that Camorra methods were just as sophisticated as any other criminal organization's, so he'd been so careful, except for Paolo. He turned his attention to that guest list again.

One family and two couples had checked into the ranch after his call to Paolo. He dismissed the family, but one of these couples could be assassins the Camorra had hired.

His killers...

If they proved successful.

"This isn't the kitchen," Aubrey said.

Startled, Luca jumped and muttered an Italian curse. Being as distracted as he was—because of her—he wasn't certain he would be as lucky as he'd been when the Camorra had tracked him down in the past.

He wasn't certain that he would be able to escape.

"I was just looking for..." He floundered for an excuse.

"For what?" she prodded him.

She had to have noticed that he was on the computer, checking her guest records. He was surprised he hadn't felt her presence, like he felt it now in the quickening of his pulse, in the tightening of his muscles.

"I thought I recognized a couple who are sitting out in the great room," he said. "But I couldn't remember their names, so I pulled up the records to check."

She tilted her head then, studying his face. "You're not a good liar," she said. But rather than being angry with him for trying to tell her a falsehood, she seemed almost relieved.

"Why would I lie to you about this?" he asked instead. She was too smart to fall for it, just as she had been too smart to fall for Warren Parker's manipulations. She hadn't given him money, at least, but Luca was worried that the man had affected her self-esteem.

"Why would you lie to me, Luke?" she asked. "Why would you lie about anything? Who are you really?"

He wanted to tell her—so very badly—but even now he could feel that he was being watched. That *they* were being watched, and he didn't want to put her in any more danger than he already had. This was that sensation he'd noticed before—in those other cities—that had made him realize that someone had recognized him or been sent for him. That was how he'd managed to escape before getting hurt. With the blizzard trapping him at the ranch, escaping wasn't going to be easy.

"I don't know what you're talking about," he insisted, and he really wished that he didn't. That he was just a regular guest with no secrets, no assassins chasing him down everywhere he ran.

He wanted to stop running. He wanted to stay with her. But he forced himself to walk away now, toward the kitchen. "I really am hungry," he said.

"That's probably about the only truthful thing you've told me," she murmured.

He turned back then, at her words, and he reached out and trailed his fingers along her jaw. "It's not," he promised her. "Every compliment I've given you has been wholly deserved and entirely truthful. You're an amazing woman, Aubrey Colton."

And it was going to kill him to leave her. But better that he left than risk her getting killed with him. He would never forgive himself if he cost her her life or even her livelihood. He knew how much the ranch meant to her, how it was the realization of a dream she'd had since she was a child.

And if the same thing happened here that had happened at that hotel or at the B and B, Luca wouldn't forgive himself for that, either. And if they both survived, he doubted that she would ever forgive him anyway.

Is it over yet?

The text finally came through his phone, service temporarily restored. The service wouldn't last, though, not with the storm kicking up again.

Colorado...

He was not a fan. Not of this state, this country and especially not of this damn assignment. At least they were inside now, back at the main lodge, and he was able to sit near the roaring fire with the woman he'd hired to portray his wife. It had been cheaper to pay her than to cut his partner in on this job. Or so he'd thought...

He didn't know if this woman was really a wannabe actress. She was overplaying her role, which was annoying him so much that he would be relieved when he killed her. And he was going to have to do it eventually, just so that nothing could be traced back to him once he eliminated his target and collected the rest of his payment.

Aubrey Colton's ex-boyfriend was proving a pain in his ass, too. But he would pay for getting in the way—not with his life but with his freedom. He provided the perfect scapegoat for the murder of Aubrey's new lover.

Luca Rossi.

No.

Luke Bishop.

Nobody here knew him as Luca Rossi, not even her, he suspected. But it wouldn't matter what name they called him.

All that mattered, in the end, was that the man was dead. And it had to happen soon, before somebody noticed him following them around.

Luca scanned the great room then, and his gaze seemed to rest on him, like he knew.

Like he suspected.

From what he'd overheard, the others might have believed that dolt ex-boyfriend was responsible for the shooting the day before and for hitting the brother over the head…

But Rossi knew the truth. He knew that no matter where he went, the Camorra was going to track him down. They weren't going to forgive and forget about him.

They were going to have their vengeance. So—before he lost service again—he quickly texted back:

It will be over soon...

It had to be if he was going to escape as he had so many times in the past—if he was going to carry out his assignment and leave before suspicion fell on him. He had to act fast.

He had to kill Luca Rossi now.

Chapter Seventeen

"You're sure you're really okay?" Aubrey asked her brother.

Jasper had insisted on talking to the nurse without her. That was why she'd returned to the front desk when she had caught Luke going through the guest records.

Had he really recognized someone? And from where?

"I'm fine," Jasper insisted. "The cut stopped bleeding, and I just have a small bump." He reached up as he said it and touched the back of his head, and then he grimaced.

Aubrey wasn't entirely sure she believed him. Just as she wasn't entirely sure she believed Luke about that couple. She glanced around the great room now, trying to figure out which one he might have recognized. Some of the couples had left, probably to return to their rooms after eating dinner.

Luke had eaten, like he'd initially claimed he had intended to. He sat at a table by himself. Aubrey ached to join him, and not just because she was hungry, too. In fact, she wasn't at all in the mood for food right now. Her stomach churned with nerves instead, over what could have been a near brush with death for her brother and with the fear that there might not be just a brush next time.

But would Jasper be the target again?

Or would Luke?

"I'm going to stay at the main lodge again tonight," Jasper said.

"That's a good idea," she agreed. That way, if he needed help because of the blow to his head, he would be closer to the nurse than if he was at his house.

"You should stay here, too," he told her.

"Why?" she asked. "I'm not hurt."

"Warren was at your place last night and earlier today," Jasper said. "He could have returned to it and be waiting for you to come back. You shouldn't be alone."

She didn't want to be alone; she wanted to be with Luke. But he hadn't asked her to join him for dinner. Instead he'd walked away from her as if he wanted some distance.

Could she blame him, with her ex-boyfriend acting so desperate and dangerous? But Luke wasn't the kind of person who seemed intent on keeping himself safe— not after he'd admitted to having researched dangerous people for his book. So she wondered if Luke was trying to stay away from her for his protection or for hers...

Which was silly speculation on her part. Probably something she wanted to believe just like she wanted to believe he was a good man and that all those compliments he'd given her really had been the truth.

"You need to stay, too," Jasper persisted. "It's too dangerous for you to go back to your house." He touched his head again, as if he needed to remind her of his wound.

She wasn't likely to forget that he'd been injured because of her. "I'm so sorry," she said.

He furrowed his brow. "About what?"

"About Warren," she said. "I had no idea when I first started going out with him what he was really like…" That his only interest had been in her money. He'd been so funny and charming when they'd first met at The Corner Pocket, a billiards bar in downtown Blue Larkspur. He'd challenged her to a game of pool with the loser having to buy dinner. He'd wound up paying that night. He wasn't a good pool player; at the time she'd thought he'd lost on purpose. Now she knew he was just that unlucky.

"I didn't see who hit me, so we don't know for sure that it was Warren," Jasper said. And he glanced across the great room at Luke now.

"I really don't think he had time to hit you and for you to have regained consciousness by the time he helped you into my house," Aubrey said in defense of her lover. She was worried that she was trying to convince herself of that as much as she was trying to convince her twin, though.

"He did help me," Jasper acknowledged. "I just think something's off about the guy."

"You liked him until Dominic talked to you," she reminded him.

"*You're* the one who talked to Dominic," he reminded her. "You're the one who asked our FBI agent brother to check up on a guest. Why, Aubrey? What's your interest in this guy?"

She shrugged. She couldn't say because she couldn't put it into words.

"You were the one who saw it first," Jasper said. "You noticed that there's something strange about him, something secretive, or you wouldn't have called Dominic."

"I shouldn't have," she said. Because Dominic had only raised more questions than he'd answered. More doubts. "A guest has a right to his privacy."

Why had Luke been looking at the guest check-in records? Was he really checking to see if he'd recognized someone? Or had he been looking for something else?

Luke stood up then, tossed some cash onto the table and headed toward the door. And he never once glanced in her direction while she had pretty much been staring at him the entire time.

Where was he going?

And why hadn't he talked to her?

Why hadn't he asked her to go with him?

LUCA WASN'T IMAGINING IT. Someone was staring at him. And it wasn't just Aubrey and her brother, though they'd been doing their share since they'd stepped into the great room. They stood together in the doorway, talking intensely.

About him?

He suspected it was. And he also suspected that whoever had really struck Jasper, whoever had really fired those shots, was watching him as well.

And he wanted that person—or people—far away from Aubrey. So he walked out without saying anything to her.

He wanted to make it clear to whoever was watching him that she meant nothing to him. Unfortunately, he was probably making Aubrey believe that, too. That he hadn't meant those compliments, that he wasn't starting to fall for her. He had meant them, and he was…

That was why he was determined to keep her safe, even if it meant he was risking his own life by going off on his own. But he wasn't unaware, like he'd been on those previous occasions.

After the Camorra had tracked him down in those other places, he now knew to be prepared. To be careful.

And he would have been if not for Aubrey, if not for being so damned attracted to the curvaceous blonde beauty. If not for her, he would have left Gemini Ranch already.

He should. But with the storm…

If the roads were unsurpassable for the police, no rideshare service or taxi would drive out to the ranch to pick him up. He should have rented a car; he would have if not for every company requiring a reservation with a debit or credit card. After he'd been tracked down before, he hadn't wanted to use those means of payment, hadn't want to lead someone to him. But he had anyway…

Or someone else, someone he'd trusted, had led that person here. Could his cousin have betrayed him like that? Even considering it made Luca feel as if he was the one hurting Paolo; he felt guilty even thinking it. He and

Paolo had always been so close as kids, more like brothers than cousins. Paolo had been a lot like him in that he'd been easily bored, so he'd gotten into some scrapes growing up. He'd made some friends he shouldn't have, friends who'd been associated with the Camorra. But Luca had never suspected that Paolo would betray him.

When Luca stepped outside the main lodge, the wind struck him in the face like a hard slap. The cold air blasted him with icy bits of snow; these weren't the big flakes that had drifted down throughout the day. It was more like sleet now, cold and sharp and slippery.

His boot skidded off the first step and he nearly fell. But he righted himself and continued down the path that led toward his cabin. It was going to be a long walk that wound through the grounds and trees.

Maybe he should have borrowed one of the snowmobiles, like Warren Parker had. But with its loud engine, he wouldn't have been able to hear what he heard now. The sound of another door opening and closing, the crunch of boots on the snow. Someone was following him.

There were other routes he could have taken toward his cabin. One that led past other guest cabins. One that went by the barn...or this one...that led through the grounds with no one around to witness whatever was about to happen to him.

He had to get a few yards farther away from the lodge, from the main garden area, for darkness to swallow the light emanating from the building and the garden lights.

Once the light was gone, plunging him into blackness, he veered off the trail. Someone must have plowed the trail earlier, leaving the snow even deeper on the sides of it—so deep that he sank far into it and could barely move. But he forced himself through what felt like quicksand pulling him deeper, and he took cover in the trees on the edge of the trail. And there, hunkered down, he waited.

He wanted to know who'd been staring at him, who'd headed out right after him. Who was trying to kill him…?

Because he had no doubt that was why the person had followed him out of the lodge, to carry out what the Camorra had probably paid him or her or them to do.

Kill Luca Rossi.

THE FLIGHT HAD been rough, the air choppy as the plane got closer to Denver, Colorado. A storm hung over the area, causing turbulence outside the plane.

Dread and fear caused turbulence inside it—and inside Paolo. What had he done?

And if it wasn't done…

If Luca wasn't already dead, he knew what the Camorra expected of him. They wanted him, instead of a failed assassin, to kill his cousin, figuring he might be the only one who could get close enough to Luca to carry out the hit on him. That was the only way they wouldn't call in the loans they'd given Paolo, the only way that they wouldn't kill him over his debts and over his cousin's exposé.

Luca hadn't called him, though. Had he figured it out? Or was he unable to call for another reason?

Because of this storm?

Or because he was already dead?

"We apologize for the rough landing," the pilot said over the speaker system. "The ground crews are struggling to keep the runways clear. We have to wait for a drift to be plowed before we can pull up to our gate and disembark, but you are now free to turn on your phones or other electronic devices."

His phone...

He'd turned it off as requested earlier. He reached into his pocket now and switched it on. It took a few moments before the screen lit up again.

And when it did, a breath of relief shuddered out of him. He'd been forwarded a text:

It will be over soon...

It had to have been sent earlier from the hitman to whoever his handler within the Camorra was. So maybe it was all over already.

Maybe Luca was already dead.

Chapter Eighteen

Watching Luke leave made Aubrey feel even sicker with nerves and fear. For a moment—a long moment—she froze as those feelings overwhelmed her.

Then she realized what he'd done. He hadn't just walked away from her. He'd put himself in serious danger.

"He can't go off on his own like that," she murmured, and she started toward the door he'd left through just a short while ago.

Jasper caught her shoulder. "Why not?" he asked. "Why can't he go off alone?"

"Because Warren thinks Luke is my boyfriend," she admitted.

"Is it true?" Jasper asked. "Is he?"

Heat suffused her face, but she shook her head. "He's not my boyfriend."

That would imply that they had a relationship of some sort. And while they'd had sex, she knew it was only sex, and that it was not going to lead to anything but pleasure.

She'd thought that by having no expectations for anything else between them, she could avoid the pain. Now she wasn't so sure, because just watching him walk away from her without so much as a backward glance hurt. Badly.

She pushed her feelings aside now to explain to her twin. "Warren was hassling me a couple of days ago, and Luke interrupted and led Warren to believe that he was my boyfriend now."

"If that was so Warren would leave you alone," Jasper said, "it sure as hell didn't work."

"No," she agreed. "It actually seems to have made him more desperate and dangerous."

"So it really could have been him who fired those shots from the Sutherland property," Jasper said. "Maybe he was trying to hit Luke."

"He could have been," Aubrey agreed. Luke's reaction had been quick; he'd knocked her down as well. He might have saved her life.

But his was still in danger because Warren was probably out there somewhere, lurking around the ranch.

Waiting either at her house, like Jasper had said, or somewhere else on the ranch, like perhaps the path leading from the main lodge to the road to her house and Luke's cabin.

"We need to make sure Luke's all right," she said. Fear had intensified in her, knotting the muscles in her stomach, and she just knew that he wasn't...

That something had happened to him.

She rushed out the door then and nearly slipped off the steps. Jasper, who'd run out with her, caught her shoulder, like he had moments ago. But he didn't hold her back; he just steadied her.

Then they both walked down the stairs to the path leading away from the lodge. "Which way did he go?" Jasper asked as he peered through the snow.

It was falling hard and fast again, sheets of it slashing across Aubrey's face, chafing her skin. She should have gotten back into her snowmobile suit. But there wasn't time.

She knew that, even before she heard the grunts and blows of a fight.

"Over here!" Jasper yelled, and he headed down the path that led through the grounds and toward his and Aubrey's houses and Luke's very private cabin.

Once they were away from the lodge, the light evaporated—leaving such total darkness that Aubrey stumbled off the path. Her foot sank deep into snow, slowing her down, and Jasper rushed ahead of her. By the time she joined him—just a few yards down the trail—she couldn't tell apart the three shadows that grappled on the ground. Jasper must have joined the fight, but which man was he?

And which was Luke?

Then one of the figures jumped up and ran off, leaving just two tangled up in the snow. "I've got you!" Jasper yelled.

"You've got *me*," Luke remarked, his deep voice a rumble of frustration. "You let *him* get away!"

"Are you all right?" Aubrey asked as she rushed forward the last few steps. "Are you hurt?"

"No." But he didn't move from the ground; he stayed lying down for a moment.

Jasper scrambled up first, but when he started off after the man who'd run away, Luke jumped up and stopped him. "Wait!"

"But he's getting away. I *let* him get away."

Luke released a shaky breath. "No. He was bigger. Stronger..."

"Warren?" Aubrey asked with shock. Her ex was not bigger or stronger than Luke.

"It—it must have been his desperation, then," Luke said. "He was going to get away even before you showed up."

"Get away?" Aubrey asked. "Were you trying to catch him?"

"I heard someone following me," Luke admitted. "And I hid out in the trees until they showed up on the trail."

"And you tried to apprehend him yourself?" she asked with fear and awe. "You could have been killed."

"I'm fine," he said, but a groan slipped out of his lips as he moved.

"You're hurt." Or had his earlier leg wound been aggravated?

"That might be my fault," Jasper admitted. "I thought he had *you*. It looked like you were the aggressor."

It had probably looked that way because Luke had been trying to catch Warren. But had that really been Warren running off?

The guy had looked taller, broader...and just as Luke had claimed, stronger.

But there was no light out here, so maybe he'd just looked bigger in the dark. "We need to get back to the lodge," she said.

"I'm going to my cabin," Luke insisted.

"No," Jasper said. "Aubrey told me you pretended to be her boyfriend, so I think Warren's after you now. You can't go off alone. None of us can."

Luke shook his head. "No. It's too dangerous."

"It's too dangerous to be alone. He's not going to try anything in the lodge. There are too many other people around. And I'm calling the police again," Jasper said. "We need to find Warren and have him arrested or at least thrown off the property for trespassing—if we can't prove anything else."

"We can't really prove anything right now," Luke said. "I didn't get a good look at the guy I grabbed."

"Since he was following you and there are only our places out this direction from the main lodge, he must have intended to attack you," Aubrey said. "He must be who shot at us yesterday."

"Caleb has that gun," Jasper said. "He's probably already handed it to the police. We'll find out if it can be traced back to Warren. In the meantime let's get the hell back to the lodge."

Aubrey shivered then—from fear and from the cold. And an arm slid around her shoulders, pulling her close to the long, lean body of Luke Bishop.

He'd ignored her earlier, but now he must have noticed that she was freezing. "You don't have your snowsuit on," he said.

"Neither do you," she said. And his clothes were

coated with snow from rolling around on the ground. "You must be freezing."

Jasper was beginning to shiver, too, so they all rushed back to the lodge, flinching at the sudden warmth inside after the cold.

"Get warmed up," she told her twin. "I'll show Luke to a room."

"I'll call the police again," Jasper said. "See if they can spare anyone yet to take a report."

"It's fine," Luke said. "Don't bring them out during a storm."

"It's not fine," Aubrey said. "You're hurt. Jasper was hurt. Warren needs to be stopped."

"Warren wasn't the one who hit me," Jasper reminded her.

"Somebody did. Somebody must be out there with him—helping him…"

"But there was only one man right now," Jasper said, and he turned toward Luke with a speculative look, like he wondered if Luke was the one who'd struck him.

Luke shrugged. "I don't know. There might have been two. I just managed to grab the one."

"And the other just let you do that?" Jasper asked.

"You guys showed up right away," Luke reminded him now. Then he shivered again.

The snow was starting to melt on his clothes, probably making him even colder as his skin got wet now, too.

She popped behind the reception counter and checked which rooms were available, jotting down the code for the lock of the closest empty suite. "I assume you already have a room," she said to Jasper, "since you stayed here last night."

He nodded and flinched.

"Go, get warmed up," she told him. "I'm going to show Luke to a room."

"What about you?" her brother asked.

She gestured at her clothes. "I wasn't rolling around in the snow. I'm fine." But she wasn't; she was shaken.

If she and Jasper hadn't headed out after Luke...

He could have been hurt, or worse. Because now in the light, she saw a red mark on his jaw. Someone had struck him. Maybe even Jasper, when mistaking him for Warren.

"I'll get warmed up," Jasper said. "But I'm going to call the police again, too."

"You can wait until morning," Luke said. "Warren isn't going to try anything else tonight."

Jasper hesitated for a moment.

"You're the one who pointed out that the lodge is too crowded for anyone to try anything," Luke said. "We're safe here. Warren is the one in trouble, if he's out there with the storm picking up again."

"Okay," Jasper conceded. "We'll wait until morning before we call the police. Hopefully, they'll send someone out then to take a report."

Aubrey didn't feel so much as a pang of embarrassment now. She didn't care if everyone knew what a fool she'd been to date a man like Warren Parker. All she wanted was to make sure that he didn't hurt anyone she cared about again.

Like Jasper…

And Luke Bishop.

She waited until Jasper left them, waited until she'd opened the door to the vacant suite and followed Luke inside before she told him, "I'm sorry…"

"You're sorry?" he asked, his brow furrowing with apparent confusion. "You have no reason to be sorry."

"I understand why you want nothing to do with me, with the mess that's my life right now," she said. "I'm sorry that you've gotten involved in it."

He closed his arms around her then, pulling her tight against his tense body. His clothes were damp and cold, but still heat surged through her along with the passion she felt every time he touched her. Or got too close to her.

"None of this is your fault," he assured her. "*None* of it."

She released a shaky sigh. "Maybe you're right. I didn't make Warren the man he is—the gambler, the opportunist, but…"

"No buts," Luke said, and as if to stop her from saying anything else, he leaned down and covered her mouth with his then. He kissed her deeply—passionately.

And she knew that she'd been right earlier. He hadn't been walking away from her for his protection but for hers.

He could have been hurt. Had probably been, because when she closed her arms around his waist, he groaned. She jerked away from him. "Are you okay?"

He shook his head. "No…"

"Where are you injured?" she asked. And she reached for his clothes then, opening up his coat and pushing it from his shoulders. Then she reached for the buttons on his flannel shirt until it hung open over the thermal top he wore beneath it.

He reached for it then, lifting its hem to drag the shirt over his head. His ab muscles rippled when he moved, but then he grunted again. And she saw the marks from the blows he'd taken.

"You're hurt," she said again. "It looks like someone hit you really hard. You could have internal bleeding or broken ribs. You should see the nurse."

He shook his head as he tossed his shirts onto the floor atop his coat. "I don't need the nurse," he said, his blue eyes so dilated that they looked black. His expression was so intense that she shivered.

"What do you need?" she asked.

"You."

Then her clothes joined his on the floor until they were both naked, tangled in each other's arms. She tried to be careful, tried not to touch any of the red marks on his flesh, but he kept pulling her closer. Skin slid over skin; they moved together, breathed together, hearts beat together…

He lifted her then and stumbled back, tumbling onto the bed.

She started to apologize again, but he kissed her, sliding his tongue into her mouth. Then he moved between her legs, and after sheathing himself in a condom, he sheathed himself inside her. He filled an emptiness in her, an emptiness Aubrey hadn't even known she had.

His hands grasped her hips, and he murmured something—something in some other language, something sexy-sounding.

"What?" she asked.

"You're beautiful," he said. "So very beautiful…"

Her hair spilled around them both when she leaned forward, when she pressed her mouth to his. She kissed him deeply and then she moved, rocking her hips back and forth, moving up and down.

He grasped her hips harder, driving her faster, driving her senseless. And he arched his back, contorting until his lips closed over one of her nipples. As he tugged on it, the pressure inside her spiraled out of control.

She bit her lip to hold in a scream of ecstasy as an orgasm shuddered through her. Then he tensed and groaned, his body convulsing beneath hers as he found his release, his pleasure.

What was this between them that any time they were alone they wound up making love? No. Having sex…

Was that all it was? Or had it already become more to Aubrey? Had it—and Luke Bishop—become an obsession?

LUCA WANTED TO tell her the truth—so badly. Warren wasn't the one who'd followed him from the lodge. He wasn't the one Luca had grappled with on the path.

That man had been bigger and stronger than Aubrey's ex-boyfriend. He'd been bigger and stronger than Luca, too.

If not for Jasper and Aubrey coming along when they had, Luca had no doubt that the stranger probably would have overpowered him.

He was grateful they'd showed up and also scared that they had, because he was worried that they were in danger now. But surely Jasper was right, surely nobody would try anything at the main lodge with so many witnesses around?

He was holding on to the hope that Jasper was right, as tightly as he was holding on to Aubrey, his arms wrapped around her as they lay beneath the covers of the king-size bed.

He closed his eyes for a moment, and behind his lids flickered the flames, the memory of the fire that had consumed that hotel in Wisconsin. There had been a lot of witnesses there, too, but that hadn't stopped the assassin they'd sent after Luca.

Luca couldn't endanger Aubrey's ranch and her life further. But he couldn't believe that the killer would take such a risk here during the storm. If he burned down the lodge, he'd have no place to go, either—not with the storm still raging outside.

The wind hurled bits of ice and snow at the windows, rattling the glass in the panes. The weather was getting worse, so the roads wouldn't be opening up anytime soon.

While the killer might have risked being witnessed, he wasn't going to risk freezing to death. He needed a place to stay as much as the rest of the guests. So the lodge was safe.

But Luca knew he wasn't.

And if Aubrey stayed with him, she wouldn't be, either. Luca had to leave her. He had to figure out some way to get off Gemini Ranch before she was hurt.

But the thought of leaving her made him ache.

HE FUMBLED WITH a lighter, the flame flickering on and off. On and off...

He could do what had been done before. He could torch the whole place, if not to kill Luca Rossi, at least to flush him out.

Luca Rossi wouldn't get far, but neither would he—not with the travel advisories and whiteout conditions. The storm was raging again. Outside.

And inside of him...

The son of a bitch had jumped him. Had taken him completely by surprise.

If he'd seen him...

If anyone had seen him...

It didn't matter. They would die.

He glanced at the woman lying beside him. The actress...

Her eyes were wide open with shock. Her lips blue, her throat red from his hands.

Whatever she'd been, she was dead. He'd come back to the lodge in such a rage, furious that Luca Rossi—a worthless reporter—had gotten the jump on him.

Nobody had gotten away from him before. He was too good at what he did.

If he wasn't, he wouldn't have survived. He would have been arrested or worse...

He would have been eliminated, just as he'd eliminated the woman. The next person he eliminated had to be Luca Rossi...

Chapter Nineteen

They had been trapped at the main lodge a couple of days now as the storm continued unabated. There hadn't even been another break like the one they'd got that morning when they'd met Caleb and Nadine at the Sutherland ranch.

Aubrey was worried about the storm. About the guests. About Warren. About her ranch.

But most of all she was worried that she was falling for Luke Bishop—even though she could see that he appeared disturbed. For the last couple of days he'd been pacing the suite, restless, on edge...

Maybe that was because he had stayed mostly in the guest room, even when she'd left to handle ranch business with Jasper. Not that she'd left him for long, since there hadn't been much to do, with everyone basically trapped at the main lodge.

Today, after all his pacing, he'd finally decided to head down to the dining room for lunch. He hadn't invited her along, but that was fine. She had things to do. And even though they'd parted ways when he went into the dining room and she'd walked away to the reception desk, his restlessness was inside her now, clawing at her. She was surprised, that after all the pleasure he'd given her over the past few days, she could have any tension left in her body.

But maybe that was why she was so tense.

So afraid...

Not of the storm but of her feelings. Those feelings were a distraction she couldn't afford right now.

At least the guests had food and the spa facilities to keep them busy.

Unfortunately, there were still the livestock to tend. And that calf. They hadn't found its mother, but it was doing well on a bottle and with the starter feed.

Kayla and the other hands had been taking care of the livestock. But with that disquiet inside her now, Aubrey stopped at the desk where Jasper was working. "I'm going out to the barn," she said.

She had to force herself to go. She would have rather stayed in bed with Luke than go out in the storm, than face the real world. But he wasn't in bed anyway. And even before he'd left for the dining room, he'd been pacing...like a caged animal. Like one just waiting for the opportunity to escape confinement.

Had she made him feel that way? Had being with her made him so tense and anxious?

"It's still nasty outside," Jasper warned.

She was afraid that it would have been nastier if she and Luke had stayed in the guest room, if she'd given in to her frustration with him and demanded the answers he had yet to give her—about his past, about himself. Maybe that was why he'd left the room.

But the dining room was not far enough away for the space she needed, for the air she needed to clear her head.

She drew in a deep breath and reminded herself of the excuse she'd given herself for leaving the main lodge. "I need to check on that calf and make sure the horses are all being well tended."

Jasper furrowed his brow as he stared at her. "Really? You don't trust the hands?"

"Of course I do," she said. "But I told them to take a few hours off from the barn, and I would take care of the calf and the horses."

"You're getting fidgety," he said. "Me, too. It's like waiting for the other shoe to drop, waiting for Warren to show up again."

He hadn't. It had been two nights since he'd attacked Luke on the path. Or had Luke attacked him when he'd tried to catch him?

Maybe that had scared Warren off, because he hadn't made another appearance. Maybe he'd left the ranch that night. If he had, she doubted they would see him again.

He had to know by now that he had no hope of ever getting money out of her. The only reason for him to stick around would be to lash out in spite. To take out his frustration and his fear of his creditors on Luke.

Before she headed outside, she glanced into the dining room, looking for Luke. He was sitting at a table by himself. He had a plate of food in front of him, but it was untouched as he peered around, studying the other guests.

Was it his writer's curiosity that had him so interested in everyone else? Or was he looking for that couple he thought he'd recognized?

There was only one couple in the dining room now, and a few single men sitting alone like Luke was. They must have lost their spouses to the spa.

Maybe Aubrey would make use of the facilities herself, after she returned from the barn. She could use a massage or a steam.

But neither of those would release her tension like Luke did. He was such an amazing lover, so thorough, so generous.

So addictive.

That was the problem. The more time she spent with him, the more she craved him. But she knew, from his restlessness, that he was anxious to move on. And she had no doubt that once the roads were cleared, he would be gone.

She drew in a shaky breath and forced herself to head toward the outside door. "You're not walking," Jasper called after her.

She shook her head. "No. I'll take a snowmobile." She hurried outside to the building where all the equipment was kept. The snowmobiles and ATVs and skis. Maybe she should have strapped on some cross-country skis and headed to the barn that way. The wind wasn't howling as loudly as it had been.

And the snow wasn't falling as thick.

Either this was another break or the storm was ending. And that meant that Luke would be leaving. So she intended to make just that quick snowmobile trip out to the barn and back.

Before he was gone…

But as she drove off, she had this strange sensation—fear that she might not have the chance to see him again.

STANDING OUTSIDE THE LODGE, Luca watched Aubrey leave. And he forced himself not to call out to her. Not to stop her.

It wasn't that he didn't want her to go. It was that he *was* going, and he was tempted to tell her goodbye. But he didn't trust himself to actually follow through and leave her if he was alone with her again. Because every time they were together, they wound up in each other's arms.

He'd never experienced such passion before—from anyone else or from himself. He'd never wanted anyone as obsessively as he wanted Aubrey Colton. But it wasn't just desire he felt for her. He admired her, too. He respected everything she'd accomplished.

She was so smart, so hardworking, so straightforward, and she deserved someone who could be as straightforward and honest with her. That was why Luca had to leave.

Just his presence near her put her and her ranch in danger. He had to leave. The weather was letting up now.

Aubrey had put on a snowsuit and taken off on the snowmobile, and he intended to do the same. But instead of heading toward the barn, like she had, he planned to travel toward town. He wouldn't wait for someone to clear the roads; he would snowmobile to town and take a bus out of Blue Larkspur. He had no idea where he would go; he knew only that it had to be far enough away from Aubrey that she wouldn't be hurt.

But the thought of leaving her made him ache...

He already felt hollow and empty inside, but he had no choice. He'd felt it again in the dining room, the intensity of someone's stare, their animosity toward him.

Their restlessness...

Whoever had been sent here to take him out wasn't going to wait much longer to act again. Not now, when the storm was letting up again.

So Luca had to leave while he could.

He couldn't leave without the things he'd left in his cabin, though. His fake identification and passport. His money. His laptop. His notes.

So once he put on the snowmobile suit and found the keys, that was where he headed first, along the path where he'd fought with his attacker.

His bruises were just beginning to turn from purple to yellow now, but his ribs were still tender. The man with whom he'd struggled that night definitely hadn't been Warren Parker, so it had to have been one of the other guests.

Or maybe a ranch hand...

He should have asked Aubrey if they'd hired anyone new sometime after he'd checked in, after he'd talked to Paolo. Paolo had to have given him up. His cousin had to be the one who'd helped the Camorra find him everywhere he'd gone to hide from them. Luca had been too careful, too paranoid about the power and the reach of the Camorra to betray himself with using the credit cards too often. He hadn't realized that the Camorra would be able to get to someone so close to him, to someone he'd considered a brother.

His heart ached with the betrayal. He wanted to make excuses for Paolo, wanted to believe it was only because he'd been threatened that he'd given up Luca. But he'd had the opportunity to leave, like Luca's mother and aunt. Paolo hadn't wanted to give up his business or his friends and family, though.

Luca had understood. He didn't want to spend his life like this, running from place to place. Isolated from everyone he cared about. But he had no choice if he wanted to stay alive and to keep everyone he cared about from getting hurt.

That was why he couldn't talk to Aubrey, couldn't ask about her employees and shouldn't have asked about her guests. But she'd caught him searching the records. There had been two couples who'd checked in after he'd talked to Paolo. And both of the men from those couples had been eating alone this morning. Both of them had been watching him...

With ordinary curiosity or that hostility he'd imagined?

He shivered now as that feeling swept over him again, like the snowmobile swept along the path. The path ended at a fork. The road to the left led to his cabin, and the one to the right led to the barn. That was probably where Aubrey had gone, to check on the calf. He wanted to follow her there, so badly that he began to turn the handlebars in that direction—to the right.

He wanted to see her again—just one more time, wanted to kiss her lips, touch her silky skin. He knew they'd be alone; he'd heard Kayla and some of the other hands in the dining room planning on using their employee discount for spa services for a massage and a steam.

So he would be able to have a private goodbye with Aubrey. That longing pulled at him so hard that he lowered his head to draw in a deep breath. And something whizzed past his head just as the sharp sound of gunshots rang out.

Somebody had followed him from the lodge and was shooting at him now.

HE SHOULD HAVE WAITED.

Until he had a better shot.

Or until Rossi had headed back to this cabin. But when he'd stopped at that fork and seemed to point the snowmobile in the direction of the barn, he'd panicked.

Rossi had gotten away from him too many times. And he'd known why the guy had hopped on the snowmobile. Rossi had seen the break in the storm as an escape.

But he couldn't escape death.

Not again.

Not as he had so many times before.

So he'd raised his gun, the Glock he'd brought since he'd left his long gun in the abandoned barn, and he had started firing.

But Rossi had lowered his head just enough that the bullet had missed. Though maybe the helmet would have protected him anyway.

He raised his gun and focused again at Rossi's back, aiming the barrel right between the man's shoulder blades. This time he couldn't miss.

Chapter Twenty

The horses reared up, pawing at their stall doors as sudden gunshots reverberated outside the barn. Warren must have come back. And with another weapon...

Aubrey ducked down but no bullets whizzed past her. Despite the volume of the sound, they weren't close. Yet.

But they must have been heading toward her direction. Aubrey ran out of the stall where she'd been playing with the calf, across the barn toward the tack room. She pushed open the door and rushed over to the cubby that had a door and a combination lock on it. Her fingers shaking, she fumbled with the tumbler until finally it clicked and the door opened.

She reached inside and pulled out a gun. Every ranch had one to protect their livestock and occasionally to protect themselves. Aubrey knew how to shoot, but she'd never had to use it for her own protection before.

Until now...

The gunshots had stopped, but now she could hear the rumble of snowmobile engines until that sound died, too. Had whoever been driving them died as well?

But then there was another noise, barn doors crashing open before slamming shut again. She rushed out of the tack room then, gun raised, and stared down the sight on it.

At Luke Bishop.

But she didn't lower the barrel. She held it on him, and her voice vibrating with nerves and fury, she asked, "What the hell is going on?"

She didn't believe the culprit was Warren—not now. Not when he'd had days to get away, to get over whatever irritation or resentment he'd felt about Luke.

No. It wasn't Warren who'd fired those shots at Luke. There was someone else who wanted him dead. And she damn well wanted to know why.

THIS WAS THE second time in a short while that someone had held a gun on him. The first time, the person had fired so many times that the shooter had had to stop somewhere to reload the weapon.

So Luca had fled to the barn. He regretted that he'd led danger right to Aubrey, but if he was going to survive, he needed a weapon. And she'd mentioned that ranchers always had guns.

She hadn't carried one on her when they'd been moving the cattle, so he'd assumed it was in the barn somewhere.

Now he knew where—trained right at him.

"What's going on, Luke?" she asked again, her voice raspy with anger and fear.

"Somebody's shooting at me," he said.

"Why?" she asked. "And you damn well better tell me the truth."

"There's no time," he said with a nervous glance over his shoulder. He'd secured the doors with the big wooden slat they'd slid over them the other night to keep out the wind and snow. But he doubted that the board would keep out the killer. "He's out there." But that wasn't where he was going to stay. "He had to see where I went."

And that was why Luca shouldn't have come here.

"I know how to shoot," she said, her voice strong and steady—just like she was. "Let him come. I just want to know who the hell I'm shooting."

Luca shivered then because it was clear that she knew it wasn't Warren who'd chased him into the barn. And her dark blue eyes had gone icy with that knowledge and with suspicion of him.

He glanced over his shoulder at those doors. They weren't moving—nobody was trying to get in. Yet. But he knew that the assassin would try soon. Luca knew that the Camorra did not give up.

Ever.

"We need to hide for now," he said. "Please, Aubrey, for your sake as much as mine."

She stared at him for another long second before she finally lowered the gun barrel. Then she turned and headed down the wide aisle between the horse stalls, past the tack room, until they reached a ladder at the end of it. "Up here," she said.

The open loft was probably a safer hiding place than the tack room. From this vantage point, they would be able to see when the assassin got into the barn. Unless he waited outside for them to leave and intended to pick them off then.

"You first," Luca said, making sure that she headed up the steps and got to the relative safety of that loft before he did.

With her gun under one arm, she climbed the ladder. Then she looked down at him as if she expected him to run. But he was already climbing up to join her among the bales of hay.

They weren't alone up there. Soft mewing noises drew their attention to where the cat—the gray tiger-striped tabby that had cuddled with the calf—snuggled with the kittens she nursed. There were at least five of them, so new that their eyes weren't even open yet. A couple of black ones, two dingy white and a little orange one. There might have been three of the black ones; they were pressed so close together, fighting over the teats on their dam's belly, that it was hard to tell.

"Oh, Mama," Aubrey murmured. "This isn't a safe place for you."

"It's not safe for you, either," Luca warned her.

Aubrey patted the stock of the gun. "I'll be fine. Once you tell me the truth."

"I can't…" he murmured. "Not without putting you in more danger."

She arched a blond brow above the rim of her glasses. "More? I'm in danger, Luke, and I deserve to know why. I deserve to know what you did that you're hiding out from someone."

"You're right," he said. Despite his best intentions,

he had put her in danger. And she did deserve to know. "I'm hiding from the Camorra."

Her brow furrowed. "Camorra?"

He nodded. "It's an Italian organized crime group that is very prominent in Naples and controls a portion of Italy."

"What did you—did you testify against them? Did you…" Her voice cracked and she swallowed hard before continuing, "…did you *turn* against them?"

His heart ached at what she thought of him, that she wondered if he could have ever been part of such an organization.

"God, no," he said. "I never worked for them. I was investigating them. I am a writer, Aubrey, like I said. My name is Luca Rossi."

Usually people recognized his name. He'd done more articles than the one about the Camorra. But then, Aubrey was always so busy with the ranch that she might not have heard of him.

But a soft gasp slipped from her lips, and she nodded in sudden realization. "Yes, I remember now. The news outlets here in America picked up the story, too, about what you'd done, how many people your investigation helped authorities convict and send to prison."

"Not enough," he murmured. "Not all of them. They're still after me, Aubrey. That's why I've changed my name, why I pay cash, why I try to stay away from people."

But it hadn't worked. He hadn't been able to stay away from her. And now, because of his selfishness, his weakness, he would probably lose her…even as he lost his own life.

"WHAT'S MISSING?" JASPER asked the housekeeper, who'd stopped him just as he was about to leave the main lodge.

"All the sheets from suite 202."

The snow had stopped but for an occasional flake and the wind was no longer howling, but travel was still not advised. "Have the guests checked out?" he asked.

Occasionally people packed up the linens and towels when they left, either for souvenirs or because they somehow believed they'd paid for them.

The housekeeper shook her head. "And we actually screwed up when we let ourselves into the suite. The guests had requested a Do Not Disturb order on it. We weren't supposed to go inside, but the maid cleaning that floor didn't pay attention. And when she went into the room, she thought it was very strange that the bed had been stripped already."

It *was* very strange, especially since the guests had not checked out.

"She found something else, Mr. Colton," the housekeeper continued.

"What?" he asked.

"Gun cases." And now she shuddered.

"Gun cases?" he repeated.

"Yes, you know the ones that have the molds inside that hold the weapons," she explained.

And Jasper's heart sank with the possible implications of that.

Nobody had signed up for hunting at the ranch. That wasn't something they offered, so why the weapons? Had one of those cases belonged to the gun Caleb had found on the Sutherland property? Had their guest been responsible for firing those shots?

Maybe Warren Parker hadn't had anything to do with that weapon or with those gunshots. Or maybe even with hitting Jasper over the head...

The front door opened with a blast of cold air, and Kayla St. James ran into the reception area. "Jasper!" she exclaimed, and there was something almost like relief in her voice. But then she rushed on, "I heard gunshots between here and the barn, and I saw two people racing toward it on snowmobiles."

Jasper reached for her, gripping her shoulders. "You're okay?"

She nodded, and her ponytail bobbed. "Yes. I turned around and headed back here to call the police. But I don't think they'll be able to get here in time to stop whatever's going on, to protect Aubrey..."

His stomach lurched with a sickening surge of fear. "Aubrey's in the barn." She'd gone out there to check on the calf and the horses.

And Luke Bishop had headed out not long after she'd left. He must have been going out to join her. And somebody was chasing him and shooting at him.

Who the hell was Luke Bishop? And was he going to get Aubrey killed?

Chapter Twenty-One

Everything Luke—no, Luca—had told her ran through Aubrey's mind. The Camorra...

They were a dangerous, far-reaching criminal organization. And he was the journalist who had recently exposed criminals at every level of local Neapolitan life as well as their connections within the government—corrupt officials who'd been taking bribes and kickbacks. Luca had disappeared shortly after his story ran, and most people believed he'd been killed as retribution.

She hadn't considered that that man could still be alive and that he could be her lover. But it all made sense...except for one thing.

"Why didn't you tell me?" she asked.

"I didn't want to put you in danger," he said.

The big doors of the barn rattled, and she knew that he was right. She was in danger.

But it didn't have anything to do with knowing the truth. Knowing the truth might have made her more prepared. Because now she knew it wasn't Warren coming after Luke, after both of them.

It wasn't some bungling gambler acting out of desperation. It was a hired, professional killer. She handed the gun to Luca. His eyes widened as he stared down at it.

"What are you doing?" he asked.

"Trusting you." And that damn well wasn't easy for her, but she didn't see any reason for him to be lying. She rushed over to the door of the loft that opened to the outside.

"Isn't it too high to jump out?" Luca asked.

But she didn't open the door. She grabbed the rope that was looped up beside the window and pulled it free of the pulley above it. That was how they hoisted up bales of hay from the wagon they would park below it.

She didn't want to hoist anything now. She intended to rope it.

"What are you going to do with that?" he asked.

"I'm better with a lasso than I am with a gun," she admitted.

"But, Aubrey—"

"Can you shoot?" she asked him.

He looked down at the gun now, undid the safety and lifted the butt of the weapon to his shoulder. "Yes."

"Good," she said. "Because he's coming…"

The board that held those doors closed broke, and the doors banged against the walls as the snowmobile plowed through them. The man stopped the machine just inside and climbed off it. He wore his helmet with a snowmobile suit. He could have been anyone, but from the way he held his gun, it was clear what he was.

He'd come here to take out Luca.

And Aubrey wasn't going to let that happen. She

whirled the rope around her shoulders. The guy must have heard it, because he looked up, and as he did, he brought up the barrel of his gun and pointed it into the loft.

Aubrey tossed the rope, dropping the circle over the guy's arms. As she pulled it tight, he started firing.

Closer gunshots echoed, as Luca fired back. Then the guy fell onto his back on the ground, the weapon down at his side. Aubrey tried to tighten the rope more, tried to link the guy's arms together, but he was too heavy, like dead weight.

"I think I got him," Luca murmured, but his voice was a whisper, like he didn't dare let the man hear that he was alive. That the shots he'd fired wildly, because of the rope tightening around his arms, had missed.

Had they missed?

Aubrey stared at Luca, looking for any sign of blood. But he seemed fine. As did the mother and kittens he stood in front of, as if he'd been protecting them with his body—like he'd protected her that day in the pasture when those shots were fired.

Naively she'd thought then that he was overreacting. Now she realized how wrong she'd been, and how much danger he'd been in this entire time.

Was that threat gone?

The man lay yet on the floor below them, perfectly still. He had to be at the very least unconscious. At the most…

She shuddered and started toward the ladder. But Luca caught her arm.

"Stay up here," he said. "Let me check."

Aubrey reached for the gun he held. "I'll hang on to this," she said.

"I thought you trusted me," he said.

"You might shoot yourself in the foot trying to get down there with a loaded gun."

And if the man was conscious, he might shoot Luca in the back as he descended the ladder. She raised the butt back to her shoulder and stared down the barrel at the hitman lying on the floor.

Had he moved?

Was he twitching?

Her heart pounded hard with fear. "Luca..." she murmured in warning. "Be careful."

But it was already too late. He was already halfway down the ladder. His back exposed to the man who lay on the ground.

When she'd picked up the gun, she'd dropped the rope, so it could have loosened around the man's shoulders, could have made it easier for him to aim his gun and fire.

If he was just faking being unconscious, if he was just wounded instead of dead...

And if he was, then he was about to have a clear shot at Luca. Aubrey had a clear shot at him, though, down the sight on the barrel of the shotgun.

Could she do it? Could she shoot another person if she had to? Even for Luca...

LUCA EASED SLOWLY down the ladder from the loft to the barn floor. It wasn't that he was afraid of the man lying on the ground—because he was pretty sure that one of his shots had struck the assassin. If not for Aubrey, Luca would have been dead already. She had thrown the rope around the killer's arms, making it impossible for him to aim and shoot. But the guy had fired a lot of shots wildly...

The mama cat and her kittens were fine, though. Luca had made certain to stand between them and the gunfire, and he'd fired back at the assassin. He'd only ever fired a gun at targets on a range—never at another human being. But he'd known that if he hadn't, the man wouldn't have stopped after shooting Luca; he would have killed Aubrey as well.

Luca's heart pounded fast with the fear he'd felt, the fear that she might have been hurt. But she was fine. He glanced up at the loft just to make sure and found her holding tightly on to that gun.

Had he left any bullets in it? Would she be able to use it if she needed to?

What if this hadn't been the only killer sent for him? What if, as Luca suspected, the guy didn't work alone?

Where was the woman who'd posed as his wife? Because surely, this person had to have been one of the couples who'd checked in after Luca made that call to his cousin.

After he stepped from the last rung of the ladder onto the concrete floor of the barn, Luca glanced back to the doors of the barn that the snowmobile had broken open. Nothing but snow, just a few fat flakes, swirled around outside.

Inside the horses whinnied and pawed at their stalls,

agitated from all the chaos. Their hearts probably pumped as hard with fear as Luca's had, as it still did.

Because even if this man was dead, Luca knew it wasn't over. The Camorra would send someone else for him—if they hadn't already. But as he turned to check on the man, he saw the shooter lift himself up, manage to raise the barrel and squeeze the trigger of his gun one more time.

The shot reverberated throughout the barn.

IT HAD TAKEN a couple of days for him to get from Denver to Blue Larkspur—because of the storm. Finally it had let up and the roads were clear enough for travel, and Paolo's cab pulled up outside a hotel. As the van stopped at the curb, police vehicles sped past it, lights flashing and sirens wailing.

"What's going on?" he wondered aloud. They could have been responding to anything—an auto accident, a fire…

But he had a strange sensation in his stomach, a mixture of nerves and dread. Over the past couple of days, he hadn't had any more communication from the Camorra.

He hadn't known what was going on—what *soon* had actually meant. Was it over yet?

The cabbie tapped one of his ears, in which he wore an AirPod. "According to the police scanner, there's been a shooting out at the Gemini Ranch."

It had to be over now. Luca had to be dead. He thought about telling the cab driver to turn around, to bring him back to the airport, so that he could go home.

But he needed to make certain—for his sake more than anyone else's—that Luca was really gone. Because if Luca wasn't dead, Paolo couldn't go home until he proved that he was…

And to do that, he might have to actually kill his cousin himself.

Chapter Twenty-Two

He was dead.

Aubrey hadn't had time yet to process everything that had happened. One minute the barn was ringing with gunshots; the next minute police and ambulances were swarming the property.

The ambulances had been too late to save him. She wasn't sure which shot had killed him—the one she'd fired when he turned his gun on Luca. Or any of the ones Luca had fired when the man first burst into the barn.

Either way, the hired assassin was dead, and unfortunately, his hadn't been the only body found on the property of Gemini Ranch. When the police had conducted a search, they had found a woman's body partially buried in the snow just off the path that ran between the main lodge and the barn. She'd been strangled to death.

Aubrey shivered at the thought of a murder taking place on the ranch. The woman's body had been wrapped in bedding that had gone missing from a guest room at the main lodge, which the hired killer had rented.

Aubrey wasn't at the ranch now. The police had separated her and Luca at the barn, driving each into town in separate vehicles to the police department to give their statements. Like they were the criminals.

Even if her shot had killed the assassin, it had been to save Luca. And if one of the shots he'd fired had killed the man, then it had been in defense of both of them. The thought of taking a life—anyone's life—had regret and pain swirling inside her, making her nauseous, yet she knew she'd had no choice. But death...

Hers and Luca's, because the assassin would have killed them both.

The police hadn't questioned them for long before they were free to go. But neither of them had been ready to return to the ranch, where they'd nearly lost their lives—where two other people had.

So they'd taken a room at one of the nicer hotels in Blue Larkspur, and Aubrey stood at the window of the room now, staring out at the street below. The snow had been cleared away, and what hadn't been plowed had begun to melt.

The storm was over.

Strong arms closed around her, and she was pulled up against a hard male body. "Are you okay?" Luca asked.

Too overwhelmed to speak, she could only nod.

He leaned down, until his face was against her cheek, his stubble rubbing sensuously against her skin. "I'm sorry," he murmured. "I'm so very sorry..."

"For what?" she asked.

Now that she knew who he was, she knew what he'd

done—how he'd worked to take down an organization of killers and criminals and exposed the corruption in government and law enforcement across a country.

"I am so very sorry for putting you in danger," he said. "That was the last thing I wanted. That was why I didn't want you to know the truth. In case they came looking for me…" He shuddered. "I didn't want them to think you would know where I was going. I didn't want you to get hurt because of me."

She turned toward him then. As much as she respected what he'd done as a journalist, she wasn't thrilled with how he'd treated her—no matter what his reasons were.

"I did get hurt," she admitted. "I blamed myself for the danger—that it was Warren—and you let me think that."

He flinched as if she'd slapped him. "I'm sorry. But I didn't know for certain that it wasn't Warren who'd been shooting at us. He'd been hanging around. I wanted it to be him rather than that I had been found again."

A pang of panic struck her heart. "Again?"

"This wasn't the first attempt on my life since I've gone into hiding," he replied. "It seems like they always find me no matter where I go…"

She flinched now—because she knew what that meant. That he wouldn't be able to stay…

Not in Blue Larkspur and not at the ranch, because the Camorra already knew that he was here. And when they didn't hear back from the assassin they had sent, they would undoubtedly hire another one for Luca

Rossi. Or Luke Bishop, since now they probably knew what he was calling himself.

"That's why we're here," she said, realizing why they hadn't returned to the ranch. "That's why you wanted to check into the hotel. You're going to leave."

He drew in a shaky breath and nodded. "While I was being questioned, a certain US marshal and FBI agent called in with the offer of new credentials for me, a new place to go…"

A pang struck her heart. "Dominic? Alexa?"

He nodded.

Were they helping him? Or her? Did they want him far away from her to protect her?

Probably.

But they couldn't protect her from the pain she was feeling. The pain that she would feel when he left. He was here now, though—with her. And she intended to make the most of that, the most of being with him.

"How long do we have?" she asked.

"Tonight," he said. "Tomorrow I have to leave."

She nodded and said, "Then let's make the most of tonight."

"You're not going to argue with me?" he asked.

"Why would I do that?" she asked. "I understand." His life was in danger—would probably always be. "I would offer to go with you, but—"

He pressed his finger over her lips. "You can't. You have the ranch. Your family. I understand."

That was what made it so hard—that she didn't think she would ever find anyone else like Luca, anyone with whom she could connect on so many levels.

She forced a smile for him. "Then I think we both understand what tonight is…"

Goodbye.

"A gift," he said. "Every minute I get to spend with you is a gift."

She smiled at his sincerity and at the sentiment. That was how she would look at it, too. With gratitude…

His breath shuddered out in a ragged sigh. "You are so beautiful…"

Usually she would have protested his compliment—because she wouldn't have believed it. Despite her knowing what he was doing, she had to admit that Warren's manipulations had affected her self-esteem, had brought back all that childhood teasing and bullying. But now…

With the way Luca looked at her, his face flushed with desire, his beautiful eyes dilated with it, she had no doubt that he was sincere.

She *was* beautiful. And she would never doubt it again.

"And you are so strong and so sexy," he continued.

She was strong; she knew that. But she didn't know if she was strong enough to survive this—to survive his leaving. But she pushed that worry from her mind, too.

All she wanted was to focus on the gift that this evening was, that Luca Rossi was.

"You are beautiful," she told him, her heart filling with warmth—with an emotion she didn't dare to identify or acknowledge. He wasn't just beautiful on the outside but on the inside as well, with his care for the calf and the mother cat and kittens.

Luca chuckled over her compliment. "I am going gray," he said, and he reached up to run his hand over the stubble on his jaw.

"It's sexy," she assured him.

He grinned, then looped his arms around her, pulling her against his body. "You're the sexy one. The things you do to me just when I look at you…"

With him holding her as close as he did, she could feel the things she did to him, the physical reaction he had to her. She arched her hips and rubbed against the fly of his jeans, teasing him.

This time his chuckle sounded gruff. "Aubrey…"

Her skin tingled at the way he said her name, with passion in his voice. Then he lowered his lips to hers, and that passion was in his kiss, in the way he made love to her mouth.

Now she tingled everywhere, her nipples taut and sensitive against the cups of her bra. Desire pulled at her, making tension spiral inside her. "Luke… Luca…"

Luca fit him better, fit the accent and the man. Tonight could be the last time anyone ever called him that, which was sad. But Aubrey refused to let sadness anywhere near her right now. She wanted only him near her—inside her.

He must have felt the same, because his hands moved to her clothes, peeling them off her body. Once he had her naked, he carried her to the bed and laid her on the plush mattress. Instead of joining her, he just stood there, staring at her as if he wanted to memorize what she looked like.

Then he stepped closer, and he ran his hands over

her, as if he wanted to memorize how she felt. And then he was tasting her...

His lips glided across every inch of her skin, lingering on her neck where her pulse jumped and the curve of her breasts before pulling gently on her nipples.

She moaned and reached for him. "Luca..."

But he moved farther down her body, and with his lips and his tongue, he built the pressure inside her even more.

She arched and squirmed on the bed, wanting more, needing more...

But he pulled back, chuckling. He was teasing her. Torturing her.

"Luca..." It wasn't a plea now but a warning. She could torture him, too.

Ignoring the throbbing low in her body, she reached for him, pulling him onto the bed with her. Then she unzipped his jeans and released his straining erection. And she teased him with her lips and her tongue...until his control snapped.

His hands shaking, he fumbled a condom packet from his jeans before ripping it open with his teeth. He sheathed himself. Then he was inside her, moving, thrusting, and the pressure broke. An orgasm gripped her with such overwhelming pleasure that tears streamed from her eyes as her body shuddered. Luca's body tensed as he joined her. But then he was shaking, his hands stroking her face, wiping away her tears.

"Did I hurt you?" he asked, his voice gruff with concern and regret.

She shook her head. "No. No, not at all. I was just overcome…"

With passion. With pleasure.

With love…

LUCA DIDN'T WANT to sleep. He didn't want to miss a minute of this magical evening with Aubrey—because he knew it wasn't going to last.

It couldn't.

Staying with her would put her in danger, too. Again. Still…

Today—in that barn—with all those shots fired, Aubrey could have been killed. He shuddered at the thought, and she murmured and shifted against his chest.

Her eyes opened, and she stared up at him. "I dozed off…"

"Shh, go back to sleep," he told her. He loved holding her like this, in his arms, her body warm and limp against his.

She shook her head.

And he knew she felt what he did—that she didn't want to waste their limited time together sleeping. He could sleep later when he was somewhere else and she was safe.

And when he did, he knew he would dream of her, of this night…

Of every kiss, of every caress, of every moment of pleasure…

It was only then that he would let himself also feel the pain, the loss of what could have been, had he been another man, had he not had a price on his head.

A knock at the door startled him, making him tense with fear. Had he messed up? Had he put her in danger by staying too long already?

"Room service," someone called out.

"You ordered dinner, remember?" Aubrey said. She must have felt his fear, too. But then her face flushed with embarrassment. "We got distracted after…"

When they'd been told how long it was going to take for their food to be done, they'd made good use of that time. Such good use that he had forgotten all about the food.

Another knock rattled the door.

"You better get that," she said. She slid out of the bed, scooped up her clothes from the floor and headed toward the bathroom, leaving him to answer the door.

He threw on his jeans and looked through the peephole before answering it. He didn't feel entirely safe. He wouldn't ever feel entirely safe again. That was just going to be the life he led from now on, one where he was constantly looking over his shoulder for the Camorra.

He opened the door and greeted the waiter who stood in the hall with a trolley of covered dishes. "Thank you." The kitchen had been about to close when he'd called, but they'd been happy to oblige them with one last meal.

That was how Luca felt. Like this was his last meal, his last day on earth.

His last moment of happiness.

HE WAS HERE.

Paolo tensed as he heard his voice; he'd been coming back from the lobby bar when the door had opened to a room on the same hall as his. He hadn't even had to see Luca to know that it was him.

Thankfully, the waiter stood between Luca and the hall, so maybe his cousin hadn't seen him, either. He would be shocked if he had, and he would know exactly why Paolo was here.

To make sure that he was dead...

Whoever was shot at the Gemini ranch hadn't been Luca. Once again his cousin's luck had held, and he'd escaped again.

If the Camorra learned about this...

If Paolo didn't do something...

He didn't have his cousin's luck. He wouldn't escape death again and again.

If he didn't finish this—if he didn't finish off Luca—then the Camorra would finish him.

Chapter Twenty-Three

Aubrey had ducked into the bathroom because she wasn't dressed. And because she'd needed a moment to compose herself…

Or she might have blurted out how she felt about Luca. That she'd fallen for him.

She didn't want this night to end. She didn't want him to leave. Ever.

But how could he stay?

His life would be in danger and hers would be as well, just as he'd warned her. Her heart ached already with missing him, and he hadn't left yet. She'd heard the deep rumble of his voice as he spoke with the waiter.

Then she'd heard the rattle of the food service cart as he wheeled it into the room. Even after she dressed and fixed her hair, which had been sticking up all over the place, she stood several long moments, waiting for the sound of the door closing behind the waiter, before she reached for the doorknob.

But when she tried turning it, it didn't budge. It was as if something was pinned beneath it.

"Luke?" she called out.

There was no reply.

"Luca?"

Had he left with the waiter?

She rattled the door, trying to dislodge whatever was pinned beneath it.

"Shh..." a deep voice murmured. "Stay in there and stay quiet."

"What—what's going on?" But she knew...even before he said it.

"You need to step back from the door," Luca said, his voice low and gruff with emotion.

"What—why?"

"Maybe climb into the bathtub or the shower..."

She glanced back at the walk-in shower. There was no bathtub. But she didn't want to step back from the door. Her hand gripped the knob even harder, but no matter how hard she tried, it wouldn't move.

"Luca..." Her heart was beating fast and heavy with fear. "What's going on?"

"It's going to all be over soon," he told her.

"What?" she asked, panic gripping her, stealing away her breath. "What's going to be over?"

Their magical evening? Their relationship? Or his life?

LUCA HATED DOING THIS, but he had no choice. With the chair jammed beneath the knob to the bathroom door, she wasn't going to be able to get out. But someone could still get inside...

Could still get to her.

This was a bad idea. All of it...

But there wasn't any time for a more elaborate plan. He'd only caught a glimpse of his cousin from the corner of his eye, but he knew why he was here.

Paolo had to make sure the Camorra hitman had finished the job, had finished Luca.

Even if Paolo hadn't seen him when he opened the door, he must have heard Luca talking to the waiter, and recognized his voice. Had he known Luca had checked into the hotel?

Or had it just been a cosmic coincidence that he'd registered at the same hotel? Fate...

Destiny that it was to end like this...

A knock rattled the door to the hallway. He drew in a breath to calm his nerves, and he reached up to check the buttons on his flannel shirt before heading toward the door. He forced a smile as he opened it, but that smile dropped along with his jaw as he feigned surprise at the person standing outside.

"Paolo!" he exclaimed. "I can't believe it's you. I thought it was the waiter." But he hadn't. He'd known his cousin was coming. That was why he'd shoved the chair under the bathroom doorknob. It was why he held his breath now, hoping that chair held.

"The waiter's gone," Paolo murmured, as he stepped inside the room and closed the door behind himself. "Just like you're supposed to be..."

He wasn't even going to make a pretense of why he was there, so Luca dropped his act as well and released a heavy sigh. "How long?" he asked. "How long have you been working for them?"

Paolo sighed, too. "A long time. I borrowed money for my business, for other things…"

Debts. Like Aubrey's ex-boyfriend, Paolo liked to gamble and must have had about as much luck at it as Warren Parker.

"I don't have a choice," Paolo said, and he pulled a gun from beneath the jacket he wore.

"Did they supply you with that weapon?" he asked.

Paolo shook his head. "Just with the money and connection to buy it from when I landed in Denver."

"They're setting you up," Luca warned him.

Paolo shrugged. "Probably. But either I do this, or I die, Luca. If I let you live, I'd be running just like you have been. And I don't have the luck you have, *cugino*. I won't be able to outrun them. So I have no choice."

"You do have a choice," Luca insisted. "You can go to the police. You can testify against whoever is pulling the strings now."

Because his cousin was so clearly just a puppet in the organization, a scapegoat they were setting up for Luca's murder.

"And then, after I testify, I would still wind up like you," Paolo said. "I would have to live like you're living, always on the run." He shuddered, probably imagining what that would be like.

"Always having to look over your shoulder, never being able to trust or get close to anyone…" Luca murmured with a weary sigh. "No, that's no way to live."

"Then maybe I'm doing you a favor," Paolo said. "I'm putting you out of your misery." And he raised that gun and pointed the barrel at Luca.

Luca held up his hands. "Do *me* a favor," he implored his cousin.

Paolo shook his head. "I can't let you live," he said. "They will kill me for certain."

"Her..." He pointed toward the bathroom door. "Don't hurt her. She doesn't know who you are. She hasn't seen you. There's no reason to hurt her."

"I'm not sure the Camorra would see it that way," Paolo said. "You know how they say 'no witnesses.'"

Luca knew that all too well. It was why it had taken him so many years to compile information and evidence for the exposé. There had been very few people alive to talk to him, and the ones that had survived had only done so because they hadn't been willing to speak. It was probably also why the hitman had murdered the woman who'd posed as his wife. He hadn't wanted to leave behind a witness.

And the assassin had died without being able to testify or to negotiate a deal to offset some of his own prison time.

And now Luca was about to do the same, to lose his life forever.

"Please, Paolo," he implored his cousin. "Just leave her be. She has nothing to do with any of this."

She shouldn't have been with him. He knew that now. Knew that he'd put her at risk from the minute he'd checked into her ranch.

Paolo tilted his head as he studied Luca's face. "It's finally happened," he said. "You've finally fallen in love."

Luca couldn't deny it, but he couldn't declare it, either. It wouldn't be fair. Not to him and certainly not to Aubrey.

"Maybe you are human after all," Paolo remarked. "So maybe this will work this time..." He motioned with the gun. "Maybe when I pull this trigger, you will die."

Luca drew in a shaky breath, bracing himself. But he also needed to brace his cousin. "When you pull that trigger, it won't just be my life that's ending. Your life—as you know it—is over, too."

Tears brimmed in Paolo's dark eyes, and the barrel wavered as if he was choking. "I won't have a life if I don't do this. They will kill me."

"Paolo..."

His cousin shook his head. "I'm sorry, Luca. I'm so sorry..."

"I'm sorry, too," Luca said. He was sorry that he had to do this to Aubrey. But like Paolo, the Camorra had given him no choice. He would gladly give up his life for hers.

Hopefully, she would forgive him.

Paolo steadied his hand even as tears streaked down his face. Then he squeezed the trigger.

He must have had a silencer on the gun because the only thing Luca heard as he fell was the sound of Aubrey screaming.

HE WOULD HAVE killed the woman, too. He'd raised the gun barrel toward the bathroom door, which was rattling from her pounding on it, when the door to the hall flew open.

"Drop the gun! Drop the gun!" a policeman yelled at him. A waiter stood next to him. He must have let the police into the room.

"You're too late," Paolo said, and his chest ached with disappointment. He glanced down at his cousin lying so still on the floor. "You're too late. He's dead."

And the woman, locked inside the bathroom, screamed even louder.

Chapter Twenty-Four

A couple of weeks had passed since that horrible night in the hotel. Since the night Aubrey had lost Luca forever...

She'd known he was going to leave. But she'd thought he was going to walk away from her, not be wheeled out of their room in a body bag. She'd hoped that wherever he lived, he'd live a full life, traveling, writing, smiling.

But he could do none of those things now. And Aubrey was barely able to make herself do anything, either. But she had the ranch and responsibilities. She couldn't let down her twin and the rest of her family. And most of all, she couldn't let down Luca's memory. He'd been so convinced that she was strong. So she needed to prove that she was—to him and, most of all, to herself.

So an hour earlier, she had walked into her mother's house with a smile on her face, intent on assuring everyone that she was fine. And she'd held on to that smile during their impromptu meeting of the Truth Foundation, so that every time someone looked at her—and they'd looked often—she'd appeared to be happy.

"Fake it until you make it," her mother remarked as she joined Aubrey in the kitchen.

In order to get away from the intent gazes of her family, Aubrey had started to clear the cups and glasses out of the family room that adjoined the kitchen. Not everyone had showed up, but with her family being as busy and far-flung as they were, it was rare for everybody to show up for a meeting. Morgan, Caleb and Nadine were here. And Gideon had showed up as well, along with their sister Rachel and her adorable baby girl, Iris. Seeing Iris usually made Aubrey happy, but today she'd just been reminded that she wouldn't be able to have one of her own with the man she'd wanted to spend her life with.

Who was the father of Rachel's baby? Her sister had never said, and with her busy career as the district attorney, she never seemed to have time to date. Maybe she'd just decided to become a mother on her own; that was what Aubrey would do, too, if she wanted children but never fell in love again.

In the family room, the meeting was still going on, Caleb assuring everyone that his and Morgan's amazing assistant, Rebekah, was on Ronald Spence's case. If anyone could find the evidence to indicate whether or not Spence was actually innocent, she would. Aubrey had wondered from the beginning if there was anything to be found.

"What do you mean about faking it?" Aubrey asked her mother. "Do you have doubts about Spence's claims of innocence, too?"

Her mother smiled and shook her head, and her blond

hair swept across her shoulders. "I have doubts about you," her mother said. "I don't think you're doing as well as you want everyone to believe you're doing."

Aubrey tried to force a smile, but hard as she tried, she couldn't pull up the corners of her mouth. She was just too tired and filled with grief.

Her mom pulled Aubrey's hand away from the cups on the counter and squeezed it. "I could always tell when you were putting on a brave face, Aubrey. You don't need to do that with me. I can tell you're hurting." And she closed her arms around her, pulling her into a warm hug.

For a moment Aubrey gave in to the comfort and let herself relax in her mom's arms. She even let her head settle on Isa Colton's strong shoulder. But then tears stung her eyes, and she knew that if she gave in to them, she wouldn't stop crying.

She inhaled shakily and pulled back. "I'll be okay," she assured her mom.

"I wish I had had the chance to meet him," her mother said. "Sounds like Luca Rossi was quite a guy and very smart."

Aubrey nodded. "He was. His exposés were amazing. So thorough that he took down entire organizations." And then they'd taken him down, using his own cousin to carry out the crime.

"I know that he was smart because he cared about you," her mother said. "He was smart to realize what an amazing woman you are."

Aubrey smiled—for real now. "Yes, I am. I get it from my mama."

Isa chuckled. "Yes, you do," she agreed. "I know all about faking that you're okay until you actually are." She squeezed Aubrey's shoulder. "You will be. Eventually."

She wanted to ask how long it took, how long she would have this hollow ache inside her before she finally started feeling whole again. Genuinely happy again. Because right now she couldn't see it; she couldn't see that far into the future.

All she could see was that image of the body bag with Luca zipped up inside it. Every time she closed her eyes, it flashed through her mind. And even now, with her eyes open, it appeared to her again. Now she closed her eyes and tried to shut it out. Tried to forget...

But she would never be able to forget that horrific night. She would never be able to forget Luca, either.

"Did you forget?" Jasper asked.

Aubrey felt a sickening lurch in her stomach and opened her eyes, shocked at her twin's question and at his sudden appearance. She'd thought she was alone with her mother in the kitchen. Jasper must have slipped out of the meeting in the family room as well.

"Forget what?" she asked him. Unlike her and their mother, he wasn't carrying dishes. He just held the keys to the ranch truck, jangling them as they dangled from his fingers.

"Did you forget that I wanted you to meet with the applicant for a ranch hand?" he asked.

Until he'd mentioned it on the drive to their mother's house, Aubrey hadn't even realized that he'd advertised for a new employee. She could understand why he thought they needed one now—to pick up her slack.

With her tossing and turning all night, she didn't have much energy to pull her weight during the day—even though she wanted to throw herself into work. Into anything that would take her mind off Luca.

But not this…

Interviewing a new ranch hand, training them, would remind her entirely too much of Luca—how he'd helped move the cattle like a ranch hand, and taken care of the calf.

Tears stung her eyes again, but she blinked them back. "I think you can handle an interview on your own," she told her partner.

He shook his head. "No. We need to both be able to get along with him. He needs to be a good fit for the business and for the family."

"It's just a minor position," she reminded her twin. "The guy's not going to become part of the Colton clan."

Jasper laughed. "You never know…"

"Are you going to marry him?" she asked.

"Let's interview him first," Jasper said. "And we'll see where it goes from there."

She laughed, too, at her brother's teasing. He'd been working really hard to keep her mind off Luca, off her loss.

"It would be lovely," their mother said, "to have more weddings and babies in this family, more happy events."

Aubrey couldn't deny that it would be good. She just knew she wasn't going to be the one personally having any of those special events.

She sighed. "Okay, Jasper, let's go interview your future spouse."

She hugged her mother again and then moved on to her other relatives remaining in the family room, assuring them all that she would be okay. Gideon tilted his head, though, and studied her face with skepticism and sympathy.

He hugged her again and murmured in her ear. "It'll take time, but you'll be okay."

She nodded. "I know." But how did Gideon know?

"Be patient with yourself, Aubrey," he encouraged her.

She nodded again and pulled back. "Now, we better get going," she urged Jasper. She wanted the hell out of there before her siblings offered any more comfort—it would just make her fall apart.

And she could not do that. Not now, not ever. She had to be strong like their mother had been strong when their father died. At least Luca hadn't died like Ben Colton—in disgrace. He'd died a hero, making certain to keep her safe.

Isa Colton had focused on her family after her husband died. Aubrey had ranch business to focus on, and when, less than an hour later, she and Jasper were back at the ranch, she breathed a slight sigh of relief.

Instead of stopping at the main lodge, Jasper drove the pickup past it. "Where are you going?" she asked.

"The barn," he said. "You can't hire a ranch hand if he doesn't know anything about horses or cattle."

"Surely you looked over his application and verified his work history and references," she said.

"We didn't do that last time," Jasper said, "with Luke Bishop, even though he didn't work for us."

She gasped as a deep pain stabbed her heart at the mention of Luca.

"Sorry," he said sincerely. He pulled the truck up outside the barn and braked. "I'm also sorry that I forgot that application and those references. Why don't you go meet him—he's waiting for you in the tack room—and I'll grab that stuff and be right back?"

Aubrey furrowed her brow and studied her twin's face. "What are you up to?" He couldn't seriously be trying to play matchmaker between her and some ranch hand applicant.

And that pang struck her again. The past couple of weeks Jasper had been so supportive and sensitive; he hadn't even mentioned Luke's name. And now...

"What is up with you?" she asked. Had it all been too much for him? Was he sick of having to do all the ranch work with her being so distracted and upset? "What's going on?"

He shook his head. "Nothing. Just go into the barn and meet the applicant. I'll be right back with his paperwork."

She hesitated a long moment before she reached for the door handle; she wasn't sure she was ready for this. Hanging out with her family at the Truth Foundation meeting at Mom's had been hard enough. Interviewing a stranger for a position she would have liked Luke Bishop to keep...

It bordered on cruel.

Not that Luke Bishop had been real, and Luca Rossi had been no ranch hand. If only...

She exhaled a sigh and opened the door. She'd barely closed it before Jasper was backing up and driving off. Maybe he was just in a hurry to retrieve that paperwork, or maybe he was in a hurry to get away from her.

Had she been that difficult to be around the past two weeks? Maybe he'd been sensing all her pain. She couldn't blame him for wanting a break from that.

She wanted a break from that, so maybe interviewing this job applicant would be a welcome distraction. She forced herself to open the side door of the barn and step inside. She'd only visited the barn a couple of times over the past two weeks. It had been hard to be in here and not think about that day—about the man trying to kill Luca. She'd saved him then.

Maybe if he hadn't locked her in the bathroom, she could have kept him alive that night in the hotel. But he hadn't given her the chance. He'd been trying to protect her.

She knew that and she loved him for it.

So she forced herself to walk to the tack room. This was another place where she had too many memories of Luca, of making love with him for the first time...

Her hand trembled slightly as she closed it around the doorknob and opened the door. The ranch hand applicant didn't turn around; he stood with his back to her. Wearing faded jeans and cowboy boots and a cowboy hat, he was tall and lean and so achingly familiar.

Was she imagining Luca here again...with her?

Then he turned, and shock staggered her, knocking

her back a couple of feet. He reached for her, catching her shoulders in his hands as if he was worried that she was going to faint.

He'd told her that he was an only child, so he had no twin. Unless he'd lied about that.

Unless he hadn't died, he couldn't be here. He couldn't be here. But when she raised her hands to his face, he felt real. Her skin tingled from the contact with his salt-and-pepper stubble.

This was Luca.

Alive and well.

"How?" she asked. But even as she asked it, she knew. He'd locked her in that bathroom and nobody had let her out until the suspect had been taken from the room, until the body had been zipped into that bag. She hadn't even been able to see him one last time before they wheeled him off.

TWO WEEKS AWAY from her had been interminably long. And Luca had known that she was alive and well. He'd just missed her—so much that he tried to reach out now. But she stepped back, and her hands fell away from his face.

Behind the lenses of her glasses, her eyes were still wide with shock. But also with knowledge...

She must have realized how he'd pulled it off. But did she understand why?

"I'm sorry," he said.

"For what?" she asked. "Sorry that you let me believe you were dead or sorry that you're alive?"

"I wouldn't blame you for being furious with me,"

he said. "I know how much it means to you to always know the truth, no secrets, no lies…"

"And still you fooled me anyway," she murmured.

His heart ached for the pain in her voice and on her beautiful face, and regret filled him that he'd hurt her. That was the last thing he'd wanted to do.

"I'm sorry," he said again. "I wasn't trying to fool you. I was trying to fool my cousin and the Camorra. And to protect you from both."

Would she understand that? Could she?

He went back to her first question now. "When room service came, the waiter was someone you know—Dominic."

She gasped. "Dominic was in on this?"

He nodded. "He put the chair beneath the bathroom door."

The FBI agent had been as determined to protect his sister as Luca had been.

"After he heard about what happened at the ranch with the assassin, he came to the hotel to provide us with protection. He heard someone mention the Italian guy who'd checked in earlier. He was worried that he was another hitman sent after me, and he came to warn me. He outfitted me with a bulletproof vest—just in time."

"So you weren't shot?" she asked.

He flinched and touched his ribs. "I was shot, but the vest stopped the bullet." Just not the force of it that had cracked some bones. But he would share that with her later, if she would give him another chance.

"And you and my brother let me believe you were dead this whole time?" she asked, her voice low with anger.

"We couldn't tell you the truth," he said. "You had to appear upset—in case any of your other guests were working for the Camorra."

She shivered as if she hadn't considered that there could have been more. The thought had haunted him, just as her screams had plagued him the past two weeks.

"We had to wait until everyone here at that time had checked out before we could tell you the truth. I couldn't risk someone hurting you to get to me," he said.

Her lips parted, as if she was about to say something. He could imagine what, so he continued, "I know that I hurt you, and if you'll give me the chance, I'd like to spend the rest of my life making it up to you."

Now her brow furrowed with confusion. "But… how…?"

"The Camorra think I'm dead," he said. And only his mother knew the truth. "We convinced Paolo of that by letting him shoot me and then the authorities declaring me dead and zipping me into that body bag." He shuddered as he remembered that feeling, one he never wanted to experience again. "They're not going to come after me anymore. In order to stay out of jail and going into witness protection, Paolo agreed to testify against everybody he knew that was left in the organization. The FBI has checked their international intel, and they don't think anyone's free to come after me. And everyone in jail believes I'm dead. I can stay here without putting you in danger. And I'd like to stay—if you want me...like I want you..." He stepped closer to her then and slid his arms around her waist. "So very much..."

"What will I call you?" she asked.

He shrugged. "It doesn't matter."

"But what name will you use here?" she asked.

"I've kept the Luke Bishop credentials," he said. "That'll work. But you can call me Luca. Or better yet, husband."

Her eyes widened. "Are you proposing?"

He nodded. "I know that I've hurt you, and that I will have to work to earn back your trust before you would consider accepting my proposal, but I love you, Aubrey Colton. I can't imagine my life without you. Please, at least consider giving me another chance."

She flung her arms around him then and pulled his head down toward hers. As her lips brushed across his, she murmured. "You have it."

He pulled back just slightly to ask, "What do I have?"

"A second chance," she said. "And my love and my trust. I love you, Luca."

HIS MOTHER'S HANDS were elbow-deep in soapy water in the kitchen sink when the phone rang, so Gideon answered it.

"Colton residence," he said.

"Gideon!" Aubrey exclaimed, her voice vibrating with excitement.

At least he thought it was Aubrey; she certainly hadn't sounded like this when she'd been here earlier. And even though she'd pasted a smile on her face, it had been painfully forced. "Is everything all right?" he asked her.

"It's perfect," she said. "Please bring Mom out to the ranch. Get everybody out here as soon as possible."

"Why? What's going on?" he asked.

And Mom, wiping her hands on a dish towel, repeated his question. "What's going on? Who is that?"

"Tell Mom that she can meet him—thanks to Dominic. All of you can meet him."

"Who?"

"Luca Rossi."

"I thought he was dead."

"He was. I guess he is, but Luke Bishop is alive and no longer has a hit out on him. He's here at the ranch with me. And I want you all to meet him. I want you to meet the man that I love."

Tears sprang to Gideon's eyes. He'd never heard Aubrey so happy. And while he was thrilled for her—that she would be able to be with the person she loved, he felt a pang of envy as well.

Gideon had been in love once.

Probably still was…

But unlike Aubrey, that person hadn't loved him back. He forced that thought from his mind, though, and focused on his sister's happiness. She deserved it, and it sounded as though she'd finally found it.

* * * * *

COMING SOON!

We really hope you enjoyed reading this book.
If you're looking for more romance, be sure to
head to the shops when new books are
available on

Thursday 3rd March

LET'S TALK
Romance

For exclusive extracts, competitions
and special offers, find us online:

JOIN US ON SOCIAL MEDIA!

Stay up to date with our latest releases, author news and gossip, special offers and discounts, and all the behind-the-scenes action from Mills & Boon...

 millsandboon

 millsandboonuk

 millsandboon

It might just be true love...

MILLS & BOON

Desire

Indulge in secrets and scandal, intense drama and plenty of sizzling hot action with powerful and passionate heroes who have it all: wealth, status, good looks…everything but the right woman.

MILLS & BOON

MODERN

Power and Passion

Prepare to be swept off your feet by sophisticated, sexy and seductive heroes, in some of the world's most glamourous and romantic locations, where power and passion collide.

MILLS & BOON
MEDICAL
Pulse-Racing Passion

Set your pulse racing with dedicated, delectable doctors in the high-pressure world of medicine, where emotions run high and passion, comfort and love are the best medicine.